PEACEMAKER: BUFFALO BRIGADE

PEACEMAKER: BUFFALO BRIGADE

•

Clifford Blair

AVALON BOOKS
NEW YORK

Western
BLA

This book is dedicated to all our grandchildren:
Rachel and Alexandria Stout, Jacob and Hannah Tisdal, and
Zachary Stephens

Chapter One

The gunshots cracked across the rolling grassland, and James Stark reined up his sorrel stallion as the sounds reached his ears. Some kind of dustup was going on at the edge of the hill country he was approaching. There were at least four guns involved, maybe five, all of them rifles. Quite a bit of lead was being thrown at something . . . or someone.

Frowning, he urged Red forward at an easy lope, taking his Winchester 1887 lever-action shotgun from its scabbard as he did so. In his mind's eye he tried to picture the lay of the land up ahead. A strip of woods and underbrush clung to the boundary of the rugged hilly terrain about half a mile ahead of him. Higher up, the hills themselves were heavily wooded in places. There were plenty of spots for a man to take cover.

Stark guided Red into a draw behind a low grassy ridge, and stepped down out of the saddle, shotgun in hand. Crouching, he went up the ridge, dropping to his belly at the crest. Only a greenhorn rode blind into gun trouble. He

1

wanted a look at what was going on before he committed himself.

Doffing his Stetson so as not to be skylined, he squinted against the spring sunlight at the wooded fringe of the hills. Four clouds of dissipating gunsmoke hung above the underbrush. Higher up on the hill, another cloud drifted over a rocky outcropping. Gunshots echoed back and forth between the outcropping and the underbrush.

Stark's brow furrowed. Some hombre was holed up in that pile of rocks, facing four-to-one odds, but making a good fight of it even so.

He watched a moment longer. Eventually the hunters could work their way up the hill under cover of one another's fire, but for now their quarry seemed to be holding all four of them at bay. Stark gave an admiring shake of his head.

He spotted the bulk of a dead horse a little ways out from the trees. Apparently the loner's horse had caught a slug and he'd had no choice but to make a stand.

Stark ducked low and slipped down the hogback towards the woods. There wasn't much cover, but he figured all the combatants would have their attention on the fight and not on their backtrail. He wasn't sure this was any of his business. For all he knew, being this close to Guthrie, the cosmopolitan capital of Oklahoma Territory, it could be a posse closing in on a desperate outlaw.

But somehow he didn't think so.

He made it to the edge of the woods and halted with a sigh of relief. Remembering the position of the four hunters, he began to work his way through the trees and undergrowth toward the nearest one. The intermittent sound of the gunshots guided him.

He moved with a stalker's stealth, although he reckoned

his prey's ears would be ringing enough from the shooting to cover most of the sounds of his approach.

At last, about 30 yards into the woods, he drew up and peered warily through a screen of brush just as another shot rang out in front of him. The shooter was crouched behind the root mass of an ancient dead tree, uprooted by its own weight. The fellow had a clear view of the outcropping, and, rifle to shoulder, he was sighted in on it.

Stark could see the edge of a foul sneer on the dark stubbled face. The man's burly shoulders jolted with the kick of his Winchester as he fired again. Eagerly he levered the rifle to jack another shell into place.

Hard case, Stark typed him—one of the violent gun-ready breed of men who often drifted through the territory on their way to the lawless Indian lands to the west.

Stark tightened his grip on the shotgun.

"This a private game, or can anybody play a hand?" he drawled before the hard case could pull the trigger another time.

The fellow jerked sharply around, straightening to his feet. Stark stepped coolly into the open, his shotgun now held loosely in his hands.

"Who the devil are you?" the hombre demanded, bringing his gun to bear on Stark.

Stark shrugged. "Just passing by and heard the shooting. Thought I'd see what the fun was about."

The man squinted narrowly at him, taking stock of another fighting man. "Ain't none of your concern," he growled, "but we got us a darky treed up yonder." He nodded in the direction of the outcropping.

Stark knew he couldn't keep the contempt off his face, so he hid it with an ugly grin. It hurt his face. "That a fact? Some kind of outlaw?"

The hard case relaxed a bit. He gave an amused snort. "Yeah, that's right, an outlaw! And we're lawdogs!" He chuckled crudely.

Still grinning his painful grin, Stark moved forward. "Let me have a crack at him."

The fellow actually stepped aside to make room. As Stark drew abreast he brought the butt of his shotgun around in a sharp vicious swipe that smashed against the man's stubbled jaw. The rowdy went down like a sack of potatoes.

Stark spared a searching glance up at the outcropping, but couldn't detect much. Whoever the quarry was, he had done a fine job of going to ground. He bent and lifted the rifle from the gunslick's unresisting hands, then backed away. This one was out of the fight, but his cohorts were still slinging lead. And before too long they'd notice their pard had stopped doing his part.

Turning, Stark legged it back out of the woods. He still didn't have all the answers, but he had enough to know he needed to take a hand in this fracas. Trying to stalk the other three hunters through the brush would take too long and carry too much of a risk, he calculated. There was a better way to play this hand.

Back on the ridge that concealed his horse, he slipped the shotgun back in its scabbard and pulled out his big Winchester Sporting Rifle. He then eased himself down on his belly, the captured rifle beside him, his own in his hands. Carefully he sighted in on the underbrush beneath the closest cloud of powder smoke. He had a moment's thought that the return fire from the lone defender up on the hill had grown uncertain. With or without their pard, the other three would be closing in soon.

His hands steady, Stark pumped two shots into the undergrowth, lined the rifle beneath the next closest cloud, and sent two more bullets winging into the brush. He reset his sights on the third gunman's position and repeated the procedure, getting off all six shots in a fleeting matter of seconds.

He had no real way of knowing if he'd scored any hits, but he wanted the three riflemen to realize they had come under attack and that the odds against them had just increased. Once the trio knew they were in a crossfire, he doubted they were of the ilk to carry on a prolonged battle.

He was aware without even looking that a betraying cloud of powder smoke now hung over his own head. He snatched up the spare rifle, scrambled several yards to the right, hit the ground, and opened fire again. When the sporting rifle ran dry, he emptied the other rifle before shifting positions a second time.

Careful to keep below the crest of the hill, he thumbed shells from the bandolier across his chest into the sporting rifle as he ran. He heard some scattered shooting from below, but couldn't tell whether it was directed at him or at the outcropping.

Considering the distance, he didn't think any of the bullets came close. The sporting rifle, on the other hand, with its three-quarter-mile-plus reach, would be giving the yahoos plenty of reason to worry. He hit the ground again and drove a couple more shots into the underbrush before pausing to take stock. In the sudden silence, the ringing in his ears was deafening.

The hard cases had stopped shooting, Stark realized. He squinted toward the outcropping up the hill, but could see nothing in the shadows there either. The gunmen's prey, whoever he was, had stopped shooting also. A twinge of worry constricted Stark's stomach. A powerful lot of lead had been thrown at those rocks.

He ran his gaze over the woods. He fancied he detected motion, and pumped a shot at it. Then he waited, finger ready on the trigger.

A handful of minutes slid past. Then abruptly, three mounted figures burst from the trees headed fast away from the hill country. The range was long, but Stark sent a final bullet winging after them. The fact that the trio was abandoning their fallen pard to his fate well confirmed what breed of men they were.

Stark held his position a little longer, watching and waiting. The three riders disappeared on the prairie horizon. At last, aware that the first hard case might be regaining his senses, Stark swung up onto Red and put the big mustang down the ridge at a gallop.

He sidetracked long enough to be sure his victim was still out of action. He dragged the unconscious man over and propped him up against a tree. He quickly bound his hands behind him around the tree trunk and confiscated his handgun and pocketknife. When he reached Guthrie, he'd have Marshall Evett Nix send a deputy out to retrieve the yahoo. Likely there was a wanted poster on the man on file in Nix's office, and Stark had a hunch the fellow the gunsels had run to ground deserved every penny of the reward.

Stark collected the outlaw's mount, which he found tethered nearby. Leading the horse—a rangy bay—he took Red wending through the woods and up the hill toward the outcropping.

"Hold your fire! I'm coming in!" he called as he drew near.

There was no answer.

Cautiously, his Colt Peacemaker in hand, he urged Red

closer. He didn't cotton to having the man he'd rescued plug him by mistake.

He reined up when he was in plain view of the pile of boulders, and sang out again. Still no response. The flutter of foreboding touched him once more. Slipping from the saddle, he catfooted forward. Behind him, Red snorted uneasily.

He edged past the outermost boulder and into the shadowy niche behind it. He scowled darkly as his eyes fell on the motionless figure sprawled on the rocky ground, fallen rifle by one outstretched hand. His fears had been well grounded. One of the attackers' bullets had reached its mark.

Sheathing his Colt, he knelt by the prone form. In the dim light he found himself gazing down into a lean black face, seamed with age. A fresh ugly wound scarred the side of the grizzled head. For a grim moment Stark thought there was no life in the old man, but then the bony chest lifted ever so slightly, and the thick lips trembled with the shallow intake of breath. He had no way to gauge the seriousness of the wound.

Stark collected his rope off Red's saddle, and led the bay as close as possible to the outcropping. Gently he scooped the victim up in his arms and straightened to his feet. The old fellow was heavier than Stark had expected. His lanky build belied a solid heft. He wore frayed overalls, a threadbare work shirt, and ancient boots. His hands, Stark noted, bore the calluses of a lifetime of hard work.

Stark glanced up at the late morning sun. This little fracas had cost him precious time, but there was still a chance he could make it back to Guthrie by noon. He had two reasons to hurry now. The old man needed immediate medical attention . . . and Prudence was waiting. The stunningly attractive face of his new bride flashed unbidden into his mind. Though he'd been away only a few days, he was anxious to get home to her.

The old man groaned and muttered a bit as Stark got him positioned in the saddle and used the rope to secure him so he was hugging the bay's neck. The bay didn't act up much. A good horse.

Stark went back to collect the old fellow's rifle. It was an ancient repeater that had seen better days, but looked to be well-maintained. Stark recognized it as an Army-issue carbine. His gaze drifted then to the Colt Dragoon holstered at the man's side. On a hunch his eyes swept the surrounding rocky ground, and he spied a well-worn cavalry hat that must have been shot from its owner's head when he was wounded.

He'd seen such a getup before—on the select group of fighting men who'd served with the 54th Massachusetts Regiment in the Union Army and later with the U.S. Cavalry . . . where they became known as the Buffalo Soldiers.

Nicknamed by the Indians they had fought because of the curly black hair which the braves likened to that of the buffalo, the black cavalrymen had earned a reputation as fighting men second to none in the West. Not many of them were left these many years after the Indian Wars.

Stark retrieved the hat almost reverently and settled it onto the oldster's head. He now knew he was in the presence of a legend.

Prudence stood outside her neat frame one-story office building and stared at the newly painted name stenciled on the door. PRUDENCE MCKAY-STARK, ATTORNEY AND COUNSELOR AT LAW.

She knew it was silly, but she couldn't resist running her

gloved hand across the hyphenated addition to her last name. She had only been Mrs. James Stark for six months, and she still felt a newlywed's thrill at the thought that she was at last a married woman. So far the marriage had been all that she'd dreamed it would be. And surprisingly, none of the problems had materialized which she and Jim had feared all the years during their strained courtship.

She smiled in genuine amusement remembering their struggle to keep their feelings for each other under control out of fear of losing a hard-won sense of personal freedom and independence. She could say now without hesitation that freedom and independence came in a sorry second to sharing every aspect of life—the joys and the problems— with a dearly loved spouse in the delicious intimacy of marriage.

Her eyes shifted to the added text stenciled below her name on the office door. JAMES STARK INVESTIGATIONS: PEACEMAKER FOR HIRE. She especially enjoyed sharing an office with Jim and knowing the details of the sometimes dangerous cases his career as a professional troubleshooter got him involved in. Before they were married she had often been left to sit and worry about his welfare without knowing when or even *if* he'd return.

She almost hugged herself in excitement. He'd be returning from just such an absence today. She couldn't wait to see him. Thankfully this trip had involved no dangerous gunplay, so she hadn't had to be overly concerned. He was away on a simple consulting job for the Cattlemen's Association in an adjoining county.

She was suddenly startled out of her daydream by a somehow familiar male voice coming from behind her.

"Well, Mrs. Stark, it appears married life is agreeing with you. You've never looked lovelier."

She whirled to find herself facing a young black man dressed in a somber broadcloth suit. Her smile of welcome was genuine as she extended her hand and stepped out across the sidewalk to greet him. "Why, Thaddeus Jenkins, it's so good to see you again! How are things in Earlsboro? Are you still the bailiff keeping order in Judge Hatch's court?"

Prudence had only the highest regard for Thaddeus. A barrister himself, she knew that he'd faced pressures far greater than even those opposing her to earn a license to practice law in Oklahoma Territory.

"I am attempting to, yes, Mrs. Stark," he answered, shaking her hand firmly. "But as is always the case with Judge Hatch, the struggle is ongoing."

Prudence laughed out loud as memories of the unorthodox judge flooded her mind. In a way she owed a vote of gratitude to Judge Hatch and Earlsboro, the volatile whiskey town in which he kept an uneasy order. It was a gun battle there resulting from a case she'd tried before the judge that had jolted Jim into proposing to her.

And it was her own feelings of jeopardy that had jolted her into accepting.

Her eyes misted as she also recalled that the jeopardy had been genuine and might have had a totally different outcome had Thaddeus not stood shoulder to shoulder with Jim and Judge Hatch to resolve it. She was tempted to again voice her thanks to Thaddeus, as she had done at the time of the confrontation. But she somehow knew that would only make the inherently modest man uncomfortable.

Instead she merely asked, "Well, what brings you to Guthrie?"

"Personal business, Mrs. Stark. I fear I have need of your husband's services."

"Please call me Prudence, Thaddeus," she insisted, sobering at his pronouncement. "We've shared too many experiences to stand on formalities. Jim's not here at the moment, but he should be returning any time now. The wire he sent me yesterday said he'd be back in Guthrie in time for lunch. Come into my office and we'll have tea while we wait."

"I'm relieved to hear the Peacemaker will be back today. I have a feeling time might be critical," Thaddeus said as he followed her inside. "As it turns out, the man I was to meet here in Guthrie hasn't made it yet. So the problem might be more acute than I realized."

Prudence bade Martha, her matronly secretary, to prepare tea, then ushered Thaddeus into her office. She left the door open so Martha wouldn't have to interrupt their conversation to bring in the tea.

When they were settled in the informal seating area in the corner of her office, Prudence again brought up the reason for Thaddeus's visit. "Exactly who was it you were meeting, Thaddeus?"

"My uncle, Caleb Jackson. He and some of his friends have started a small business up in the panhandle area, and are facing some opposition from the locals. He got in touch with me hoping there might be something they could do legally to end the harassment. But the more I learned, the more obvious it became that they needed intervention in ways far beyond what the law could provide. That's why I suggested my uncle meet me here and enlist your husband's aid."

"And since your uncle isn't here yet, you suspect he's run into trouble."

"Exactly. I only hope he hasn't come to any harm. He's a tough old soldier who's been battling overwhelming odds all his life. And, by the grace of God, he's always come out on top. So I guess I shouldn't get too worried yet. His luck has held so far."

"And it's still holding," a voice drawled gruffly from the doorway. "But this time that old man has a lot to thank the Almighty for."

Prudence knew the voice well and was on her feet even as she turned to welcome him. "Jim! I'm so glad you're back!" she hurried into the arms he opened wide in greeting.

She blushed becomingly at his warm hug, then turned back to gesture toward Thaddeus. "Look who's here to see you."

Stark kept her in the circle of his arm as he extended his hand to Thaddeus.

Concern was evident on Thaddeus' face as he gripped Stark's hand. "You sound as though you've already encountered my uncle, Peacemaker."

"Well, we haven't been formally introduced, but I heard enough of your story as I entered the building to suspect that the man I just dropped off at the doctor's office has got to be your uncle. And you're right about one thing. He's a tough old fellow, all right. As tough as they come."

Chapter Two

Over lunch in one of Guthrie's swank restaurants, Stark filled Prudence and Thaddeus in on the attack on Caleb Jackson.

Prudence's expression grew more alarmed as the story unfolded. "I'll swear, James Stark!" she exclaimed at last. "You can get yourself into more trouble faster than anyone I know. Here I was thinking I didn't need to worry about you this trip, and all the while you were out there trading gunfire with four outlaws!"

He couldn't resist teasing her a bit. "It goes with the territory, my sweet." He leaned toward her as though he intended to kiss her on the cheek.

She blushed fiercely and pushed him away. "Will you please behave yourself!" she hissed. "This is serious business. Thaddeus' uncle was almost killed!"

Stark couldn't deny the truth of what she said. Even though the joy of seeing her had taken the edge off the events of the morning, they remained a grave matter. The concern evident on Thadddeus' face bore witness to that.

"Don't worry, Thaddeus," he hastened to voice a reassurance. "Doc Walker said the bullet just grazed him. He assured me he'd be good as new once he came around—and he was starting to do that even before I left. The doc gave him something for his headache and told me we could see him after he'd slept for a couple of hours." He glanced at the ornate clock on the restaurant wall. "It's been about that long now. What say we mosey over and find out the story behind the attack I interrupted."

The doctor was out on a call when they got there, but his cheery nurse showed them into the back room he used as an infirmary. Caleb Jackson appeared to be asleep on one of the cots set up there.

"He's feeling much better now," the nurse whispered. "I checked on him a bit ago and he said he felt fine except for a bad headache. And I'm afraid that's liable to be with him for a few days. The doctor wants him to stay here overnight, and he'll be free to go tomorrow morning."

"Is it all right if we try to talk to him?" Prudence asked quietly.

"Of course. Just don't tire him out. He really does need to rest."

The old man stirred then and opened his eyes. "What's all that jabbering about over there?" he growled. "Can't a man have any peace to get a little sleep."

Thaddeus smiled in genuine relief at the old man's tone. "Why, Uncle Caleb, here I was worried about you, and you're back to normal already—as cantankerous as ever."

"That you, Thaddeus boy?" Caleb squinted in their direction. "Well, come on over here, so I can see you better."

Prudence helped the nurse slip another pillow behind Caleb's shoulders as he struggled to sit up. A white bandage covered one temple and lingering pain lurked in his dark eyes, but even so he looked a lot healthier than when Stark had last seen him.

His face split in a wide grin as he and Thaddeus shook hands. "Well, nephew, what's happened to your manners? Ain't you going to introduce me to your friends?"

"Yes, sir, I fully intend to. This is Mrs. Prudence Stark. She's one of the few lady lawyers in our territory. And she's married to this fellow, James Stark, also known as the Peacemaker. He's the one we came here to talk to, and coincidentally the one who saved your bacon and brought you here."

"Obliged, Mr. Stark, I surely am." Caleb extended a steady hand.

Caleb's grip, Stark noted, carried the strength of a much younger man. "Glad I happened along when I did."

"I reckon I am too. I recollect you opening fire from up on the ridge. I couldn't tell who you were, but I was mighty pleased to have you take a hand. I figured we just about had those boys ready to turn tail, when one of their shots caught me. Don't remember much after that."

"Who were they, Uncle Caleb?" Thaddeus inquired.

Furrows ridged the old man's brow. "Can't say for certain, but I reckon they were hired guns belonging to Morg Hagen."

Stark settled his shoulders against the wall. Prudence stood close beside him. "Who's Morg Hagen?" he asked.

"He's the big curly wolf around Beaver."

"Town up in the Panhandle area," Stark mused aloud. "No man's land."

"A fellow could make a mighty good argument that it's all Morg Hagen's land," Caleb spoke with an edge of bitterness. "He owns most of the town, and has his finger in what he don't own. That is, all but the Buffalo Freight Line.

That's a little enterprise run by me and a couple of men I served with in the cavalry, Jeffrey Tyler and Hollis Kelso."

"Not much business for freight lines anymore," Stark commented.

He knew that during the past couple of decades the area known as the Panhandle Region, consisting of the southwestern quarter of Kansas, the Texas Panhandle, and the strip of no man's land between, had been crisscrossed by such freight routes as the Fort Supply Trail, the Tascosa-Dodge City Trail, and the Jones and Plummer Trail. Along these avenues of commerce moved the freighters with their lumbering wagons, branching out from Dodge City to supply the entire area.

Stark had heard the old tales of the hundred wagon trains hauling tons of supplies, dry goods, medical supplies, foodstuffs, and settlers into the remotest areas of the huge region. They had provided lifelines to the military bases, communities, ranches, trading posts, and homesteads scattered across the rolling prairie. Without the freight lines, the Panhandle Region would've remained a desolate wilderness, fit only for coyotes, antelope, and outlaws.

But with the incursion of the railroads and the telegraph lines into the area, the need for freighters had dwindled and all but vanished. Now most of the old trails were marked only by weathered ruts worn deep into the prairie sod by the passage of thousands of wagons carrying the loads of bygone days.

Stark figured traces of them would still be stretching across the grassland a hundred years hence, and maybe even longer.

"Naw, there ain't enough business to support a big freight line," Caleb's agreement brought Stark out of his reverie. "But there's enough ranches and towns and settlers that the railroads ain't reached yet for a small line to get by all right. Jeffrey Tyler had the knowhow so's we could set it up. He spent a spell as a muleskinner after he left the cavalry."

Caleb's dark face grew more sober. "Anyways, we picked up some old wagons and got them in working order. Times was rough at first, but, shoot, that ain't nothing new for any of us. Eventually folks came to know they could rely on us. What with that, and us being former pony soldiers, we managed to get the mail service contract for a good part of the area, along with standing orders from most of the big ranches in the lands. We haul a few passengers, to boot, and keep the trading posts and farmers supplied. We were starting to do right good."

"And Morg Hagen didn't like it," Stark surmised aloud.

Caleb shot him a shrewd look. "That's the straight of it. You know him?"

Stark shook his head. "No. Just others like him. So Hagen started putting the spurs to you, did he?"

"The spurs and the whip," Caleb confirmed with feeling. "Once he realized there was a penny or two being made that wasn't going into his pockets, he started doing his best to buy us out. Course, we wouldn't sell, even when he offered a halfway decent price. We decided we'd worked hard to make something worthwhile, and we couldn't let it go just 'cause some fellow was flashing some greenbacks at us."

Thaddeus patted the old man's arm encouragingly. "I said he was stubborn as a mule, didn't I?"

Caleb grinned tightly. "And just as hardheaded. Lucky thing too." He reached up and gingerly touched the bandage on his head. "Anyway, Hagen wouldn't give up. At first it wasn't much—just some hoorawing by his hands. Nothing we couldn't handle. Then accidents started happening. A wheel broke on one of the wagons while Hollis was carrying a full load across the creek. Banged him up some when the wagon went over. We lost most of the load and had to make good on it."

Caleb shook his head bleakly. "When we got to looking we found the wheel had been part sawed in two. Somebody done it deliberately. Then one of our sheds burned down. We barely got the wagon out in time. It smelled powerful of coal oil thereabouts."

"You posted guards, I reckon?" Stark asked. He glanced at Thaddeus. The younger man's face was hard.

Caleb nodded. "Yessir, we did. But we was already shorthanded, and keeping one of us on sentry duty just spread us thinner. And things didn't get much better. A couple of times somebody threw lead our way when one of us was on a run. Nobody got hurt, but them shots came mighty close. Like a warning, you might say. Then while all this was going on, Hagen started up his own freight line. Never got much business." He smiled with bitter pleasure. "But now he's undercutting our rates. He can afford to operate at a loss for a spell. We can't."

"Is there any law in the region?" Prudence inquired.

Caleb shook his head. "Not so's you'd notice, ma'am. It's in the Indian lands, so we're pretty much on our own. Beaver's got itself a town marshall, but he's in Hagen's hip pocket."

"And you think Hagen is the one who hired those gunslicks who ambushed you?" Stark asked.

Caleb smiled tiredly. "Reckon he did. Must've figured I was going for reinforcements. Folks has heard me talk about Thaddeus, about how he's a lawyer and such. Hagen don't want the law and the courts to come to that area.

There's things going on up there I ain't told you about."
Caleb licked his lips with the first sign of nervousness he
had shown. "A few days ago we done found a cross burning
just down the road from our stable."

Beside him, Stark heard Prudence's sharply indrawn
breath.

"You talking about the Klan, Uncle Caleb?" Thaddeus
asked quietly.

"Looks that way, son. Ain't never had no signs of Klan
trouble before, but there's tales of it from other black folks
who've come into the territory from the Southern states.
Could be it's spreading into these parts too."

Tension tautened Thaddeus' shoulders. He turned his
head toward the window, and Stark couldn't see his face.
"Hoped we'd heard the last of that sort of poison," came
his whispered words.

"We're all of us good men," Caleb continued, "and we
ain't ever run from a fight. But we never faced the likes of
all this at once before. We're not even sure who all we got
as enemies, but they got us outnumbered and outgunned.
At this point we're not doing nothing but holding ground
on the battlefield. If we don't do something more, we'll
end up losing the war—and that means losing everything
we've worked for."

For the first time he centered his gaze on Stark. "That's
where you come in, Peacemaker. Thaddeus told us you
were good at fighting the likes of Hagen. But now you've
seen personal what we're up against, and I wouldn't blame
you if you decided not to get involved. We can't pay much
right now, but we'd be happy to make you a partner in the
Buffalo Freight Line. If we get back to where we were
before all this trouble started, that could be a right smart
amount."

"Don't worry about paying me," Stark said tightly. "I'm at the point in my career I can afford to take some jobs for the pure pleasure of it. I've grown up hearing tales of the Buffalo Soldiers, and I figure I owe you—one fighting man to another. So it would be a pleasure to help you fellows out after all you've done to settle the West for the rest of us. We'll leave for Beaver as soon as you're up to it."

"I'm going along too," Thaddeus said tightly. "I've already made arrangements with Judge Hatch to be away for a few weeks."

"I'm coming as well," Prudence spoke up. "I know these cases you take for pleasure, James Stark. They're the ones where you take the most chances. I want to be there to protect my interest and ensure I don't become a widow prematurely."

Stark bristled. "Now see here, Prudence, things could get really dangerous on this trip, and I don't want you at risk."

"I'm no stranger to risk," she asserted stubbornly. "You know I can handle myself in a tight situation. Heaven knows we've faced enough of them together already. Now, I'm going, and that's that."

They'd had this argument many times before, and Stark had yet to win it. He knew that if Prudence had her mind set on going to Beaver, she'd get there one way or another . . . with or without his help. She'd shown up more than once in situations where he had forbidden her to go. And more than ever now, he knew he couldn't let her go wandering about on her own. She knew it too. He was trapped—unless he could come up with a way out.

He continued to scowl darkly at her as his mind searched for an angle. This situation *was* a bit different. Usually Prudence was the one who brought him in to handle security on cases she was involved in. And this time it wasn't one of her clients he was working for. His employer should have a say in what went on, and Prudence would have no choice but to listen.

He turned hopefully to Caleb Jackson. "Mr. Jackson, you know more about this situation than I do. Perhaps you can tell my wife whether or not there are even any facilities for her at your place. You certainly have a right to decide who comes along with us."

For the first time a touch of humor lurked in the depths of Caleb's eyes. "Now, don't pull me into this go round. Whether Miss Prudence comes along is strictly between the two of you."

"But you surely have a preference," Stark prodded irritably.

"Well," Caleb chuckled, "if you really want me to say . . ."

Stark's hopes rose. "I do. And be honest."

"Okay." Caleb's smile was full-blown now. "I reckon it would be good if she came along. I can think of one problem in particular that Miss Prudence could handle better than any of us."

Stark was still feeling the sting of being outsmarted when they stepped back out on the street. Prudence smiled indulgently and slipped her arm through his. He glowered down on her and she ignored him.

"All this talk of the Klan is pretty frightening, isn't it?" she ventured. "I must admit I've had very little experience dealing legally with such racism."

Stark sensed that she wasn't merely trying to distract him with this change of topics, but was also expressing genuine concern and frustration. "Then maybe we should talk to someone who has," he suggested.

Prudence looked puzzled at first, then nodded as understanding dawned. "George Perkins. Of course." She turned to Thaddeus. "George Perkins is a black lawyer who moved here to Guthrie a few years ago from Arkansas. He owns his own newspaper, is very active politically, and is quite vocal on the issue of racial equality. He's been dubbed 'the African Lion' because of his strong protests against the Jim Crow Laws passed by Arkansas and some of the other Southern states. You really should meet him."

"I'd like that very much," Thaddeus agreed.

They found Perkins in his office at 524 south Second Street. He welcomed them in jovially. "Peacemaker and Mrs. Stark. Good of you to come calling. What can I do for you?"

"We have a legal matter we want to discuss with you," Prudence began, "and we wanted you to meet our friend, Thaddeus Jenkins. Thaddeus is also a lawyer. He assists Judge Hatch in his court down in Earlsboro."

"Ah, yes," Perkins acknowledged as he and Thaddeus shook hands. "I've heard of you, Mr. Jenkins. You have a right to be very proud of your accomplishments. You have an excellent reputation for being a fair and knowledgeable jurist."

"Why thank you, Mr. Perkins. I count that as high praise indeed," Thaddeus said humbly.

"Now, what is the other matter you wanted to discuss?" Perkins asked.

Briefly Prudence outlined the problems Caleb and his partners were facing in Beaver, particularly the Klan activity.

Perkins listened with a thoughtful scowl on his face.

"Since the Klan operates in such secrecy, it's very hard to bring legal action against them," he said at last. "The hoods pretty much guarantee anonymity. Besides, what you're describing sounds pretty mild compared to what the Klan has done in other areas. Lynchings and outright murder aren't uncommon in some parts of the country. So far here in Oklahoma Territory black people have enjoyed equality and fair treatment. Guess I was hoping it would continue. But as more and more folks come here from other states, they're bound to bring their bad tendencies and beliefs along with them. I fear things will only worsen as we move toward statehood."

"Maybe not," Stark spoke up. "I travel around these parts a good deal, and in most places folks are living peaceable side by side. The schools I've seen are taking in kids of all colors."

"And ideally that's the way it should be," Perkins asserted. "But Southern Democrats are moving into political prominence here in the territory, pedaling their propaganda about segregation, trying to get grandfather clauses inserted into the law to prevent colored people from voting. It doesn't look good."

"Yes," Prudence murmured. "I've been reading your editorials urging black people prevented from voting to file suit in District Court. If there's ever any way I can help you with litigating such cases, I hope you'll call on me."

"I'll keep that in mind," Perkins replied. "And I do appreciate the offer. Unless I'm totally misreading them, the Twelfth, Thirteenth, and Fourteenth Amendments to the Constitution protect the civil rights of *all* citizens. I guess it remains to be seen if the courts will interpret them fairly or not."

"Well, we'll never know until we file a few test cases

and push them through the system, will we?" Prudence asked coyly.

Perkins threw back his head and laughed heartily. "I like your attitude, Mrs. Stark. I'm glad you're on my side of the issue. I'd hate to come up against you in court."

"It's truly an experience," Thaddeus confirmed with a smile. "The town of Earlsboro barely survived the case she tried there."

"For a fact," Stark said flatly. "All that lead flying around rattled me so badly I up and proposed to her. I figured she made so many enemies she needed a live-in bodyguard."

He neatly sidestepped the elbow she aimed at his ribs and escorted her, sputtering her protests, from the office, leaving George Perkins laughing heartily in their wake.

Out on the sidewalk, she jerked her arm free and stood glowering up at him. He glowered back, figuring he'd evened the score for her earlier victory at the doctor's office when she'd finagled her way into coming along on this mission.

Chapter Three

T here she be," Caleb announced, pointing proudly. "The Buffalo Freight Line."

Located on the outskirts of the Indian Territory town of Beaver, the handful of frame buildings making up the freight company's headquarters were backed by a tangle of scrub brush with open country beyond.

Stark saw what had once been a stable, to which a newer lean-to had been attached. The stable had seen numerous repairs. A neatly painted sign with the words BUFFALO FREIGHT above the silhouette of a buffalo, hung over the entry. A few outbuildings, including a blacksmith shop and a small warehouse, were scattered nearby. A sectioned corral held several mules and a couple of horses. A neat frame house, newly whitewashed, stood off to the side.

Five large wagons of varying makes and age were lined up in a row near the stable. A blackened patch of ground, with greenery just beginning to reclaim it, marked the site of the burned shed, Stark figured. Whatever debris had been left by the fire must've been hauled off, he noted with approval. A clean headquarters spoke well of the outfit that ran it.

Caleb was dividing his expectant attention between him and Thaddeus, Stark realized. Thaddeus gave the older man an agreeable nod.

"Nice bivouac, sergeant," Stark murmured, and put his horse forward.

Because of Caleb's injury and since time was critical, they had made the major part of the journey by train, with their horses riding in the stock car. Caleb had insisted on paying everyone's fare out of the reward money from the man Stark had captured—which had turned out to be a sizable chunk of change.

At Caleb's suggestion they had gotten off at the stop before Beaver and had swung wide of the town, so Stark had been given little impression beyond that of the community's isolation out here in the rough plains country.

"Hagen will know the minute we ride through town," Caleb had explained. "No point letting him see we brung in reinforcements just yet."

Thaddeus narrowed his eyes, but made no comment.

"Hello, the stable!" Caleb called out as he spurred the bay up alongside Thaddeus' mount. Stark fell in behind, beside Prudence, dropping a hand to the butt of his Colt just in case.

"Pull up there!" a voice called in command from within the gloom of the stable. "Who's that riding with you, Caleb?"

"They're all friendly," Caleb called back in easy tones. "They'll do to ride the trail with."

Deliberately Stark moved his hand clear of the Colt. A tall lanky figure appeared in the double doorway of the stable. Stark noted the familiar stubby length of a sawed-off double-barrel shotgun tucked conveniently under one long arm. A holstered pistol hung from a plain belt encircling a lean waist.

Stark switched his eyes to the face beneath the drooping slouch hat, and saw features that were as thin as the rest of their owner. At the moment they were splitting into a wide grin.

"Been worrying about you, Sergeant. Thought we was going to have to send out a search party. You're the prettiest sight I've seen in a month of Sundays."

"Your vision must be doing right poorly in your old age, Private Tyler," Caleb said, and performed a military dismount as neat as any Stark had ever seen. He went forward eagerly to clasp hands and forearms with his friend.

Stark continued to take stock of Jeffrey Tyler. Despite Caleb's dig, Tyler was considerably younger than the other ex-soldier, which would've made him just a pup when he had ridden in the cavalry. There was an air of likable good humor about him, but in the newly etched lines of his face, and the barbed wire tension of his muscles, Stark could detect the strain he must've been operating under of late.

"Where are Hollis and your young'un?" Caleb asked after the introductions had been made and they were leading their horses to the stable.

A brief shadow seemed to touch Tyler's face. "Off making a short run to one of the ranches," he advised. "They left before daybreak this morning. Should be pulling in here about nightfall."

"Any trouble since I left?"

Tyler shook his head. "Felt like a coyote waiting for the trap to close on my paw, but it ain't happened yet. Things have been right quiet." He cocked an eye at the healing wound on Caleb's temple. "Appears as though you had some rough riding."

Caleb briefly recounted what had happened.

Some of Tyler's good humor slipped away as he shut the last stall door. "Maybe that's why Hagen didn't stir up no trouble here," he surmised aloud. "Guess he figured those four backshooters would take care of you, and we'd have to knuckle under to him." He looked Stark over speculatively. A faint twinkle returned to his eye. "You aiming to give us a hand, Mr. Stark?"

"I'll do what I can," Stark responded.

"Obliged, I guess," Tyler said dubiously. "But I'd put a lot more stock in you if I didn't figure you were a little bit tetched in the head for letting yourself get roped into this mess."

Stark gave a snort of laughter. "Didn't they teach you nothing about gift horses in the Army?"

"Not enough to keep me out of trouble, I reckon," Tyler said with a laugh of his own. "I'll see to the horses if you want Caleb to show you around the homestead."

"We done got this old stable and the land for a song, and we fixed it up to our liking," Caleb explained as he escorted them through the structure. "We added this here space for a tack room," he told them as they left the stable through the sturdy lean-to. "We plan to keep on building as need be."

The shadows were stretching long when he finished leading them through the other buildings. Everything looked to be clean and orderly, Stark reflected, like a military base before a visit from politicians or dignitaries. He smiled a little bit at the thought, and looked over to where Thaddeus was inspecting the forge in the blacksmith shop.

Outside again, Stark nodded at the tangle of scrub brush

backing the stable and other structures. "Need to get that brush cleared," he commented. "Makes too good a cover for hostiles."

"Yessir, Peacemaker," Caleb agreed. "We been meaning to do that. Just ain't had the time, as yet."

"Coming in!" bawled a distant voice from down the road. Caleb cocked his head. "That'll be Hollis and Tyler's young'un. I'd recognize that bull's bellow anywhere."

They stood waiting as a heavy Schuttler wagon hove into view. Six mules loafed in the traces of the empty wagon. They perked up when one of the figures on the seat snapped out an arm and popped a bullwhip over their backs. Stark thought the other, bulkier figure chided him for the stunt.

As the wagon drew closer the speaker was revealed as an aging black man with a pair of shoulders and a chest that might've led him to be likened to a buffalo even without the short curly hair visible under the brim of his flat-crowned hat. He didn't look to be very tall, but the bulge of biceps swelling the rolled sleeves of his shirt bespoke a strength diminished little, if any, by the onset of years.

The wagon rumbled to a stop, and the driver dropped the reins and clambered agilely out, leaving it to his older companion to secure the lines. Stark surveyed the youth who bore a definite resemblance to Jeffrey Tyler. None of Tyler's sly humor, though, lurked in his manner or in the flashing eyes he cast appraisingly at Stark and Thaddeus, and lastly, Prudence. He wore baggy clothes and an old slouch hat pulled low on his head.

The stocky man who'd been riding shotgun lumbered forward, grinning. "You're looking good, Sarge," he greeted Caleb. "We was afraid you'd turned into buzzard bait somewhere along the trail."

"Not quite, but almost," Caleb responded, indicating the

healing scar on his temple. "Come on over here, Hollis, and meet these folks what come to help us out. This here's James Stark, also known as the Peacemaker. He's the man I went to Guthrie to hire. Reckon he would've made a pretty fair Buffalo Soldier himself. And this is his missus, Miss Prudence. Then this fellow's my nephew, Thaddeus Jenkins. He decided to take a hand in this mess too."

Hollis stuck out a callused hand to Stark first, and Stark could tell by his grip this wasn't a man worried about proving his strength. There was no open belligerence in him, but there was a deep-set challenge in his dark eyes just the same. He was packing an old revolver that gave the impression of being an afterthought. Stark guessed that this man relied on his own physical power more than he did firearms, and had been doing so for a good long spell.

"Glad to have you along," he allowed gruffly, and Stark read the lingering reservation in his tone, particularly when his eyes drifted to Prudence. "Nice to meet you, too, ma'am," he said, touching the brim of his hat respectfully, then nodding a greeting to Thaddeus. "Good to have you here as well, Thaddeus."

"We had a clean run," Hollis told his partners as he turned away. "No manmade trouble, but the fords are running deep on the rivers. I let Pete here take the lines for a spell on the way back. The kid's getting to be a right good hand."

For the first time there was the hint of a smile on the youngster's face as he ambled forward. Stark sensed there was something he was missing in his assessment of the kid, and it was Prudence who spotted the problem.

She stepped forward to greet the youngster. "Pete doesn't sound appropriate for a young lady," she chided. "I'll bet it's a nickname, right?"

Stark tried to hide his surprise as the girl swept the hat off her head allowing a single long braid to tumble down her back. "That's right, ma'am. My real name's Patricia." There was an air of rebellion as she added, "But I like Pete better."

Beside him Stark saw an expression of equal shock settle onto Thaddeus' face. The girl's disguise, whether intentional or inadvertent, had been a good one. There was nothing in her clothes or mannerisms to give away her gender or her age. Stark guessed her to be around 20.

Prudence's expression remained warm and friendly. "Then Pete it is."

Jeffrey Tyler appeared out of the stable just then. "Good to have you back, Hollis. Pete, why don't you see to rustling us up some grub while we look after the team."

Pete appeared ready to object when Prudence slipped an arm around her shoulders. "Come on, Pete. I'll lend you a hand."

Pete shrugged away from her and trudged away toward the house. Prudence continued to smile patiently as she winked at Stark before following along.

With a comfortable ease born of practice, Tyler and Hollis fell to unhitching the team as Caleb sidled up to Stark and nudged him with his elbow. "See why I wanted your missus to come?"

"I'm beginning to, yes," Stark muttered. "What happened to the girl's mother?"

"Died of the fever right after Pete was born. Tyler never quite knew what to do with a little girl, so's he raised her as best he could, dragging her with him from town to town, job to job. Taught her the things he knew, but those ain't the things she needs at this point in her life. Neither one of them's seen that yet, though."

"So you thought you'd help them out, huh?"

"Well, it wasn't in my original plan, but when Miss Prudence seemed so set on coming, I sensed the good Lord working in His mysterious ways again. Won't hurt Pete none to see a strong woman who's ladylike *and* good at what she does."

Stark scowled. "Well, the good Lord and my wife have got their work cut out for them."

"Ain't it the truth," Caleb chuckled as he moved off to help lead the mules away. Thaddeus followed along.

Tyler hung back as the others entered the stable. "Tell your wife thanks for trying with Pete," he said walking over to Stark. "I never wanted her to wind up such a tomboy. Just ain't been many women along the roads we've traveled since her mother died."

Stark looked at him in surprise. Apparently Tyler's thoughts of late had run along the same lines as Caleb's.

"I ain't never encouraged her to be more ladylike neither," Tyler continued. "Always thought it was safer for her this way."

"Reckon you were right," Stark agreed. "Guess you've kept some pretty rough company over the years. Caleb said you were the one with the know how in the freight business. What outfits did you work for?"

"Well, after I left the pony soldiers, I signed on as cavvy boy, looking after the livestock, on a little ol' local line. Did that for a spell, then worked as a bullwhacker, all the time watching the way the muleskinners handled the teams. Finally, I asked the wagonmaster for a chance to fill an empty slot. I was a hard worker, and he gave me a chance driving a team. I've taken wagons down all the old trails, worked for all the big freighters and plungers at one time or another, even Mister P. G. Reynolds himself. There was a man, sure enough."

Stark had heard of the straight-laced livery stable operator who had built an empire around the delivery of mail, passengers, and freight in the Panhandle Region some two decades before. Reynolds was known to have operated a station on the Underground Railroad which spirited slaves to freedom during the War Between the States. Nevertheless, he had earned the respect of Confederate raider William Quantrill such that, during his infamous raid on Lawrence, Kansas, the renegade had attempted to keep any damage from coming to Reynolds' property. Tyler had apparently learned his trade from the best.

"I've walked many a mile driving oxen, eaten, I reckon, a ton of dust, and frozen my legs more than once working in flood waters to free a mired wagon. And I've put I don't know how many thousand miles under the wheels of wagons I've driven." Tears filled his eyes. "I left that life for farming when me and my missus got married. We had a right good start on building a nice spread when the fever took her. After that, I just couldn't make a go of the place by myself. So I had to go back to the only way I had to earn a living, and I took Pete with me. Maybe I should've tried harder at farming, then she wouldn't have turned out thisaway."

Stark reached out and patted his arm. "I don't know, Tyler. Seems to me she's the type who would've just put on a pair of overalls and followed you out into the fields to help with the plowing. Can't see much difference in that and in driving a freight wagon."

Tyler laughed in spite of himself. "I guess you're right, Mr. Stark. Appears you're right good at reading people. Never thought about that before."

"She's old enough to be making her own decisions about the direction her life takes," Stark opined. "You can't be taking a whole lot of credit either way at this point. Besides, my wife has a powerful way of influencing people . . . whether they want to be influenced or not. Let's give her a chance to work on Pete for a while. Could be the girl will end up wearing a dress and a ribbon in her hair before too long."

Tyler's laugh this time was full and hearty. "That'd take a miracle for sure—one I'll look forward to seeing."

"Well, I can't make any guarantees, you understand," Stark backpedaled. "But I have seen stranger things happen. So, tell me how you fellows got the Buffalo Freight Line started."

Tyler took up his account again, "Well, I managed to put away a little money working for other freighters. Then when I figured I had enough dinero to make a start, I rousted Hollis to see if he was a mind to go in as a partner. A freight line ain't no job for one man, and I knew I could trust Hollis with my life. Done it plenty of times when we rode under Sarge. And Hollis is mighty good with animals. Knew he'd take good care of the stock."

Stark nodded, looking over at the corral where the sleek mules milled around. He'd never seen a better kept string.

"Anyway," Tyler continued, "then we ran into Caleb. He didn't have much to call his own, but he was willing to put what he had into the pot. Things was going fine, and I figured I was building a business that could support Pete like she deserved. When she was a kid she used to talk some of going to college, and I had hopes of sending her. All of us has had our fill of fighting in our day, and we thought we'd put that all behind us. Then all this trouble started with Hagen, and now it looks like everything comes right back down to the fighting again."

Stark scowled at the thought of the injustice of this, and the other similar situations involving decent people that kept him in his line of work. "One way or another, there's always going to be fighting needed to keep anything worthwhile," he said aloud.

"Guess you're right, Mr. Stark. And like I said, none of us is any stranger to it. But being soldiers, we just need a battle plan. Think you can come up with one?"

"I'll do my best," Stark promised, hoping Tyler wouldn't press for details.

"Come and get it!" Pete shouted from the back porch of the house bringing an end to the conversation. Stark felt almost relieved.

Chapter Four

T hem was hard times," Caleb mused reflectively as he stretched his long legs out in front of him and leaned back in the rickety straight chair he occupied. "Thirteen dollars a month, and all the fighting, riding, boredom, and hard work you could ask for, along with all the beans and hard-tack you could eat."

The three ex-soldiers were seated with Thaddeus in a ragged circle out in the yard under the night sky relating stories of their past. Relaxing beside Prudence in the porch swing, Stark studied their faces. Even in the poor light, he could tell that all of them were caught up in remembering the old days when they'd ridden together in one of the toughest fighting forces the West had ever seen.

Made up solely of black soldiers, except for their commanding officers who were white, the 9th and 10th Cavalry Regiments had played major roles in taming Texas and the Plains country following the close of the War Between the States. They had battled Indians, desperadoes, and the elements themselves on a nonstop basis for over 10 years.

Those redoubtable soldiers had fought the Apaches, the Kiowas, the Comanches, and other hostile tribes to a standstill. They had held the lawless regions against marauding gangs of owlhoots, and labored to build forts and protect the settlements that sprang up around them. In so doing, they had helped mightily in making the Southwest safe for settlers and civilization. It had been their enemies, the Indians, who had dubbed them "buffalo soldiers" because of their strength and tenacity as fighting men, and because of their appearance.

Stark shifted his weight a bit and slipped an arm around Prudence. She sighed and settled contentedly into the curve of his shoulder. Supper had filled his belly comfortably. The mingled scents of food, dust, muleflesh, and the grassland teased his nostrils. The coolness of dusk felt good on his face.

Following the meal, they had moved their chairs outdoors to enjoy the evening, careful to stay clear of the lighted doorway, which might silhouette a target for a lurking sharpshooter. Pete prowled restlessly on the outer rim of their gathering.

"Yeah, they was hard times, right enough," Tyler agreed easily with Caleb's comment. Some of his good humor had returned during dinner following his talk with Stark about his daughter. "I guess I'd have to say you couldn't pay me to live through them again. But then, you couldn't pay me to have missed them either!"

Even Stark grinned. He felt some honor to be on the fringe of a gathering of such men as these. The Buffalo Soldiers had been the stuff of heroes and legends.

"The Tenth Regiment of the U.S. Cavalry, reporting to Colonel Benjamin Grierson," Caleb murmured. "I still have our old standard, you know that? Kept it all this time. Carry it sometimes for luck. It flew proud."

Hollis shook his head. "All I got is a Lipan arrowhead still in me." He rolled his powerful shoulder as if to work out lingering stiffness. "Pains me now and again when it's fixing to rain. Caught it at Mount Carmel."

"Mount Carmel," Caleb echoed reflectively. "No coats, and water freezing in our canteens. Mules kept slipping and falling into the canyons. But we tracked them braves down and whipped them when they turned on us. Before we made it back to Fort Clark, I thought I'd never be warm again."

"As I recall, we was always either freezing our bones or burning our tails," Tyler said dryly. "Remember the Staked Plains? We was after the Comanches. If Old Nick ever had a stomping ground in the world, it was them plains!"

"Eighty-six hours without water," Caleb said tonelessly. "We couldn't swallow food because our throats were too dry. Men were falling over in their tracks, or wandering off half-crazy. And in the back of our minds we were wondering whether the Comanches might not finish us off before the heat and the sun did first. But Captain Nolan drove us on, and Private Howard told us jokes even when his mouth was so dry he couldn't do more than croak the words out. If we hadn't made it to Double Lakes when we did, I don't reckon none of us would've lasted another hour."

Even Pete had stopped her restless prowling to listen, Stark saw. The girl's face was unreadable in the dimness.

"And just think what all we might've done if they'd given us decent horses and gear," Tyler said laconically.

"Second-rate rations, third-rate guns, and fourth-rate nags," Hollis agreed in a low rumble. "We got the castoffs of the other regiments, and we still did the jobs none of them could do." A bitter pride echoed in his tones.

"You even whipped Victorio and his Apaches, didn't you?" Stark asked to keep the conversation going.

"We whipped them, overtook them when they run off, and then whipped them again," Hollis confirmed.

"We skirmished them and lost a good man," Caleb took up the account. "Private Willis Tockes it was. He went down firing right and left into a swarm of braves. They faded away into the desert after that, but Colonel Grierson reckoned Victorio would be trying for Rattlesnake Springs to get water. That was some sixty-five miles away, and them Apaches could cover ground in the desert at a pace that'd kill most men within a few hours."

Caleb hesitated for a long moment. Stark sensed that reminiscing about old times and past battles wasn't always pleasant for these seasoned veterans.

"Colonel Grierson started us moving at three the next morning," Caleb went on at last. "He kept a range of mountains between us and the route Victorio was taking, and we *marched.* Covered that sixty-five miles of desert in twenty-one hours. When Victorio did get to the Springs, we was there waiting for him. He had to turn south without water, and eventually headed into Mexico where we couldn't follow him."

Stark realized he'd been holding his breath. He had heard of that legendary trek when black troopers had outmarched the Apache warriors on their own ground, but to hear one of the men who'd been a part of it recount the tale was a privilege he counted high.

"Yep," Tyler said wryly. "And here Morg Hagen thinks he's just tangling with a bunch of old men. He must not know we're genuine heroes!"

Stark saw Pete turn sharply away and disappear into the darkness.

"All that was a long time ago," Caleb reminded quietly.

No one answered him, and after a moment he pushed himself stiffly up out of his chair. His face was in shadow. "I expect we better see to setting guard duty and then hitting the sack."

With all of them taking turns, the shifts at guard duty were short. Stark pulled his in the small hours of the morning, when dawn was casting a crimson fire just beyond the horizon.

The others were up and stirring by the time it was full light, readying gear and animals for the day's work. But it was Stark, keeping an eye on the road, who first spotted the tightly bunched group of horsemen headed their way from town.

"Company calling," he sang out.

Caleb reached his side quickly. He squinted in the growing light then gave a resigned grunt. "Ain't wasting no time, is he? That's Morg Hagen leading the pack."

"Then I guess we better be ready to welcome them," Stark surmised. "Hollis, you and Pete get out of sight in the stable. Keep us covered. Tyler, you watch out for anybody trying to sneak in on us across the field. Caleb, you, me, and Thaddeus will do the talking." He turned to Prudence who had appeared on the porch wiping her hands after doing the breakfast dishes. "Prudence, just stay in the house out of sight for now."

Prudence scowled and appeared ready to object, but finally nodded reluctantly and went back inside. As everyone moved into place, Stark put his attention back on the approaching horsemen, narrowing his eyes to study the lead rider.

Morg Hagen was a cocky little man who sat his big appaloosa stallion with an arrogance having nothing to do with his stature, but everything to do with having a passel of gunsels at his beck and call. Sharp eyes and a blade of a nose showed above a gray goatee that came to a precise point below his chin. His lips were so thin that there seemed to be only the merest slit between mustache and beard. He wore a fancy tailored suit, a low-crowned hat, and a revolver in a cutaway holster that meant he probably knew how to use it.

The men behind him were of the same ilk as those who had ambushed Caleb. Eight in all, they were bristling with pistols, a handful of long guns, and even a couple of sawed-offs. Watchful eyes moved restlessly in grim tight-lipped faces. A disreputable bunch, Stark gauged them, and more dangerous than a den of rattlesnakes. He was just as glad Prudence was out of sight.

Hagen hauled his horse out of its canter to an abrupt prancing halt. As if on signal, the riders spread out to flank him on either side so they were no longer bunched in a tight group. Stark's eyes narrowed even further. He curled his fingers a little tighter in the lever action of his shotgun, but left it hanging at arm's length.

Hagen's piercing eyes flicked dismissively over the others and settled on Stark. The slash under his mustache curled down in a brief frown.

"I got word you were back, Caleb." His voice was surprisingly deep, and his eyes didn't leave Stark until after he'd started speaking. "You have a good trip?"

"Passable," Caleb said tersely.

"Your head looks like you ran into trouble."

"Nothing that couldn't be handled," Caleb said tonelessly.

Hagen reared back a little bit. "Is that a fact? Well, who're your friends here?"

"This here's my nephew, Thaddeus Jenkins, and this fellow goes by James Stark." Caleb nodded at each as he gave their names.

One of the hard cases, a two-gun hombre in a black vest, urged his horse forward a little and squinted closely at Stark. He gave a thin smile then eased his mount back in line. Hagen's eyes darted in his direction. A few of the other gunsels glanced curiously at their comrade.

"Your partners don't seem too sociable this morning," Hagen commented, as though the interruption hadn't occurred. "Why not call them out so we can parley?"

"Got nothing to parley about."

Hagen's dark brows grew together. "I thought we had an offer on the table—a good one, in hard cash. More than this two-bit outfit is worth. I was hoping maybe your trip might've given you a chance to chew things over, and be a little more reasonable."

"You might say my uncle and his friends have made me their business manager," Thaddeus spoke up for the first time. "I'll do any dealing that's to be done on their behalf."

"Ah, yes, you must be that fancy dan lawyer Caleb's been jawing about. You sure you want to deal yourself into this hand, boy? Law books and freight lines don't exactly mix. Could get a little dangerous for you. I been hearing about a lot of *accidents* happening to these fellows lately."

Thaddeus subtly pulled back the coattail of his jacket to reveal the pistol holstered at his side. "I'm not all that accident prone myself. I tend to believe a little planning and anticipation can go a long way toward *preventing* accidents.

Now, the Buffalo Freight Line isn't for sale. You might as well accept that and be on your way."

Stark could tell Hagen was angered by Thaddeus' manner and precise cultured language. His head drew back a little. The two-gun hombre's horse stirred restlessly.

"You talk mighty big for an uppity darky. I own this town." Hagen gestured about him with a short arm. "I own these men and plenty more like them, almost like your kind used to be owned. Why, if I ordered it, my men could run you off right now."

"You could try," Stark said coldly.

Hagen's eyes shifted to him. "What's your stake in this, cowboy?"

Stark shrugged. "Just a hired hand."

"I've heard of him, boss," the two-gun rider spoke up. "This is the fellow they call the Peacemaker. He's got quite a reputation as a hired gun and bounty hunter. Works outta Guthrie."

Hagen appraised Stark shrewdly. "That true?"

"Just talk."

Hagen's head swung toward his hired gun. "You willing to find out if all the talk is accurate, Sanger?"

The gunman smiled slowly. "Just say the word, boss."

Stark tilted the barrel of the shotgun up just a little. He noted Sanger's matched guns. They were hung for doing serious business. Stark had no doubts he was good. It just remained to be seen how good.

"See what I mean?" Hagen boasted. "These men are mine!"

"You may own these sorry yahoos," Stark said deliberately, never taking his eyes off Sanger. "But you don't own Buffalo Freight. So like the man said, accept it and get going."

"Shoot, boss, don't let these darkies and this two-bit gun-slinger get the bluff on us!" The speaker was a burly hard case who edged his horse forward a mite as he spoke.

Bearded, hatless, and balding, he wore a vest without a shirt under it, despite the morning's chill. Mats of filthy black hair covered his broad chest. He would've made two of Hollis Kelso. A long-barreled shotgun lay across his thighs.

"I don't figure to let them bluff me, Mauler," Hagen said with a superior sneer. "So you're ready to take them on, too, huh?"

"Like Sanger said, just say the word."

"Chain up your dogs, Hagen, or you'll be the first casualty," Stark said with deadly intensity.

Hagen's sneer remained in place, but he made a jerking motion with his head, and Mauler relaxed with a disgusted sigh.

Stark had never completely taken his eyes of Sanger. The gunhand caught his gaze, and gave a nod that was almost companionable.

"Thaddeus—was that your name?—I think you and your bunch need some more time to consider my offer now that you see more clearly what you're up against. I'm a big believer in making carefully considered decisions."

"We've already given your offer all the consideration it deserves," Thaddeus said bluntly.

Hagen touched a mocking forefinger to the brim of his fine hat. "Well, then I guess the negotiations are at an end and it's time to move on to other forms of persuasion."

He turned his big appaloosa neatly about. His men followed. Sanger was the last. He backed his sorrel expertly for a half-dozen yards to keep Stark in front of him. Then he wheeled the animal on a nickel and clattered after his cohorts, head turned just a little back over his shoulder as he rode.

Stark could have sworn he was smiling.

Chapter Five

"The train will be arriving in town later this morning," Caleb said as they all gathered to watch Hagen and his crew disappear down the road. "We'll need to send a wagon to the depot to meet it. We're due to pick up a load of supplies for one of the ranches up north."

"I'll go," Hollis grunted.

Stark had watched the sullen glower grow in the big man's eyes since Hagen had departed.

"Now, don't go looking for trouble, Hollis," Caleb advised.

"Sure, Sarge," Hollis rumbled.

"I'd like to go along," Stark offered. "I need to get a look at the town."

"Guess that'd be all right," Hollis allowed. "I'll go hitch up a team."

Stark turned to Caleb. "We need to fort up the stable and the house. Why don't you all get busy with that while we're gone."

"Sure thing, Peacemaker. Been thinking along them lines

myself. The house is in purty good shape already. We just need to start closing the shutters over the windows at night. It won't take much to nail up boards across the windows in the stable with slots for firing. If there's any side of the building where we don't have a clear field of fire, we'll cut rifle ports in the walls. We'll bring in some buckets of sand, too, for putting out fires, and we'll lay in plenty of drinking water."

"Sounds like a good plan," Stark agreed. "Hollis and I'll stock up on food and ammo while we're in town."

"Good, good." Caleb paused reflectively. "When we're done with fortifications, we can start clearing that brush away from out back. Might be we should delay making any more deliveries until all this work is finished."

"We can get it all done today, Sarge," Tyler predicted. "Why, it'll be just like a work detail at Fort Supply in the old days. You reckon Hagen'll try to hit us here, Peacemaker?"

"Maybe so, maybe not," Stark temporized. "But I don't aim to get caught napping if he does."

Tyler flashed Stark a tired smile. "Well, at least now you see how things are here. We're sitting on a powderkeg, and Hagen's got a fire and the matches. Sorry you signed up for this hitch?"

Stark flashed a smile of his own and slapped Tyler on the back. "Naw, I still consider it an honor to serve with an outfit like this one. And despite what Hagen thinks of his own importance, he ain't nearly the opponent Victorio was. So before you fellows get too discouraged, you need to remember you've licked better than him lots of times."

The look of sly humor crept back into Tyler's eyes. "That was lots of years ago, Peacemaker. Lots of years. Right, Sarge?"

Caleb chuckled. "Don't seem near as many now as it did a few minutes ago. Thanks for the reminder, Mr. Stark."

The wagon Hollis chose for the trip to town was an old Conestoga, which Stark figured had probably seen service as a prairie schooner hauling pioneers in the early days of Western settlement. It still looked to be plenty sturdy.

Hollis took the lines without comment and headed the three double teams down the short stretch of road toward town. Seated beside his short solid bulk, Stark settled himself into the familiar jolting rhythm of the old wagon.

The sun was high enough to be warming things up, and flies hovered persistently over the mules as they plodded along. Ears and tails flicked irritably to scatter the pests when they lit. Hollis twitched the lines to help when one of them came into range. Stark saw a horsefly as big as the end of his thumb settle down near the bony spine of the palomino mule in the lead team, just clear of the twitching tail.

Hollis let out a short grunt. One-handed, he plucked a coiled bullwhip up from beside his booted foot, and sent it snaking out with a single snap of his arm. The horsefly disappeared in a spray of crimson. The mule gave a lift of its head as if in thanks.

"Good aim," Stark remarked.

"Don't like nothing getting after my mules. That there's Jenny." Hollis tugged on the line to indicate the palomino. "She's a fine one. Makes a mighty good bell mule. She won't never roam far at night. Always stays near the wagon. Put a bell on her so's the other mules can hear it, and they'll stay right near her." Hollis hesitated a moment, then added almost gruffly, "You ever handled mules?"

"A little bit," Stark allowed.

"Me, I fancy a team of mules any day over a team of

oxen. Sure, them oxen winter a little bit better on the open range, and they ain't likely to stampede, but they're slow as all to get out, and their feet are always giving them trouble. Now, you take a mule like old Jenny there. She'll outlast an ox in hot or cold, move faster, and take less water. And she's a sight smarter to boot."

"Sounds like you know your animals."

"I should. Seems like I always pulled duty tending the livestock at the forts where we were stationed. Tyler told me once it was because I was so much like an old ox myself." He gave a little snort of a chuckle that was the first sign of humor Stark had heard from him.

An eerie wail drifted from the grassland as they skirted Beaver's Main Street on a rutted track lined with shabby hovels. "There's the train," Hollis said. "We're right on time."

The big old Baldwin locomotive was just pulling up at the depot in a cloud of cinders and smoke as Hollis guided the wagon to the far side of the loading dock. What looked to be a large frame warehouse stood adjacent to the depot. Beyond it was a turnaround for the train.

Towns like Beaver, Stark knew, were often the end of the line for the railroads. Supplying the needs of ranchers and settlers in the surrounding territory was what kept outfits like Buffalo Freight in business. Of course, whether Buffalo Freight could remain in business with Morg Hagen looking to corral it, was anything but a sure bet, Stark thought bleakly.

A few passengers got off the train. Hollis signed a receipt, and he and Stark started shifting sacks, crates, and drums from one of the freight cars to the Conestoga. The engineer and other railroad employees straggled off toward the cafe for coffee.

"There. That should do it," Hollis said at last as he hefted the final keg of nails into the wagon with a flex of arm and shoulder. He vaulted off the loading dock, and Stark joined him. Sweat gleamed on Hollis' dark skin.

"We got company," Stark commented.

Hollis swung about. Ambling toward them was the burly shirtless Mauler and a trio of strapping hard cases.

"Where's the law in this burg?" Stark asked, keeping his eyes on the approaching foursome.

"Outta sight, I reckon. He wouldn't put a stop to this anyway." Hollis was studying the hard cases as well. "They ain't armed," he said, and something like satisfaction was in his voice.

Mauler had discarded his shotgun, and the waists of his cronies were clear of gunbelts. Brawlers, Stark thought. Rough-and-tumble boys. By refusing to pack guns, they could keep this on the kind of terms they obviously wanted: Fist and boot, with the odds two-to-one in their favor. Stark rolled his head about on his neck and hitched his shoulders in anticipation.

"Well, if it ain't the gunslinger and his darky friend." Mauler halted three yards distant and crossed his thick arms across his vest. On his feet, beside the other rowdies, his true height and mass became evident. "What're you boys doing in a white man's town, anyway?"

"Pull in your horns," Stark advised coldly. "We didn't come here for trouble."

"Well, it appears to me you found it, just the same. Me and my pards don't take to the notion of black folks and them that hangs around with them taking on airs and acting like they're regular people. What business have them old slaves got owning a freight line? They shouldn't be allowed to own nothing. They ought to just be working for their betters, and grateful for maybe getting some crusts to eat and a stock shed to sleep in, just like in the old days." His cronies muttered agreement.

"Stand aside," Stark said levelly. "We're ready to pull out."

"Not yet you ain't." Mauler smiled with ugly enjoyment. "We're going to teach you a lesson, teach you some respect for your betters, and put a little something else onto the bargaining table for Mr. Hagen."

"Looks like Hagen done cut loose a few of his cur dogs," Hollis said in a tone that was little more than a deep rumble in his chest. "It shouldn't take much to send them yelping back to their master."

"What's that you say, boy?" one of the other three brawlers snarled. He was the smallest of them, but he was still pretty hefty.

Stark sighed. He let his eyes roam quickly about. He fancied he saw a spare figure lurking just within the entry of the neighboring warehouse, but no one else was in sight. They weren't going to be able to sidestep this, he concluded sourly. After some of the words that had been spoken, he wasn't sure he *wanted* to sidestep it. The odds were against them in a brawl, but he wasn't prone to haul iron on un-armed men.

So, maybe he could lower the odds.

He let an expression of fear and worry cross his face, and cut a quick glance at Hollis before stepping forward, open hands extended, palms up.

"Count me out," he said, still moving forward. "This ain't my fight." Behind him, he heard Hollis grunt in surprise.

He halted in front of the foursome, conscious of their sneering contemptuous grins, but too caught up in what he was doing to let it bother him much. "Look, fellows, I got no quarrel with you. I earn my pay with my gunhand. I don't want to risk busting it up in a fist fight."

"Big bad fighting man," the smallest said scornfully. "He turns yellow when some real men show up."

"Like I said, this ain't my fight." Stark knew he was playing a dangerous game by getting this close to the four of them, but he was betting it was worth it.

"About what I expected from you, gunslick," Mauler added.

Stark expected something from them, too, and he got it.

"You ain't walking that easy, fancy dan," the smallest one said, and stepped arrogantly forward, fist cocked.

Instantly, before he could cut the punch loose, Stark swung his booted foot hard in from the side. The edge of the sole smashed against the brawler's lead ankle just as his weight came down on it. The man cried out as his leg buckled. Both of Stark's open hands shot forward to lock behind the fellow's neck and yank him down and forward. His face plunged to meet Stark's rising knee. Stark hooked his right fist savagely to the hinge of the jaw as the fellow went down like a head-shot mule.

No such thing as dirty fighting against these odds . . .

Mauler let out an enraged bellow and lunged forward. Rather than dodge, Stark tried to shove the falling rowdy into him. It was the wrong move. Mauler swept his collapsing crony aside with a single swing of one tree-trunk arm. The other arm swept out to envelope Stark and crush him against the giant's half-naked chest.

Stark had a brief impression of the other two hard cases rushing past to close in on Hollis. He didn't have time to worry about the ex-soldier. He had enough to do worrying about surviving Mauler's bear hug.

It was like being pinned against a tree. Stark felt his ribs bending, and thought his chest was about to collapse. Snarling, slobbering, Mauler ducked his head and tried to ram his bald dome up under Stark's chin. Stark glimpsed the scars of old brawls on the grimy scalp as he twisted his head aside and heaved his weight backwards. Mauler lurched to keep his balance, and Stark tangled the fingers of both hands in the filthy matted hair of his bare chest and yanked with all the strength he could muster.

Mauler's howl of anguish deafened him. The big man's arms snapped open. Stark staggered loose. With his feet under him, he used his right fist, hooking twice to Mauler's ear, twisting it each time as it landed. Switching arms, he sank his left into the hard flab of Mauler's gut.

Mauler shuddered under the blows, but he didn't back off. His name suited him, because he was a wrestler, a grappler. He clamped a hand with fingers like ice tongs on Stark's shoulder and jerked him forward, shoving a flat palm of his other hand full at Stark's face. Stark ducked his head just before Mauler's palm blotted out his vision. He took the jolting impact on his forehead. His hat went flying. He ripped an uppercut to Mauler's jaw. The beard cushioned the blow, but Mauler wavered, and Stark, with a convulsive twist of his body, tore free of those grasping fingers.

Mauler pivoted toward him. "I'm going to tie you in knots, gunslick," he growled.

"Start tying," Stark said, and flashed in with an overhand right that rocked Mauler's head on his bull neck.

Stark backstepped as Mauler's arms reached out. He felt his spine come up against the edge of the loading dock, and understood Mauler had him cornered. Mauler understood it too. Barbaric pleasure gleamed in his eyes as he bore in. Stark knew if Mauler ever got hold of him for very long, he would be bent and broken and crippled—that is, if Mauler let him live at all.

The big man lunged. Stark shifted his body sideways in a feint, wheeled in the other direction, and ducked clear of Mauler's closing arms. He drove a right and a left into Mauler's side, shot another right against his ear, before Mauler tried to take his head off with a sweeping back-handed swing of his outstretched arm.

Stark got under it, and went to work with both hands as Mauler completed his turn. He felt his fists sink into the solid suet of Mauler's body, and bang against the hard bone of his skull. Too late, then, he tried to dance clear.

Once more Mauler caught him, this time by both shoulders, fingers sinking deep into flesh and muscle. He yanked Stark forward, trying to smash his forehead down into Stark's face. Again, Stark ducked his head so that it was Mauler's face, driven by the combined force of his attempted butt, and the yanking pull of his arms, that ran into the top of Stark's skull.

Stark felt like he'd been kicked by one of Hollis' mules, but the impact had to have been even worse for Mauler. His grip on Stark's shoulders loosened. Stark pumped both fists at the same time into Mauler's body, then drove them up in a twin uppercut to the jaw. Even the heavy beard couldn't absorb all of that double impact. Mauler actually rocked back a step. Stark threw a straight right square between his eyes, twisting his shoulders into the blow.

Mauler's knees buckled just a bit, and a fierce rejoicing rose up in Stark. Mauler was hurt! Stark set himself to fire another punch. But even hurt, Mauler was dangerous. Blindly he flung his whole bulk into Stark, not trying for a hold, just wanting to knock him flat. Stark went down bruisingly beneath Mauler's heaving, flailing mass. He felt as though his spine had snapped. Panic roiled up in him. Mauler's barbaric face snarled at him; Mauler's huge hands fumbled and battered at him; Mauler's crushing weight smothered him.

Desperately Stark bucked and heaved, but the whipcord strength of his body was no match for Mauler's layers of muscle and flab. In the last moment before blind panic overcame him, he realized that to give in to it would mean the end. His mind snapped into a feral clarity bent only on survival.

Openhanded, he swung his outstretched arms up from the ground and clapped his palms against Mauler's ears. He saw a grimace of pain flash across Mauler's brutish features. The huge paws groping at him lost some of their coordination. Stark shot his left hand up to grasp Mauler's beard and yank his head back. He ground his right fist in under the beard, pressing and twisting it against Mauler's exposed throat until Mauler reared back out of reach.

Still down flat, Stark writhed backwards to get his legs clear. Mauler loomed hugely over him. He jerked his right knee back, then drove the heel of his boot up to the bigger man's low-set brow, like he was trying to kick down an oak door.

On his knees, Mauler reeled, his upper body swinging in a complete circle. Stark flung himself erect. Mauler, too, was trying to rise. Stark stepped in and battered at his skull, kneed his face, drew back and launched another kick, driving his leg straight out, the thrust of his whole body behind it. His boot smashed Mauler's head back so he was looking at the sky. The force of his kick sent Stark lurching past as Mauler toppled awkwardly onto his side and lay still.

Stark had no time for celebration. He spun, his breath

rasping in his lungs. His sweat-blurred vision took in one of the other brawlers sprawled senseless in the dust. Beyond him, the fourth was squared off with Hollis, fists raised.

As Stark blinked his vision clear, the hard case swung a sledging right hand that Hollis, arms sagging, looked too tired to avoid. Still, he appeared to roll with the blow, but not enough to keep it from dropping him to one knee. Gloating, the rowdy stepped close to finish the job.

Stark darted forward, but before he could reach the combatants, Hollis came suddenly to life. As the brawler towered over him with fist cocked, Hollis lunged upwards. One hand clamped on the fellow's thigh; the other, reaching higher, closed on his shoulder. With a strained roar of effort, Hollis lifted the writhing hard case clean off his feet, then dashed him to the ground with enough force to raise a cloud of dust about his form.

Next, Hollis was on him like a bobcat on a rabbit. He caught one arm, twisting it cruelly as he slammed a heavy boot down on his victim's chest to pin him in place.

"You hear me, boy?" he spat. "I want you to call me sir. You understand? Say it!"

"Hollis, that's enough!" For a moment it was as though Stark's words had frozen Hollis in place. Then the stubbled head came about in a series of slow jerks, and Stark found himself staring into a pair of wild glaring eyes.

He met their gaze levelly. "Enough," he repeated.

Hollis blinked. The glare faded. He shook his head and slowly eased up on his victim. Released, the rowdy scrambled away on hands and knees.

"Yeah," Hollis croaked. "I guess it is."

His broad shoulders were heaving, and sweat ran in rivulets down his broad face and thick arms. This old soldier had just polished off two much younger opponents, both of whom were seasoned brawlers. Cuts and bruises showed on his lined face.

"I couldn't get ahold of that one," he explained between breaths. "I had to trick him into getting close and standing still. He fancied himself some sort of boxer, I reckon."

Stark was suddenly glad they'd been on the same side, and that it hadn't been him tangling with Hollis Kelso.

A dog's abrupt barking brought Stark around. "It ain't over," he advised hoarsely. Hollis grunted as he followed Stark's gaze.

A dozen more rowdies were coming purposefully toward them from the direction of the saloon. Most of them were toting ax handles. Hagen had sent some reinforcements. The odds had just gotten worse.

Chapter Six

Mauler still lay where he had fallen. Striding swiftly, Hollis went past his motionless bulk toward the wagon. When he turned he had the coiled bullwhip in his hand. Near the warehouse, the dog's barking grew more frantic.

The dozen new hard cases had spread out in a little circle as they closed in. One of them was slapping his ax handle rhythmically into the palm of a leathery hand. They halted as Hollis drew even with Stark. Most of them were packing iron.

"Pick up your pals and haul them off unless you want a taste of something even worse than what they got," Hollis ordered.

The rhythmic slapping of the ax handle came to a stop. "I don't reckon we're of a mind to do that," its owner said.

"We'll see." Hollis stepped clear of Stark and let the coils of the whip drop to the ground, the butt still gripped firmly in his fist. He flexed his arm so the braided leather writhed lazily along the ground. One of the rowdies edged a step backwards.

"Come on, boys. There's just two of them," the spokesman said. He moved in confidently, hefting the ax handle.

Hollis stepped forward, and his arm lashed out fast as a pop of sound split the air. The hard case's ax handle was snatched from his fingers. The wooden shaft spun high, then dropped a couple of yards from Hollis' feet.

Hollis laid about him left and right, and the whip writhed and snapped and hissed in his grip. The rowdies retreated before him, one of them crying out as the touch of the lash shredded the fabric of his sleeve and drew blood from his forearm beneath.

Stark felt a tingle of foreboding. The rowdies were tough, and they didn't cotton to being backed down by one man. They spread their ranks even wider. Motion caught the edge of Stark's vision. His eyes shifted to see an ax handle, flung by one of the hard cases, spinning end over end toward Hollis. Hollis sidestepped, the cadence of his strokes broken. For a heartbeat, the whip lay limp in the dust, and their attackers rushed forward.

Stark's arm came about in an arc, and the Colt Peacemaker was in his hand. The shot cracked and the ax handle shattered in the air, the pieces raining down on the pack of yahoos. The rush came to an abrupt halt.

Stark leveled the Peacemaker at the men facing him. "That's far enough. The rules of this game just changed. Now clear out."

Again the leader spoke up. "Come on, fellows. We can't let him and that old darky get the best of us. He can't get off more'n one shot before we reach him."

"That one shot will be the last sound you ever hear," Stark warned, bringing the Colt to bear on the leader.

The braggart's confidence slipped a little. Stark felt the

first glimmer of hope that he could pull this off without getting himself or Hollis seriously hurt.

But before the men could react, three rifle shots slammed through the morning air, one after the other in a continuous roll of sound. The attackers' attention shifted to the source of the fire. Stark looked around to see who'd taken a hand in the fracas.

"That's enough, you men!" a firm voice called. "I'll not have this sort of brawling on or near my property!"

A spare nondescript figure had emerged from the warehouse, a lever-action rifle held competently at waist level. He strode boldly forward. "That's enough, I said! Now, clear out. Go on back to the saloon."

Reluctantly the rowdies backed off. A few of them helped their fallen comrades to their feet.

The spokesman was the last to retreat. "This ain't over," he warned Stark. "We got us a man who's good as you with a gun—maybe better." With a final glare at Stark, he turned his attention to the newcomer. "Mr. Hagen will hear about this."

"Go on. Get out." The man moved the rifle barrel for emphasis.

Muttering, the fellow stalked away after his companions.

"We're obliged to you, Mr. Shuttle," Hollis said, coming forward. He still gripped the whip absently in his hand. The savagery which Stark had seen in him had passed.

"I'm not sure you gentlemen needed any assistance, but things looked to be getting out of hand."

"Mr. Stark, this here's Oscar Shuttle," Hollis did the introductions. "He owns the warehouse there. Does a little bit of business with us from time to time."

Shuttle wasn't impressive at first glance. He was starting to show some age. His slender build, sallow features, and thinning hair added to his unassuming appearance. He wore town clothes, but the grip of his hand in Stark's carried surprising strength. He didn't offer to shake hands with Hollis.

"Hope you didn't buy any trouble with Morg Hagen by helping us out," Stark told him.

Shuttle shook his head as if dismissing the notion. "Morg and I do some business together. He knows I won't stand for his hired guns causing trouble on my property." He cocked his head curiously at Hollis. "You boys aren't giving in to his offer to buy your company, I take it."

Hollis nodded. "That's the truth. We reckon to stay on. We'll keep Buffalo Freight going, all right."

Now Shuttle's curious probing gaze was turned on Stark. "I understand you and another—gentleman—are helping them out."

"That's right." Stark watched as Hollis recoiled the whip. It looked like the news was all over town, and they'd just arrived late the day before, he reflected.

"So are you and your hired hand partners in Buffalo Freight?"

"He's my friend," Stark said shortly, "not my hired hand. In fact, in a way I'm working for him. He's an attorney. He arranged for me to get this job."

Shuttle cleared his throat. "I see. Well, we're always glad to have new faces in town, particularly when they're helping out a struggling business. That makes for a good economy, and that helps us all." He broke off with a frown. "I am sorry about the trouble with Morg's men here today. I don't like seeing brawls like that in our town. Bad for the town, and I'm no fighting man to have to defend myself or others."

Stark kept silent. Shuttle hadn't handled that rifle like any tenderfoot he'd ever seen.

He noted that a medium-sized dog with short brown hair had advanced halfway from the warehouse and was standing quite still, watching them warily. He recalled the barking that had alerted him to the approach of the second bunch of attackers.

"That your dog?" he asked Shuttle.

Shuttle glanced around in surprise. "Him? No, he's just a stray that's been hanging around. Some of my loaders feed him scraps when they're working." His tone judged the animal as of no consequence.

Stark was studying the dog closely. "Mind if we take him?"

"No, haul him off if you can catch him," Shuttle invited. "I'll be well rid of him."

"Here, fellow," Stark addressed the dog. Leaving the other men, he went slowly forward, continuing to speak to the animal.

The dog lowered his head slightly. Stark could see the feral tension in his gaunt body. The poor mutt hadn't been living easy. His ribs were clearly visible beneath his ragged coat, and several engorged ticks clung to him. A partially healed scar, probably left by a grazing bullet, angled across his hindquarters.

"That's a good dog," he whispered, stretching his hand the last few inches to stroke the coarse fur. At his touch, the wariness drained out of the gaunt body. The tail began to wag faster, and the fanged mouth opened in what Stark figured was a smile. Some care and food would put the animal back good as new. He wondered idly how the mutt had ended up here in this remote prairie town. He might ask the same question of himself, he concluded wryly.

With the dog trotting happily at his heels, he returned to the other two men. The animal shied away from Shuttle, but went directly to Hollis, who roughed up his ears a little, and gave Stark a faintly puzzled look.

"Thanks for the help and the dog," Stark told Shuttle.

"I'm sure I'll be seeing you about town. Good day." The man headed back toward his warehouse, rifle carried loosely at his side.

"Now we've got us a watchdog," Stark explained to Hollis as he boosted the canine into the wagon.

Hollis nodded with understanding. "Not a bad notion," he conceded. "Might give us some help standing guard duty. He sure sung out when those other yahoos showed up." He reached back to pat the dog's head. "We'll name you Watcher," he declared. "I do hope you live up to your name."

With the newly christened Watcher perched on the bulging grain sacks just behind the wagon seat, Hollis headed the mules back down the road.

"You're pretty handy in a fight." Hollis cut a sidewise glance at Stark. "You laid out that first hombre right neat before lighting into Mauler. I wasn't any too sure I could handle Mauler, but I was fixing to give it a try. Turned out, there wasn't no need. How'd you learn to fight thataway?"

"I picked up a few tricks here and there." Stark flexed his shoulders and winced. Too bad he hadn't picked up a few more tricks, he reflected sourly.

Hollis appeared to relax by degrees as they left the town behind. "You stuck your neck out today for me and Buffalo Freight. I appreciate that, I surely do." A glimmer of mirth shone in the old man's dark eyes. "I wasn't too sure about you at first, but now I'm about to change my mind. You'll do to ride shotgun for us, I reckon."

Stark gave a snort of laughter. "All I can say is it takes a heap of effort to win your approval."

The stable area was abuzz with activity when they pulled up to the storage shed. Caleb was busy sawing lumber, while Pete and Prudence nailed the newly cut boards in place. Tyler and Thaddeus were already at work on the underbrush with ax and sickle. Once the wagon was unloaded, Stark and Hollis pitched in.

Stark stopped behind Prudence inside the stable and reached around her to hold a bulky piece of lumber in place. She pulled a nail from the pocket of her divided riding skirt and gave it a competent whack.

He leaned in closer and said teasingly, "I had no idea I was marrying a master carpenter."

She elbowed him sharply in the ribs as she pulled out another nail. "I have many talents you have yet to discover."

Beside them, Pete tried to hide a smile. She offered Stark her hammer. "Here you go, Mr. Stark. Why don't you help Miss Prudence finish up here, and I'll go rake up the brush Dad and Thaddeus have cut so far."

Stark watched as she balanced a rake on her shoulder and walked away. He picked up a nail from the can on the floor to finish securing the board. He nodded toward Pete. "Making any progress with that one?" he asked Prudence.

She wrinkled her nose fetchingly. "Can't tell. I've been sticking to her like glue, but she hasn't opened up to me yet. She's very unhappy and troubled about something, though."

"Yeah," Stark agreed. He went outside to fetch the board Caleb had finished cutting. He noticed Pete had chosen to rake the brush closest to Thaddeus, rather than that which her father was working on. The pair seemed to be talking companionably. Both were smiling. When he went back into the stable, he paused behind Prudence and said in a low voice, "Find some excuse to go outside and have a look at Pete and Thaddeus."

Prudence laid down her hammer and went out to the water barrel to have a dipper of water. She came back in wearing a smile. "I think we might be witnessing the blossoming of a romance. I must admit, they would make a handsome couple."

"Yeah," Stark agreed again. "That might be a way to reach her, huh? She might want a woman's advice on how to become more attractive to a man . . . especially since she's apparently got a particular man in mind."

"Yeah." Prudence began nailing the board he held in place. "I hope she's not going to end up with a broken heart."

"What do you mean?" Stark asked, puzzled.

"Well, Thaddeus, of course. You really think he's interested in getting involved romantically?"

Stark grinned. "Whether a man's looking for romance or not falls by the wayside when the right woman comes along. Look at us. Last thing I wanted when I met you was to end up hitched. Yet, here we are—two old married people, settled and boring."

Prudence gave him another sharp jab to the ribs. "Settled and boring, huh? I'll remind you of that next time the bullets start flying or Morg Hagen sets his bruisers on you."

Her words brought the events of the morning back to him with gripping clarity. They were in a deadly struggle here. The aches left over from Mauler's beating were a painful reminder of that.

Tyler was almost as good as his earlier boast. By the time the afternoon shadows stretched long, all the revisions to the stable and outbuildings had been made, and a sizable section of the underbrush had been cut down.

Watcher, after having been fed and watered by Pete, had kept an interested eye on things, darting after varmints flushed from the shrinking stand of brush or barking at passersby on the road.

"Good idea, bringing that pup back," Caleb told Stark once in passing.

The sharper note of the dog's barking made Stark straighten from using his hand ax on a stubborn scrub oak. He'd moved out to the field to help Thaddeus and Tyler when the women went in to start supper. The hard work had done a lot to rid his body of the aches and pains left by Mauler's punishing grip, but he felt at least as old as any of the ex-soldiers as he came erect.

Two riders had just turned onto the short cutoff leading to the freight line headquarters from the main road. Stark straightened a little further in surprise as he recognized the small arrogant figure of Morg Hagen and the two-gunned silhouette of Sanger, his pet gunslinger.

Shifting the hatchet to his left hand, Stark moved to meet the pair. He saw Thaddeus and Caleb also headed in that direction. Tyler and Hollis, he noted with approval, were hanging back to keep an eye out and provide cover if need be.

Hagen's sharp eyes darted about, taking in the changes to the buildings and grounds. Stark didn't doubt but that the town boss grasped their significance.

"You fellows expecting company?" Hagen's first mocking question confirmed Stark's hunch.

"Just doing a little spring cleaning," Caleb drawled. "The two of you look mighty lonesome out here all by yourselves."

"I came alone for a purpose," Hagen said, ignoring Sanger's presence. He stepped down smoothly from his appaloosa.

"Nobody asked you to light down," Caleb pointed out.

Hagen paid no heed to the remark. Deliberately, he advanced until he was some five feet from the trio confronting him, just far enough so they wouldn't be looking down at his lesser height. There was no sign of fear in him. He put his hands on his hips and addressed Thaddeus and Stark as though Caleb wasn't present.

"I came to talk business. We've butted heads now. I don't know who came out on top, but I hear you're mighty handy with fist and boot, Stark. My man, Mauler, is still in sorry shape."

"Oh, I'm so sorry," Stark drawled sarcastically.

Hagen's eyebrow lifted angrily. "Yes, I'm sure you are. I'll pass along your regrets. At any rate, after that unfortunate business this morning, we all know that everybody's serious. I can appreciate that. So I'm willing to up my offer just a bit. I'll go four thousand dollars, no more."

It was a lot of money, Stark acknowledged to himself. Enough to tempt most men.

"No deal," Caleb spoke up. "And no need to keep upping the offer. If we're ever interested in selling, we'll let you know. Otherwise, leave us alone. And if you keep throwing your hired hands at us, they'll get hurt. Now, ride out."

Hagen's nostrils were flaring. His mouth had all but disappeared between his mustache and goatee. "Who do you think you are to talk to me like that, old man?" He bit out the words. "You're nothing but a bunch of muleskinners. I could roll over your sorry outfit like a freight wagon over an anthill anytime I choose."

"Whip up your team and come ahead," Stark invited. "But you'll need a sight better men than you've got now."

"You think I need my men at all? You think I need him?" Hagen tossed his head back at Sanger. "Sure, I hire men to do my fighting for me. I can afford it, but I don't have to do it." He brushed back his coattail with a movement that made Stark stiffen. His pistol in its cutaway holster was revealed. "You see this? It's a double-action Colt. Fires when you pull the trigger. No need to cock it first. That means it shoots fast, faster than the single-action irons most folks carry hereabouts."

Stark put his eyes on Sanger. The gunslick sat his saddle loose and relaxed. He gave a friendly smile that raised the hairs on the back of Stark's neck.

"If I wanted to," Hagen continued to boast, "I could face off with any of you two-bit muleskinners, and you'd never clear leather. I used to make my living with this gun."

Caleb's eyes were downcast. " 'The wicked have drawn out the sword,' " he murmured almost to himself, then lifted his eyes to Hagen and spoke with chilling softness. " 'Their sword shall enter into their own heart.' " His hand moved to hover over the old Colt Dragoon. "Maybe you'd like to try facing off with me right now?"

Hagen chuckled harshly. "That's just the point, old man. I don't need to. And you're right about one thing. There's no deal now. My new offer is this: Sign Buffalo Freight over to me, get out, and you'll live."

Caleb met his gaze unflinchingly and continued the quotation. " 'For the arms of the wicked shall be broken: but the Lord upholdeth the righteous.' You best be watching out for your arms, Hagen. And your neck."

"It'll take more than scripture to stop me, boy," Hagen spat.

"The Lord provides," Caleb said serenely.

Hagen wheeled and strode to his appaloosa. He mounted, and put the big horse around without looking back.

Sanger shifted in his saddle. "You favor toting a hand ax now, do you, Peacemaker?" he asked wryly, nodding at the hatchet still in Stark's fist.

"It's a handy tool to have around."

"You ain't holding it much like a tool."

"Depends on what job I have to do."

Sanger smiled again, performed his stunt of backing his horse away, then spun the animal and cantered after Hagen's retreating figure.

Stark hefted the hatchet and looked at Caleb. The ex-sergeant's aged features were alight with staunch determination.

Chapter Seven

Caleb paused in the shadows by the stable before continuing his rounds, accompanied by the faithful Watcher. He was grateful for the dog's alert presence. Watcher was proving himself a worthy addition to their little force. He chided himself for not having thought of getting a watchdog himself.

He wondered bleakly if he might be chiding himself for other, more costly, oversights before this ugly business was over. The weight of command seemed a lot heavier on his shoulders than it had all those years ago when he'd been in charge of far more troops than this handful of men. Maybe, back then, he hadn't been able to realize just how much stood to be lost if he made the wrong decision. Age had given him perception. Had it also robbed him of his nerve?

And there would be plenty more decisions to make in the coming days. Buffalo Freight had to keep operating, even if only on a limited basis. Otherwise, Hagen would've won without a shot being fired. Continued operations meant that wagons had to go out. And whatever men were driving those wagons would be plenty vulnerable to attack. But it was a risk they had to take.

In his mind's eye he reviewed the map of the Panhandle Region and the various routes the wagons followed in making their deliveries. The recollections were slow in coming. Of late, he'd noted, his memories of the old days in the cavalry, and the War Between the States, and even his childhood as a slave, stood out in his mind with startling clarity, while other, more recent memories were fuzzy. The realization bothered him, but there was little he could do about it. That awareness filled him, at times, with an unaccustomed sense of helplessness.

The run scheduled to leave in the morning, he recollected at last, headed north up a piece of the old Jones and Plummer Trail, across the wide Cimarron River into southern Kansas, and thence to scattered ranches and farms. Three days, maybe four, to make the entire run. And longer runs would be forthcoming, he knew.

Who to send, he wondered. He reckoned Stark, with his undoubted abilities in just about any sort of fracas, was the logical choice to ride shotgun. So, whose life to put on the line along with his?

He sighed heavily. His circuit of the grounds was completed. Time to mount to the roof to have a look-see from up there, he decided. The soft sound of the tack room door opening made him halt. In a moment, a short broad shape took form out of the gloom.

"Anything stirring?" came the quiet voice of Hollis Kelso.

"Just me and the dog," Caleb answered. He cocked his head a little. "Your watch ain't for a spell yet."

Hollis' broad shoulders shifted. "Having a little trouble

sleeping. That old Lipan arrowhead pains me some these days. I can feel it in there just kind of burning. And adding them boards and such to the windows makes it sort of stuffy inside there."

"Yeah, I sure appreciate you and Tyler giving up your room in the house to the Starks. Tyler resting okay?"

"Yeah. He's sacked out. I reckon I ought to be right tired myself, what with you working us all day, and that dustup me and the Peacemaker had in town." He shook his head wonderingly. "I tell you, Sarge, that man is a ring-tailed rounder in a fight."

"He don't appear to shy away much when trouble finds him," Caleb agreed.

"I'd say it's found all of us this go round," Hollis rumbled. "That was sure something the way you backed old Hagen down today."

Caleb remembered the cold glitter in the eyes of the town boss. "I'm not so sure I did," he said almost to himself.

Hagen had been doing more than just shooting off his mouth. Caleb was certain the man believed every boast he'd made to the freighters. And Caleb was equally certain that the double-action Colt had seen use, likely more than once. Could he really have taken Hagen using his old Colt Dragoon, he wondered. Had he been the one bluffing? He'd never been a gunfighter. And, of late, his gunhand, like Hollis' old wound, had taken to cramping and paining him at odd times.

"Him standing there threatening you, and you quoting the Good Book to him," Hollis was recalling with immense enjoyment. "I never seen the likes of it." He grew suddenly sober. "But you always did have the faith, Sarge. Truth to tell, I always kind of wished I had faith like yours. Then, maybe, I wouldn't get the killing fury on me when I fight.

Stark had to all but pull me off one of them jaspers today. Otherwise, I likely would've killed him, or, at least, crippled him up a mite."

"All you have to do is reach for that kind of faith, and it's yours," Caleb advised. "Just let go of that rage you're holding so tight to, and reach for it."

"Never looked at it like that," Hollis mused thoughtfully. He extended his long arms and stretched, then yawned hugely. "Starting to feel some tiredness now. I'll be pondering on what you said, Sarge."

"Do that." Caleb listened as Hollis returned to the lean-to, then he continued on his way to the ladder to mount to the roof of the stable. He slung his carbine and climbed, his joints creaking.

From the vantage point of the roof he could command a view of the entire area. A single lantern shown from an anonymous window in town. The ghostly plains stretched away into darkness in all other directions. Overhead, the moon gleamed a dull silver, and revealed occasional flashes of its face from behind a racing curtain of clouds blowing high above the grasslands. More rain coming, Caleb thought.

He relaxed a little and settled down on the gentle slope of the roof. The scent of sage touched his nostrils, and the phantom shape of an owl floated past not far over his head. The talk of faith with Hollis had soothed his worries some.

His nostrils flared involuntarily, and he raised his head as the familiar scent wafted to him on the breeze blowing in off the prairie. Coal oil. At the same moment, Watcher's frantic barking sounded from the edge of the compound.

Caleb faced into the breeze, straining his eyes against the gloom shrouding the grassland. He fancied he heard a man's voice, and then a spark of light flared out there on the plains. The spark grew larger. It raced up and down and sideways.

In a matter of seconds the distinctive outline of a cross was etched in fire against the blackness beyond.

Caleb sucked in his breath. The night's breeze seemed to turn as cold as a blue norther. Below the flaming outline, white-robed figures pranced and capered on the edge of the darkness. The Klan was paying a call.

Caleb scanned the compound, blinking against the glare left in his eyes by the distant flames. He saw nothing else to alarm him, nothing to confirm the momentary stab of fear that the cross was just a diversion to cover an assault on the grounds.

Quickly, then, he raised the carbine to his shoulder, resisting the savage urge to sight it on one of the grotesque figures under the cross. But that would be a little too close to murder in his book. Instead, he lifted the barrel a bit and squeezed the trigger.

The flash and crack of the carbine split the night, sounding the alarm to the men below. Caleb felt a fierce satisfaction. They'd served notice now to the varmints out under the cross that Buffalo Freight wasn't going to knuckle under to their ugly brand of hatred. With swift precision, not even needing to look, he cocked and reloaded and fired again, punching another shot over the heads of the robed figures.

Below him, Stark's voice called a quick inquiry. Caleb sank to one knee and fired again, shooting almost blind now. His eyes, dazzled by the muzzle flashes, could no longer detect the robed shapes of the Klansmen. He thought they had scattered from about their totem, and he blasted a fourth shot to send them on their way. Perversely, he found himself hoping that one of his high shots had accidentally found a target. He rid himself of the unholy notion with a quick shake of his head.

Other voices were shouting nearby. From close to the corral, a long gun—probably Stark's—opened up, sending lead screaming across the prairie. Caleb scuttled along the roof. He'd been in one place long enough. A determined sharpshooter could've targeted his position by now.

But no return fire came. The Klansmen had scattered. Not too surprisingly, he reflected contemptuously. Human trash of their ilk wanted victims, not opponents.

Stark stopped firing. Caleb shouted answers and orders down to the questions hollered up at him. With the men dispersed to secure the area, he stayed where he was, watching for any further signs of attack.

But none were forthcoming. The cross had burned to a mere red silhouette. Satisfied at last, Caleb clambered down the ladder.

Stark appeared out of the darkness, his face grim. "You hit anything?" he asked tersely.

Caleb shook his head. "Wasn't trying to."

"Me either." Stark looked toward the fading outline of the cross. "Maybe we threw a scare into them."

"Maybe," Caleb said. And that made one more thing he wasn't any too sure about.

"We'll hook these two up tandem," Caleb said, indicating the pair of Schuttler wagons in their small fleet. "It'll take an extra couple of teams to pull them when they're loaded, but Tyler's handled double rigs like this many times before."

Stark moved to inspect the two wagons Caleb had pointed out. Built by cheap convict labor in Jackson, Michigan, the short hitches of the Schuttler vehicles made them well-suited to tandem work. With Caleb, he checked the spindles, wheel rims and siding. The pair of vehicles looked sturdy enough to survive the rigors of the trail.

"We got a visitor!" Pete's voice called from where she stood lookout atop the stable. "It's Mr. Shuttle from town."

Stark and Caleb waited, squinting against the morning sun, as the warehouse owner headed his buckboard down the cutoff from the main road and pulled to a halt before them. A pair of fine black geldings was in the traces.

"Morning, gentlemen," Shuttle greeted.

Stark nodded a companionable welcome.

"Light down, if you're of a mind to," Caleb invited.

Shuttle stepped agilely from the buckboard. He looked fresh and dapper in his city clothes. Stark noted his Winchester riding in a specially crafted boot beside the buckboard seat. Other than the rifle, Shuttle looked to be unarmed.

"I had a few items that came in on the train to be delivered to some folks up north," Shuttle explained, indicating a small stack of bundles in the bed of the wagon. "I remembered you fellows were about due for your run up that way. I'll pay the usual delivery fee, of course."

"We're pulling out today," Caleb confirmed. "I reckon we can accommodate you."

Shuttle stepped aside to give him access to the buckboard. "I've got to say I admire you boys for the way you're hanging on in spite of all the trouble."

"Shoot, we was all born to trouble, Mr. Shuttle." Caleb turned with the packages and bundles balanced in his arms. "I'll just see these are added to the inventory. Tyler and Hollis are getting that all wrote up now." He headed toward the storage building.

"Any ill effects from yesterday's fisticuffs, Mr. Stark?" Shuttle asked.

Stark shifted his shoulders where soreness still lurked from the crushing grip of Mauler's hands. "Nothing to speak of, I guess. Might've been some different if you hadn't taken a hand."

"Least I could do for neighbors and business associates." Shuttle grew serious. "I understand there was more trouble out here during the night."

Stark tensed. "Just some varmints lighting up a bonfire out there a ways. We threw some lead to discourage them."

"A terrible thing. Everybody in town is talking about it."

"You have any idea who might be behind it?" Stark asked.

Shuttle's brow furrowed. Slowly he shook his head. "Hard to say. You know, Beaver's a fine town, for the most part."

Stark cocked his head skeptically.

"It's the truth," Shuttle assured him quickly. "Oh, Morg Hagen tries to run roughshod over folks now and again, but, by and large, the citizens are fine upstanding people."

Stark didn't voice his thoughts about the citizens who'd been out under the burning cross. "You ever have any other trouble with the Klan?" he asked instead.

Shuttle frowned as if he didn't like hearing that name linked to his community. "Never to my knowledge. Of course," he added almost apologetically, "until recent, we never had the, uh, circumstances around here that would give rise to that sort of thing." He glanced pointedly in the direction Caleb had taken.

"Looks like you've got them now."

"Things will settle down," Shuttle predicted with confidence. "Like I said, Beaver's a fine town. Used to service the old Jones and Plummer Trail when the big freight lines were running. A man named Jim Lane opened a road ranch in a sod house for just that purpose here at the river ford. That's how Beaver got its start."

"You've lived here a spell, have you?"

"Oh, a few years. Now, I'll grant you, Beaver used to be a lot rowdier place than it is now. With the big wagons pulling through, and the muleskinners and bullwhackers looking to have a good time. But we took things in hand. We built us a jail and hired some tough marshals. What they couldn't handle, the vigilance committees did."

"You talking vigilantes?" Stark drawled.

Shuttle nodded firmly. "Sometimes there's no other answer to lawlessness. A man like you, a bounty hunter, is bound to know that." He pointed eastward. "Off that way a couple of miles is a big old oak tree. Stands all by itself. Not another sizable tree for miles. I'll tell you, in the old days it bore its share of gallows fruit." His spare features split in a mirthless grin. "There's no appeal from the court of Judge Lynch."

Stark wondered how many men, guilty or otherwise, had danced out their lives at the end of a rope on Beaver's lynching tree.

"Here's your receipt, Mr. Shuttle." Caleb reappeared with a scrap of paper which he handed to the townsman. "We'll see your goods get delivered."

"I'm sure you will." Shuttle mounted once more into the buckboard. He tipped his hat then put the geldings around. Stark watched him take the cutoff back to the main road into town.

"Everything's ready to load," Caleb told him. "Let's get these wagons hitched and get you and Tyler on your way."

With all of them pitching in, the work was completed in

jig time. Before the morning was much further along, the two loaded wagons stood, hitched one behind the other, with the five teams of mules in the traces. One of the pair in the lead team twitched an ear and let out a loud bray.

"Hear that?" Hollis grinned. "She's ready to go!" Watcher stood near him, observing all the goings-on with interested eyes and lolling tongue. "You take it easy on them mules," he cautioned Tyler, "and be mighty careful."

"Don't worry. We can handle it. Right, Peacemaker?" Not waiting for an answer, Tyler clambered up onto the driver's bench and took the lines, threading them between his fingers. "Come on! Let's move out."

Thaddeus smiled broadly and slipped a long arm around Caleb's shoulders.

Stark turned to Prudence standing off to the side. "You be all right while I'm gone?"

She smiled. "Sure." She cut her eyes toward Pete. "I've got an assignment of my own to keep me busy, remember?" She placed her hand fleetingly against his chest and reached up to kiss him lightly on the cheek. "Come back to me," she whispered.

Stark felt an unaccustomed tightness in his throat. He caught her hand and squeezed it. "Yeah." He bent awkwardly and gave her a peck, then climbed up beside Tyler on the seat.

Some of Caleb's bleakness had faded. "I'll be praying for you," he promised.

Tyler let off on the brake, jigged the lines, and set the teams to moving. Stark glanced back once as they pulled onto the main road. The group watching their departure looked like a mighty frail force to be left holding down this particular fort.

Stark turned his thoughts back to the job at hand as they

left the town behind. He scanned the grassland stretching out before them. Clouds were building above the horizon. He scowled. It looked like they were going to be in for some rain.

Prudence stood at the kitchen window washing dishes in the enamel pan that stood on the bare counter. She wasn't used to limiting her activities to the domestic side of life, as she had been doing since they arrived here in Beaver. Normally, she would have insisted on standing guard duty and taking a turn at the other rigors of life that went along with running a freight company. But in this instance, she felt it was important to model to Pete some of the more feminine traits that went along with womanhood on the frontier. The girl obviously had had enough experience on the other side of the issue.

She felt a bit awkward being left in the midst of strangers with Jim gone, but she knew it couldn't be helped. After all, she had gotten herself into this by insisting upon coming along.

Over all, she was glad she'd done it. It had given her and Jim more time together than if she had been content to sit and wait back in Guthrie. And through their years of association, she had come to almost relish these opportunities to help him intervene in unfair circumstances and bring the odds a little more in balance. She just wished they hadn't had to separate. He'd only been gone a few hours, and she missed him terribly already.

She left the tin plates and coffee cups to dry on a dishtowel and wiped her hands. Today she planned to try to corral Pete into going in to the general store in town to look at dress goods. She hadn't sewn in years, but it was a discipline drummed into her through years of finishing school. And she was sure she could still manage to make a presentable garment—particularly with Pete's help. It might even be fun and provide an arena where Pete would feel comfortable opening up and sharing with another woman.

She crossed to the back door and movement caught her eye. Hollis had just relieved Pete from her stint of guard duty, and the girl was walking away around the corner of the stable. Once there, she looked surreptitiously over her shoulder and then darted away toward a stand of trees across the cleared area behind the compound. Prudence waited until Hollis disappeared behind one of the outbuildings then followed along in Pete's wake, too curious to let the incident go uninvestigated.

Once in the woods, Pete stopped and pulled a bundle from under a dead tree. Then she kept moving through the undergrowth to a plowed field on the other side. As she started across the field, she called a greeting, which was answered by a joyous chorus of children's voices. Prudence watched from the shelter of the trees as five stair-step children tumbled out of the ramshackle shanty on the far side of the clearing and ran to meet her.

Laughing, tugging on Pete's hands, scuffling with one another for position, the children led her over to a large cottonwood tree in the yard where they all collapsed in a merry heap on the ground. Pete then opened her bundle and pulled out a tattered book, a slate, and some odds and ends of chalk.

Prudence sank into the shade and watched what could only be termed as an outdoor classroom. The children took turns reading, copying alphabet letters on the slate, and doing simple addition and subtraction problems. After about an hour, Pete rose to a chorus of regrets, gathered her meager supplies, and began an effortless lope back toward the woods.

Prudence scrambled to her feet and waited. Pete turned to give a final wave to her pupils, before entering the dimly lit woods. It was then that Prudence made herself known.

Pete gasped as Prudence stepped into view. "Miss Prudence! Where did you come from?"

Prudence laughed. "I followed you." She reached out impulsively and gave the girl a hug. "You were great with those kids. Pete, you're a natural born teacher! Have you ever thought of going to college and getting some training?"

Pete pulled away, scowling angrily. "Of course I've thought about it. It's just not possible, that's all."

Prudence hadn't expected such a reaction. "I don't understand. Why not?"

"I'm a poor black woman—the daughter of ex-slaves. What chance would I have to get into college?"

"Maybe more than you think. Thaddeus managed to do it, and even go on to law school."

"That's different!" Pete cried, then quickly diverted her eyes. "He's a man."

Suddenly a lot of things became clear to Prudence. "And you wish you were too."

Chapter Eight

Prudence followed a sullen Pete back through the woods. A tight-lipped Hollis was waiting as they emerged from the trees.

He solemnly blocked Pete's path. "You been visiting that sharecropper's kids again, girl?"

Pete nodded, staring at the ground.

Hollis shook his head. "You know your daddy told you not to go over there no more until this ugly business with Hagen is finished. It's too dangerous."

"I was careful," Pete said defensively. "School starts in just a few weeks. If I don't keep working with them, they won't be ready to start. They weren't allowed to go to school where they moved from. They're really far behind."

"I know all that," Hollis said, his tone softening. "But right now it can't be helped. It's not only your life you're playing around with. If Hagen were to get ahold of you, this fight would be over. We'd have to give up this whole shooting match to get you back."

Pete nodded again, and turned abruptly to stride off toward the house. Prudence hurried after her.

She caught up with her on the porch steps. "Pete, wait."

The girl swung around angrily. "I don't need another lecture."

"No. No lectures," Prudence said softly. "Just talk. Let's go inside."

Once in the kitchen, Prudence set the kettle on the old cast iron stove and hurriedly brewed some tea. Pete fidgeted as Prudence set two cups on the table and motioned for the girl to take a seat. Prudence prayed silently for the right words. She knew she'd pushed Pete pretty far already.

"About what you said in the woods," Prudence began hesitantly, "I understand exactly how you feel."

Pete lifted a skeptical eyebrow. "I don't see how that could possibly be."

"No, I mean it," Prudence said sincerely. "When I was a youngster, I wanted to be a man, also. Because ever since I can remember, I've wanted to be a lawyer, like my father. And all the lawyers I knew were men. So I wore pants and learned to ride and compete in sports. I was determined to do *everything* a man could do . . . *only better.*"

Prudence paused to take a sip of her tea, watching for some indication she was getting through to the girl.

Pete drummed her fingers impatiently on the table. At last curiosity overcame her irritation. "Okay, what happened?"

Prudence reached across and patted her hand. "Well, finally my father sat me down and asked me why I was wasting my time and my energy trying to do *everything* men could do when I was actually only interested in doing *one thing* men could do. That sort of brought my life into focus.

"After that, I cut out all the activities except the ones I really enjoyed. I was then able to relax and enjoy who I was and concentrate on becoming the best lawyer I could become. It wasn't easy, and I did end up competing with men all along the way, but it was on my terms—not theirs. I won in the end, and I didn't have to sacrifice my *femininity*."

Pete glanced down self-consciously at her own clothing. "I suppose you're suggesting that I should do the same?"

"In regard to achieving your goals, yes. All the incidentals, including the way you choose to dress, are up to you."

Pete shook her head from side to side, as if trying to clear her mind of confusion. "Don't get me wrong, ma'am. I'm not trying to belittle what you've accomplished. I don't doubt it was hard. *But you're not black.*"

"I am," came a voice from the doorway.

They both turned to see Thaddeus standing there. "I didn't mean to eavesdrop," he apologized, then looked directly at Pete, "but I overheard enough to know that Prudence is giving you some very good advice."

Pete looked back at him just as directly. "I can only repeat to you what I said to her. I know you haven't had it easy, but you're not a *woman*."

He smiled kindly. "You're at a real crossroads here, *Patricia*. Prudence and I have both stood here ourselves. And I can only say this to you. You can either spend your time finding excuses why you can't do what you want to do, or you can start looking for ways to make it all work out."

"Quite a bit of rain these last few days," the scraggly homesteader commented, looking up at them on the wagon. "Glad it finally let up so's I could get some work done."

As he gazed past the man at his sorry spread, Stark wondered just when the last time had been that this fellow had done any work at all. A dugout with a flimsy lean-to over it constituted home for a slatternly wife and an untamed pack of kids who seemed to be squabbling on even terms with chickens and a grunting porker.

The homesteader ignored it all, grinning a hideous gaptoothed grin. "What you got for me, nigra?"

"A couple of boxes of ammo, and a few other things, Mr. Grissard," Tyler answered with tight-lipped courtesy as he passed the packages down. "Mr. Shuttle had us deliver them. You're our last stop."

Grissard accepted the bundles with ill grace. "Been waiting for these shells. Need them to keep varmints off the place. Where in thunder you been, boy? You're more'n a day late on your usual run thisaway."

"Rain's been hard on the roads," Tyler said shortly. "Made the going slow."

"You didn't let these shells get wet none, did you?"

"No, sir. Had everything under the tarps."

Grissard grunted and looked past Tyler to Stark. "Who're you? What's your business here?"

"I work for Buffalo Freight."

"Huh. Things must be mighty hard up for a white man to be working for a bunch of darkies."

Stark swept his gaze pointedly over Grissard's own rundown homestead. "Yep, pretty hard up," he agreed.

"What's your moniker, boy?" Grissard snapped.

"James Stark."

"Oh," Grissard said with obvious recognition. He backed off a couple of steps, sneered, then turned and stomped away toward his dugout, not bothering with any good-byes.

"And it's a pleasure doing business with you, too, *sir*,"

Tyler muttered. He popped the whip more violently than was necessary.

Stark eyed him askance, but held his peace Grissard's belligerence was the biggest threat they'd encountered over the whole route, and he was feeling grateful for that fact. Steady rainfall had made the trek unpleasant. Frequent stops had been necessary to ensure the load stayed dry. More than once they'd had to wrestle a bogged wagon out of a mud hole. When they weren't doing that, they were huddled under their slickers on the seat, or trying to find dry spots to sleep at night under the wagon.

Once north of the Kansas line, they had left the well-established roadway of the Jones and Plummer to swing across a wide circle of territory on lesser roads, some of them all but impassable in the rain. Unlike other smoother stretches of prairie further south and east, this region was rough country, often cut by rugged draws and gullies, now running with water deep enough to swallow a wagon. By necessity, the makeshift roadways wound irregularly around and about these miniature chasms.

But Tyler had done his job skillfully, allowing Stark to spell him only occasionally. Stark knew the strain of wrestling the teams over the rough terrain had taken its toll on him, but he had stood up well under it.

Stark kept his eyes peeled for trouble, ceaselessly scanning the surrounding countryside, shotgun in hand. But other than a handful of wandering cowpokes, and a family or two of Indians, they had encountered few other folks on the road. It was understandable since the weather had been such a discouragement to travel.

Things had been quiet, he reflected, almost too quiet.

He questioned silently if Hagen and his boys had cooked

up any trouble back at Beaver in their absence. Or, had the ugly presence of the Klan made itself known again?

He tipped his sodden hat back off his forehead. Before too many more miles, they'd hook up again with the main trail not far from where it forded the Cimarron. After that, they'd be on the final stretch home. He figured he'd have his answers soon enough.

"He knew your name, right enough," Tyler opined, and Stark realized the man was still chewing over their stop-off at the Grissard place. "Reckon he'd heard how you put the licking on Mauler and them other yahoos."

"Oscar Shuttle and Hollis had a hand in it, too," Stark reminded.

"I know," Tyler acknowledged. "But without you, Hollis wouldn't of stood a chance, and I doubt Shuttle would've lifted a finger to help him. Thaddeus told me some about you. Said you took on a whole gang of outlaws in his town, and did away with most of 'em single-handed. That true?"

"Yep. What of it?"

"Considering all that, I was just wondering how you keep your temper under control when you run into a lowlife like Grissard."

Stark chuckled. "Oh, it ain't that hard. Fighting and killing is something you do when there's no other choice—in order to protect yourself or others, or to right a wrong that's too big to be overlooked and that can't be made right in any other way. What Grissard and his kind say usually don't matter much. If you start looking for a scrap over things like that, you're likely to end up getting yourself killed for something that ain't nowhere near worth it."

"I guess that makes sense," Tyler acknowledged grudgingly. "It sure is hard to ignore such as him, though."

"It sure is," Stark agreed. "It sure is . . ."

They rode in silence until they reached the main road leading to the Cimarron. Stark concentrated on watching for danger. They were getting closer to home now, and closer to Morg Hagen's stomping grounds.

Tyler pulled to a halt. "Never seen that old creek running so wide before," he said with an edge of awe in his tones.

In normal times, Stark knew, the river wasn't much more than a sandy stream meandering down a wide riverbed. Now, choked by the recent heavy rains, the Cimarron was a churning, muddy flood, its reddish waters filling the bed from bank to bank, a stretch of a good three hundred yards, he estimated. With its shifting sandy bottom and treacherous patches of quicksand, the Cimarron had sealed the fate of more than one unwary traveler over the years.

"Is there any better ford downstream?" Stark asked.

Tyler gave a negative shake of his head. "Nope. This here's the best spot. Even with all the rain, it shouldn't be running too deep for us to handle. The banks get narrower going either way. Makes the water deeper and faster. Since the wagons are empty, we should be able to take both at once, rather than taking one across then coming back for the other. The extra weight of that second wagon might even help anchor us some."

Stark knew Tyler's estimate of the situation was accurate, and that the man was expert at handling the teams. Yet, out there in the river, with the hills lining both banks, they'd be at their most vulnerable to a sharpshooter.

Stark squinted, studying the opposite hills on the rim of the river valley. The distance was too great to make out the details, but there were some scattered stands of trees and underbrush that could serve to conceal an enemy.

One last thought occurred to him. "What about the

mules? Will they handle all right?" Mules were notorious for acting loco in water.

Tyler remained confident. "They'll do fine." He shifted the reins impatiently.

Stark shrugged his doubts aside. "Take her across."

Tyler put the mules down the muddy road, riding the brake on the slope. As the ground leveled out, the wheels sank a little deeper into the mire. They splattered through small pools of standing water. From eye level, the river looked even wider and more daunting. Debris of all sizes slid past, half-submerged in the muddy torrent. Overhead, the sky hung dark and foreboding.

Leaving his position on the seat, Stark clambered into the bed of the lead wagon and made his way to the rear to eyeball the hitch connecting the tandem wagon. Everything looked to be secure. He was back in place by the time the lead mules splashed into the shallows. The river deepened gradually, so they were well out into the ford by the time the water reached the axles.

Stark could see the muscles beginning to flex beneath the hides of the mules, and he knew the animals were feeling the pressure of the tide pushing steadily against them and the wagons they pulled. Tyler kept them moving slow, his hands steady with the leathers, and none of them balked. Occasionally one wheel would drop into a submerged hole then jolt out of it.

The water rose higher. One of the mules wasted its breath in an unhappy bray. Stark could look over the side and see the water lapping less than a foot below the rim of the wagon. Much deeper, and they'd run the risk of being swamped. He tried to keep his attention on the shoreline and the hills above it, sparing a few glances back over his shoulders.

He felt the change in momentum and looked about as Tyler slowed the mules to a near halt. Twenty feet in front of the lead team, a good-sized tree, uprooted by the flood, swept sluggishly past, naked roots and leafy boughs clawing at the air. Stark didn't like to think what might've happened if the floating trunk had struck the team or either of the wagons broadside.

Tyler urged the mules gently forward. His face was set in concentration. Stark knew he was driving by feel and memory, trying to keep the mules centered in the shallow stretch of bottom that created the ford.

It wasn't shallow now. The heads of the mules, and their pumping shoulders, were all that was visible. They were half-swimming, half-walking on the bottom. The wagons were floating. Stark felt the rear Schuttler wag slightly beneath the steady push of the current.

They were almost to midstream, but the far shore seemed to draw nearer with painful slowness.

Finally, a little more of the mules' forequarters began to emerge from the water. The forward movement became more stable. The wheels bit into soft bottom mud. Stark drew a breath of relief. They were past the deepest point. The worst was over. Seeming to sense it, the mules surged ahead.

Stark saw the small splash off to the side, and it was a moment before he realized what it was. In almost the same instant a faint dull report came rolling across the water from the hills on the opposite shore.

"Get your head down!" he shouted above the rushing of the water. "Keep those mules moving! Someone's throwing lead at us!" He glimpsed the flash of Tyler's startled expression.

As he unlimbered his shotgun he saw a couple more of

the small splashes made by bullets striking water. A pair of bushwhackers, he understood, but they'd started firing too soon, while the range was still too great for their rifles.

Tyler lashed the mules as Stark snugged the butt of the shotgun against his shoulder, trying to keep his balance on the swaying seat. He cracked off four shots, firing almost blind, knowing only that their ambushers must be located in the fringe of brush and rocks clinging to the nearest hill. They needed to know that their prey wasn't going to roll over without a fight.

At the sound of his shots, the mules bucked and plunged in a spray of water. Before he could fire again, the rear wagon gave a tremendous lurch. The lead vehicle shifted sideways and tilted alarmingly so Stark had to grab at the back of the seat to keep from being dumped into the river.

"We're stuck!" Tyler shouted. "Quicksand!"

Looking back, Stark saw the back half of the rear wagon sagging out of sight below the water. Its weight had pulled the lead wagon to the side. As Stark stared, the rear Schuttler settled another six inches beneath the water, and the lead vehicle tilted even further. A bullet struck the water with a small splash beside Stark.

Tyler fought the lines, coming half to his feet, exposing himself even more fully to the aim of the drygulchers. He yelled, hauling back hard on the leathers, working them expertly, and the mules gradually quieted. As they did, the sliding, shifting motions of both wagons stopped. They were stranded in mid-river, with the rear wagon half-submerged, the lead vehicle's back wheel trapped, and the mules helpless to pull them free.

A bullet thudded into the wooden side of the wagon.

"Secure the reins! Take cover!" Stark yelled.

He took his own advice, vaulting into the bed of the

wagon and ducking behind the shelter of the seatback. Tyler joined him an instant later, his own rifle in hand.

Now that they had a still target, the two sharpshooters began to pepper the wagon with greater accuracy. Splinters flew, but Stark didn't think they were in much danger for the moment. The range was still too great for any sort of consistent marksmanship. But they were pinned down, and, at any time, the pull of the river bottom might suck the rear wagon even deeper into the shifting sand, pulling them and the team along with it. Water in the wagon sloshed around Stark's boots. He inched up for a look-see.

His back against the rear of the wagon seat, Tyler was checking the load in his Winchester. "They're too far away to hit us!" he echoed Stark's own assessment.

"They don't need to hit us," Stark said tightly. "Look there. We got company."

Tyler followed Stark's pointing finger. A pack of horsemen had burst from the woods on the hillside and were making for the river's edge. The plan was obvious. While the snipers kept them pinned down, the mounted outlaws would ride out into the river to get close enough to finish the job.

Tyler levered his Winchester. "Those blamed riflemen will keep us held here like treed varmints!"

"No, they won't," Stark told him, and picked up the sporting rifle from behind the seat. With quick deft movements he withdrew the long-barreled gun from its sheath, and unwrapped the oilcloth he had bound about it to protect it from the rain and moisture. He prayed the protection had been enough.

Thumbing shells into the breech, he raised up far enough to scrutinize the distant hill. Rifle fire from the sharpshooters was continuing. Stark narrowed his eyes, scanning the terrain. He picked out two clouds of powdersmoke, and after a moment he spotted a brief movement behind a boulder fronted by a fringe of brush.

Good enough. He rested the barrel of the sporting rifle on the seatback, estimating wind and distance. While too much for most repeaters, the range was only fair for the big gun.

Ignoring the bullets continuing to fly, the oncoming riders just reaching the water, and the unnerving tilt of the wagon, Stark set his sights on the distant hillside and waited. After a handful of seconds came another flicker of motion, and Stark touched off the sporting rifle. Its blast and kick were jarring.

"There he goes!" Tyler yelled a pair of seconds later.

A tiny figure, flushed by the near miss of Stark's shot, had leaped to his feet and darted to new cover. The next shell slid into the breech a clocktick too late for Stark to bring the rifle to bear. Conscious of the critical passing moments, he trained the sporting rifle on the rifleman's new position. Not waiting for betraying movement this time, he fired. Again his target was up and dodging for different cover. Stark blinked through the powdersmoke, led the running figure, and fired again. A moment later the rifleman went down as if swatted by a giant hand.

Tyler let out a whoop and reared up to open fire on the horsemen. Bullets were flying faster now, but the riders were mostly using handguns. They were still too distant for any sort of accuracy from the plunging backs of horses breasting the floodwaters.

Stark fed more shells into the sporting rifle, and swung the barrel to where the remaining cloud of gunsmoke still hovered. He didn't bother aiming high and low to get his opponent targeted in. He had a pretty good grasp of the range now. All he had to do was let the bullets fly.

The mules shied at the increased gunfire, but held steady. Stark fired again, ramming the shot home in the same general spot as the first. He sent a third after it, then waved away the smoke. No more shots came from the targeted position. Either the sharpshooter had taken a hit, or he had lit out.

Stark shifted his stance in the tilting bed of the wagon and brought the sporting rifle to bear on the pack of horsemen splashing toward them. Tyler's fire had slowed them, but didn't seem to have done much damage. There were no empty saddles, and they were still throwing lead, some of which was zipping uncomfortably close.

Stark chambered another big cartridge. Abruptly, the leader of the riders threw up his hand and hauled his horse to a rearing halt. He then threw a quick look over his shoulder in the direction of the silenced sharpshooters. He made a sweeping motion with his arm, ordering his followers to fall back, as he swung his horse about. He obviously wanted no part of riding full into the fire of Tyler's Winchester and Stark's sporting rifle without the cover of the bushwhackers up on the ridge.

Tyler yelled in triumph and pumped more shots after their retreating backs. Stark dropped the hammer on his gun one more time to send them on their way a little faster.

"Work those mules," Stark ordered. "I'll keep an eye out in case they come back." He reloaded the sporting rifle as he spoke.

Tyler clambered to the seat, released the brake, and freed the lines. "Yaw! Move, you mules!" He worked the lines from side to side, having the teams haul left, then right, then straight ahead to dislodge the mired wagons.

The bed shifted and rocked beneath Stark's planted boots, but the rear Schuttler held firm. Tyler sent the whip popping out, yelled again, sawed the lines back and forth. The lead mules surged hard against the traces. Stark flung a glance back. If anything, the bogged wagon looked to have settled even deeper.

Up front, panicked by their driver's demands and their inability to respond, the lead team began to buck and thrash in the traces, necks bowed, hooves flailing, braying in fear. The panic was contagious. The other teams started acting up as well. If they weren't careful, Stark realized, they'd have some drowned mules on their hands.

He laid a hand on Tyler's shoulder. "We'll have to unhitch the rear wagon. Once we get this one into shore, we can bring the teams back out to try to work the other one loose."

Tyler gave a reluctant nod, and drew back hard on the lines to quiet the mules. "Whoa! Whoa up, now!" Slowly the mules subsided, and he shoved the brake lever down. "I'll unhitch the wagon while you keep us covered."

Tyler scrambled to the rear of the first wagon and gazed over the tailgate at the tandem hitch. He shook his head, then dropped over the side into the muddy swirl of water. His head and shoulders remained above the surface. Stark knew he couldn't trust his full weight to the uncertain river bottom. Instead, clinging to the wagon, he worked furiously to free the hitch with his free hand. Stark couldn't see what the problem was. He had to divide his attention between Tyler's efforts and the shoreline, empty so far of any threat.

Finally, Tyler let down the tailgate, pulled himself back aboard the wagon, got hold of a hammer, and, lying flat on his belly, used both hands and the hammer to complete the job.

Stark felt the lessening of the drag as the rear vehicle came free. Dripping, Tyler regained the driver's seat. He was panting from his exertions, but he shook his head to refuse Stark's offer to handle the lines. He took them himself, entwining them through his fingers.

At his command, the teams surged forward again. Now only the wheel of the lead wagon remained to be freed from whatever underwater hole held it. "Go, mules! Get up! Pull!"

Once more the mules lunged forward in unison. Briefly the stuck wheel held. Then, with a lurch, it was free, and the wagon was moving forward. Eager now, the mules breasted the flood. As the team neared the shore, Stark vaulted off into the shallows, long gun in hand.

No riders swept down upon them. The mules hauled the lumbering wagon up on the muddy bank with much snorting and tossing of heads. Stark kept his eyes peeled as Tyler unhitched the teams. Stark's gaze went to the spot where he'd placed the second bushwhacker. Was the yahoo still alive, maybe even now drawing a bead on them?

"They're loose!" Tyler called. Like a farmer behind a plow, he worked the lines to turn the dripping mules back toward the water. They balked and brayed at the prospect of reentering the flood.

With a last searching look at the hills, Stark laid his rifle back in the wagon. It was going to take both of them to go back out there and hitch up the remaining wagon. He went alongside Tyler as he yelled and hoorawed the teams back into the river.

The water pushed and tugged against him as it mounted up his legs. The bottom was shifting and uncertain beneath his feet. His six-gun was going to need some serious cleaning tonight, but he didn't want to leave it behind. Besides, for the moment, that was the least of his worries.

He gripped the harness of the nearest mule, and let the strength of the animals draw him along. Ahead of them, across the surface of the rushing water, he could see the front end of the trapped wagon angled upward. Had it settled even deeper?

Of a sudden, one of his feet sank deep into the river bottom, and an awful suction tugged at his leg. He was thankful for the power of the mules as they pulled him free.

"Turn them around!" he shouted to Tyler as they neared the wagon. "I'll get them hitched."

Once the mules were turned about, he worked his way along the traces back toward the wagon. One of the mules brayed deafeningly as he passed. Another turned and snapped angrily with blunt yellowed teeth. He thumped its nose with his fist, and its head jerked back.

He reached the rear of the teams. Tyler, handling the lines, had backed them as close as he dared to the wagon. Any closer, Stark knew, and the beasts themselves might become mired in the quicksand. The water was up almost to Tyler's armpits. He looked apprehensive but determined.

Letting go of the harness, Stark half-waded, half-lunged across the intervening space to reach the wagon. He had no idea how he was going to hook up the teams to the uptilted tongue.

As his hand grasped the rough wood of the wagon, the sand beneath his boots shifted, and the wagon began to slide from sight. It was being swallowed up completely, Stark understood in a single bleak moment. The water and sand pulled at him, and he knew that the suction of the wagon would drag him down along with it.

Desperately, he threw himself back at the mules, stroking hard with his arms, kicking frantically to clear his feet of the grasping sand. Tyler yelled and flipped one of the lines to him. His grasping fingers caught it, and Tyler shouted the mules forward. Stark was slowly drawn free of the sand. He got his feet under him, and managed to get hold of the traces, flicking the line back to Tyler.

Looking over his shoulder, he saw the tongue of the wagon slide from sight beneath the brown water. The wagon was gone, locked into a coffin of sand that had almost been his as well. Even after the river went down, it would be months or years before an effort could be made to salvage the vehicle. That is, if it could be located at all. The underground currents might eventually move it far downstream.

Sopping wet, they staggered out of the river in the wake of the mules, and dropped breathlessly to the ground.

Tyler looked up toward the hills where the outlaws had vanished. "Those sorry owlhoots didn't get to rob us, but they sure cost us a wagon. Don't seem right somehow."

"They weren't trying to rob us," Stark cut him off.

"Huh? What do you mean?"

"Think about it. If they'd wanted to rob us, they would've done it early in the trip, when we had both wagons loaded. Then they would've been sure of getting something for their trouble. As it is, they had no way of knowing how much cash, if any, we were packing. And they were fools to attack us when we were mid-river. Whatever money we had could've been swept away. They should've waited until we were ashore." Stark shook his head solemnly. "This wasn't any try at a stickup. They were out to kill us. If they hadn't started shooting too early, we'd likely be dead now.

Chapter Nine

"Where you headed, Peacemaker?" Caleb asked.

Stark finished tightening the cinch on Red's saddle. "Figured I'd have me a talk with the law."

"Marshall Tallworth?" Caleb snorted. "I done told you, he don't jump unless Morg Hagen says frog.'

Stark shrugged. "Having that run-in yesterday at the river got me kind of interested in the law enforcement in these parts."

Caleb snorted derisively once more. "What law enforcement?" he muttered before ambling away.

Prudence had followed Stark out to the corral and was leaning thoughtfully against the rails. "I need to ask you something," she said at last.

He let the stirrup down and slapped Red on the shoulder. "Okay. What's on your mind?"

"Well, talking to George Perkins back in Guthrie started me thinking. So I brought a couple of law books with me, and I've been doing some research."

"And what did you find out?"

"It seems the area of civil rights law might offer some remedy in this situation as well as the areas he mentioned."

"How so?"

"Well, I could make a pretty good case in court that the owners of Buffalo Freight are being harassed solely because they're black, especially since the Klan has chosen to take part in the intimidation. And if the town marshal won't move to protect them, that would open the door for Federal Marshals to move in. I talked it over with Thaddeus, and he agrees that *in theory* it's a viable legal tactic."

Stark rubbed his chin and took a moment to ponder the matter. "Interesting train of thought, all right."

"Unfortunately, *in reality,* as short-handed as Evett Nix is, there's not much likelihood that would happen."

A slow smile split Stark's face. "Yeah, but Marshal Tallworth doesn't know it's unlikely. Wouldn't hurt none to give the good marshal something to worry about. I think maybe you and Thaddeus are the ones who need to talk to the law. Go get him while I saddle your horses."

Prudence's smile hinted at a plot of her own. "Could we take the buggy and ask Pete to go along. For reasons I won't take time to explain, I believe this is something she needs to see."

Red was feeling frisky after being cooped up during the time Stark and Tyler had made their freight run. Stark held him in as he rode beside the buggy the short distance into town. He had no trouble spotting the frame building on Main Street with the crude sign reading MARSHAL above the door.

In the Lands, a town could hire a law enforcement officer, as the residents of Beaver had apparently done. But whoever occupied the office had no real legal standing outside the community and exercised only the authority the townsfolk were willing to grant him.

Stark dismounted, keeping a lookout for Morg Hagen's rowdies. He didn't see anybody who looked particularly threatening, although some of the citizens were eyeballing their little group curiously. He saw the steeple of a church toward the far end of town.

He took Prudence's hand to help her out of the buggy, then offered his hand to Pete, who accepted it awkwardly. He stepped up onto the sidewalk and opened the door to the marshal's office. He moved aside and motioned the others to enter ahead of him. Prudence and Thaddeus strode inside, but Pete shook her head no and sank down onto the bench outside the door. Stark left the door open so she could hear what went on.

The man behind the rickety desk jumped just a little as they entered, making him miss the coffee cup into which he was pouring a liberal dollop of whiskey. The amber liquid splashed on the scarred desktop. The odors of whiskey and fresh brewed coffee mingled in the stale air of the room. A stove sat within arm's reach of the desk. A flimsy cellblock took up the rear of the building.

The lawman set the bottle down with an angry thud. "Waste of good whiskey. What the deuce you all want?" Then recognition brought a scowl to his sallow features.

"You the marshal?" Stark asked.

"Cal Tallworth, that's me. You're that gunslinger working for them coloreds, ain't you?" Tallworth sipped at his whiskey-laden coffee and leaned back in his chair. His body was gaunt and fleshless. Stark couldn't guess his age. A holstered revolver was on his belt. His eyes swept over the others. "And who might you good folks be?" he asked with sarcastic courtesy.

Thaddeus took up the introductions. "I'm Thaddeus Jenkins. I'm an attorney, and my uncle, Caleb Jackson, and his friends have asked me to handle their legal interests. And in that respect, I've asked my colleague, Prudence Stark, to represent them if we decide to bring legal action against the town of Beaver and you personally."

The marshal's scowl deepened and he leaned up to lock eyes with Thaddeus. "Legal action? Are you threatening me, boy?"

Prudence stepped forward with a confident smile. "No threat intended, Marshal . . . at least at this point. We're merely here to ask you if you've made any effort to find out who's behind the Klan activity around Beaver. In particular, we're interested in the cross burning out behind Buffalo Freight the other night."

"No reason for me to check into that," he drawled indifferently, and for the first time Stark detected a faint southern inflection to his accent. "Got no laws against that sort of thing. Just some good upstanding white folks letting their feelings be known. Somebody threw lead at them, howsomever. We got laws against that."

"Sounds like you were there," Stark suggested.

"Wouldn't have been nothing wrong with it if I was." Tallworth sucked at his coffee and grinned mirthlessly up at them.

His empty desktop had a layer of dust over most of it. The floor of the office hadn't seen cleaning anytime recent. Stark held himself in check. "You get voted into office, Marshal?"

"Got hired," Tallworth asserted. "Town council pays me to keep the peace."

"The town council," Stark reflected. "That'd be Morg Hagen?"

"Him and others," Tallworth confirmed. He eyed Stark with cold speculation. "I think you got me all wrong, gunslinger."

"Is that a fact?"

"Yep, it is," Tallworth said bluntly. "I ain't in any man's pocket. Never have been. I sure ain't in Morg Hagen's, no matter what you think. I've worn a badge in towns that would've eaten you alive and spit out the bones. I grew up in the South after the war, when there wasn't no law to speak of!" Bitterness edged his tones. "I pinned on a star because it had to be done, and I been wearing one, off and on, ever since. I've given my life to law and order, and if there's one thing I've learned, it's that there's different ways of keeping the peace in a town."

"Such as?" Stark prodded.

Tallworth finished his whiskey and coffee, then set his cup down with a solid thump. "Such as throwing a loop around every hellion that spits in the street or cusses in public, and keeping the cellblock full, and your own life in danger all the time."

Stark thought of Evett Nix and his stalwart band of deputies. "There's some that says that's how it's to be done."

"And that's the way I done it in my younger days, till I come to know better."

"I'm listening."

Tallworth gave a nod, as if such was his due. "Mark it down, boy. A smart lawman figures it out, if he plans on staying alive in this trade. Best way to keep a town peaceable is to see that the bigshots—the ones the other folks look up to, the ones who own the businesses—are kept happy and always get their own way. You do that, and they'll see to it that a town runs smooth. Be shooting themselves in the foot to do otherwise. Get my drift?"

"Like a frog soaking up sunshine," Stark said wryly.

Tallworth gave him a sharp look. "You got business with me, or did you just come to flap your jaw?"

"Business. I want to report an attempted robbery of one of Buffalo Freight's wagons."

"Attempted, you say? Where was this?"

"At the river ford on the Cimarron north of here. Happened yesterday around noontime."

"Out of my jurisdiction," Tallworth declared. "I don't get paid to ride herd on the Lands, just the town limits here."

"Don't guess you noticed a large group of rowdies riding out about that time and coming back minus some of their members?"

"Naw, can't say as how I did. Cowpokes come and go around here as they please. Ain't no law against coming and going."

"Marshal, it seems as though you have a better grasp of what's *not* against the law than what is," Prudence said pointedly.

Tallworth bristled. "What's that supposed to mean, lady lawyer? You got something to say, just say it."

Prudence met his gaze unflinchingly. "Very well. I'll begin by reminding you that the Twelfth, Thirteenth, and Fourteenth Amendments to the Constitution guarantee black people the same rights as any other citizens of this country. That includes the right to own and operate a business. As a law officer, you're sworn to protect the rights of *all* citizens. Now, if it could be proven that you failed to give the owners of Buffalo Freight the same protection under the law that you give to white citizens, you could be charged with dereliction of duty. And that would open the door for Federal Marshals to move into Beaver, remove you from office, and enforce the law equally."

Tallworth rose from his chair, rested his palms on the desk, and leaned forward menacingly. "I ain't scared none by your fancy law talk, lady. Federal Marshals got a lot more to worry about than a bunch of old colored slaves who can't make a go of a two-bit freight line. And I'm doing my job just fine, plenty good enough to please everybody around here that counts."

Prudence also rested her palms on the desk and leaned toward him like a tiny David facing a gaunt Goliath. "Well, the law says everybody counts, Marshal. So perhaps we should just move forward with this case and let the courts decide."

Stark caught the first glimmer of unease in Tallworth's eyes. "You do what you want, lady. Won't make a bit of difference to no one in these parts. Now you all get on outta here. I got things to tend to."

Prudence smiled pleasantly. "As you wish, Marshal. We'll keep you informed as we move forward with our case." With that she turned and flounced out of the office. With a courteous nod, Thaddeus followed in her wake.

Stark hesitated just long enough to touch a mocking finger to the brim of his Stetson. "Be seeing you in court, Marshal," he drawled. As he pulled the door shut behind him, Pete rose from the bench outside the door and followed him to the buggy. He wondered what she'd thought of the exchange she'd overheard.

Prudence glanced nervously down at him as he handed her into the buggy. "You think we did any good in there?" she asked.

He gave her a smug smile and a wink. "Oh, I think you

shook him up plenty. Remains to be seen whether the shock waves run in the direction we want."

Prudence still looked worried. "Well, to hedge our bets, I think we should send a couple of telegrams."

Stark scowled. "You realize copies of them will most likely end up in the hands of Morg Hagen."

She smiled for the first time. "That's what I'm counting on."

From the window of his office, Morg Hagen watched the group from Buffalo Freight leave the marshal's office and stop a short way down the street at the telegraph office.

Where in blazes had that woman come from? And what about the kid? Why had Stark chosen to bring them along? When the bunch first appeared, Hagen had assumed Stark just wanted to report the attack on the freight wagon the day before. But they'd stayed much too long for that. They'd clearly talked to Tallworth about other matters as well.

Hagen only hoped that fool marshal had been able to keep his wits about him. He'd been meaning to speak to the aging lawman about his drinking. Luckily, it was still too early in the day for Tallworth to be too liquored up to let anything incriminating slip.

Hagen had purposefully kept Tallworth at arm's length—wanting to maintain some semblance of propriety as far as Beaver's law enforcement went. But Tallworth had a sly cunning about him, Hagen acknowledged, and was bound to know more about Hagen's operation than the town boss would have liked.

Rising from his cluttered desk, Hagen moved closer to the window, turning at an angle to peer down the road so he could be sure Stark and his bunch were in fact returning to Buffalo Freight.

Even mounted, Stark's lanky figure bore the kind of relaxed assurance that Hagen knew all too well from having been around men who were no strangers to powdersmoke and lead. He was sure he himself still had that same assurance about him.

He'd done a little checking since Sanger had recognized Stark. The man had some skill with a gun, all right. And Hagen had ready evidence among his own men that Stark knew how to handle himself in a fight. *So what was Stark's stake in Buffalo Freight? Why was he willing to put his life on the line for a bunch of coloreds? Was it because of his friendship with that black lawyer, or worse, some misguided loyalty to that group of old cavalrymen, particularly that old ex-sergeant?*

Caleb Jackson. Hagen clenched his gunhand as he recalled the arrogant way the old man had stood up to him. Why, even today, no colored man could match guns with him and walk away from it. Maybe he didn't practice as much as he had back in the wild times, and maybe the years were creeping up on him, but he could still get his double-action Colt into play with a speed that would shame plenty of younger gunhawks. Neither Stark nor Jackson could teach him anything when it came to dropping the hammer on a six-gun.

His gun had given him his start. He'd begun by selling his gun and operating sometimes on one side of the law, sometimes on the other. Eventually he had accumulated enough in his poke to come out here where there weren't many rules and set himself up in the newly founded community of Beaver.

He'd bought into the two-bit saloon already operating in

the town. A year later, negotiating over the barrel of his gun, he'd taken over his partner's interest. From being a saloon owner, he'd branched out, offering cheap loans to new business owners in the community. Then, one way or another, eventually he obtained control of their shops and stores. In this way he'd acquired the stable, the general store, and the hotel.

He'd learned a lot from hiring out his gun. Just as you couldn't let the other side hire too many gunhands without doing something to reduce their number, so you couldn't allow any competing business interest to be too successful if you wanted to stay on top of the heap.

And you couldn't afford to let anyone buck you or stand up to you and get away with it.

He'd missed a good bet, he admitted to himself now, in not recognizing and seizing on the need for a small freight line in the area. When the black partners had started their business, however, he'd been quick to see the possibilities in it, and had moved just as quickly to secure himself an interest.

But the freighters hadn't wanted to sell, and didn't want him as a partner. Further, his own efforts at competition had made him look like some sort of tenderfoot.

He could see the danger well enough. When a sorry outfit like Buffalo Freight stood up to him and got away with it, then his hold on the entire community was weakened. And worse, the door was opened for other competitors to come in and try their luck against him. Soon, he'd be spread too thin, be facing too many enemy guns. This upstart enterprise needed to be nipped in the bud. A lot was riding on it.

So once more it came down to hard case tactics. It was humiliating that he'd let the other side bring in their hired guns, and so far he hadn't been able to do much about it. Fuming, he watched the buggy, with Stark riding alongside, turn into the gate at Buffalo Freight.

Simultaneously, the door to the marshal's office was jerked open, and Tallworth strode across the street toward him. *Great!* Now he'd have to deal with that dolt of a lawman.

He crossed his office to the door and yanked it open. "Get Sanger over here, pronto!" he snapped at Tallworth before the startled man could speak.

"But, Mr. Hagen, that gunslinger just left my office—"

"I know. We'll talk about it when you get back. Sanger's probably over at the saloon."

Hagen paced impatiently while he waited. Lighting a cigar, he puffed furiously in time with his steps, filling the office with clouds of smoke.

He disdained having a clerk or secretary, not wanting anyone to become overly familiar with his varied interests. There lay another possible danger. Once he'd become a somewhat legitimate businessman, he'd seen opportunities to expand into other not-so-legitimate fields that were proving equally lucrative. Now these other enterprises looked to be at possible risk as well.

Hagen met Sanger and Tallworth at the door. He motioned the marshal inside then stepped outside, out of Tallworth's hearing, to give Sanger terse instructions. "Go over to the telegraph office and bring me copies of all the telegrams that have gone out today."

Stepping back inside, Hagen closed the door and sank into his desk chair to glower up at Tallworth. "Okay, fill me in."

Tallworth's eyes darted about nervously. "Well, that gunslinger showed up with that colored lawyer and a woman who claimed to be an attorney too. They were spouting all sorts of highfalutin' nonsense about coloreds being guaranteed the same rights as white folks and talking about having Federal Marshals move in and force me out of office 'cause I wasn't protecting them old slaves like I should."

Hagen filled his voice with condescending calm. "Relax, Tallworth. They're just trying to rattle you. No Federal Marshal's gonna waste his time getting involved in something like this. This is No Man's Land. We're responsible for enforcing our own law up here, remember?"

"Yeah, I remember," Tallworth said sarcastically. "I remember that's how it used to be before you started messing with them old muleskinners." He swept his battered hat off his head and ran his fingers nervously through his greasy hair. "For all we know maybe they can get Federal Marshals to move in. Who'd of ever thought they'd wind up with a gunslinger the caliber of Stark. And that lady lawyer knows what she's talking about too. You can tell by just being around her."

Hagen hid the seething contempt he felt for the washed-up lawman. "Like I said, Marshal, they're just trying to rattle you. Don't worry. If there's any trouble the town council will stand behind you. You've done a passable job of keeping order here. I've heard no complaints from the townspeople."

Tallworth appeared somewhat soothed. "Thank you, Mr. Hagen. That's good to hear."

"Now, you best be going," Hagen said dismissively. "Keep me posted if they make any other threats."

"Yessir, Mr. Hagen. I'll do that."

Sanger entered as Tallworth skulked out. His easygoing grin was in place as he handed Hagen a fistful of telegrams.

He leaned nonchalantly against the wall as Hagen went through the messages, crumpling and discarding all but three.

Hagen's anger rose as he read the short missives. One was to U.S. Marshal Evett Nix in Guthrie:

Please advise as to procedure to request a state of Marshal Law be declared in Beaver. Ku Klux Klan activities and other conditions suggest gross Civil Rights violations. Signed, Prudence Stark.

Prudence Stark! So the lady attorney was the gunfighter's wife. That explained her involvement. Apparently the affinity for lost causes ran in the family. As to how good she was, that remained to be seen. Women lawyers were an oddity in Oklahoma Territory. So it shouldn't be too hard to get a line on her.

The second telegram was to an attorney named George Perkins, also of Guthrie. It read:

Please advise if you would be willing to serve as co-counsel in a lawsuit alleging Civil Rights violations by the city of Beaver, its town council, and its employee, Marshal Cal Tallworth. All seem to be conspiring to wage a concerted and carefully orchestrated campaign of terror and intimidation against the black owners of a local freight line.

Hagen crumpled that missive with particular ferocity. He'd heard of Perkins, all right. He was that uppity black politician who was always preaching about coloreds getting involved in elections and running for office. As if any of them had sense enough to run the government on any level!

The third telegram was to a Judge McKay up in Kansas:

Dear Father, I find myself embroiled in a case of land-mark importance legally. Please advise as to procedure for bringing charges of Civil Rights violations in Federal Court and also inform me which District Court would have jurisdiction in such a case. Much love, your daughter, Prudence.

Hagen had heard of Judge McKay during his early days as a gunhawk. The old man was as hardnosed as they came in cases tried before him. If the Stark woman was his daughter, she'd likely had the best of schooling and had a good share of clout on her own in certain political circles— particularly when she chose to bring her father's name into play, as she had now.

This game had just gotten a lot more complicated.

"I read those telegrams on the way over, boss," Sanger prodded. "Sounds like they mean business. Want to turn up the heat a little?"

Hagen puffed harder on his cigar, his mind going at a gallop. "I ain't sure what our next move will be, but I want you to make certain nothing goes on at that freight company that we don't know about. You hear me?"

"I got a man watching."

"Put another on the job along with him. And I especially want to know the next time they're shorthanded. Savvy?"

"Sure, I savvy." Sanger tried to look thoughtful, but Hagen could read him well enough to know he'd just been looking for an excuse to say what he did next. "Might be I could prod Stark into something. Then they'd be short-handed for sure."

"That is, if you beat him," Hagen said dryly.

"I can beat him."

"Maybe. But there's no point in risking a head-on confrontation for now when there's a smarter way to play this. You've got my orders. Just keep me informed, and I'll tell you when the time is right to move."

He puffed on his cigar until the end glowed red-hot. "And rest assured, that move will come a long time before they can bring in Federal Marshals or file any charges in court."

Chapter Ten

Caleb sat in the broad breezeway of the stable rubbing oil into the harness and trying to decide the freight runs they should make in the coming week. The responsibility remained oppressive, and his mind was resisting the task.

Here he sat in the calm twilight doing mundane chores that made the danger they were facing seem a million miles away. Through the open kitchen door he could see Prudence and Thaddeus, law books spread out on the table before them, engrossed in discussing the legal strategy they'd threatened to use when they'd confronted Marshal Tallworth earlier that day.

As battle tactics went, it was an interesting diversion. But he had a hunch all this would be settled long before any court could take a hand in it.

His eyes shifted to where Hollis and Tyler sat on the porch. He could hear snatches of their conversation, and knew the talk centered again on their time as Buffalo Soldiers. The Peacemaker had done good by shifting their focus back there. Recalling the victories had helped lift the despair that had hovered over the outfit of late.

Pete was sitting alone in the porch swing, a brooding look on her face. As Caleb watched, she rose, picked up her father's carbine, and walked toward him.

"Hi, girl," he greeted as she walked up. "Your turn at watch?"

She nodded. "In a few minutes." She leaned against the doorframe. "Uncle Caleb, can I talk to you about something?"

"Sure thing, honey. What's bothering you?"

"Have you ever thought about how unfair it is to be colored—I mean, slavery and all that?"

"Slavery's behind us now. We got to move on."

"But it was white folks that forced it on us."

"It was also white folks that started a war to end it."

She nodded slowly. "Guess I never thought about that."

"And we got white folks standing with us now—siding us in a fight that ain't none of their responsibility."

"You mean Mr. Stark and Prudence? Yeah, I know. You should've seen them both today, Uncle Caleb, standing up to Marshal Tallworth. Especially Prudence. It was a sight to behold."

"I'll bet it was, child. I'll bet it was. They're good folks."

She nodded again. "You know, before they came here, I pretty much hated all white people."

"You got to fight against feelings like that, and see each person as an individual. Otherwise, you line up alongside Hagen and the Klan and all their kind. You don't want to be in that camp, do you?"

"Of course not," she snapped. She stared at the ground

thoughtfully for a moment. "Uncle Caleb, how have you come through all you have and not grown bitter?"

"I've had lots of good times along with the bad. Got lots of things to be thankful for. Nice place to live, good friends, my freedom, my faith . . . .Hope in tomorrow."

"I guess it's the hope I'm short on."

"Oh, you can't let go of that, honey. You got to keep hold of hope in the future so's you can pass it on to the next generation. Otherwise, things'll never get better for them."

She looked even more peeved. "I have enough to do worrying about myself. Why should I care about the next generation?"

"It's like planting a tree, sweetheart." He nodded toward the big tree standing outside the kitchen door. "Take that old elm there. Must be nigh onto fifty-years-old now. Think how much we've enjoyed the shade from that tree. Now what if the person who planted it all those years ago had selfishly decided not to just because he wouldn't be around to enjoy it."

The girl smiled in spite of herself. "I get your point. Well, guess I better go relieve Mr. Stark. You know, you're a tricky one, all right, Uncle Caleb."

Caleb watched as Pete disappeared around the corner of the stable. He drew a heavy breath. He hoped the girl was right. He hoped he still had a few tricks left up his sleeve.

The mantle of leadership settled heavily upon him again. Hollis and Tyler were seated only a few yards away, but he still felt all alone. With a sigh, he closed the can of oil and rose to hang the harness back in the tack room.

Awkwardly he took a jar of liniment from the shelf holding various medications for the livestock. He scooped out a healthy dab and methodically worked it into the crevices and callouses of his right hand. He almost relished its sting-ing bite. The medicine seemed to be doing some good. His hand felt more flexible and no longer ached as much when he made a fist or handled a gun.

He slowly massaged the hard knob of his enlarged mid-dle knuckle. He'd broken it on the jaw of an unruly private during an unofficial training session behind the barracks, which had settled, once and for all, that the sergeant really was the toughest man in the outfit.

Then there was the pale line across the back of his hand caused when he'd raised it reflexively to deflect an Apache arrow aimed at his face during the wild storm of battle.

And there were other scars, the origins of most forgotten over the years. Some scars on his heart too, he reckoned. In his mind's eye he saw a pretty smiling face, a slender feminine figure. A soft voice seemed to whisper again in his ear. Dear sweet Bonnie. The war had torn them apart. When he did get back to look for her, her family had moved on. He hoped she'd been happy all these years. Hoped she didn't have a big empty hole in her heart like he did. Some wounds never healed. They just hurt a little less over the decades.

He sighed once more. Didn't do no good to let his mind wander down that path. It was better, more productive, to dwell on the positive things in life—just like he'd told Pete. He set the jar back on the shelf and moved off to join Hollis and Tyler.

Stark watched from the corner of the shed as Pete made her way toward him across the yard. Though she still wore denim pants and a work shirt, the shirt was tucked in neatly and her braid hung down her back. A few wisps of dark hair were visible under the slouch hat. They curled becomingly around her face.

Prudence appeared to be making some progress, but the girl was clearly struggling with sorting out all the issues she'd been confronted with lately.

She paused in front of him, carbine held loosely in her hands. "Anything moving out there?" she asked with a smile.

"Nope, nary a thing so far. Guess I'll grab a cup of coffee and check in with the others."

"Mr. Stark, wait. I need to ask you something."

"Okay, shoot. I'll help if I can."

"Well, Uncle Caleb just accused me of being as prejudiced against most white folks as some of them are against us. And I guess maybe I am. I mean, all my life I've watched my daddy struggle to make ends meet. He's worked twice as hard as most people, and he hasn't got much to show for it. And now that he and his friends have a chance to own a little something, people are coming from all sides to try and take it away from them. It's just not fair."

Stark was silent for a moment, trying to find the right words. "You're right," he said at last. "Your assessment is right on the money, and I agree wholeheartedly that it's not fair. But then again, life's not fair. That's one of the first things a body has to come to grips with in order to get along in this world."

"That's easy for you to say," the girl retorted irritably. "But I wonder if my daddy would agree."

"Why don't you ask him." Stark watched the girl's startled reaction. She clearly thought he was joking. "No, I mean it," he assured her. "I'll bet if you asked him, he'd tell you that overall he's had a good life."

"Uncle Caleb just said something like that about himself," Pete admitted. "But to me, it seems ridiculous."

"Well, it's not. Because Caleb sees himself as a winner. Granted, he's fought a lot of hard battles that he arguably shouldn't have had to fight. All those old soldiers have, for that matter. But I'll wager they'll all say just what Caleb did. They came out of each skirmish stronger and wiser—better equipped to handle the problems of life and end up on top of the heap. In fact, I'd be willing to bet my horse on your dad's answer—and I care a lot about that horse."

Pete still looked skeptical, so Stark went on. "What? Don't you consider your father a winner?"

"I guess I never thought about it."

"Well, he is a winner. And you can be too. That's really what all this talk is about, isn't it? You're looking for an excuse not to make a grab for that brass ring that's dangling out there so tantalizingly in front of you, right?"

A worried frown played across her face, then she nodded. "I guess I'm scared. Miss Prudence and Thaddeus keep talking about me going off to college and changing the way I look. . . . It all sounds like a foolish gamble to me—a gamble that probably won't pay off anyway, since so many of the people I'll have to deal with will be wanting me to fail."

"You're right again. It's going to be a struggle, with no guarantees you'll succeed. And it *is* a gamble—probably the biggest one you'll ever take. But if you don't try, won't you always wonder what it would be like to own a brass ring?"

A spark of hope flared into her eyes. "You really think I can do this?"

"I'd bet my horse on you too. Don't forget, you've also got lots of folks in your life who'll be wanting you to succeed—people who've walked this road before you and will be cheering you on. They should all be an inspiration to you." He nodded toward the house. "Look over there and tell me what you see."

Pete's eyes swept over Prudence and Thaddeus conferring over the law books spread out on the kitchen table, then moved on to the old Buffalo Soldiers gathered on the porch. "A lot of people holding brass rings?"

A smile split Stark's face. "Right again. Just remember, the way to win when you're battling unfair circumstances in life is just to show up on the battlefield each day. You take whatever blows the enemy throws at you, and you keep toeing the line. You don't flee the battle or make excuses to stay in your tent and nurse your wounds. You just get out of bed each morning, put on fresh bandages, and make your way to the front lines."

Stark paused to let his words sink in, then went on. "And eventually you'll win the respect of your enemies, the admiration of your colleagues, and . . ." His gaze shifted to the group of old soldiers. ". . . maybe even a place in history."

"Hagen's pet gunsnake is coming down the road," Thaddeus sang out from atop the stable.

By the time all of them had emerged into the early morning sunlight, Sanger was slouching his horse down the cutoff from the main road. His lips twitched in an affable grin as he spotted Stark. He reined to a halt, all but ignoring the others. Stark got the sensation that the grin was a ploy meant to unnerve possible foes. It came darn near to working.

Sanger reined up. Stark knew Caleb would have an eye out for any other of Hagen's hirelings lurking in the area.

Hollis and Tyler faded aside to take positions of cover in the outbuildings. If Sanger noticed—as Stark was sure he did—he paid no heed.

"Still riding for the losing side." He regarded Stark with a rueful shake of his head. "These boys paying you gun wages to side them?"

"Top dollar," Stark responded.

Sanger snorted in disbelief. Despite his relaxed stance, Stark could read the violent tension coiling in the man. But none of it sounded in Sanger's drawling tones. "Morg sent me out here to see if your employers had changed their minds about accepting his offer."

"He pays you to run his errands, does he?" Stark queried.

Sanger's easygoing smile widened. "I been paid to do worse."

Stark didn't doubt it. He nodded toward Caleb. "You'll have to talk to him."

"What about it, old man?" Sanger spared only a brief glance at Caleb, then shifted his eyes back to Stark. Watcher had appeared from somewhere to snarl silently at the gunslinger.

"What gives your boss the notion we might've changed our minds?" Caleb queried shrewdly.

"Oh, he just thought maybe circumstances had changed . . . maybe you'd taken stock of things and found some reason to deal."

"Nope, nothing's changed." Caleb's tone was flat. "You're wasting your time, and your boss' money."

Sanger gave a careless hitch of his shoulders. "He's got plenty of it to waste. But maybe you answered too quick. Maybe you better take some time to mull it over. I'll tell Morg you're still thinking about it. That would be the *smart* thing to do, I'll guarantee." Sanger looked back at Stark with a lazy half-grin quirking his lips. "Too bad we're on opposite sides of the fence. Who knows? Otherwise we might've been pards."

Despite himself, Stark almost laughed. "Not likely."

"Maybe you're right." Sanger used his left hand to sketch a simple salute from the brim of his Stetson. He backed his horse a couple of steps, flashed one last affable grin, then wheeled the animal and sent it back out to the road at a relaxed canter.

Caleb watched him go with a speculative frown. "Could be Hagen knows something we don't."

"Could be," Stark agreed as an uneasy feeling played up his spine. "We better take a turn around the place. Look things over real good."

As Caleb moved off to check the wagons, Stark strode toward the house. Prudence was waiting for him on the back step.

"What is it?" he asked with a worried scowl.

"Pete's not here," she said nervously. "I checked her room, the well house, and the chicken coop. She's none of the usual places she goes on her chores."

"That's not good," Stark gritted. "Sanger was just here playing some sort of game—like he knew something we didn't. They've got some trump card they're getting ready to play."

"Well, maybe there's nothing to worry about. I think I know where she is."

"Lead out," Stark said tersely.

Prudence led the way into the woods down a dimly visible path. "There's a sharecropper's cabin in a clearing through this stand of trees," she explained. "They have a whole slew of kids, and Pete's been helping them get ready for school." She bent and peered under a fallen tree. "Pete keeps her supplies in here. As I expected, they're gone."

"Fool girl," Stark growled. "Why'd she pull something like this. Hagen's bound to have had his men watching our every move. They would have spotted her for sure."

Prudence was almost running now. "Well, maybe she managed to sneak past them. She's done this before, and I've only caught her one time. I saw her leave and followed her. Hollis was waiting for us when we got back. He told her how dangerous it was and forbid her to go again, but she's really worried about those kids being ready for school when it starts."

"That's all well and good," Stark allowed. "But it's still a fool stunt."

"Granted," Prudence responded, "but you know young people. They always think they know best. Besides, things have been quiet the last couple of days. She probably thought it was safe to venture out."

"Just the opposite," Stark growled. "This is just the calm before the storm."

At the edge of the trees, they looked out on a pastoral scene. A group of ragtag kids ran and played innocently around a rundown cabin. Stark pulled out his Colt Peacemaker. "You go talk to them," he said tersely. "I'll keep watch from here. Walk easy."

Prudence nodded. She waved and called a friendly greeting as she approached the kids. They stopped playing and clustered together shyly as she talked to them. After a few sentences, she waved good-bye and walked quickly back toward Stark.

"She never got here," she told him as she entered the woods.

He nodded, and turned to retrace their steps. Close by

the fallen tree, he spotted what he was looking for. He lifted a low-hanging branch and indicated the marks in the dirt. "Signs of a scuffle. This must be where they grabbed her." He followed the marks easily enough. One set of heavy bootprints was clear and distinct. The second smaller set was smeared and irregular. Her captor had half-carried, half-dragged Pete to his horse. There the struggle stopped. Stark felt a chill. Pete had probably put up such a fight, the hard case had had to knock her out. He wouldn't have risked her escaping while he tied her up and got her aboard his horse.

Prudence bent to pick up Pete's packet of school supplies lying in the grass. "They'll hold her hostage to force the sale, won't they?"

"They'll try," Stark said tightly. "Let's get back to the compound. The sooner I hit the trail, the sooner I get her back."

Chapter Eleven

"I'm going with you, Peacemaker! No arguing! We're talking about my little girl!"

Stark studied Tyler across Red's back as he tightened the cinch. The man was understandably upset, but he didn't have time to be tactful. "That's not a good idea, Tyler. I'll be traveling hard and fast. Besides, you're needed here."

Tyler bristled. "What you're saying is I'm too old."

"What I'm saying," Stark said coldly, "is you're needed here. Hagen's watching this outfit like a hawk. If we leave it too shorthanded, he'll have his forces move on it pronto. Together, you, Caleb, and Hollis can hold them off. With you gone, the odds of that happening drop by a third."

Desperation glittered in Tyler's eyes. "Look, I can't just sit here and do nothing!"

"I know how you feel. But they took Pete to goad us into doing something stupid. You want to oblige them?"

A look of resignation settled on the man's features. "I guess you're right."

Stark's voice softened. "Look, I'll bring Pete back to you. I give you my word."

Tyler nodded, then turned silently to walk away.

As he left, Thaddeus appeared out of the stable. He was dressed in trail clothes and leading his horse. "I'm going with you," he said swinging up into the saddle. "I heard all the reasons you gave Tyler, and none of them apply to me. I can keep up with you, and I'm not all that vital to the defense of the outfit."

"Well, I don't have time for another argument, so do as you please." Though he couldn't say so out loud, Stark was glad for Thaddeus' company. They'd sided each other before, and worked well together.

Prudence then came out of the house carrying his saddlebags, which she'd been packing with provisions. He strapped them on behind the saddle and turned to take her into his arms for a brief hug. "Stay in the house as much as possible," he instructed, "and keep your gun handy."

She nodded. "Be careful," she said softly. Her eyes swept up to Thaddeus. "You too."

The young lawyer smiled. "I'll watch his back."

The three Buffalo soldiers had gathered to stand shoulder to shoulder behind Prudence.

Stark locked eyes with Caleb and sketched a salute. "They ain't licked us yet, sergeant."

Caleb returned the salute. "You got that right Peacemaker. Ride safe, boys. I'll be praying."

"Appreciate that." Stark looked at Thaddeus. "Let's slope."

It was late afternoon when Stark tracked his quarry to ground. He lay prone beside Thaddeus on a slight rise staring down on a collection of ramshackle structures that looked to be all that was left of an abandoned farm.

The draws and gullies of the rough terrain had given them cover as they worked their way nearer the rundown homestead. Stark hadn't spotted any lookouts. Likely the men who occupied the deserted farm felt confident enough at this remote site to not be too worried about trespassers.

Stark had to admit it was by sheer luck, or, more likely, because of Caleb's prayers, that they had found the place. They'd lost the trail several times on the rocky ground, which, no doubt, Pete's captor was counting on. But the man had made the mistake of traveling too consistently in one direction. Stark had seen the tendency early on. He'd only had to keep heading in that direction himself, casting about as he rode, to pick up the trail again.

They'd watched the comings and goings of the dozen or so men for half an hour now. Several of the hard cases and their mounts in the nearby corral looked familiar to Stark. He recognized them as the same group who'd attacked him and Tyler at the river ford.

"Well, what's the plan?" Thaddeus asked in a low voice.

Stark squirmed back down off the promonotory before he answered. "I don't have one at this point. I need to move in closer on foot to see where they're holding Pete. We'll probably have to wait until after dark to get her out."

He stood and stretched to limber up, then walked over to his horse to retrieve the sheathed hatchet from his gear and affixed it to his belt. He left both his long guns in their scabbards.

"Stay here out of sight and keep the horses quiet. I'll be back as soon as I can."

As Stark worked his way toward the buildings, he

jumped a coyote. The little prairie wolf fled, and Stark hoped its flight wouldn't be noted by suspicious eyes.

The broken ground leveled out about 50 yards from the outermost shed. Stark lay on his belly in the grass for a spell while he studied the layout. The central structure was a big two-story farmhouse. It sagged alarmingly. The other buildings were in little better shape. What might've once been a chicken coop had folded into a pile of rubble. The barn still looked serviceable, and makeshift repairs had been done on the corral so it could hold the outlaws' horses. This place probably dated back to the days when certain tribes had farmed these lands before the opening of the territory to white settlement.

The men slouched about lazily in groups of two or three. Clearly, they thought they had no reason to be concerned. Stark's gaze settled on a man alone sitting outside one of the outbuildings with a rifle across his lap and a cigarette hanging out of the corner of his mouth. As Stark watched, the owlhoot finished his smoke, leaned back in the rickety chair, stretched his long legs out in front of him, and tilted his hat down over his eyes.

Stark guessed Pete was being held under the man's guard. He snorted derisively to himself. *Some guard!* He and Thaddeus shouldn't have any trouble affecting a rescue come dark. He decided it'd be best to give Pete notice to expect them. He figured it was safe to crawl through the grass to the back of the outbuilding.

He had no shade from the sun. The minutes wobbled past as he elbowed his way forward, careful to keep his head down. Impatience prodded him like spurs. He wished Thaddeus were here to cover him.

When he had the outbuilding between him and the lounging hard cases, he came up into a crouch and darted up to the back. Through a crack in the weathered boards, he could see Pete sitting on the edge of a filthy bunk with her head in her hands.

He tapped lightly on the wood, and her head came up abruptly, her eyes casting about for the source of the noise. He repeated the tapping, and she rose and moved cautiously toward him. He took a step away from the building so she could see him through the crack, then moved in close again.

"Mr. Stark!" she whispered. "How'd you get here?"

"Tracked you. We'll come in after dark and get you out. Be ready to move."

She nodded. "I'll be waiting."

Stark crouched low again and made ready to work his way back to cover. Before he could move, a new voice called out from some distance down the road, "Hello the house! I'm coming in, and I got me a prisoner "

Stark heard the yahoo on guard thump his chair back to ground and come to his feet. He peered around the corner of the outbuilding and saw Pete's guard moving off to join the others waiting for the man who'd hailed the house.

Stark's heart sank as he saw the sorry-looking figure mounted on a sorrier-looking horse riding herd on the lone captive who led Red and another familiar mount. Somehow, probably by not watching his back, Thaddeus had let himself be surprised and taken prisoner by one of the outlaws. Thaddeus' holster was empty, and his captor rode with a Winchester centered lazily between his prisoner's shoulder blades.

As the little procession halted in front of the house, the outlaws gathered around them. Thaddeus was in deadly danger, maybe only moments away from death or some form of brutal interrogation. Stark licked dry lips as he listened to the talk.

"Rode right up on him, big as life, hiding out in a draw back yonder a little ways," the captor was recounting. "Never even saw me coming. Had him covered almost before he knew I was there."

"Who are you, boy?" one of the others demanded. "What are you doing in these parts?"

A tall man shouldered his way to the front. Stark recognized him as the one who'd led the charge on the wagon at the river crossing. "I seen him hanging around the freight company with them other darkies last time I rode into town to palaver with the boss," he growled. "He's probably here to try and rescue that girl. You come alone, boy?"

"No, you're surrounded!" Thaddeus responded coolly.

The leader's backhanded knuckles exploded alongside Thaddeus' jaw and drove his head sideways. Thaddeus lost his balance and fell to his knees.

"Mr. Stark, we've got to do something!" came Pete's urgent whisper. "They'll kill him!"

Stark had almost forgotten the girl in his concern for Thaddeus. His mind was churning furiously. Maybe this diversion could work for their benefit, depending on how Thaddeus played it.

Thaddeus knew he was here and likely was watching for him. Since the attention of all the outlaws was focused on their prisoner, Stark risked letting Thaddeus know where he was. He drew his gun and stepped quickly into the open, then back behind the shed again.

Peering around the corner, he caught the lawyer's almost imperceptible nod. Hopefully Thaddeus could keep the owlhoots distracted long enough for him to get Pete out—provided he worked fast.

He holstered his gun and unsheathed the hand ax. He inserted the blade between two of the wide planks and pried with all his might. The rusted nails in the weathered wood came out easily enough. He slipped the ax back in his belt and grabbed the loose edge with both hands to wrench it free. Setting it aside, he grabbed another board. Pete was squeezing through the opening even before he had the second plank completely off.

Stark grabbed her arm and thrust her behind him as he flattened himself once more against the back wall of the shed. "Don't move until I tell you to, then be ready to scramble," he whispered. He drew his Colt Peacemaker again and concentrated on the action unfolding out in the yard.

Thaddeus was just regaining his feet. Apparently he'd stayed down longer than necessary, pretending to be more addled by the blow than he actually was. Stark hoped the yahoos had bought his act. He noted that Thaddeus grabbed hold of his horse's reins as he rose, on the pretext of steadying himself.

"I asked you something, darky!" the leader snarled. "Who's this other horse belong to?"

Thaddeus' captor still had the rifle trained on his back. The man posed the most threat. None of the other outlaws even had their guns drawn, probably not seeing their prisoner as much of a threat.

Thaddeus started to answer the leader's question in some fashion. His reply was lost in the explosion of Stark's .45 as he aimed and shot the captor out of his saddle.

Before the falling body hit the ground, Thaddeus vaulted into his saddle and grabbed the reins of the man's horse. Red had stood steady as he was trained to do. Thaddeus leaned down and grabbed the stallion's reins too as he spurred toward Stark and Pete, dragging the two horses in tow.

"Get on that extra horse and ride like your life depends on it," Stark ordered Pete, "because it does!"

Stark darted into the open, throwing lead at the owlhoots even as they were diving for cover. He heard a couple of cries of pain above the uproar of startled yells and curses, and figured he must've scored some hits.

Thaddeus dropped Red's reins and held the bridle of the other horse while Pete scrambled aboard. "Yaw, horse!" Pete yelled as she reined the balky horse about, drummed heels against its side, and sent it pounding away after Thaddeus.

Stark emptied the Colt at the darting owlhoots, holstered it, and wheeled to mount Red. A foot in the stirrup, a surge, and he was aboard. He plucked the shotgun from its scabbard, levering it with a jerking motion of hand and wrist. A gun snapped and a bullet zipped past him. He had an instant's view of the outlaw leader triggering a six-gun from the corner of the house. Stark's own bullet tore splinters from the wall beside the man, and sent him dodging out of sight.

Stark fired off one last shot, then put Red into a run, concentrating on staying low in the saddle as more bullets whizzed past him like angry wasps.

Thaddeus and Pete were just disappearing into the mouth of a draw ahead of him. Stark sent Red racing in their wake. The grassy sloping walls of the draw shut off his view of the house and its confounded occupants.

His near-loco attack, with its element of surprise, had won Pete's freedom. But it would be only minutes before the outlaws had thrown saddles on their horses in the corral and set out after them like hounds on a scent.

He pushed Red up alongside the others in the narrow

draw. Pete flung him a glance that was all mixed-up fear and relief.

"This way!" Stark peeled off into the mouth of another draw, taking the lead.

They had ridden into a maze of rough gullies and defiles deep enough to conceal a rider. But if they weren't careful, the maze was just as likely to double back and lead them into the laps of their pursuers as to take them to freedom.

Stark wasn't fooling himself. They had a rugged trail to ride. Thaddeus was unarmed, Pete was mounted on a horse that looked to be half-winded already, and they had a mighty big stretch of countryside between them and safety.

When they were well clear of the outlaw compound, Stark slowed the pace a little. Keeping his bearings in the maze of gullies was near nigh to impossible. Somehow he had to get a better grasp of the lay of the land.

A short distance farther on he signaled a stop and risked dismounting to ascend the steep bank. Mentally he mapped a route out of the badlands and onto smoother terrain some quarter-mile distant as the crow flew.

As he started to ease back down off the rim, a rifle's flat report sounded, and a bullet struck the ground close by. He didn't wait to spot whatever sharp-eyed rifleman had targeted him.

"Come on!" he shouted to Pete and Thaddeus as he threw himself astride Red and led the way at a gallop along the path he'd picked out. Another shot followed, but the bullet came nowhere close.

Nose to tail, they raced down a narrow gully, swerved around the base of a hill, and broke out into open country. Stark spared a look back, but there was no visible sign of pursuit yet. He glanced at Pete's mount. The animal appeared to be well past its prime, but for the moment it was matching Red's headlong gallop.

Ahead of them, the prairie stretched away in gently undulating waves. Stark eased Red up into a dead run. Pete's horse tried valiantly, but Stark and Thaddeus pulled on ahead. Stark reined in, letting Pete once more pull alongside.

Stark's pledge to bring Pete back to her father unharmed weighed heavily upon him as the girl urged her mount on with urgent words and pounding heels.

Chapter Twelve

Stark kept an eye over his shoulder. They'd covered more than a mile when he saw the first tiny shapes of horsemen appear behind them. He slowed, squinting rearwards. The outlaws' ranks had been thinned by two, but there were still somewhere around a half score of men riding after them. Gravely, Stark faced front.

When he looked back again, the mounted forms were a little larger. The gap was closing. They raced on beneath the cloud-scarred sky. Pete's horse was giving it everything it had, but Stark was forced to hold Red in to keep from outstripping the beast.

The gap was narrowing dangerously. Stark fancied he heard the first shot. A waste of lead at this range, he thought bleakly, but soon the outlaw pack would be close enough to throw lead with a purpose. He cast his eyes westward. The day was almost done. If they could outdistance their pursuers for a spell longer, nightfall would give them some protection. But at this pace, they would be overtaken long before then.

Stark scanned the countryside ahead. A rugged hogback ridge rose in the near distance a little to the left of their present course. He indicated it with pointing finger.

"There!" he shouted. "Make for that ridge!"

Thaddeus shot him a surprised look, but glanced in that direction and nodded.

They slanted toward the ridge. Pete's horse was beginning to labor. The slight change in direction let the outlaws gain a bit, but Stark calculated they'd still reach the ridge well ahead of the pack. Stark gritted his teeth and put Red up the steep slope to the crest, hoping the other horses could survive the climb.

At the top of the ridge, Stark sprang out of the saddle, hauling the awkward length of the sporting rifle from its scabbard. As he opened his saddlebags to retrieve extra ammo, he watched Pete slide to the ground and stand on wobbly legs. For the first time the stress of the ordeal showed on her features, and tears began to flow down her cheeks.

Wordlessly, Thaddeus stepped down from his horse and enfolded her in his arms. She rested her head on his chest and began to sob. Thaddeus held her tighter and bent to kiss her softly on the forehead.

The tenderness of such a moment in this unlikely place stabbed at Stark's heart. The memory of the first time he'd held Prudence came flooding back to his mind. In that moment he made a decision. He pulled a compass from the saddlebag and caught up Red's reins.

Thaddeus' horse looked okay, but Pete's horse was standing with head down, mouth wide open, and sides heaving. Stark left the shotgun in its scabbard and led Red over to the couple. He handed Red's reins to Pete, then pulled the .38 hideout gun from his waistband and thrust it and the compass at Thaddeus.

"Take these, mount up, and get out of here," he said gruffly.

"You mean take your horse and leave you here?" Thaddeus protested. "What about you?"

"I'm going to buy us some time, lower the odds, and," he jerked a thumb at Pete's horse, "give that old fella some time to catch his breath. We'll be along in a jiffy. Use the compass and head southeast. You should pick up the main trail into Beaver in about ten miles. You can slack off on the pace after that."

Stark looked pointedly at Pete then locked eyes with Thaddeus. "Now quit wasting time and get going!"

Thaddeus nodded his assent as understanding dawned. He urged Pete up on Red and hurriedly mounted his own horse. "We'll have to slow down after dark. You catch up to us in time for supper?"

Stark looked over at the winded horse and smiled. "Better make that breakfast."

As they tore away down the back of the slope, Stark moved quickly to the rim and squinted out over the grassland below. Pete and Thaddeus were pounding away from the ridge, and the outlaws were slowing down as they realized their prey had separated. Stark figured to give them something else to slow them down even more.

He knelt and hefted the sporting rifle to his shoulder. He adjusted the brim of his Stetson, then lined up the long barrel through the sight. The range would have been too great for the shotgun he'd given Thaddeus, but he figured the sporting rifle could handle it.

For a second he hesitated, sorry to have to drop the hammer on men who, for the moment, couldn't fight back.

Then, with grim resolve, he sighted carefully for one of the tiny nameless figures and pulled the trigger. The blast rocked him, the big gun jumping in his grip like a live thing.

Far off, he saw his target disappear from the saddle. Stark's mouth tightened. The outlaws were drawing up short, shaken by this killing from long range. They hadn't learned their lesson from facing the sporting rifle at the river ford. Stark set his sights again and cut loose the big gun's thunder. He waved the smoke away. Another man was swatted from his saddle like an insect.

The rest of the outlaws started to pull back or turn tail. Stark sent a third target tumbling over his horse's head as they tried to flee. For good measure, he hurled one more big slug whistling after them, but could see no effect from the shot.

They regrouped out of range, and after fanning the smoke aside, Stark noted for the first time that one of them hadn't retreated. Instead, the man dismounted and seemed to be standing boldly near one of his fallen comrades, a long gun raised to his shoulder. Stark saw a puff of smoke from the barrel. It was tiny at this distance.

Understanding dawned on him a fragment of a second before something tore over his head like a miniature cannonball. He ducked instinctively and scuttled sideways. One of the owlhoots was packing a long-range piece of his own. And he was plenty good with it.

Automatically, Stark looked for Thaddeus and Pete, fearing they would be the next targets. He spotted the pair galloping far out of reach of the owlhoot's gun. He could pull back himself, Stark thought, but he didn't cotton to having a marksman like that hombre riding on their backtrail armed with whatever piece he was packing.

Dirt and grass exploded from the face of the ridge less than a foot below Stark's position. The faint rumble of the shot reached his ears a second later. The outlaw hadn't been fooled by his change of position, he realized. The man might have been expecting it. And one high shot and one low meant he was about to get Stark targeted in.

Run or fight, Stark told himself. As he reloaded he saw his opponent stride a few steps closer. Stark felt a twinge of reluctant admiration. The marksman had no cover, but he was coolly doing his best to keep Stark from having time to target him between shots. The rest of the brigand crew sat their horses further back, watching the duel. As Stark finished reloading, the outlaw sharpshooter sent another heavy slug whistling somewhere nearby. Stark waited for him to take three paces forward and halt, then he sent a shot of his own drilling back.

Almost in the same instant that he fired, Stark saw the sharpshooter drop to one knee, and knew he'd missed. He shook his head in disbelief. It was uncanny. Had the outlaw somehow known or sensed the moment he was going to fire?

He lifted the sporting rifle again and figured the distant figure was doing the same. He ducked and the whine of a big bullet passed close over his head. Let the outlaw marksman have his own unnerving doubts now, he thought with a fierce satisfaction. Then he lined up the sporting rifle and fired.

For a moment the smoke and afterimage of the blast blocked his view of his target. Then his blinking eyes made out the shape of the outlaw sprawled like a crushed bug far off on the prairie below.

He turned his attention to the remaining members of the band. Counting the two yahoos back at the deserted farm, they'd lost six men now, he calculated. The gang had been near cut in half.

And the rest of them weren't any too eager to ride into his range of fire, he saw. He raised the barrel slightly and threw a slug at them, trying for as much distance as the big gun could give him. He didn't hit anything, but it was still enough to make up their minds for them. Almost as one, the distant riders turned their mounts and made tracks back the way they had come.

Stark waited until the outlaws disappeared in the distance to be sure the retreat wasn't a ruse. The day was drawing fast to a close. Even if they tried to double back now, he estimated, they wouldn't be able to cut his trail in the dark.

An ugly business, he thought, but the gang had paid a high price for butting heads with Buffalo Freight.

Stark walked over to the horse. It had caught its wind, and looked back at him alertly. He peeled back the horse's lip to ascertain its age. In surprise, he found it wasn't as old as he'd figured. Just must be in poor shape, he thought to himself.

To its credit, it had stood steady during all the gunfire, and it had given its all in their desperate escape flight. He gave it an affectionate pat on the neck. A good horse, he allowed. It had a lot of heart. Under Hollis Kelso's care, he had a hunch the animal could be successfully reconditioned. Then Buffalo Freight would have a fine buggy horse.

He slipped the sporting rifle into the empty scabbard on the saddle and swung aboard his new mount. He put the horse into an easy lope down the back side of the ridge.

He drew a deep breath and felt some of the tension drain out of him. Stars were winking in the night sky above. It looked to be a beautiful evening.

Even if he let the horse set its own pace, he should easily catch up to the others in time for breakfast. He smiled. Some bacon and biscuits would taste mighty good, he admitted.

"Sarge!" Tyler's voice was low. He slipped into the stable, staying to the shadows.

"Here." Caleb came awake with a surge, and sat up on his pallet of hay. "What is it, Private?"

"We got intruders on the perimeter."

Caleb used his carbine to push himself to his feet. "Identity?"

"Not sure. They're trying to sneak around quiet-like, but I spotted them. Watcher's got his back up. He knows they're out there too. Whoever they are, I figure they're trying to get positioned to open fire."

"Or give cover to some saboteur trying to reach the wagons and disable them," Caleb voiced his thoughts aloud. "Any of them moving toward the house?"

"Not that I saw. You think we need to alert Mrs. Stark?"

"I don't think we can without letting the intruders know we're on to them. We got the house forted up good, and she's got her handgun and one of the extra rifles. She told me she knows how to use both of them. I have a feeling there's going to be enough racket in a minute to cause her to wake up on her own."

Tyler snorted. "Bet you're right about that, Sarge."

"Get back out by the wagons," Caleb ordered. "Give me a couple of minutes to rouse Hollis, then when you think you've got one of the enemy spotted, throw some lead his way. No point waiting for them to commence hostilities. Maybe we can put them to rout before they get positioned."

"Yessir." Tyler vanished once again.

After a few steps, some of the stiffness disappeared from Caleb's gait. Sleeping on the floor wasn't easy these days, but he was glad now he'd chosen to spend the night in the stable instead of the house. Hurriedly, he entered the lean-to and roused Hollis, explaining the situation as the man collected his carbine and some extra ammo.

The old confidence that always came with action stirred anew in Caleb. "Tyler's out by the wagons. You stay here, Corporal, and I'll man the stable."

Almost before he finished speaking, a pair of shots cracked from outside in the direction of the wagons. For a moment the whole night seemed to hang silently. Then, abruptly, came a withering fusillade of rifle fire from what sounded like a dozen different points.

"Okay, let's draw some of that fire off Tyler," Caleb snapped.

Hollis was already cutting loose through one of the newly installed rifle ports as Caleb ducked back into the stable. Taking a position at one of the slots, Caleb peered out.

Angry red fireflies winked at him from the darkness. He chose one as a target and sent a carbine slug tearing through the night. He ducked low as bullets thumped into the wood in answer. He moved to another port and sought another target. No more muzzle flashes came from the first point he'd fired at, but he didn't know if he'd scored a hit or just spooked the ambusher into changing positions.

He kept firing, switching from port to port. With him in the stable, Hollis in the lean-to, and Tyler near the wagons on the opposite side, they had the compound pretty well covered, he noted with satisfaction. Tyler was the most exposed. Caleb hoped he was staying under cover. Barricaded as they were, he felt like they could stand off a small army for a spell. And that was pretty near what they were doing. The enemy fire tapered off. Some kind of palaver going on, Caleb surmised. Gunsmoke and dust hung in the stable, making his eyes smart. His ears reverberated from the repeated discharges in the closed area.

"Corporal?" he called. "Status?"

"Here, sir. Unhurt. What about Private Tyler?"

"Still near the wagons," Caleb told him. "Look sharp." He threw another shot just to give their attackers something to chew on. As yet, he had glimpsed only vague shapes. There was no burning cross this time. That let the Klan out. No doubt these were Morg Hagen's hirelings come calling, probably led by the affable gunslinger, Sanger.

"What you figure they're planning, Sarge?" Hollis called.

"That," Caleb said flatly as the flare of flame he'd been half expecting suddenly shone out in the darkness. Simultaneously all the enemy rifles opened up again, pouring fire on the defenders.

Coolly Caleb ignored the bullets chopping and chewing into the wood. He saw the torch move, and faintly discerned the figure holding it as he drew back his arm for a throw. Caleb's carbine roared. The shadow figure reeled away, the torch dropping to the ground where it flickered eerily. No one moved to pick it up.

Another flaming brand sailed out of the night toward the wagons, but fell woefully short. Likely its thrower had been too worried about catching a bullet to make a good cast.

The light of the two torches cast an uncertain illumination that hindered the movements of the attackers. Caleb triggered at a skulking human form, and thought he had a hit. A few more shots came in return. Gradually they waned. No more shadows crept on the outskirts of the uneven areas illuminated by the torches. Caleb's ears were too deafened by the gunfire to be able to detect the sounds of any retreating hoofbeats.

A stillness settled over the compound. The torches burned slowly down. Impatience gnawed at Caleb to check on Tyler, but still he waited.

"You reckon they're gone, Sarge?" Hollis asked from the far end of the building.

"Yep, I reckon," Caleb told him. "But we'll let those torches go the rest of the way out before we venture into the open. I don't cotton to giving any of those boys a target just yet."

After both torches had flickered out, Caleb emerged from the stable. In a moment Tyler and Watcher appeared from the direction of the wagons.

"You all right, Private?"

Tyler's grin was broad. "Sure am. I just hunkered down in one of them wagons till the enemy sounded retreat. No bullet could reach me there. It'd take a field piece to dent them old prairie schooners."

Hollis joined them, and there was some congratulatory backslapping and handshaking. A stirring fulfillment touched Caleb's spirit. It had been satisfying to lead good men to victory in battle for a just cause, even in a skirmish such as this. Thanks to good security and preparations, they had repulsed a raid that could've all but destroyed Buffalo Freight.

"Peacemaker sure knew what he was talking about when he said they was just waiting to catch us short-handed," Tyler opined.

"He's been right on the money about lots of things lately," Caleb agreed.

After checking with Prudence and making sure everything was all right in the house, they all stood guard the rest of the night. However, there were no further hostilities.

With morning's light, they examined the damage done to the wagons. There were bullet holes, but a lot of the opposing firepower had been directed at the buildings. All the wagons would take some patching, but they were still operational. Caleb grunted with satisfaction as they completed their inspection.

"They'll think twice before they try that again!" Hollis snorted.

"They'll for sure be a lot more careful," Caleb allowed. "But as long as Morg Hagen's alive and has the dinero to hire more gunhawks, they'll keep coming. Speaking of which, how many casualties did we give them?"

"Not sure," Tyler said. "Let's have a look-see."

A search failed to give them any definite answers. They found a couple of dark stains on the ground large enough to indicate quite a bit of bleeding. But the bodies, if any, and the wounded had been removed when their comrades quit the field.

Hollis added up the score. "I'm sure you did for the one with the torch, Sarge. And Tyler's bound to have nailed a couple too, I'd wager, since he was so close to the action."

Movement out on the road caught their attention. "That's Oscar Shuttle," Caleb muttered. "Wonder what he wants."

They went to meet the visitor as he pulled his buckboard to a halt. His spare figure sat trim and erect, peering about intently.

"Good morning," Shuttle greeted. He made no effort to release the reins so he could shake hands.

"What can we do for you, Mr. Shuttle?" Caleb inquired.

"The whole town is talking about the ruckus you had out

here last night." Shuttle looked around again. "I'm glad to see there was no major damage, and, I trust, no casualties?"

"Nary a scratch on any of us. We came through just fine."

"I see." Shuttle's black geldings danced in the traces. He stilled them sharply. "I have come to offer my sympathy and, ah, my assistance, if need be."

"You might assist us if you could tell us who attacked us last night," Caleb responded deliberately.

Shuttle looked at him with keen eyes. "I have no idea who would do something this extreme," he said flatly. "For the most part, we have a nice community here. There's a rowdy element, of course, but you'll find that in every town."

"You won't find the Klan in every town," Tyler ventured.

"We'd be obliged if you'd let us know if you hear anything about the men who shot us up last night *or* the Klan," Caleb spoke up quickly. "And we do appreciate your offer, but I reckon we got things under control."

"Very well. And rest assured I will bring the matter of this shameful attack on your holdings before the town council." He jigged the geldings around and headed them out at a trot.

A scowl settled on Caleb's face as he watched him go. "Kind of strange, him being so concerned about us, ain't it?"

"Why do you say that?" Hollis asked with a puzzled frown.

"Just strikes me as funny, him coming out here thataway, like maybe he was checking on the damage so's he could report back to somebody."

"You don't really think he's in cahoots with Hagen do

you, Sarge?" Hollis asked. "You recollect he helped me
and Peacemaker when those rowdies jumped us."

Caleb nodded a reluctant acceptance of Hollis' conclusions. Maybe, he reflected sourly, along with getting slow
and old, he was getting a mite too suspicious of folks.

"We ain't hardly had a chance to palaver since you and
Thaddeus and Pete got back," Caleb said quietly from behind Stark.

Stark looked around, trying to hide his surprise. He had
come to marvel at how silently the old man could move
when he wanted to. "I was just thinking that myself," he
confirmed. "You got a minute now? We'll bring each other
up to date."

Caleb leaned against the rail of the corral and recounted
the raid of the night before as Stark continued to groom
Red.

Stark listened as best he could while running the stiff
brush briskly over the horse to remove the caked sweat and
trail dust. He was bone tired, and it took an effort to concentrate. He'd taken time to eat in the hour since they'd
pulled into the freight company, but he didn't want to turn
in until he saw to Red.

All the horses had had a tough trip. Stark glanced across
the corral to where Hollis was cleaning up the new horse.
Stark felt satisfied to see the animal already looked better
after a good portion of grain. As he had expected, Hollis
had taken an instant shine to the horse after hearing the
part it had played in Pete's rescue.

Likewise, Tyler was working on Thaddeus' horse, allowing Thaddeus to go ahead and hit the hay. The young lawyer wasn't as used to hard riding as Stark was, and the trip
had taken a toll on him. He and Pete both were exhausted.

"Sounds like you three gave Hagen's crew pause to think," Stark confirmed as Caleb finished the account.

"We held our own," Caleb allowed. "And after the way Pete says you lit into them varmints what took her, Hagen's likely too busy licking his wounds to want any part of Buffalo Freight for a spell."

Stark frowned. "Don't count on it. He's in too deep to back off now. It might take him a few days to regroup, but he'll keep coming at us."

Caleb grew thoughtful. "Then you think we might better take advantage of this time to make another haul?"

Stark nodded. "Yep. I think it's important to keep the wagons running. Tyler and I are slated to make a run come morning, right? That'll give me the rest of the day and evening to get a good rest. We'll move out at first light. Any more rumblings from the Klan while we were gone?"

Caleb shook his head. "I reckon they're just biding their time too. I expect we ain't seen the last of them either."

Hollis turned the new horse loose, and it trotted hungrily over to the hayrack. Poor critter was half-starved. But it wouldn't be long before it was as sleek as Hollis' mules, Stark thought with satisfaction.

"Townfolk coming," Hollis called as he emerged from the tack room after putting away his brushes and curry-comb.

Before leaving the corral to meet the visitors, Stark released Red and gave the stallion a slap on the rump to send him over to the hayrack with the other horses.

Hollis reached to take the brush Stark had been using to groom the horse. "That fellow driving the buggy is the Reverend Jeffrey Keller from the church," he advised. He then went on and identified the others in the vehicle. The pastor was accompanied by the burly town blacksmith, a barber, and a local farmer. "I'll be watching from the stable," Hollis continued, moving off to take up his post.

Stark nodded and went to stand beside Caleb to welcome the newcomers. The pastor was a youngish man with regular features and a sincere direct gaze. A little surprisingly, Stark thought, he wore regular work clothes. and, except for the absence of a gun, could've passed for a small-time rancher. A look at his callused hands told Stark that he might be no stranger to that sort of work.

The churchman's companions made equally good impressions on Stark. Here, he guessed, were some of the salt-of-the-earth folks who had helped make Buffalo Freight a success in these parts.

Prudence appeared from the house to link arms with Stark. After Caleb introduced all of them, the four men accepted Prudence's invitation to light down from the buggy and share in some lemonade.

"I should've come calling sooner," the reverend said once they were settled in the shade. "But my deacons here wanted to accompany me so that you'd know we're all of a mind on this. We're not unaware of what's been happening to you and your business. Not just the pressure that Morg Hagen's been putting on you, but the other persecution you've had to bear as well."

"We don't hold with any of it," the blacksmith spoke up in a rumble. "None of the folks in the church do."

"We're sorry it's happening in our town," the barber added.

"Not everyone in this area is owned by Morg Hagen," the farmer asserted in his turn, "although he likes to think otherwise."

Stark could sense the frustration in them. They were Godfearing decent men, faced with a situation that left their hands tied. Violence wasn't their way. They would be no match for the likes of Hagen and his crew. And the Klan, cloaked in its armor of secrecy, was immune from punishment.

"Besides our prayers, if there's anything we can offer—" Keller began.

"You just keep praying for us, Brother Jeffrey," Caleb cut him off. "It means a lot to us. The Good Book says that the prayers of men like the four of you carry a mighty lot of weight."

"We've knowed all along the townfolk haven't been against us," Tyler informed them. "We wouldn't have stayed otherwise."

"If we could catch them varmints that burned that cross the other evening, we'd ride them out of town on a rail," the blacksmith promised. The farmer and the barber muttered agreement.

Brother Jeffrey looked a bit discomfited, but he didn't contradict his parishioners' statements.

Their support was heartening, Stark reflected. However, although he was the last one to ever dismiss the power of a righteous man's prayer, he wasn't sure just how much help these allies would be when it came to facing up to the guns of Morg Hagen and the evil prejudice of the Klan.

Chapter Thirteen

Morg Hagen sat scowling, beating his fist gently, rhythmically on the surface of his desk. "So how many men do we have left?"

"Well, we lost three in the raid on the freight company and Stark killed six of the men stationed out at the farm," Sanger reported. "That's near half our force.'

"We can recruit others."

"Not around here . . . not fast enough, anyway. Word's sort of gotten around. Mauler and his buddies lit out right after Stark licked him so bad."

"Cravenly cowards," Hagen muttered. "They were just street brawlers anyway. Saloon riffraff. We need professional gunhawks. Men who aren't afraid of a good fight."

"We had us a pretty fair fighting force before all this started," Sanger reminded. He paused. "Guess we shouldn't of taken the girl, huh?" he needled subtly. "That's what got them all riled up and put Stark onto the boys at the farm."

"Kidnapping the girl was a good plan!" Hagen insisted.

"It would have solved everything if those bungling fools hadn't let her escape."

"Those boys didn't bungle much before Stark came on the scene," Sanger prodded. "That Stark must be the devil come calling when he uses that long-range rifle of his."

"He'll be dead come calling before this is over," Hagen vowed viciously. "They all will. I'll see to it that their sorry freight company is burned to the ground. Then I'll build my own on the ashes."

"That ain't going to happen if we let them get forted up there like last time," Sanger assessed coldly. "They ain't so bad with rifles themselves, shooting in the dark, to boot."

Hagen held his fist still. "They won't be forted up," he prophesied menacingly. "Just let me know the next time Stark is away from the freight company."

"He pulled out this morning. Him and one of those darkies are off making a run. The man I got watching just reported in."

"Good, good." Hagen lit a cigar. It gave him something to do with his hands so he wouldn't start the slow methodical pounding again. "Get word to the men at the farm to move in closer to town so they can side us on short notice. And on your way, stop by the marshal's office and tell Tallworth to get over here."

Sanger hesitated, clearly wanting in on the plans. Hagen cocked a hard eye at him.

"I'll see to it," Sanger said reluctantly. He left the office with poor grace.

Hagen puffed on his cigar. The news that Stark, almost single-handed, had cut the outlaw pack to pieces, coming on top of the loss of three men in the abortive night raid, had rasped his nerves to a raw edge. He could feel control of matters slowly slipping out of his hands. He had to act once and for all to finish off Buffalo Freight.

His cigar hadn't burned down much when Cal Tallworth responded to his summons. The lawman slouched into the office. His eyes were wary, but he was respectful enough. Hagen leaned far back in his swivel chair and regarded the man. He knew he needed to be a little careful in how he dealt these cards. "Like I said the other day, Marshal, you've done a pretty fair job as lawman around here," he began. "You were smart enough to figure out how things operate in Beaver and not interfere. So I've mostly been able to let you alone to do your job. Makes things look better that way."

"That's how I always figured it," Tallworth agreed carefully.

"And I respect that. But there's one area I'm not sure you're aware of where some trouble might develop." Hagen waited, but Tallworth didn't rise to the bait. At last Hagen said, "I'm talking about the way you've handled the Klan activity."

Tallworth frowned. The fingers of his gun hand trembled, and Hagen read a sudden danger in the man. "Wasn't nothing about the Klan I needed to handle. They just been hoorawing them coloreds a mite is all. Didn't figure no harm was done there."

"I agree," Hagen said hurriedly. "I didn't mind it, because it just put more pressure on them boys to pull up stakes."

Tallworth snickered. "Figured that's how you'd see it."

"The Klan's outlawed in a lot of places," Hagen went on deliberately. "But I never raised no fuss about it operating around here, even though I could've generated some heat for whoever's taking part in these activities. You might say I've done the Klan a favor. Understand what I'm saying, Marshal?"

Tallworth's eyes narrowed. "I understand."

"Now, I ain't implying you're involved with the Klan, but it seems to me a man in your position would have some method of contacting these people if there was a way they might repay a favor that had been done for them."

"I'm listening." Curiosity was now mingled with the caution in Tallworth's eyes.

"Well, you listen good to what you're about to hear." Hagen put some danger into his own tones. "I need that whole bunch of darkies out of their headquarters for a spell tomorrow night while their hired gun is away on this freight run. Now, if the Klan could accomplish that, all favors would've been repaid, and I'd be mighty beholding."

An unholy fire seemed to light Tallworth's decadent features. "I ain't saying I know anything about the Klan, but I reckon as how something like that might be arranged, providing there wasn't going to be no repercussions afterwards."

"There would be none," Hagen promised flatly. "You have my word on it."

Tallworth chewed it over. "We—that is the Klan—wouldn't want to go tangling with them fellows head on," he cautioned.

"I'm not asking you to fight them. My crew will be on hand to take care of that if it's necessary. I'm just asking for something that will have them all out looking for you, and leave their place unguarded. The Klan's good at striking and disappearing. That's what I want. And I've even got an idea as to what you could do that'd bring them coloreds after you."

Tallworth let out a little panting breath. "Let's hear it."

* * *

Sitting high atop the wagon seat, with the darkness of night cloaking him, Stark felt close enough to the starglow overhead that he wanted to reach up and run his fingers through it. Tyler dozed beside him, his body relaxed. The creak of the huge wagon and the jingle of the traces seemed muted by the night.

Stark could smell the fresh scents of the prairie on the breeze, and the more pungent ones of the mules. Threaded between his fingers, the lines of the six two-animal teams were almost slack. The mules knew they were headed home, so they weren't interested in acting up.

Tyler stirred, muttered something incoherent, and awakened. He stretched, then gazed at the stars. He peered about him for landmarks. "How far out are we?"

"Not far from home," Stark told him. "We'll be pulling in soon."

"You want me to take the reins?"

"Naw, I'm fine."

"Glad we done it this way," the older man commented. "It'll put us home near a day early."

Stark nodded without answering. Even easy conversation seemed a shame in the peace of the night. The run itself had been a peaceful one. There had been no problems with equipment or animals, and no sign of the outlaws or any other of Hagen's men. They'd made such good time, he and Tyler had decided not to stop at dark, but to push ahead on the last leg of the trip. They'd be home in half an hour now. Stark wondered how things had fared at the freight company in their absence.

Suddenly another sound reached him over the peaceful noises of the night. He sat up straighter. It sounded like a low moan. The next moment his eyes discerned the shape of a wagon pulled off the side of the road in the brush. Stark jerked back sharply on the reins, even as Tyler's startled exclamation rang in his ears.

Securing the lines, he clambered down from the wagon's height. Tyler was on his heels. They found Hollis lying in the dirt beside the wagon. The large lump on the back of his head was visible even in the dim light.

Tyler caught his friend's arm and helped him to his feet. "What in the world are you doing out here, man? What's going on?"

"They took Thaddeus," Hollis rasped groggily. "They just dragged him off!"

"Who took him?" Stark asked urgently.

"The Klan! They just appeared out of nowhere and surrounded the wagon."

Stark felt the night turn cold. "Tell us what happened."

Hollis made a visible effort to steady himself. "A load of feed came in on the afternoon train for one of the ranches right outside of town. The owner wanted it delivered today. He offered a bonus. Seemed like easy money. I handled the team, and Thaddeus rode shotgun. We should've been home by dark, but it took the ranch hands longer than we expected to stow the feed away."

"That figures," Stark gritted. "Go on."

"Well, we was driving home all peaceable and such, and suddenly the Klan was all around us. They grabbed the team and led the wagon off the road. Then they pulled Thaddeus down off the seat, and one of them rode up beside me and hit me alongside the head with a rifle butt— not hard enough to knock me out, but hard enough to addle me good."

"Do you remember anything they said?" Stark asked urgently.

"I don't know. . . ." Hollis rubbed his head gingerly. "I think one of them said something about gallows fruit."

For a freezing moment Stark seemed to hear the voice of Oscar Shuttle saying, "There's no appeal from the court of Judge Lynch."

"This is important," he said tautly. "Can you tell us how many of them there were?"

"I think about a dozen."

"All right. You up to taking this wagon on home, Hollis?"

"You bet. As thick as my skull is, weren't no permanent damage done."

"Good." Stark gave him an encouraging slap on the back. "Go on to Buffalo Freight. Tell the others what happened. Tell them to come after us. We might need them."

"Where are we going?" Tyler asked urgently.

"To the old hanging tree." Stark knew it was a bet born of desperation, but there was nothing else to put their money on.

As Hollis raced away into the night, Stark and Tyler hit the seat of their wagon at the same instant.

Stark loosed the reins. "You know where this hanging tree is?"

Tyler nodded. "I know." He pointed. "That way."

"Yaw, mules!" Stark popped the lines against the beasts' hindquarters to get them moving.

Startled, they lunged into their traces. Stark hauled hard on the lines to turn them in the direction Tyler had indicated. After two days behind the reins, he had the feel of the huge wagon, but he'd never driven it at any speed before. The earth seemed to shake as the mules hauled the wagon off the road.

Beside Stark, Tyler sent the bullwhip singing out. "You think we'll be in time?" he shouted.

"Don't know," Stark shouted back.

"We just got to be!" Tyler insisted. "Before we left, Pete told me her and Thaddeus been talking about getting hitched. I couldn't face her if anything happens to him. That'd turn her bitter for the rest of her life."

Stark nodded and urged the mules on with increased urgency. He had his hands full working the lines. The team hit a rough gallop, the tons-heavy wagon jolted and bounced and careened across the prairie in their wake. Stark's seat cleared the bench and thumped painfully back down. Tyler clung with one hand and plied the whip with the other.

Each mule had a separate rein. Those for the beasts on the left were threaded one-by-one between the fingers of Stark's left hand. His right hand gripped the reins of the other animals in the same fashion. It was all pull and jerk and slack off on the lines to keep the mules in some semblance of control while guiding them over the rough terrain and around the steeper ridges and slopes.

More than once Stark felt as though an arm had been yanked out of its socket by a turn of the animals or the impact of the ironshod wheels bouncing into an unseen pothole. His shoulders ached. The lines were damp and slippery with the sweat of his palms. Desperately he hung on and worked the reins by reflex and skill, hoping the wagon would hold together.

"There!" Tyler shouted hoarsely when a couple of miles of prairie grass had passed beneath the spinning wheels.

Stark tore his eyes away from the team and the dimly seen terrain flashing past under their wheels. Tyler's pointing finger drew his gaze to an eerie wavering glow coming from behind the steep hill off to his right. He recognized the glare of firelight, and sawed the mules hard in that direction.

The steepness of the slope slowed them some, but he still had to haul back on the lines and kick the brake on to keep them from going over the crest and down the other side in a pell-mell rush.

For a span of heartbeats he and Tyler took in the barbaric scene spread out in the valley a couple of hundred yards below.

By the light of an enormous flaming cross, a circle of grotesque hooded forms surrounded a slim figure beneath the reaching branches of a towering old oak.

"Oh, my Lord!" Tyler gasped. "They're fixing to hang him!"

Thaddeus' hands looked to be bound behind him, and a pair of hooded figures held him immobile. There was a buggy along with some buckboards and saddle horses, but none of them were being used for the bloodthirsty enterprise at hand. A rope had been tossed over a thick branch of the tree, and a noose put around Thaddeus' neck. The other end of the rope was in the hands of a half-dozen robed Klansmen. At some given signal, they would simply haul Thaddeus kicking off the ground to slowly strangle the life out of him. Even for a lynching, Stark thought, it was a deuced ugly way to kill a man.

"Get in back with your rifle!" he ordered Tyler. "Give me some cover fire when we go in. Leave the whip on the seat."

Tyler didn't argue. He clambered into the open bed of the wagon. Its thick sides were almost as good as armor. The levering of Tyler's repeater sounded in Stark's ear.

Seconds were valuable. Stark shifted his right-hand reins

to his left, gripping all of the lines in that fist. It was a foolhardy way to handle any wagon, much less one as big as this freighter, but Stark wanted his right hand free.

He let off the brake, staring intently down the darkened slope ahead of them. An unseen draw or gully could capsize them. Rising to his feet, Stark caught the butt of the bullwhip in his right hand, then sent its length whistling around his head before it straightened to lick at the mules with a pop of sound that merged with his challenging yell.

The mules went plunging down the slope, and the big wagon followed like an avalanche. Feet braced, arm taut with the reins, Stark plied the whip and yelled his throat raw, as the wind of their passage rushed into his face. He felt the sidewards shift of the wagon beneath his feet, and understood that it was perilously close to overrunning the mules. If that happened, it would roll over and take the mules and its passengers tumbling to the bottom of the slope in a splintering wreckage of wood and bone and flesh.

He couldn't reach the brake. He could only redouble the fury of his whip for greater speed, and offer up a desperate wordless prayer. The mules lengthened their stride at the kiss of the whip and the growing thunder of the monster behind them. Miraculously, the wagon steadied.

The ugly scene below appeared to rush at them in a jumbled series of images. The Klansmen were just starting to react. The report of Tyler's rifle cracked above the song of the whip and the rumble of iron-shod wheels. Stark had no idea how the muleskinner managed to handle the rifle in the rocking bed of the wagon, but another shot followed close on the first, then another. Tyler yelled, but his words were torn away by the wind.

Then they hit level ground, Tyler still firing, and from among the figures ahead rifles spoke in answer. But the panicked mules were bearing down upon the Klansmen with hardly a slackening of speed, the wagon coming out of the night like a behemoth. Stark saw their ranks start to break.

As the flaming totem of the cross loomed ahead, Stark dropped the whip and caught the reins in both hands. He hauled back hard, leaning his body into it, just as the churning wheels clipped one of the buckboards, smashing it to kindling.

The wagon rocked wildly, sideswiped a buckboard and spun it aside like a child's toy, it's horses bolting free. The impact lessened the wagon's momentum. Hooded figures scattered from in front of it, but a horrifying cry clawed up from beneath the massive wheels.

Feeling the heat of the cross, the mules swerved. Somehow Stark was aware of Tyler vaulting from the wagon as it slowed. He lifted his boot and stomped down hard on the brake lever. As its drag worked against the mules, he bailed out himself in a rolling dive that jolted the teeth in his head and brought him staggering erect, Colt in hand.

Chapter Fourteen

Madness reigned under the hellish flame of the cross. Hooded figures were fleeing. Others were down in the rubble of the smashed buckboards. Yells of fear and excitement mingled with the roar of gunfire. Merciless, Stark snapped a shot at a grotesque shape that bolted in front of him. The Klansman lurched but didn't go down. He staggered on and was lost in the confusion.

Stark swiveled to seek new targets. He saw Tyler in a crouch, repeater at waist level, squared off against a trio of rifle-toting Klansmen. Even as Stark's gaze took in the scene, muzzle flames stabbed back and forth between the combatants.

It was over in a flashing handful of seconds. Tyler shot from the hip, and one Klansman spun away. While his victim fell, Tyler dropped to one knee, rifle to his shoulder, as his opponents' bullets chewed the air over his head. Again his rifle cracked; a second Klansman buckled on collapsing legs. Tyler flung himself flat, firing from prone on his belly. Almost as one, two shots blasted from the barrel of his repeater before it ran dry. He dropped it, rolled sideways, and came back up on one knee, revolver already in his hand. He didn't need it. The third Klansman was falling atop his comrades.

Stark caught a vivid image of Thaddeus, off to one side, hands still bound behind him, trying to stay out of the line of fire. Then Stark swung his Colt tracking across the area illumined by the burning cross, firing furiously until the gun ran dry.

The rest of the Klan members had quit the field on foot or on horseback. Only their conveyances and the sprawled shapes of several of their kind lay in evidence of their presence.

Stark rushed to Thaddeus' side, pulling the Bowie knife to cut the ropes binding the man's hands behind his back. "You all right?"

"Yeah, I'm fine." Thaddeus laughed shakily as he stripped the noose off his neck. "You couldn't have cut it much closer, though. What's the matter? Couldn't you get that wagon going any faster?"

"Very funny," Stark said dryly. He looked about for the wagon. He spotted its massive bulk a little distance away. Slowed by the brake, the mules hadn't run far.

Their attention was snagged then by four mounted silhouettes appearing atop the hill. Stark tensed, then relaxed as Caleb and Hollis pounded to a halt before them, with Prudence and Pete following a few strides behind.

"Guess we're a little late," Caleb greeted.

"We got here in time," Tyler told him, "thanks to the Peacemaker driving that wagon like I never thought nobody could drive it."

Caleb nodded. "Mighty obliged. We better secure the area."

The flames of the cross were dying as the men hurriedly walked among the abandoned buggies and wagons checking for wounded and collecting the rifles of the fallen Klansmen. Stark felt a chill as he stopped beside one splintered buckboard and hefted the half-empty can of coal oil sitting in the bed.

Caleb paused beside him looking equally grim as his eyes took in the conveyance. "They likely used that to light up the cross."

"Yeah." Stark set the can down again. "Wish we had time to chase down the rest of those hooded yahoos."

Thaddeus walked up behind them then rubbing his wrists. "You and Tyler reduced their number significantly tonight, Peacemaker. There can't be that many of them left."

"There's at least one," Caleb muttered.

Stark nodded. An ugly notion was prodding him. "We need to get back to the freight company." He strode over to Pete. "Can you bring the wagon?"

The girl looked puzzled, but nodded.

"Stay with her," Stark told Prudence.

"But, Jim, why—"

"Could be this was all just a diversion to draw us away from headquarters and leave Buffalo Freight unguarded," Caleb explained. "Peacemaker's right. We best be getting back, if we ain't already too late."

Prudence smiled reassuringly at Stark. "Don't worry. We'll be fine."

He nodded. Hollis and Tyler had rounded up three riderless horses. Stark swung aboard one and urged his mount over beside the wagon as Pete tied her horse on behind and climbed up on the seat.

"The team is pretty winded," he told the girl. "Get home as soon as you can, but don't push them too hard."

"Sure thing, Mr. Stark," she responded, threading the lines through her fingers in expert fashion, which reassured Stark somewhat. Despite Prudence's words, he still felt nervous about leaving the women on their own. But as Thaddeus had pointed out, judging from the number of bodies scattered about on the ground, the Klan was in no shape to be much of a threat to anyone.

Stark was relieved to see Prudence was wearing the sidearm he'd trained her to use. On impulse he pulled the hideout .38 he carried at the small of his back and handed it to Pete. "You know how to use that?" he asked.

She nodded, sticking it in her belt.

Caleb leaned far down off his horse to secure a pole from the wreckage of one of the buckboards. He patted the breast of his shirt. "I brought along the old standard for luck. Looks like we might need it!"

Stark had already retrieved his shotgun from the wagon. On impulse, he now retrieved the sheathed hatchet from under the seat and secured it to his belt along with the Bowie knife. Sanger had jeered him for the way he held it, but the hand ax, Stark had learned through hard experience, wasn't so different in weight and heft from an Indian tomahawk.

A look of firm resolve settled on Caleb's face. His arm swept down to point, and he led out at a gallop. "Forward ho!"

Stark's horse had the feel of a good one. Riding through the darkness, his companions sitting alert and erect in their saddles with the unmistakable carriage that bespoke the cavalry, Stark felt a curious sense of near reverence pass over him. The ex-soldiers rode with a confidence and pride that made them loom large and formidable in the gloom. So must these men and others of their ilk have ridden to face overwhelming odds in years past.

Like beings out of myth, the Buffalo Soldiers rode again.

They drew nearer the freight headquarters, and Stark saw Caleb reach inside his shirt and produce a square of fabric that unfolded to flap in the wind of their passage. With sure hands he threaded it onto the pole he'd secured from the wreckage. Then he lifted it high. For a moment the starglow caught and fixed in Stark's mind the image of the buffalo there. Once more, the standard of the 10th Cavalry flew proud.

From out on the plains they saw the wavering glow of flames. Caleb's uplifted arm brought them to a halt. "That's one of the sheds burning," he opined. "They ain't got the stable yet."

"I think you're right, Sarge," Hollis agreed.

Dimly seen figures, some afoot and some mounted, moved back and forth in the light of the fire. A dog's frantic barking could be heard. Watcher must be doing his dead-level best to defend the homestead, Stark thought.

"How many you make it, Corporal?" Caleb snapped with a crispness that was unfamiliar but strangely natural to him.

"Ten to fifteen, Sarge," Hollis answered.

"One last charge, Sergeant?" Tyler asked with a voice gone suddenly tight.

"Yes, Private," Caleb answered. "We don't have time for anything else." He raised his voice. "Form up!"

The ex-soldiers fell into line side by side a dozen feet apart. Stark found himself at one end, next to Thaddeus. The young lawyer sat proud and straight in the saddle with a look of stern determination on his face. He carried one of the rifles Stark had collected.

Stark pulled his own shotgun and levered it one-handed with a snapping flick of his arm. The blood seemed to race hot and heady in his veins.

"On my command, gentlemen," Caleb said from the center of the line. He raised his arm. For a moment he held there, poised. Stark fancied he saw him glance once at the standard waving in the night breeze. Then he set his eyes on the glow ahead.

His arm dropped. *"Charge!"*

Stark was almost caught napping, so fast did the ex-soldiers respond. Then he laid heels to his mount, and within seconds was sweeping across the prairie in their ranks. Somehow, he thought he heard the sound of a distant ghostly bugle in his ears.

Neck and neck, the horses stretched out, and the dark shapes of the buildings, backlit by flames, grew larger before them.

"Rifles!" Caleb's voice sounded above the hoofbeats.

Nearly as one, Stark saw the soldiers lift rifles to their shoulders as they rode, still controlling the reins. Stark did the same, and glimpsed Thaddeus following suit. Ahead of him, he could see frantic movement beginning among a few of the raiders as some awareness of the attack reached them.

"Fire!"

The volley of rifle blasts split the night.

"Fire at will!"

Stark got off another shot as the line of horsemen swept in upon the compound. He kept shooting as they tore past the buildings. Some gunfire came back at them from the raiders, but it was hurried and mostly unaimed. Stark saw one of the enemy knocked from his horse. He didn't know whose bullet had scored.

He snapped shots of his own at the running, dodging shapes. A snarling bearded face seemed to appear almost beneath his horse's hooves. Pistol fire blazed up from the desperado's fist. Stark thrust down hard with the butt of the shotgun, felt it smash bone as his horse carried him past, its hooves striking flesh. Then he was through the compound, hauling his horse hard around.

"Regroup! Charge!"

Once more the mounted line raced through the compound with a drumming of hoofbeats and gunfire.

"Dismount! Skirmish line! Fight on foot!"

Stark saw the others of Caleb's command swinging from their saddles. Gun flames stabbed at them from among the buildings, but there was no organized plan to the resistance.

On foot, gripping his Colt Peacemaker, Stark advanced in a crouch, snapping shots as he went, seeing men fall. He drew gunfire from the corner of the burning shed. Pivoting, he returned it, and the gunman lurched forward and fell on his face.

Stark darted to the cover of the shed. Kneeling, he began reloading. Gunfire crashed about him. He could feel the heat of the burning outbuilding on his face. Dust and smoke hung in the air. He'd lost track of Caleb and the others in the confusion.

Suddenly a figure lunged toward him. He drew the Bowie with one smooth sweep of his arm and hurled it. It caught the hard case in the chest. The man staggered backward and collapsed.

He finished reloading and took a second to pull the hatchet from its sheath and stick it through his belt. As he moved forward to retrieve the Bowie, a horseman burst out of the night like a maddened centaur, spouting flame from one fist. Bullets whipped past Stark. He had a vivid memory of the fate of the man he'd ridden down. He didn't want to share it.

A lean fierce face leered at him from the charging horse. Desperate, Stark hurled himself sideways, landing hard on shoulder and hip, triggering up at the outlaw's mounted form thundering past. The outlaw leaned back with a tremendous yank at the reins to haul his horse up short.

The animal reared, hooves flailing as its rider fought for control, silhouetted against the burning shed. Still lying on his side, Stark thrust his arm straight and fired thrice in a single burst. The outlaw fell sidewards from the saddle and landed an instant before his horse's front hooves thudded back to the ground beside him.

Head buzzing, breath rasping in his lungs, Stark scrambled up on one knee. In some automatic part of his mind that calculated such things he knew his Colt was empty. Still shaky, he rose to his feet, reaching for shells in his cartridge belt.

"Hey, Peacemaker! Try me!"

Stark whirled. The grinning figure of Sanger confronted him, and the gunslinger's hands were already filled with his weapons. Dead drop. Sanger wasn't even going through the motions of a fair fight. Sanger's teeth gleamed behind his leveled gun barrels.

Stark tensed for a last futile play. Then a dark snarling streak burst out of the night and dove at Sanger's leg. The gunslick howled as Watcher buried his fangs in his calf. Cursing, Sanger kicked the dog aside.

Stark dropped his empty six-gun and ripped the hatchet from his belt, his movements smooth and sure, all weakness gone now under the prod of danger.

Sanger tried to line the guns again, and Stark threw the hatchet cartwheeling through the night. Firelight glinted off its spinning blade. Sanger reeled back with the hatchet embedded in his chest. Stark snatched up his Colt and dashed forward, thumbing a live round into the cylinder. He skidded to a halt with the revolver thrust down at Sanger's face.

But the gunslinger was almost finished. "Blasted dog," he managed, then grimaced wryly. "And a stinking hand ax."

"Handy tool to have around," Stark said.

Sanger managed one last eerie grin even as he died.

Caleb's dismount after his command to fight on foot was almost as smooth as it would've been 25 years ago. He noted that fact even in the heat of battle. Rifle at hip level, barrel moving in wide sweeps, he went into the fray, levering and firing his Army carbine at the enemy.

The two charges through the compound had thrown the enemy's ranks into disarray, but the raiders were hard cases and gunhands to a man. Disorganized or not, they were still willing to fight.

A hatless figure appeared in front of Caleb, pistol leveled for aimed fire. Caleb dropped to one knee, rifle lifting as if of its own volition. Just like on the firing range, he thought, and drilled the fellow dead center.

"Sarge! Watch out!" the deep voice of Hollis Kelso bellowed.

Caleb had a bare glimpse of a man lunging at him from the side, knife in hand. Caleb tried to swing his rifle, but knew it was too late. He was too stiff, too slow, too old . . . .

Hollis Kelso plowed into the knifeman like a charging buffalo, driving the man aside in a stagger, the knife spinning out of his fist. The butt of Hollis' rifle pounded the fellow down sprawling on the ground. Hollis' teeth were bared, his eyes wild. He swept the rifle up for a final killing drive at his senseless foe.

Then, poised there, he faltered, powerful arms trembling. Some of the madness faded from his face. He lowered the rifle and turned toward Caleb.

His grin was one of triumph. "Like you said, Sarge. Just got to reach for the faith!" He sobered. "You okay?"

Caleb rose. "Fine, Corporal. Carry on."

Hollis disappeared into the dust and smoke. Off toward the stable Caleb saw a small figure running from a fire just kindled at the corner of the building. He frowned in recognition. Morg Hagen himself must've led the raid on Buffalo Freight. And now the town boss was deserting his troops. Caleb lifted the rifle and drew a bead. His finger tightened on the trigger.

No, he thought with sudden determination. He wanted— needed—to face his enemy. Dropping his rifle, he ran at an angle to intercept Hagen's path.

He was old and tired, and his joints popped and creaked, but Hagen was no spring chicken himself. Panting, Caleb closed on him.

"Hagen!" he shouted in his command voice.

The town boss slid to a halt and wheeled. "You!" he gasped. He was no longer the arrogant, cocky little man who had ridden up to Buffalo Freight on a fine appaloosa. He was desperate and disheveled and cornered at last. "You and your filthy partners are ruining me!"

Caleb caught his breath. "A bunch of muleskinners, you called us." He gestured about him. "See what some muleskinners can do?"

"At least you won't live to brag about it!" Morg Hagen's hand swept for his double-action revolver in its cutaway holster.

Caleb pulled the big Colt Dragoon with a hand that gripped it sure and true and without a trace of stiffness. Faster, Hagen's gun burst clear of leather, firing as it came up. The first shot kicked up dirt at Caleb's feet. The second went singing past his side, and a third might've gotten him. But the Dragoon spat fire in Caleb's hand, and Hagen's second shot was his last. He buckled and fell.

Caleb lowered the smoking Colt. Around him the sounds of battle were dying. He advanced on heavy feet to stand over his victim. Hagen snarled up at him.

"You still got time to repent before you meet your Maker," Caleb told him sadly.

Then he saw that he was wrong. Hagen was dead.

"I don't think he would've done it anyway," said the voice of James Stark.

Caleb looked around at him. The younger man was unharmed, he saw with relief. "Reckon not," he agreed.

"We licked them," Stark reported. "Your command's all present and accounted for.

Caleb gazed once more at Hagen. "Let's get the fires out. Then I guess it'll be over."

Stark shook his head. "Nope. Come morning we got us one last piece of business that needs tending to."

It took Caleb a moment to catch his drift. Then he nodded bleakly in agreement.

Chapter Fifteen

The town of Beaver was astir with the happenings of the night before when Stark and Caleb rode up to Oscar Shuttle's warehouse. Rays of the early morning sunlight slanted down Main Street, backlighting the train that had just pulled into the station. Murmurs of excited conversation arose from the small groups of people scattered about the railroad platform as the pair dismounted.

"I reckon word has spread," Caleb commented, glancing about.

"Looks like it," Stark agreed.

A crowd of townspeople had converged on Buffalo Freight the night before to help extinguish the fires after the battle. Identification of some of the outlaws among the dead had caused quite a stir, as had the death of Morg Hagen. Some of the hirelings of the town boss had been rounded up. They had corroborated much of what the muleskinners reported.

"Let's get this done," Stark said looping Red's reins loosely over the hitching rail.

"Yeah," Caleb grunted. His face was set in stern lines, his movements were stiff.

Watching him, Stark thought the ex-sergeant looked old and tired and grim. Stark felt that way himself. As they mounted the steps, the door to the warehouse office opened, and Oscar Shuttle's spare figure was framed there.

"Something I can help you gentlemen with?"

Stark studied the man closely, but shuttle's features were bland and unassuming.

"Planning to stay here big as life and bluff it out, are you?" Stark asked easily.

Shuttle's eyes narrowed, but his expression showed only polite puzzlement. "I'm not sure I understand."

"Yeah, you do," Stark said in harder tones. "You didn't catch a bullet last night, so you just decided to get rid of your hood and robe, come back to town, and pretend nothing happened. But it ain't that easy."

Shuttle drew himself up stiffly. "I'll have to ask you to explain yourself."

"You're head of the Klan hereabouts," Stark accused flatly. "Or at least one of the ringleaders. You led them last night when they kidnapped Thaddeus. Hollis told us he heard someone mention 'gallows fruit'—the term you used when you were singing the praises of the old vigilantes. I'm betting you said it again last night. That's how I knew where to go looking. I remembered what you said about the hanging tree, and it was easy to figure what you were planning to do. I also reckon you were somehow in cahoots with Hagen."

Shuttle's eyes narrowed even further into a glare of wordless hatred. "That's nonsense! Fool's talk!" he spat. "I've gone out of my way to be friendly to those—those *darkies.* I helped you and that other colored against Hagen's men."

Stark nodded. "And you did that just so you could stand here and deny any involvement with the Klan if the truth started to come out. And I expect you didn't want trouble of any sort involving Caleb and his pards to take place in broad daylight next door to your place of business. Might make you look bad. The Klan has always liked operating in secret anyway."

"You don't have any evidence to back this up!"

"No? It was easy to spot your pair of black geldings in the traces of one of those busted up wagons out there under the hanging tree. There was even a half-empty jug of coal oil in it. You probably used that to light the cross."

"I don't have to listen to this! My team was stolen. You can't prove—"

"Maybe he can't prove it," a voice cut in, "but I can."

Stark turned to see the approach of Reverend Jeffrey Keller, backed by two of his deacons, the blacksmith and the postmaster. They had been close enough to overhear the conversation. And behind them, other townsfolk were converging on the scene.

"You stay out of this, Pastor," Shuttle growled. "Don't you forget I'm a regular contributor to your church!"

"Buying your way into heaven won't work, Oscar," the pastor said sadly. "If you'd attend and listen to the Word, you'd know that."

"I don't need your sermons! And what do you mean, you can prove what this filthy gunslinger and his darky are saying."

"Last night a friend of yours, Marshall Tallworth, showed up in town badly wounded," Keller explained regretfully. "Seems he caught a bullet at the lynching tree.

He was wanting help, but the doc said it was too late. He'd lost too much blood."

"The work of some outlaw," Shuttle sputtered, moving forward to the edge of the dock.

Keller shook his head ruefully. "You're the real outlaw in this piece, Oscar. Marshal Tallworth went to get his just reward, but he didn't do it with his sins unconfessed. Before he died, he told us what happened out there, as well as some other things that have gone on. He named names. Yours was one of them. You're from down South. You brought some ugly baggage up here with you. It was you who organized the Klan when Caleb and his partners opened Buffalo Freight. You did your best to run them out of town. Tallworth told us all about it. I'm no lawyer, but I think that's what's called a deathbed confession."

"I *am* a lawyer, and you're absolutely right, Reverend," a new voice spoke up. "A deathbed confession will stand up in any court in the land."

The crowd parted then, and Stark saw George Perkins and Evett Nix making their way to the front.

With an oath, Shuttle turned to lunge for the door of his office. He drew up short at the figure of Caleb Jackson blocking his path. He spat an ugly racial epithet, and turned at bay like a rabid animal.

"We'll take over, gentlemen," Keller said. A grim murmur of agreement arose from the ranks. "We'll lock him up until we get a new marshal—a good one this time—and then we'll hold us a trial."

Stark took hold of Shuttle's arm and wrestled him to the edge of the platform. "We appreciate that, Reverend." He nodded toward Nix. "This here is Evett Nix, U.S. Marshall. I reckon he can lend you a hand in getting all that done."

"Be glad to." Nix reached up to take charge of Shuttle.

"Just lead the way to your jail, folks, and we'll have us a little talk. I know lots of good men who'd be right for the job of town marshal."

Shuttle began to curse. Spittle flying, he spewed forth a vile stream of racial slurs and foulness as they hustled him away.

Keller was the last to go. "You cleaned up the town," he addressed Stark and Caleb. "We won't let it get this way again."

As he walked away, Stark jumped down off the dock and shook hands with George Perkins. "What brings you to this neck of the woods?" he asked.

Perkins laughed. "Your wife's telegrams, of course. Evett and I figured you must be running some sort of bluff, and we thought it would be worth taking a couple of days vacation to help you pull it off. I see we arrived too late to be in on the fun."

A grin pulled at the corners of Stark's mouth. "Yeah, it was great fun," he said wryly. "Here, let me introduce you to Caleb Jackson, then we'll collect Evett and get back to the freight company. I'll fill you in on all the details on the way."

"We've identified the Klansmen who were killed," Reverend Keller said as he sat beside Tyler across the picnic table from Stark, Caleb, and George Perkins. "They were mostly local riffraff. One was a farmer, name of Grissard."

Stark grimaced. "He's got a wife and kids, if he's the same one we delivered rifle shells to. You might check on them."

"Already taken care of," Keller assured him. "His widow's planning to sell the farm and go back down South to live with her family."

Stark wasn't surprised that the pastor had already seen to such matters. He was proving to be a fine man. A lot had been taken care of in the two days since the raid on Buffalo Freight. Marshal Nix had felt the call of duty and headed back to Guthrie on yesterday's train, but Perkins had lingered to take part in the cleanup activities. Stark could tell the man was enjoying this glimpse of life at its best. The dark and gruesome battle with the Klan and Hagen's gunmen seemed a distant memory now.

Stark looked about at the collection of picnic tables piled high with grub which had been prepared by the local womenfolk.

The potluck dinner was the women's contribution to the workday declared by the citizens to repair the damage done by the raiders. After a morning of rebuilding the burned shed and making other repairs, the crowd of men had retired to the tables for lunch.

"I suppose you folks will be heading out shortly, Mr. Stark," Keller speculated aloud.

"I reckon so," Stark conceded. "Buffalo Freight should have smooth sailing from here on out."

"I've done give up trying to make him a partner," Caleb spoke up. "I keep telling him us old codgers could use some new blood in our Buffalo Brigade."

"Old!" Stark echoed with a wry snort. "That coming from the man who outdrew Morg Hagen."

Caleb shook his head. "Didn't outdraw him," he corrected gently. "Just outshot him." He lifted his right hand and clenched and unclenched it, smiling at some personal satisfaction.

Hollis Kelso ambled up to the table, a half-eaten piece of fried chicken in his thick fingers. Watcher trotted hopefully at his side. "I'll be looking forward to listening to some of your preaching, padre," the big ex-soldier stated. "I need to be hearing more of that sort of thing."

He glanced at Caleb, and Stark could've sworn he winked before biting into the chicken with great relish. Caleb looked even more satisfied.

Stark felt a mite satisfied himself. The affair had taken on a holiday atmosphere. The weather was pleasant. Children ran and played. The tables were crowded, and the women, Prudence and Pete among them, bustled about keeping food coming to the hungry men.

Pete looked like a different person today—truly feminine in a new gingham dress with her braid coiled becomingly atop her head. He watched now as Thaddeus walked up to her, caught her hand, and pulled her off to the side for a private exchange. Prudence was right. They did make a fine looking couple.

Stark felt a sudden surge of pride in Prudence. She had remained steadfast throughout this ordeal in her dedication to helping Pete achieve an acceptance of her womanhood.

Until now, he realized, he had never fully appreciated his wife's skill at blending her own professional life with her personal one. For in all the years he'd known her—and loved her—there had never been any doubt that she was all woman, and proud of it. He now knew what a difficult path that had been to navigate successfully. And she had been one of the trailblazers. All the professional women who came after her, Pete included, would have it a little easier because of her success.

Yep. He was a truly lucky man.

As if she felt his eyes on her, Prudence separated herself from the other women and came over. He made room for her to slide in on the bench beside him.

She plunged into the male conversation with the same

ease she had exhibited when talking to the ladies. "Well, George, do you still think we're headed for racial tension here in the Territories?" she asked teasingly.

The African Lion grinned as he glanced around the gathering. "I must admit, times like these give a man pause to reconsider, all right." Then he sobered. "But, yes, I'm afraid I do. However, I don't think it will ever reach the proportions that exist in the South. Territory folks are an independent lot. They tend to look more on a man's character and inner traits than on his outward appearance. I guess, in the end, it all remains to be seen."

She looked over at Keller. "What about you, Reverend?"

He too looked troubled. "Well, before all this ugly business with the Klan, I would've thought the matter settled by the War Between the States. Now I fear the battle's not yet over."

"But we won this skirmish," Stark spoke up, "and that's how we'll eventually win the war—one battle at a time, with good people of all colors fighting side by side."

"That's the way the Good Book tells us to live," Caleb opined, "one day at a time, taking care of the troubles and enjoying the blessings of that particular day. Now, as to this day, it's looking to be a mighty fine one—all a man could ask for."

Stark reached for Prudence's hand under the table. He had to agree with Caleb's assessment wholeheartedly.

Yep, a mighty fine day, indeed.

Shen 05

THE PILLAR OF FIRE

Karl Stern

THE PILLAR
OF FIRE

New York

HARCOURT, BRACE AND COMPANY

Contents

Foreword

A FEW years ago, at a psychiatric convention, I ran into a girl with whom I studied medicine and with whom I interned in the Neurological Department of one of the municipal hospitals in Berlin. We met in a big hotel in Chicago. It was a most fortunate meeting and we were both overjoyed. We had not met for fourteen years, and had heard little of each other. She had the same halting, absent-minded way of speaking, as if she were always thinking of two things at a time. She looked older and there were lines in her face which had not been there before. There was so much we had to tell each other. While she spoke of her didactic psychoanalysis in Zurich, her marriage, her child, her practice, about mutual friends who had perished in Europe, I was asking myself: "Shall I tell, or shall I not tell?"

If I were to say to her, "Since we last met, I have become a Catholic," it would be a statement entirely different from any other I could make. We both had many startling and unexpected things to tell; it could not be otherwise with two Jews who had parted in Germany in 1932 and met again in America in 1946. But the fact is that with that simple sentence, "I have become a Catholic," there arises a cloud of estrangement. No matter how much one attempts to break this estrangement down to the elements of social or political separation, of prejudices from childhood, and so on, there is something additional which cannot be explained so easily. What is it?

While the conversation was as far removed as possible from speculations of this kind, I told her of this decisive event in my life. She paused for a moment and then said simply and shortly: "Oh!" Her polite exclamation contained a cosmic abyss. It is about this "Oh!" that this book is being written.

When I meet a friend with whom I used to work in the Zionist Youth Movement or in a group of radical students, I realize the extraordinary fact that, when we come to the bottom of things, I have not really departed from their ideals. There is a core to their beliefs which I still share with them. It is contained in my belief. What must appear to them as a betrayal, is to me a fulfillment. I still understand everything they are talking about, but they cannot possibly understand me. This is what makes these scenes, as human encounters and as a meeting of friends, so agonizing. We talk about the Histatrut (the Labor Unions in Palestine), about the Poale Zion (Left Wing Zionism), the Kibbuz (the movement of cultivation of the land in Palestine, without private property), about my brother who lives as a teacher in one of those co-operative settlements, or of old friends who were killed as Trotskyites, as Social Democrats, or simply as Jews—and then it comes.

"What has happened to you?"

"I have become a Christian."

Some of my friends even pale and their pupils dilate. A common world falls asunder.

There are sometimes surprises, however. I remember the following unexpected exchange:

"What has become of Paul?"

"He was living in Brazil when I last heard of him."

"What has become of Rose?"

"She went to Russia, and I heard that she was killed in the Purge of '36."

"What has become of Yosha?"

"Yosha? Now this is something you would never guess. When we last heard of him, he was in England and had entered a monastery!" Laughter. ("Shall I say it now?")

To write the story of a conversion is a foolish undertaking, for the convert, the "turned-around," is a fool. He is a fool in the sense in which Saint Paul uses this word. All stories of conversion appear to have something subjective-arbitrary, some tragic secret. The communication contains something incommunicable. Even the story of Saint Augustine, told by a powerful spirit in the crystalline, translucent atmosphere of the Mediterranean, contains that foolish, devious something, the element of dark solitude.

All true love is subjective and unique, and at the same time creates communion. Here, as always, love of the sexes is an image of divine love. There is something about falling in love which cannot be re-experienced by the outsider; it is something lonely: the lovers leave everything behind them. Yet love is not true love when it is only unique and lonely; it must also create community. The Tristan and Isolde of Wagner are abandoned to death but the Tamino and Pamina of Mozart enter through the Gates of Life. What is true of those who love is also true of those who know. It is no coincidence that in Hebrew the word *Yadoa* is the word for knowing and for the physical consummation of love.

In spiritual love the two forces of solitude and community create power like the two poles of an electrical element. If the Christian religion were lived only in the cell of a Saint John of the Cross, it would become something lunatic and asocial. And if it were concerned only with the existence of the parish, it would soon resemble any business concern. In religion, if we must share the horrible cosmic solitude of the night of Gethsemani, neither must we refuse to belong to the multitude which is fed on bread and fishes.

Seen "from outside" a conversion is something adventurous and anarchic. We know from the story of poor Don Quixote how foolish it looks for someone to take ideas so seriously that he really rides away from home. However, the fact that the first voyage of Columbus appeared like a gigantic Quixoterie did not disprove the existence of the sought-for continent. If there are certainties, one must be able to find them.

That one simple question, whether Jesus of Nazareth was God incarnate, becomes increasingly decisive between people, as history moves forward. Dostoievsky once said that it is the one question on which everything in the world depends. The answer to this question cuts into human ties and seems to reflect even on the nature of inanimate things. What if all that is folly in the eyes of the Greeks, and scandal in the eyes of the Jews, is Truth?

I

BAVARIAN YOUTH

1. The Cattle Market

THE SMALL town in which I spent my childhood is one of the oldest in Bavaria. Not far from the Bohemian frontier, it lies on a hill over a vast river valley, and everywhere on the horizon are the delicate bluish mountain ranges of the Bavarian and Bohemian Forests. Part of the old wall and some of the medieval fortifications are still there and, in a nearby village, in the churchyard of a thirteenth-century Gothic church one can behold, through an iron grill, an "ossarium"—thousands of skulls and bones from bygone centuries stored in orderly piles.

All my ancestors, as far back as we can trace them, lived in Bavaria in parts of which there had been no Jewish immigration since the Middle Ages. At Floss, a peculiar town built on a tower-like hill, with columns of houses surging upward as if designed by El Greco, there was one of the oldest Jewish congregations in Bavaria. Several of my ancestors were Rabbis in that town. I went there only once, but I have a vivid memory of the narrow streets and the synagogue surrounded by a moat which could be reached only by crossing a little bridge.

In contrast to this somber town on a steep hill above the dark forests, our town was bright and gay, with its silvery river, the endless valley, and the mountains beckoning from afar. Since it held an intermediary position between the forests and the world outside, its business was very much concerned with

timber. But the Jews had little to do with timber; they were
not to be granted even the slightest activity associated with
nature and the land. This was the more remarkable since there
were a few Jewish families in nearly every small Bavarian town;
they belonged to the picture as an integrated part, and were
so regarded by the rural population. Josef Filser, a creation of
the famous Bavarian humorist Ludwig Thoma, is a cunning but
semi-illiterate peasant who represents his district in parliament,
and in his *General Observations,* a treatise which deals with
political and religious problems, Filser sums Judaism up in one
sentence: "The Jews have a friendly religion and are mostly
hop merchants."

In our area Jews were not even hop merchants. They had retail
stores for such things as textiles, or wholesale stores which supplied the shoemakers in the villages with leather or tools. Thus
they were middlemen between the big cities and the country.
So there existed in our lives, when we were children, a peculiar
discrepancy of which we became conscious only later. On the
one hand we were rooted in the country; the valley, the river,
the woods, the old little town, and the peasants in the villages
had a determining influence on our development. (My brother,
who after the Hitler revolution had a good deal to do with
Jewish children from the industrial regions of Northern Germany,
used to say that Man ought to originate in a small town in the
Bavarian Forest.) On the other hand, we lacked active relation
to the soil, to the stuff of which things are made, and to the
making of things. One could argue that there are also intermediary occupations among non-Jewish people; of course, only
a small portion of the retail shops in our town belonged to Jews.
However, the non-Jewish store owners were single members of
a chain which was otherwise composed of craftsmen and farmers.
They stood, as it were, on the shoulders of the others. As far as
we were concerned, no matter whether one looked back to our
ancestry or around among our relatives, there was nothing of

peasantry or craftsmanship visible. This discrepancy explains why, when the so-called "Jewish problem" had become so acute under Hitler, people like my brother regarded vocational re-orientation, settlement in the country, and craftsmanship as primary prerequisites for working towards a solution. I am sure that he was influenced by the experiences of our childhood, even if he was perhaps not aware of it. Of course, the purpose of the present story makes me emphasize differences, colors and depths of which we were hardly aware in those years. Actually, our Jewishness was woven imperceptibly into the background of things, much more imperceptibly than it might seem from the way I am writing now.

When I think of the house of my childhood it is as a limitless universe, inhabited chiefly by four people—my grandfather, my father, my mother and, for nearly ten years, by only one child, myself. First, there was the store. Its threshold was made of stone and contained indentations for the iron bolts with which we fastened the safety door at night. From this door one could see the Saint Florian fountain only three yards from the house. It was made entirely of granite, the stone of our mountains: the vast basin, the eighteenth-century statue of the saint, the two spouts flowing day and night, fed by what seemed an infinite source but was really an iron pipe which refed the same water. Across the street were the houses of the watchmaker and the plumber.

All this was linked by what struck my eyes as a continent of cobblestones, sidewalks, and gulleys in which the rain water collected. The intersection was called Rindermarkt (cattle market), and here on certain Saturdays the farmers brought their cattle to market. On those Saturdays I used to be awakened by mooing animals and sharp bursts of bargaining, haggling and chaffing. When I looked out of the window I saw a throng of men and beasts, heaving and milling in an endless stream. By afternoon one could hear the fountain again, but the store was

full of customers. Many farmers converted their cash immediately into goods, corduroy and buckskin for the men, woolen
and cotton clothes for the women, flannel for underwear, and
bed linen.

To me the store, the street and the square represented Outer
Space. It was vast, open, bright and contained no riddles. Behind the store was the office—the "comptoir" as it was called in
those days—where Father and Grandfather worked. Behind this
was the storeroom, where the bales had their ever so faint but
characteristic differences of smell: various shades of a faintly sour
mustiness, bales of thin prints, of herring-bone cloth, of chintz
and of velvet. In the backroom these bales were anonymous; in
the store and on the counter they received life. They were meas-
ured and tightly rolled again and lay there in Outer Space.

Upstairs was Inner Space. In my memory it is as unlimited as
the entire outer world. There were the bedrooms, the kitchen,
a large living-room, a small sewing-room and the drawing-room
or "salon." On the third floor was the bedroom which I used
during my teens and which later became the maid's room. Above
this was the attic, under a slanted ceiling. There were changes
in the rooms from time to time. Partitions were built or spaces
enlarged, and all this seemed to correspond to chapters in our
family history.

In the evening we often sat in the sewing-room around a small
table. The lamps had green shades with curtains of pearl-strings;
one could lower them by a pulley. When I think of our evenings
I remember the family clustered in a ring of light.

The salon was hardly ever used. It contained a cupboard
with books and thick easy chairs with useless tassels. Its only
window, curiously enough, had been walled off and one had to
turn on the electric light even during the day. Outside a fake
window had been painted, a meaningless artificial eye facing
the street. In the salon there were three huge albums called *The
Nineteenth Century*, with pictures of Beethoven, Alexander

Graham Bell, Wagner, Verdi, Napoleon, Lincoln and Goethe. There was also Meyer's *Konversationslexikon* in which one could secretly study "Reproduction in Man," with color plates on the development of the embryo.

My grandfather was a man of medium height, broad-shouldered, with a potato nose and a walrus mustache. To us children he was a source of never-ending hilarity, and it seemed to us that his whole life was devoted to jokes. He was conscious of this belief on our part, and whenever we were around he "got going." When a farmer's wife came into the store he would walk up to her with the measuring rod and slap her gently with it; then he would immediately act as if he were smitten with feelings of guilt and regret. I was a grateful audience for this sort of thing. I remember no instance in which the customer reacted badly. On the contrary this increased Grandfather's popularity. He addressed every farmer who came to the store for the first time as "Sepp" (Joseph), and all peasant women "Kati" (Katherine), and since these were the most frequent Christian names in our area the customer was often overwhelmed by joyful surprise.

In our region, in which much beer was consumed, commercial custom required us to devote several evenings a week to drinking beer. Each innkeeper had a definite evening. My father and Grandfather hated this, and I often observed Grandfather looking around furtively for a place, usually a flower pot, to pour his beer. Obviously these barkeepers needed more blankets and buckskin than we did beer, or this extraordinary barter system would have made no sense.

A different kind of memory is also associated with beer. Instead of a synagogue the Jews in our small town had a prayer-hall which was rented from the brewery. In order to get there you had to walk through corridors piled with beer barrels. There seemed always to be pools of stagnant spilled beer, and the place had a special scent which I remember very well. Since smells seem to have a greater power of association than other sensory impressions, even today whenever I enter a brewery, it all comes back: a certain spiritual mood, melodies, liturgical texts, Friday evening with its atmosphere of peace, the Psalms (*Leho lerananu*), and the beautiful hymn *Leho dodi* of Yehuda Halevy.

While my grandfather could be incomparably funny to us children, he was at the same time a strict and authoritative man. In fact, we would not have enjoyed his clowning as much as we did, had he not been a man of such patriarchal authority. He came from Franconia where he had grown up as the youngest of twelve children of a poor family. As a young man he had begun to study to become a Rabbi but had given it up. Then he peddled china in his home country (we frequently called him "Porcelain Moses"), and even after we had the store, he would visit the country fairs in the neighborhood and put up a stand.

My grandfather was the only one in our congregation who had received Jewish instruction. He was, for instance, the only one besides the Cantor who knew the liturgy well enough to conduct part of the service during the holidays. For as long as I could remember, he had been the president of the congregation, which consisted of about twenty families including some from neighboring villages. Yet he was not at all orthodox, and assumed the somewhat lax attitude of compromise frequent with Western Jews. For example, he kept his store open on Saturdays, and took it for granted that his children did not keep the Mosaic dietary laws. On the other hand, he never missed a service except during sickness. He participated in three Sabbath services, those on Monday and Thursday mornings, many annual memorial services for the dead and, since there were such things as semi-holidays, it happened not infrequently that he went to the synagogue seven times a week. Whenever we thought he went to prayer-hall too often we called him "Frau Witzelsperger," after a neighbor who went to daily Mass and all other devotions.

In religious questions he had towards the younger generation

an attitude which is hard to describe. Whatever was a vital law
to him was not at all binding to those who came after him. His
own children lived in a world which consisted of a strange mixture of political liberalism, agnosticism, Lessing's religion of
tolerance, Goethean, and even Nietzschean ideas. He seemed to
regard it as a fundamental law of life that the generation of
"enlightenment" must follow the generation of "religious tolerance." This went so far that my grandfather did not seem to like
having his children emulate him. When I, his grandson, later
turned to Jewish Orthodoxy he was hostile and sarcastic. Was
he perhaps not convinced of the truth of his religious position?
I do not think so. I believe I understand him quite well now,
but I do not want to overburden this story with "psychology."

At any rate, this gave rise to some funny incidents. At one time
he was with his children, who were still young, in a station
restaurant; they had to wait for the next train, and there was
only one item on the menu: pork goulash. The children were
extremely hungry, and he ordered the meal. The children, who
apparently suspected something, insisted on knowing what they
were eating. In his plight he named the very first thing that came
into his mind—stewed pears. These "stewed pears" became proverbial in our family.

It is no coincidence that I have described my grandfather before saying anything about my parents. When I come to think
of it, I remember my parents only as my grandfather's children.
My father was my grandfather's oldest child and, according to
tradition, had continued my grandfather's business. However,
Grandfather actually never let go. In the office behind the store,
there was a huge oldfashioned writing-desk with two surfaces
sloping off on either side, in a roof-like manner. There Grandfather and Father sat opposite each other on high swivel stools,
whenever they were not occupied in the store.

Whenever I had done anything wrong my father would shake
his head and say: "You just wait until Grandfather hears about

this!" It never occurred to him to punish me himself. One day, for example, I decided to test my marksmanship by throwing one of the measuring rods at a clerk. The man quickly posted himself in front of a huge pane of glass which formed the back of the show-window. I gave him a firm order not to duck; he informed me that he would most certainly duck. Having just read the Song of the Nibelungen, I thrust the measuring rod at him as if it were a spear. The clerk ducked, and the glass pane broke with a tremendous crash. I ran into the office at the back. Father was sitting alone at the desk. He looked at me sadly and said: "You just wait until Grandfather hears about this. I would not like to be you." I ran quickly upstairs into the bedroom, threw myself on my knees and implored God to prevent Grandfather from hearing about the accident, or to perform some other miracle to spare me from punishment. I had barely time to finish my prayer when Grandfather came in, lifted me up by the back of my blouse, and carried me downstairs like a kitten. For some reason (he had never heard of Professor Pavlov), he always gave me my spanking in the same corner of the house.

Besides running the store we employed traveling salesmen who visited small retail stores in the villages of the Bavarian Forest. They also showed samples of merchandise to the farmers and returned at the end of a few weeks with their order-books. Father quite frequently traveled in a similar manner, and this may have increased my impression that he worked for Grandfather. The fact that he had the privilege of the first-born seemed to keep him always in subjection—that was the way I came to see it.

The second oldest son, Uncle Felix, had studied engineering and later law, and become an outstanding patent lawyer in the United States. The third son, Uncle Julius, became the co-owner of a lithographic institute. While my two uncles were like mythological figures, Father's life seemed to represent drab reality. Of Uncle Felix's existence I had at that time little more tangible proof than a popular edition of *War and Peace* whose margins he had illustrated with the most charming pen drawings in the style of the German painter Menzel.

Uncle Julius appeared, from time to time, on short visits and told us about experiences on business trips to India, North America, or France. It seemed somehow extraordinary that he, my father's brother, supplied Chinese merchants in Ceylon with perfume labels and that in his suitcase were literary reviews from Paris. He came traditionally almost every Easter. He made fun of Grandfather's paschal ceremonies. On Easter Sunday morning he recited the "Easter Walk" from *Faust,* and in the evening at some unexpected moment he would quote the words of the Night Hymn from *Zarathustra.* He recited softly, with the peculiar restraint characteristic of the most progressive actors of his youth. He was a bachelor, probably the only man from our little town who spoke French and English fluently. He was Grandfather's favorite. It was taken for granted that his life was not guided by the same rules as life at home. Grandfather suspected him and Friedrich Nietzsche of something which he called "social democracy," and it would be impossible to enumerate all the things which were summed up under that heading.

My father was the opposite of all this. He was a man of natural humility and simplicity. He was probably the most guileless person I have ever seen; this was the more striking since in his rôle of submission to that sadly inverted right of the first-born, there would have been, under the best of circumstances, hundreds of possibilities of resentment, envy and jealousy. If he had been merely simple he would undoubtedly have become entangled in all this. I later encountered other people who appeared to have chosen a small corner of life. It was as if there had occurred a simple willful act of choice quite early, at the very dawn of a person's history. His rôle of my grandfather's son, and the contrast between this rôle and the dazzling world of his brothers, were embarrassing to me.

The only thing which seemed to link him with the faraway fantastic world of my uncles was his beautiful stamp collection. I still see him bent, with magnifying glass, over those colorful little pictures from the Transvaal, Peru, or the Dutch East Indies. Instead of bringing home, like Uncle Julius, dressing-gowns from Japan or illustrated magazines from London, Father brought me, every week, a bar of chocolate which he had purchased in the station restaurant in Miltach near Straubing.

2. *Feast Days and Rudolf*

THE PEOPLE of my parents' generation were almost entirely cut off from Jewish tradition. They hardly understood Hebrew, and therefore were unable to follow the liturgy. The time between 1870 and 1914 was a secure period which produced in most people a feeling of material happiness. Although everybody adopted an "attitude" on ultimate matters, nobody bothered about formulating it. If someone had compelled my mother to define her view of life with words, the result would have been an amiable mixture of political liberalism, Goethe's "Noble be man, helpful and good," and Lessing's conciliatory Deism. Had she lived in a big American city instead of a Bavarian country town, she might have joined one of the Ethical Societies. I must conclude, however, from some of her remarks, that at times she was interested in Quakerism.

I know that my mother was deeply familiar with the pathos of solitude, of suffering and of self-denial, but she was too restrained with herself and with us ever to use such words. Perhaps she never reflected upon these things and only lived them. It was part of her tolerant eclecticism that she helped with the preparations for all the beautiful religious ceremonies in the house. She enjoyed getting ready a Friday Evening or a Seder table but she liked equally decorating the Christmas tree for the maids and the children. Christmas was always celebrated because Mother was afraid lest it cause me anguish if all my friends in the neighborhood enjoyed a feast full of joy and light while we were sitting in a dark weekday room. To be "different" and "outside" has a permanent sad influence on children; if one is sure of one's cause, then one cannot spare one's children this injury. But was the generation of our parents sure of its Judaism?

At times it happened that Christmas and Chanukkah coincided. Chanukkah is the Jewish feast which commemorates the conquest of the temple after it had been defiled by the Greeks under Antioch Epiphanes. This re-inauguration of the temple is commemorated by a feast of one week beginning on the twenty-fifth day of the Hebrew month Kislev. In every Jewish house the lamp of eight candles was lit—one additional candle each night. After returning from the synagogue we would walk into the living-room. Grandfather sang the prayers of benediction and lit the Chanukkah candle. Quite often he let me sing the benediction and light the candles. I am sure I did not understand very much of what I sang, and what it was all about, but I can still hear the melody in which I thanked God for having "protected our fathers in those days and in that time." This was followed by the old Hebrew hymn whose verses and melody are so full of familiar sentiment to every Jewish child.

In the meantime Mother had prepared the Christmas tree and the presents in the adjoining salon which she kept locked. I returned to my room and, after another hour or so, I heard the fine tinkling of a bell. This was the sign. I remember that, before leaving my room to go to the salon, I used to look through the window into the dark winter street. It would be completely abandoned, though one could see the lights of Christmas trees in windows. Somehow I did believe that the Christ child had silently passed from house to house.

The salon had thousands of smells. Besides its usual mustiness, arising from bric-a-brac, velvet and books, there was the smell of pine, of burning wax, of fresh pastry. After I had received my presents it was the employees' turn. They used to stand around awkwardly. Since we had a textile store they had their free choice, and each knew beforehand what he was going to have. The fact that there was no thrill of surprise in their gifts disappointed me. Then Mother intoned *Silent Night* and we all joined in.

I was never aware of any conflict or discrepancy in all this. Since most Christians as well as Jews had forgotten about the spiritual meaning of their feasts, it did not matter much anyhow, and the two celebrations fused for the child into one mood of winter poetry, kindness and friendship. Of course the story of Christmas seemed more concrete and understandable. Often I went with my friends from the neighborhood into the churches to see the crib with the Christ child, the Blessed Virgin, Saint Joseph, the shepherds, the angels and the animals. Little did I realize that on the eve of Chanukkah I had prayed in ancient Hebrew with David: "To Thee, O God, I have called, and Thou hast prepared my salvation." Not long before Mother's death I found out that each year on Christmas Eve she used to go, secretly, to the poor of our town with meat and other things. Not even Grandfather or Father knew about this. In her later years she made me help her, because she was ill, and probably in order to set me an example. I remember the meat particularly because we had to pick it up at the butcher's shop before making the rounds.

Christmas was the feast of the Christ child. Saint Nicholas came on the evening of the fifth of December, the eve of his feast. He appeared to go from house to house, often accompanied by his servant Ruprecht. Saint Nicholas had a long beard and carried birch rods, heavy iron chains, and a big bag full of gifts. I had to wait in the sewing-room until I heard the clanking of chains

in the street and the noise of heavy boots slowly coming upstairs. Finally the door opened, and he was there. He always
displayed an amazing knowledge of one's behavior during the
year, and it was a question of either birch rods or gifts. Finally
he left his gifts, a shower of apples, nuts, figs, dates, candies.
From the noises going on in the streets it seemed that there were
several Saint Nicholases. We had a heavy black felt blanket,
the sort of thing one used on horse-drawn coaches. Saint Nicholas
was draped in that very blanket and he wore Grandfather's boots.
I believe I was almost eight before this struck me as an extraordinary coincidence.

I received my first schooling in the kindergarten which in our
little town was conducted by nuns. Here, too, my mother broke
with tradition. Up to that time no Jewish child had ever been
sent to the Catholic kindergarten. Thus my first formal religious
education was Catholic. We had no catechism but we were entertained with stories from the Bible, particularly from the New
Testament, which were illustrated with colored pictures on the
wall. There was also a little prayer now and then. I must have
been impressed by the pious atmosphere; I have only vague recollections of the stories, the pictures, the May devotions, and our
Christmas play in which I had a rôle. Soon I moved on to public
school.

Here, as in the kindergarten, there was the important fact that
children of all social classes were together. Since the poor are
everywhere in the majority, they gave everything a characteristic
pattern. As a whole you can say that in the small towns and
villages of a rural country many problems of formal education
are solved in a natural way, questions about which ponderous
theses are now being written. At present everybody is interested
in the "problems" of education; I have heard very clever people
make speeches about it. Even with all we now know about the

matter of education, I still think our country schools were quite good.

For instance, it now appears a very important fact that we were taught to love beauty. This was done in an informal, not at all planned way. The things most deeply rooted in my memory were obviously not contained in the curriculum but derived from the teacher's own inclinations. Whenever we had been particularly good boys, Herr Gradl, the *oberlehrer,* read to us. This was our reward. We were then allowed to bake our apples in the huge tiled stove in the classroom and the old teacher with a crown of white hair read "Rock Crystal," a short story by Stifter. In this story there are two children who get lost in the snow, spend the night on a mountain and are found next morning. Stifter is little known in Anglo-Saxon countries; he was a poet of deeply hidden powers whose real greatness was recognized only by Nietzsche. Stifter had lived not far from us in the Forest area. Although his great art is more than just "idyllic" and "full of local color," I still associate his name with teacher Gradl, the smell of apples baking in the stove, and a snowy winter in the Bavarian Forest.

Teacher Gradl was in private life an enthusiastic botanist. During the summer he used to take a group of pupils with him on some of his excursions in the vast meadows of the Regen Valley. There we would collect plants and identify them. He liked to be visited in his house during vacation. Then he would read from Schiller's poems and dramas, or poems of medieval romanticists of the late nineteenth century. At that time all German philology professors had broken out in an acute attack of drama, epic and lyrics; it was as if millions of Wilhelminian sofa cushions had to be covered with a crochet of knights, pages, monks and ladies. Oberlehrer Gradl's cheeks would flush when he read the epos "Thirteen Linden Trees." I have a dim recollection that he read poems of his own to me; at any rate I am sure that he wrote poetry.

Another teacher, in fact my very first one, was Kaspar Russ. He was a giant out of a fairy tale; everything about him seemed much too big—his skull, his mane, his hands, which looked like an unwieldy arrangement of ham and sausages, his feet, his snuff box, his handkerchief with colorful flower patterns, and especially his nose, which resembled a huge silo filled with snuff. He was deeply religious, musical, and there was something clumsy and giantesque about his goodness; his benevolence seemed inexhaustible. He was organist in the parish church and choirmaster of the St. Cecilia Verein. He came originally from another town not far away, and one of his friends there had been another schoolteacher, the father of the composer Max Reger. He had an intimate love for the theory of harmony, and he coached his people zealously in the boring church music of Rheinberger, sparingly interspersed with Mozart and Haydn. Traditionally he performed Haydn's *Seven Last Words* every Good Friday at church. He was proud of this, and I was always invited.

Like many people of unwieldy build, he was shy. He was clumsy but it was not difficult to find camouflaged behind a cloud of snuff a heart full of charity. He had a particular love for the Jewish children. This went as far as a display of favoritism.

I have said that everything personal, spontaneous and improvised in our schooling stuck much better in my memory than those things which correspond to the official curriculum. It was always like this, even later at high school and at the university. Just as the stories by Stifter and the botanic excursions with Gradl had a decisive influence on us, I found later that those teachers influenced us most who showed a good deal of improvisation outside of, or instead of, the curriculum; these were teachers who gave one something personal by means of a personal approach. One of the greatest dangers of present-day education is the impersonal dishing-out of the "teaching material" by an official. It is apparent that growing industrialization has produced a depersonalized type of education. Here, as in many other things, decentralization is perhaps the solution, though of course, one cannot reconstruct small Bavarian country towns of 1912 and equip them with synthetic Kaspar Russes.

Many of the problems of education which are now taken so seriously lost much of their ponderous significance in our school. For example, there was corporal punishment, but I do not believe that it did me any harm. As a whole the punishments were standardized. The teacher had a cane (a so-called "Spanish cane"), and we received slaps on the palm of the hand, a definite number for a particular type of misdemeanor. When the entire class had misbehaved, we all had to file past Russ and put our hands out. Teacher Schmaus had a ring with an ivory seal which he used for boxing our heads. Behind the school were the railway tracks, and whenever I turned around to follow a gorgeous freight train the ivory seal dropped down on me.

The beautiful days of the child in a small town: the smoke of burning potato leaves in the fires of autumn, rising over the cool misty meadows; the smell of washed laundry drying on the lawn in the summer sun; the cool moldiness underneath the town walls; the smell of the old wooden beams beneath the roof; the sensation of hot slate roof under hands and feet; or the eternal lure of pale blue mountains far away. Then there are the dark experiences, the days when we approach for the first time the frontiers of life: sex, lunacy, crime and death. One morning the boy who had been sitting in front of me at school did not come in; he had been drowned the day before. I still see the empty place with photographic accuracy, the pattern in the wooden plank of his bench. The first sensation of death, the awareness of it, moves into the center of the child's retina like a gray spot.

One day all along the river there were groups of people chatting excitedly, because over in the dark forest a poor old man had hanged himself from a tree. I had known the man. The forest was suddenly tinged with strange significance. I also remember the girl in the neighbor's house who was so deeply entangled in

sin that she painted her face. Nobody seemed surprised that she
was soon stricken with consumption and died. Then there was
the old peasant woman with a discharge running from her eyes
who came screaming into our store, telling us of her visions; she
had seen Hell. The world of twilight and darkness always at-
tracts children much more than the bright and orderly world of
the drawing-room.

Rudolf, my best friend in the neighborhood, was the son of a
little shoemaker who was always drunk. Their house was overcrowded with children, and it stank indescribably. I was impressed by the fact that one of Rudolf's brothers, incidentally the
most industrious and decent one, was a true hunchback. I was
equally impressed by the fact that Rudolf stole and lied. He did
not seem to be subject to the regular laws of life, and I admired
and revered him. Even the fact that my most beautiful toys disappeared did not matter. Rudolf was our leader when we played
soldiers; when he ordered it we remained lying on our stomachs
in the mud. He told us about large gymnastic halls in his house,
with many bars and climbing ropes which were installed exclusively for him and his brothers, and although we never saw
those halls we believed in their existence. Father and Grandfather called him "the devil"—nobody except myself ever used
his real name. All except Mother looked with misgivings upon a
friendship which could bring nothing but perdition. Mother, for
some reason or other, maintained that one should not interfere
with a child's friendships; she left me entirely to Rudolf whenever
I wanted to be with him. Later, when we had grown up, he did
land in jail.

That autumn I urged my grandfather, whenever we were on
our way to the synagogue, to tell me when the candle feast
would be (Simchath Torah, the feast of law-giving). This is a
feast during which children make a procession through the
synagogue, holding candles and singing hymns. He kept putting

me off until the actual date of the feast would arrive. One evening I came home late from the fields with glowing cheeks, broke into the room, fell on my mother's neck, and shouted with pride and joy—Rudolf had promoted me to the position of captain. Everyone looked at me in a cold and strange way; I had missed the feast, the procession and the candles. Grandfather looked stern and sad; obviously there was nothing one could do against the devil.

Since I had entered school, things concerning religion had changed. At school the Jewish children stayed away during the hours of religious instruction, and had their own religious class on a free afternoon. There were only a few Jewish children and the class was therefore composed of several age groups, the beginners and the advanced pupils. There was no Rabbi in the town, only a Cantor. Our Cantors at that particular time were far removed from the ideal of a pastor of souls. I remember the first one very well, a short young man whom we disliked for some reason which I cannot remember. When the First World War broke out he was drafted into the army. We children used to stage plays in which one of us acted as sergeant major and bullied the Cantor in a most miserable way; only then were we satisfied.

In religious things children separate the human and personal aspect from the spiritual in a much more natural way than adults do. The hateful Cantor was the first teacher since the nuns to convey "religion" to me. And yet this circumstance had no influence on my religious development. The external features seemed as repulsive as possible; there was the miserable Cantor, and the bare prayer-hall inside the old brewery. Nevertheless, I was again attracted to this spiritual sphere, and it was precisely in this environment that my religious growth was nurtured. Finally, after an interlude of several other Jewish schoolmasters, a Cantor arrived who was to stay in our small town for almost twenty years, until the Hitler revolution.

Cantor Mohrmann was more awe-inspiring than the previous ones, he seemed to sing with more beauty and fervor and, while the others had been bachelors, he brought a Biblical household with him—at least it looked like this because there were three generations. My grandfather was his only friend; apart from this he was rejected by the entire congregation. Mohrmann was a "personality." He introduced a children's choir and enlivened the service with beautiful songs. He aroused in us glowing enthusiasm for the beauties of liturgy; the "Hear Israel," the Psalms, the Eighteen Prayers. We learned to translate from the Hebrew, word for word, entirely without grammar.

This translating was like some sort of unwrapping. I remember very well that during certain parts of the Morning Prayer I felt as though I was taking jewels out of a box, unwrapping them and letting them shine in all their color and golden beauty. I had the experience of unfathomed mystery whenever he took a few of us aside and showed us a Talmud volume or a Scroll of the Torah, with unpunctuated Hebrew words. Whenever he read all this fluently he seemed to us like one initiated in some esoteric cult. Everyone, even among those who know nothing about it, is esthetically impressed by a Talmud print. There are the beautiful characters, the noble spatial arrangement of columns printed in varying magnitude, representing the text, the commentary, and the commentary of the commentary—the style of an early aristocratic humanism.

Certainly Mohrmann was not initiated in an esoteric cult. Any true Hebrew lay-scholar could have easily shown him up. However, he did not claim to be a scholar, and it was not his fault that he impressed the children as if he were one. Anything mysterious and full of implications is spiritual food for children. I remember well how deeply impressed I was when he told us that the Old Testament had prophesied wireless telegraphy. There is some text, I believe in the Psalms, which says that the Word goes around the earth with the speed of air.

We were not at all disturbed by the fact that Mohrmann at the same time was like a man of vices, full of pride and vanity. He played expensive card-games throughout the night, with a dark passionate addiction. Perhaps he had some peculiar attitude towards money. Father and Mother were very much disturbed by all this; they did not want to accept the word of God from a man like that. To us children this did not make any difference, since children are much less inhibited than adults by the personal element in their religious experiences. There is another thing which I saw again later in other children—the natural way in which children associate the ascetic ideal with the spiritual. Our parents had brought us up without teaching us the laws of diet, and had observed just enough of them so as not to hurt other people's feelings. The moment we learned about these laws in our religious lessons we began to impose them voluntarily upon ourselves. We did as much of it as we could. The discipline of supernatural obedience to which one has to submit in the choice of food and in the life of Sabbath—all this was to us children quite naturally tied up with the more poetical values of religion. I am inclined to take this child-like tendency as a sign that there is a true and an organic inner relationship between praying and fasting. These tendencies of children seem in a peculiar way linked with the true nature of concepts. Psychoanalysis has shown how the child, during the years preceding adolescence, counters sexual impulses by imposing on himself rules of discipline. As far as the natural plane of things goes, this is a profound observation. But this natural history of asceticism does not tell us anything about the true value and meaning of ascesis.

It was probably also an ascetic feature that made us feel that the bare and poor prayer-hall in the brewery was better than the parish church with its interior of golden baroque. On Corpus Christi there was always a procession through town, with several open-air altars, one of which was invariably set up opposite our house. It was a grand feast when the various asso-

ciations of young men and young maidens passed by with colorful banners. The priest came dressed in white and golden vest-
ments, walking underneath a canopy carried by four men, and
stopping at the altar opposite our house. Unlike our neighbors
we kept the windows closed, but watched from behind the curtains. I am sure we never gave these matters much thought, and
of course they take up more space in this narrative than they did
in reality. Nevertheless, if someone had examined us closely at
the time he would have found that we considered all these colorful ceremonies as pagan and that we considered ourselves closer
to truth with our poor and undecorative forms of worship.

On the morning of the fifth of December, 1915, the eve of
Saint Nicholas, Father woke me up and said: "Come over to
Mother's bedroom." I said I would but went on sleeping. He
came again and made it more urgent; it was half-past five in
the morning. When I entered the room, Mother had a peculiar
smile and said: "You've got a little brother." I dropped on the
floor and looked underneath the bed. I had some dim idea that
babies were "thrown" (the German expression used for the birth
of animals). However, he was in the bed lying right next to her,
a bundle of fresh-smelling linen. Through a small round hole I
saw a tiny area of pink skin. I probably thought a serious word
was expected from me at this moment, and presently I addressed
pink-skin in the following way: "You are my little brother. If
later the big boys should ever threaten you, just call on me!"
Later in life the big boys threatened him quite a bit, but he
never called me.

On this day, contrary to tradition, no Saint Nicholas came to
us. One big event a day was apparently enough. In the evening
I heard the clanking of chains in the streets. Saint Nicholas
was going into the houses. The new little brother was such a
thrill that I was torn with conflict. I ran quickly to the neighbors,
couldn't wait for Saint Nicholas, and rushed back home to be
present when baby brother got his bath. They first called him

Wilhelm after the Kaiser, but mitigated it, at the last minute, and
named him Ludwig after the King of Bavaria.

3. *Munich: Music and Civil War*

IN OUR little town there was no high school. Therefore, all those
who did not want to take over their father's business or trade
had to be sent to a bigger town for "studying." Some went to
big boarding schools. Most of them were taken in as boarders by
families, either alone or with one or two more boys. The schoolboy as boarder is a rather typical Southern German institution.
The little paying guest even plays a rôle in literature; he occurs
in the books of Ludwig Thoma and Hermann Hesse, and in
books less known. Curiously enough, he is always a tragic figure.
Even in Ludwig Thoma's humorous stories there is a faintly tragic
undertone whenever he is dealing with the little boarder, an
undertone distinctly discerned by any boy who ever lived
"abroad" (the expression commonly used). These boarders usually lived with families of subaltern officials who in this way supplemented their meager monthly salaries; or with widows, or
teachers who were on the staff of the school to which the boarder
belonged.

I went "abroad" at the age of ten. Ebenburg is a drab industrial
town in the east of Bavaria, not far from the places of origin of
the composers Gluck and Reger. It is really drab and sad, not
only in my memory; I was able to convince myself of that much
later when I revisited it.

We were boarders at the Jewish teacher's home. The high
school was just across the road. Our teacher was a brother of our
Jewish teacher at home, but the brothers were on bad terms.
This astonished me; I had been wont to believe that it belongs

to the very definition of family to be on good terms. It is difficult
to imagine anything more oppressive than the life of such a
Kultusbeamte (cult official). He had hardly any religious education, and there was not very much of the living fire of the
Torah. I can still see him, a man of medium height, a little
rotund, with a tiny goatee. This was during the First World War
and he was in uniform. The tie of such Cantors with Jewish tradition was only external and historical, their function purely social.

This mediocrity and apparent lack of inner content in people
who are professionally concerned with religion makes a re-
volting impression, particularly on agnostics and atheists. Those
who don't believe in God make high demands on those who believe in Him; particularly on those who "make a living out of
it." Our poor teacher would have presented an ideal victim for
the wrath of the godless. There was hardly anything left of the
world of Isaiah—just a little establishment for circumcisions, for
funerals, and for the singing of prayers on certain days. We lived
on the second floor of a dismal building which contained the
synagogue, and the prayer-hall was right below my bedroom.
All we had to do to attend a service was to climb a staircase.

We were three boys—Leo, sixteen; Alec, eleven; and I, ten.
We lived together in one room and came from the same town.
Mother had warned me that life in Ebenburg was to be quite
different from things as I had known them at home. She left on
the evening of the day of our arrival, but Alec's mother stayed
for a few days.

On that evening I was alone with Leo, while Alec spent some
time with his mother. Leo took me to a window and pointed
at the building across the street. "See the lighted window in the
basement? That is the janitor's apartment, where Grete lives, right
in that very room." He told me that Grete was sixteen and his girl
friend. We looked intently across the street towards the lighted
window. After a while I began putting my things into drawers,
but Leo kept looking. Without even turning, he asked me if I

knew that it was scientifically proved that hair kept growing on
corpses' heads after they were buried. This, he said, had been
established beyond doubt in people who had been exhumed. I
asked what "exhumed" was, and he explained it to me. I said that
Alec was lucky that his mother was staying on for a few days.
Leo replied that Alec was a sissy and that I seemed to be a
sissy too.

Suddenly he exclaimed: "Look, quickly!" I rushed to the window. A girl had emerged into the street, apparently from the
house. She walked slowly away and Leo, panting with excitement, said: "See how she looks up to me?" I pressed my face
against the window pane but could only see her walking away. I
wondered what made Leo certain that she looked up to our window. This was repeated every evening like a ritual. Leo made
us believe that there was an adventurous link between him and
the janitor's daughter. But this link remained mysterious. What
Mother had told me was true: everything here was different
from the world at home.

The Cantor would suddenly appear in the morning in our
room, pacing up and down with his hands folded over his back;
this happened whenever his wife had thrown him out. At least
this was the explanation given us by Leo. There was the Cantor's
wife who had appeared so fashionable to me when she met my
mother in the drawing-room, and yet everything seemed to be in
disorder after my mother left. There were so many mice that
they even ate the bread which I kept in a bag suspended near
my pillow. There was a maid to whom Leo used to talk in obscure and meaningful allusions. He was able to say things which
we could not understand and which roused peals of laughter
from the Cantor's wife and the maid; we admired him for that.

Everything seemed alien, bad and terrifying, and I believed
that it was so utterly different that I could not possibly make
it understandable to Father and Mother. Gradually I developed
the idea that "abroad" had to be something altogether different

from "at home"; it was another cosmos which one forgot completely the first minute of the holidays. Thousands of other boys had to go through this—like soldiers who, while on active combat, do not meditate on the philosophy of war.

Vacations had developed into something which you might call furlough in heaven. From my window on the top floor of our house, just underneath the attic, I was able to see, beyond the neighbor's house, the distant mountains. I had only to run down two stairs, and I found myself in the homely sphere of Father, Mother, Grandfather and little brother. There were only a few steps to my friends' homes. We spent our days swimming or with a book, or we visited the old schoolteacher, or we hiked in the woods. The dark world was hundreds of miles away; but the more the golden days advanced, the more that darkness approached.

After one year I was sent to Munich. I was again a little boarder, this time with people of quite a different kind. I lived with an orthodox Jewish family, a widow with three children. Frau Kohen was the widow of a banker. All members of the family were midget-like, so much so that whenever I visited other people I felt for a moment as though I were among giants. The entire Kohen family exhibited a really bee-like industriousness; everyone contributed to the household. Even the son, only two years older than myself, made some money by giving lessons. Herr Kohen had died a sudden death and had left the family in a helpless condition. Moreover, one of the daughters, a private teacher, suffered from epilepsy. In spite of all these hard blows of fate, there was an atmosphere of security in this home which is often found among pious folk.

Munich, in spite of the war's shadow, in spite of *ersatz* goods, dried vegetables and lack of fuel, had lost nothing of its incomparable charm. I had been there once before with my father, at the age of eight, when he took me to see the puppet play of

Doctor Faust. A magic world was now opened before me; all the things of which I had read a lot were at hand—the museums, the operas, theaters, concert halls, churches, parks, the Isar valley, the mountains and lakes. That Munich does not exist any more. But cities, even if we disregard our nostalgic sentiments, have something like immortal souls. Munich meant some sort of harmonious synthesis of North and South, of East and West, of Art and Nature, of rural and urban civilization, a vanguard of serene Latinism in the gloomy North, a Gothic sentry in front of the porch of Italy. With the exception of Paris there has never been a town which had so much individual expression, so little of the artifact and so much of natural growth.

At this time an influence came into my life which has remained a most powerful and decisive one—Music. Since this book is intended to describe the journey of a spiritual discovery, I must talk about music. From the beginning to the end it has been for me the most immediate expression of spiritual realities. "To talk about music" is a miserable paradox, and contains in four words an admission of incongruity. I remember the embarrassed feeling I had when I read Kierkegaard's somber theological speculations on Mozart and *Don Giovanni*. Is *Don Giovanni* not just a "charming" opera which has a place on the repertoire somewhere with *Carmen* and *The Barber of Seville?* Or is it something entirely different, opening up the fathomless abyss of human existence? There is a hierarchy of values, the validity of which cannot be proved by what one calls ordinary means. In this respect, as in others, the Good and the Beautiful are intimately related. To me Mozart's quartets and Bach's *Well-tempered Clavichord* are in essence much more closely akin to Saint Thomas' *Summa* than to Wagner's *Götterdämmerung*, although the latter is music and the *Summa* is not.

I had started with music in our hometown. Kaspar Russ as a rule gave no lessons but for some reason he made an exception for me. In vain did he try to convey to me his enthusiasm for

the theory of harmony. He tried to do this simultaneously with
the elementary teaching of piano. Even today, when I hear something about a diminished seventh or about enharmonic transformations, the smell of snuff and the sensation of his huge
hands comes back to me. Counterpoint played no rôle at all.
Nevertheless, he came to the lesson one day with a sad face:
"Yesterday the greatest contemporary musician died." I said:
"Wagner?" He shook his head sadly and said: "Reger." I understood nothing about his theory of harmony, and all I was interested in was how to play the piano. I loved sonatinas by
Dussek, and the play of bells from *The Magic Flute*, and I har-
monized *Lorelei* with the most luscious chords long before we
had ever reached diminished sevenths. At the Cantor's in Ebenburg there was no musical stimulus outside a melodramatic song,
"The Seaman's Fate," which seemed to fit in with the dust-catch-
ing furniture and the oil prints in the drawing-room.

Munich seemed like a second birth. There was the Hoftheater
in which opera was played every night. I saw it perhaps twice a
year. We had to begin queueing at five in the morning, and at
ten the box-office was opened. Then we went home, and there
was a whole day of beatific expectation. This reached its climax
during the last half-hour when we were sitting in the top gallery,
waiting for the various curtains to rise—the second one (with
Guido Reni's "Aurora" which seemed to indicate what was going
to happen later) and finally the last one which separated the
audience from the stage and which was to rise after the Overture.
The tuning of the instruments, the gradual dimming, the appearance of the conductor and the last seconds of silence; all these
were phases full of significance, meaningful like those of an esoteric cult of antiquity. I was equally impressed by everything, no
matter whether *Lohengrin, The Barber of Seville,* or *The Magic
Flute.* However, Wagner dimmed more and more and my love
for Mozart deepened as the years went by. This love became a
decisive factor in my life, going far beyond the realm of music

With concerts it was rather similar. Every year at All Souls'
there was the *Missa Solemnis,* and during Holy Week *St.
Matthew's Passion.* Here, too, the thrill was heightened by
queueing in the early morning. I remember the annual performances of the *Missa* in every detail. I know now that they exerted
a powerful influence upon me which was reinforced much later
in a somewhat different direction. The late Beethoven, he who
wrote the *Missa* and the last string quartets, is an awe-inspiring
phenomenon, not only musically but in the history of mankind.
Is it not extraordinary that this Promethean, whose life crosses the
epoch of the French Revolution and Napoleon, should arrive at
the end in some space of mystic loneliness? Nobody who has
heard the last quartets and the "Benedictus" can deny that the
composer entered into a sphere which has found its verbal expression in Saint John of the Cross. It is a platitude to say that
Beethoven in his last quartets was far ahead of his time; actually
he was there ahead of Time altogether. What an astronomic span
in one man's life! What if those were right who say that geniuses
anticipate the course of history?

At that time I was far removed from such speculations. I
possessed a small reading score which still contained as a printed
heading Beethoven's original motto: *"Von Herzen, möge es zu
Herzen gehen*—May heart speak to heart." These words touched
me in a very special way. Beethoven had called the *Missa*
his greatest work. In this connection this dedication is particularly moving, as if he had been concerned with the act
of communication, of correspondence with the hearer. This was
precisely how I felt. From the first majestic D-major chord
which introduces a longing Kyrie to the "Prayer for Internal and
External Peace" of the Agnus Dei with its naive operatic inter-
mezzo of the Miserere and the final bars of supernatural happiness, there is nothing like it in the history of art. It is as if you
beheld European man, a late estranged European man, already
half cut-off from his moorings, just once more stirred in the

depth of his heart by an experience of infinite importance. I knew from books that Beethoven had the text of the Mass translated to him word by word, and that he attempted to interpret its content verbally; thus I followed the text as closely as possible. The experience was overwhelming every year. I remember well that for a few hours after leaving the Odeon Hall the world seemed altogether changed. People in the street, even the tramway cars, everything seemed in a state of transfiguration, everybody appeared to be reconciled and full of peace. Later, after the religious world of Bach and Mozart had opened itself to me, I maintained that particular personal relation to Beethoven's *Missa*, in the way one may feel towards some person who has played an important part in one's destiny. By chance my wife and I, just before our departure for Canada in 1939, heard the *Missa Solemnis* in London under Toscanini. This was our farewell to Europe.

During my first few years in Munich, I was under the influence of two currents which have nothing to do with each other. At Kohen's I came for the first time in contact with the world of Jewish orthodoxy; on the other hand in Munich during the armistice and the post-war years I found myself on the stage of the social revolution. In Munich everything was to occur which had happened on a large scale before in Russia, and which was later to happen on a large scale in Germany.

The Kohen family belonged to the orthodox congregation of Munich which had its center in a small, inconspicuous synagogue at the Herzog Rudolf Street (the "canal" synagogue). The liberal congregation was by far the bigger one. It had a big "reformed" synagogue in the center of the city. This synagogue resembled a big, fashionable Protestant church, and contained an organ. The canal synagogue, however, was a gray house, hardly distinguishable from the poor houses of the neighborhood. Contrary to the liberal synagogue it was always full to capacity, and had unbelievably bad ventilation. Jewish orthodoxy, like all orthodox religions in the world, does not keep pace with modern hygiene. There were assembly rooms, and schoolrooms for children and adults in a side wing, and you could be sure that something was always going on. Moreover, the orthodox families chose their dwellings near the synagogue (if only not to be forced to use vehicles on Sabbath day) so that the synagogue became a living center, the heart of the congregation.

What attracted me as a child was not any particular detail of the doctrine but the entire atmosphere. It is quite true that in exploring religious truth you have to exclude all emotional influences. Nevertheless, all religions have a way in which they are lived by people rather than thought, they have their gestures and elements which cannot be formulated; all this has an overwhelming, penetrating power which no child's heart can resist.

Take, for instance, the Sabbath. From the late afternoon on Friday to the first stars on Saturday evening, it was as if time and space had become a spiritual enclave. From the time when good tiny Frau Kohen put out the white linen, with the solemn cutlery of silver, and the candles, until Saturday night, when the Week was welcomed with a special ritual, there was an atmosphere of peace and enchantment. Life seemed to continue within a strange outer space in which it was subjected to laws different from those of the world. There were hundreds of little, seemingly senseless Talmudic precepts. You were not allowed to go on a vehicle, to write, to switch on any electric light (this was done by the maid!), you were not supposed to carry anything in your pocket, not even the key. Erwin, the son, even had his handkerchief pinned to the lining of his coat so that it would be part of his clothing, and not "carried." This was the famous "fence around the Torah" which the Wise had erected so that not even a shadow was possibly darkening the Law of Sabbath. This entire time-enclave was used for service, for private devotions, for the study of the Torah and the rabbinical Fathers.

All these activities were interrupted only by gay meals, Hebrew round-songs, and occasional short walks.

It is remarkable that even the poorest orthodox families cele-brated the Sabbath in this manner. For in many cases this meant a great financial sacrifice. Many stores had to remain closed on Sunday so that the merchants lost the income of another weekday. This was one of the reasons why many Jews said that for practical reasons one had to conform with the times, and that orthodoxy was impossible in a "modern world."

Service in the orthodox synagogue was, of course, entirely dif-ferent from anything I had seen until then. Even the outward appearance differed, because here the men wore their prayer-shawls over the whole body. In liberal synagogues the men wear their prayer-shawls folded up around the collar like mufflers. This is done in a sort of diffident way to conform with the times. Many prayed for themselves without paying attention to their neighbors, often without reference to what the Cantor was doing. Many closed their eyes in devotion and made characteristic rhythmic movements forward and backward. This diminished the danger of distraction. Everybody seemed to know the liturgy by heart and followed the reading of Torah and Prophet with the most amazing knowledge of detail. Anyone from the con-gregation might be called upon to read from the Prophets. Al-though you never knew beforehand whose turn it would be, everyone was apparently able to recite any Prophetic text with perfectly accurate intonation. This is an art in itself practiced from early youth. The synagogue was an organic continuation of religious life in the family; whoever had finished the Eighteen Prayers earlier than the Cantor did some religious reading or talked to his neighbors.

The Munich orthodox congregation was at that time under the leadership of old Rabbi Ehrentreu. Doctor Ehrentreu was an extraordinary man, of a type I have never encountered again in life. He looked as if Rembrandt had known him, a stooped, thin

old man with a long silver beard. I still see him leading the
Sabbath procession of the Torah, wrapped in his prayer-shawl,
so that only his face was visible. There was something non-
physical about him; whoever remembers him remembers a con-
spicuously high and broad forehead and huge gazeless eyes
which seemed to behold something which was not visible. He
preached rarely and, contrary to the liberal and reformed synagogue, the sermon played a very unimportant rôle with him.
Whenever he spoke at all he gathered the men and discussed
some very technical Talmudic problem. Although he confined
himself to dry special questions, everybody felt the undercurrent
of wisdom and goodness.

I thought of that much later when I read what Franz Rosenzweig said of Jewish orthodoxy, of its rough, almost indigestible
shell which contains such a rich and sweet nucleus. Somewhere
underneath this seemingly impenetrable crust of formalism the
essence is buried; there you find, says Rosenzweig, words such as
"Love Thy Neighbor as Thyself," words which are seldom expressed, as if out of some pious diffidence. Here he makes a
strange comparison with Christianity which, as he says, exhibits
its sweetness on the surface. The interesting thing is that in Christian orthodoxy, too, the onlooker often sees nothing but empty
formalism behind which one cannot see the "Christian ideas" any
more. Here, too, the Catholic Church represents the most direct
development from Jewish orthodox tradition. Doctor Ehrentreu
was a typical son of those Eastern Yeshivoth–Jewish centers of
teaching which had an atmosphere of extraordinary spiritual intensity. Some Russian Christian philosopher once said that the
Yeshivah is an incarnation of the Hegelian Absolute. You must
have seen Yeshivah disciples to be able to understand this remark. I am not speaking of unequaled virtuosity of memory and
knowledge. There were men who knew the Bible visually so well
that when you pierced the book with a pin they were able to tell
you through which word on each page the pin was stuck. I am

rather speaking of an absolute and perfectly natural way in which everything material became secondary, a pure means for a purpose; how these people are, into their innermost biological strata, possessed in the literal sense of the word. There is a famous short story by Perez of a Rabbi and his disciple who, while slowly starving to death, discuss Talmudic problems, with red eyes and glowing cheeks; these types really exist, I have seen them. With all this the Western orthodox congregations were only a shallow reproduction of what existed in the East.

It is quite natural that I was then much more attracted by the aura of religion without understanding much of the details. In all religion the unexpressed and the inexpressible are as important as all those things which are verbalized in prayer-books and treatises. Within the whole structure the air-filled spaces are as significant as the pillars. This must be one of the main difficulties for the people who study "comparative religion" with "scientific methods." All they get are marble slabs, pillars and blocks but no interspaces. The interspace is an emotional element organically interwoven with the rational structure. There is nothing purely rational which is strong enough to bind the heart of man.

I had not started early enough to study scripture. All children around me read Hebrew without effort, with or without punctuation. At that time I knew hardly anything of the true liturgical content of the Day of Atonement, nothing of the Sacrifice of the Scapegoat, nothing of the incomparably beautiful Isaiah chapters, hardly anything of the Book of Jonah; I just knew barely enough of the prayers of contrition which are mechanically repeated all day long while the entire congregation, men, women and children pound their chests. But what I grasped entirely was the gesture of the day, and this penetrated my limbs as it does every child's. The ten days of preparation, and then the solemn eve of the Day of Atonement!

The entire congregation resembled a white sea because the married men wore not only their prayer-shawls but also the

shrouds in which they would one day be buried. No one was to
enter the house of God with shoes on his feet. When the ceremonies began with the solemn Kol Nidrë, twice repeated, there
was a faint rustling going through the crowd. Would the next
twenty-four hours bring a remission of sins? None of the grown-
up men left the synagogue from morning till night. Some supplemented the twenty-four hours' fast by some special penance, for
instance, standing during the whole day. In the evening we children were so hungry that from this alone we concluded that our
sins must be forgiven.

When we came home, Frau Kohen had prepared the food. I
felt good, and I thought that life was beginning anew on a spot-
lessly clean new page.

Similarly profound was the experience of Passover. Here, too,
the preparation was important. Frau Kohen and the maid
needed days to purify the house according to the precepts of
Passah. Finally the first Seder evening arrived. The Seder plate
was prepared, the horse-radish (the bitterness of Egyptian
slavery), applesauce (the clay of Egypt), the lamb, and other
symbolic objects. I knew the Seder from Grandfather. The
Hagadah was recited by Erwin, the son; I, the youngest, had to
put the famous question: "*Mah nishtanah haleilah haseh micol
haleiloth?*—What is the difference between this night and all
other nights?" Everybody ate and drank a lot, and as the evening advanced Erwin, who interrupted the Hagadah with con-
siderations from Midrash, seemed more and more admirable
to me. With all this we got clear chicken broth with balls of unleavened bread in it, and many other delicious things. Whenever
the ritual of the Hagadah prescribed the drinking of wine, we
children drank too; we dipped our fingers ten times into the
wine, corresponding to the ten plagues of Egypt. Towards the
end I had too much wine, and the final round-songs seemed
outrageously hilarious to me; the lamb that was eaten by the
cat, the cat by the dog, and so forth, until the Angel of Death

appeared to slay the butcher who had slain the ox. From then on for one week there was only unleavened bread, for the commemoration of the Exodus. Everything had to be eaten from dishes which were not used otherwise during the year.

Thus, life was arranged according to some high order; there was the rhythm of weeks and Sabbaths, of seasons and of feasts, and there was the profound symbolic separation of "pure" and "impure" which reached down into every profane activity.

Simultaneously with the aura of piety something else penetrated my life, of an altogether different nature—my contact with the social revolution. Although I was only twelve at the end of the war, I remember very well the scene of the post-war revolutionary period in Munich.

It all started with a book. Uncle Julius, on furlough from the front line, made a casual remark of praise about Barbusse's *Le Feu,* a war book which then was being widely read in all belligerent countries. I read it, and it was as if scales had dropped from my eyes. A new world was opened up, a world of new insights and feelings. I was at the age during which children develop the spiritual organs of emphatic perception; i.e., at the age when for the first time the strange neighbor in the street car becomes a feeling human being, a person who has the same eyes, the same sense of smell, the same brain, the same sensations as I myself. It is the age during which the range of sympathy suddenly extends far beyond those nearest to us, in fact it runs for some time the danger of cosmic dilution.

Until then war had been something distant, something that happened "out there"; it had been a matter of geography, of little colored flags pinned on maps. Now for the first time I saw what it really was: the dirt of trenches, the rain, the snow, floods, rats and corpses, the death of so many single human beings whom I might have known personally, and it was a fact that innocent human beings killed one another. The fact that all

these people could just as well have been personally acquainted
with one another, and could have been friends, was the most
stunning insight. It seemed due to an immoral clique of murderous capitalists and industrialists that these workmen, artisans,
clerks and peasants were sitting in mudholes for four years,
waiting to kill one another. Barbusse described with terribly
penetrating power, because he was devoured by a deep sense
of justice. At the end of his book he exhorted the soldiers with
the wrath of a prophet to make an end of a world of filthy op-
pression of which all the bourgeoisie, the society of bankers, professors, lawyers, priests, were guilty. The taximan of Berlin and
the factory-worker of Paris would have been good friends, had
they been living in the same street. Now they sneaked up on
each other until one could find an opportunity to shoot a bullet
into the other's head. I understood that this senseless deviltry
was somehow deeply associated with the faults of our society
and with the position of money in the world.

It was Karl Liebknecht who on August 1, 1914, had cried
"Down with War" in the streets of Berlin. It was Jaurès who had
been assassinated around the same time for his internationalism.
I read the letters of Rosa Luxemburg from prison. I read the
pre-war Reichstag speeches of Karl Liebknecht, in which he
compared infantile mortality in the rich and in the poor quarters
of Berlin. Liebknecht was shot from behind; Luxemburg's head
was bashed in with a rifle butt and her body was thrown into
the Landwehrkanal. All this was to me quite obviously connected
with the Berlin taximan and the Paris factory-worker; even the
most brutal crimes had to be committed to prevent their becoming friends, because this was dangerous for those who had accumulated much money.

I myself lived in the sheltering atmosphere of the middle-class,
the world to which my parents belonged. I experienced little of
the misery of the masses during the post-war years except for
what I saw in the industrial quarters of Munich and in the trains

during my home journeys. But misery, hopelessness and injustice were like a cold fog which creeps through tiniest fissures and through your very clothes.

Henri Barbusse had opened a door. In later years I wanted to get to the bottom of all this, and I began to study Karl Marx, and even the fundamentals of Hegelian philosophy. It seems strange that those two worlds, the world of Piety and the world of Revolution, were then not at all irreconcilable. I met many people with whom it was very much the same. Karl Marx has strongly Old Testament features of which we are not usually aware because of the disguise of nineteenth-century frills, Feuerbach's materialism and all that. If one were able to study him as a human being, one would probably find that his "opium for the people" is nothing but fury over those who use religion as opium for the people. His anger at industrial slavery, his apocalyptic concept of history are fed from the eternal well of truly prophetic anger. He had a glowing sense of justice, but he lacked metaphysical sense altogether. A justice which is of this world, a justice not at all transcendental, is something very dangerous. This I did not see at the time. Therefore, Karl Marx and the religion of the Old Testament represented two reconcilable ideas; in fact, their compatibility was not even questionable. Later I asked myself how it came about that I saw no contradiction between the world of Rabbi Ehrentreu and that of Karl Liebknecht. When, much later, I read what Berdyaev had to say about the prophetic-Messianic character of Marxism, I appreciated more fully my sentiments of that time.

The great religious philosopher, Martin Buber, must have been thinking of something similar when he called Gustav Landauer a "Jewish Prophet." I remember Landauer from a workers' parade, a haggard man with a long beard. He belonged to those who were brought in contact with politics after the war, during those years of misery. They were driven into politics, or at least into something they thought was politics. Before that he had

written a monograph of two volumes on Shakespeare. Later he
became the fiery representative of an non-Marxian socialism, the
Utopian ideal of Proudhon and Fourrier; he foresaw that a Marxist revolution would, in the end, give birth to a monster which
would far outdo Capitalism in lack of humanity and outright
cruelty.

Around Easter, 1919, there existed in Munich a short-lived
Soviet Republic. The Communists had become impatient because the World Revolution had stopped too long (two years)
at the frontiers of Russia. Wanting to speed things up a bit,
they chose two more or less rural lands, Hungary and Bavaria—
one of those poor jokes of the demon of history.

I was then thirteen, and I just caught one of the last trains to
leave Munich before the beleaguered city was in the midst of
a civil war. I was eagerly awaited at home. Although it was
usually a journey of half a day, it took us almost two days to
reach our destination. Journeys like these brought us bourgeois
children in contact with a life which seemed to be outside the
pale of protection. I had to sleep on the floor of a railway station
between workers with tin cans and peasant women with bundles.

On this particular occasion people asked me where I belonged, and without further explanation took me to a small town
in Lower Bavaria, where they sheltered me for the night in their
house. I saw that they were butchers with a small inn beside
the shop, as used to be the custom in Southern Germany. I was
taken through dark and musty corridors into a room without
windows in which there was a high bed with an oil print of the
Blessed Virgin above it, and a small lamp. The next morning
an old cook woke me up at five, gave me breakfast and showed
me the way to the station. When I arrived home I realized that
I did not even know the name of my hosts, nor could I have
found their house again.

My arrival was expected eagerly because this was to be my
Bar Mitzvah (feast of confirmation). This solemn feast is cele-

brated when a boy is thirteen and approaches for the first time the scroll of the Torah to pronounce the formulas of benediction. In houses with religious tradition the boy recites from the Torah and from the Prophets himself. This is done after he has been coached carefully in the proper intonation. My grandfather had given me the necessary instructions during the preceding vacations, and there were several rehearsals with the scroll which is written in Hebrew without punctuation.

Another boy happened to have his confirmation on the same Saturday. He had a peculiar lisp. The Cantor said to me: "Whatever you do, don't laugh. You are peculiar—even while you are serious you look as if you were laughing."

Finally the appointed day came. We put on dark blue suits, white shirts with collars and ties. At home the women busily prepared a gorgeous meal. There were many guests from abroad. The boy with the lisp said only the formulas of benediction. Nobody understood Hebrew or knew anything about the meaning of the texts, but this was a solemn moment; I suddenly heard myself sing with a loud voice, while the entire synagogue seemed strangely silent. It was in March, and the prophetic text of that Saturday was from Ezekiel:

The hand of the Lord was upon me, and brought me forth in the spirit of the Lord: and set me down in the midst of a plain that was full of bones. And he led me about through them on every side: now they were very many upon the face of the plain, and they were exceeding dry. And he said to me: Son of Man, dost thou think that these bones shall live? And I answered: O Lord God, thou knowest. And he said to me: Prophesy concerning these bones: Ye dry bones, hear the word of the Lord. Thus saith the Lord God to these bones: Behold, I will send spirit into you and you shall live. And I will lay sinews upon you, and will cause flesh to grow over you, and will cover you with skin: and I will give you spirit and you shall live, and you shall know that I am the Lord. And I prophesied as he had commanded me: and as I prophesied there was a noise, and behold a commotion, and the bones came together, each one to its joint. And I saw, and behold the sinews, and the flesh came up upon them:

and the skin was stretched out over them, but there was no spirit in them.

And he said to me: Prophesy to the spirit, prophesy, O Son of Man, and say to the spirit: Thus saith the Lord God: Come, spirit, from the four winds, and blow upon the slain, and let them live again. And I prophesied as he had commanded me: and the spirit came into them and they lived: and they stood up upon their feet, an exceeding great army. And he said to me: Son of Man: all these bones are the house of Israel: they say, our bones are dried up, our hope is lost and we are cut off. Therefore, prophesy and say to them: Thus says the Lord God: Behold I will open your graves and will bring you out of your sepulchres, oh my people, and will bring you into the land of Israel. And you shall know that I am the Lord, when I shall have opened your sepulchres, and shall have brought you out of your graves, oh my people. And shall have put my spirit into you, and you shall live and I shall make you rest upon your own land: and you shall know that I the Lord have spoken, and done it, saith the Lord God.

When I came home, Aunt Clara said it had been beautiful, she had almost cried. This was an attempt to be sarcastic. There was a gift table with the collected works of Schiller, Kleist, Uhland and Eichendorff, and numerous works on Polar expeditions and on Tibet. The dining table was drawn out to double its length. I said the thanksgiving for dinner. After that one of my cousins played Wagner's "Magic Fire" from *Valkyrie* on the piano.

By the time I got back to Munich the Soviet Republic had collapsed. Wagons full of soldiers were racing through the streets; the soldiers had white badges to show that they fought Communism, some had swastikas. The Communists, incidentally, had persuaded Gustav Landauer to join their government. After much hesitation he agreed. He must have known that the things he had to do were mostly the opposite of what he was thinking and saying. When the counter-revolutionary troops entered Munich, Landauer was killed. He was kicked with soldiers' boots and hit with rifle butts until he was dead.

4. Youth on the Move

THESE were the years of the German Youth Movement. On all country roads during the summer you saw groups of young people with long blouses made of some sort of dyed burlap, similar to Russian peasant shirts, tied with laces over the chest and reaching down to the knees. These *wandervögel* wore leather belts, rucksacks and heavy boots; some carried mandolins, guitars or flutes. They spent the nights in youth hostels and barns, or in the houses of peasants whom they helped with the harvest. During the winter they met in cheaply rented houses in the big cities, in converted garages or stables; they wore their strange costumes only during the summer when they began to migrate. While they gathered around fires in the forests or in the fields they practiced eurythmia, played ball games, or they "read." There was always something heavy, problematic and solemn about that reading. They read Plato and Ibsen, Dostoievsky's "Great Inquisitor" and Nietzsche's *Zarathustra.* There were Ultra-Nationalists (they undoubtedly formed the nucleus for the Hitler Youth to come), Catholics, Communists, Zionists and many others—and just plain *wandervögel* who did not bother with any "ism."

All of them had one thing in common: a rebellious attitude against their parents' generation, or at least against the mode of living of that generation. There was a sort of ascetic protest against everything "bourgeois"—no drinking, no smoking, no smart clothes. One boy denounced another as "bourgeois" because he ate chocolate candies filled with liqueur.

In the summer, incidentally, they did not migrate aimlessly; there was one central aim, the bundestag. It was the climax of a year; boys and girls of one bund from all over the country congregated, and there were speeches, resolutions, dancing, plays, singing, games and "reading" until late in the night around the fire.

Looking back at it now, we see what profound spiritual restlessness had seized the heart of Europe. For some unknown reason, the relationship between generations, particularly that between father and son, seems much more problematic in Germany than in Anglo-Saxon countries. Generalizations like this are usually questionable but here there is something quite characteristic, if one could only put one's finger on it. A teacher who was loved by his pupils was a great exception. As a whole, the relationship between teacher and pupil was quite different. In German funny magazines, in short stories, in Wilhelm Busch's poems, and on the stage, the teacher was always a victim of aggression and hostility. He was attacked by means of glue on the chair, stink bombs in the stove, noises of mysterious origin. It was not always funny. In reality, to some teachers life was hell on earth, they were ill-treated until they became sick. One has only to look at Wilhelm Busch's *Max and Moritz,* a children's book which has the same importance in Germany as *Alice* has in Anglo-Saxon countries. There the two boys play pranks, some of them murderous, on adults, and only adults, never on other children. Gunpowder is put into the teacher's pipe so that he literally explodes after lighting it and only his charred body remains. The lunch of an old widow is being lifted through the chimney by means of line and hooks.

Incidentally, that extraordinary significance of the struggle of generations, that most peculiar biological revolt is nothing new in German history. It existed as "Sturm und Drang" in the eighteenth century, it is immanent in the story of the Reformation, in other words, in the entire history of that German "protest" of which Dostoievsky spoke. There is no doubt that the anti-Christian attitude of the great and tragic Nietzsche was rooted in that sphere of personal experience. It was, more than anything else, something resembling a neurosis, a revolt against the father's house, with its delicate, bourgeois, somewhat emasculated Christianity of the nineteenth century. Other ministers' sons of the nineteenth century became evolutionists, vitalists or materialists; Nietzsche, however, made fun of God and tried to decapitate Him, acting just like Max and Moritz.

In the German Youth Movement which began before the First World War with the foundation of the *wandervögel,* youth par excellence—the Platonic idea of youth, so to speak—found expression and a specific form. Youth aspired to be more than a stage of development or a miniature edition of adulthood; it was something *per se.*

You could see that even in the Jewish Youth Movement in Germany. In Poland and in Russia there were Zionist youth associations the main function of which was to spread Zionist ideas and to prepare young Jews for life in Palestine. There was an immediate connection between the group in Poland and the settlements in Palestine. When it came to "Blau-Weiss," that Jewish *wandervögel* organization which was originally the strongest of its kind in Germany, the whole thing was quite different. More than anything else "Blau-Weiss" was reaction against middle-class culture, against a parent-generation, against a colorless form of liberalism and assimilation, against the "German citizen of Jewish denomination." There were, to be sure, individual cases of emigration to Palestine, but those who had emigrated abandoned the Youth Movement as their moral and cultural basis. By the time youth ended, movement came to an end too.

However, it was not always like this, as we shall see presently. The "Jung-Jüdischer Wanderbund" (Young Jewish Wanderers) to which I belonged was similar to "Blau-Weiss." In the beginning it claimed to be neutral in its political tendencies; you could be Zionist or anything. This changed as time went on, perhaps under the influence of growing anti-semitism. When I belonged

to it, one might have called the whole thing pluralistic. Some
of our older leaders were strong personalities. They were not
chosen on account of any particular allegiance, either German
or Zionist or Socialist, but merely because they happened to be
good at softball or literature. Due to this fact, the bund had something loose, free and mobile, something really youthful. Almost
every one of us had a leader whom he followed. They were
usually university students whom one could ask for advice.

Our "home" was in the Thierschstrasse, next to Hitler's original
headquarters, above an old garage. Here we had our evenings
and our courses. I gave a course on *Macbeth* for girls. In summer
came migration and the bundestag which was usually held in
Franconia or in Thuringia, preferably in a castle. Off we walked
into the mountains or along the Main and Rhine valleys. In
retrospect I must say that the dances, the softball, the tour, and
the nights in the barns were the most beautiful parts of it all.
But that is not the reason why I dwell on such details. I do so
because, with all that playfulness, there was a general mood
which seemed to point at events which later came to pass. Latent
in the situation were sorrows, questions and doubts pointing towards the great Jewish catastrophe—or rather the great European catastrophe with which the fate of the Jews was interwoven
in so mysterious a fashion. Let me take as examples the stories
of three of us, which are fairly representative.

There was, for instance, Erna, a girl of fifteen from Munich.
She came from a typical Jewish middle-class environment; her
father was a lawyer. She was a slim, tall girl with blue eyes and
brown hair, which she wore in long braids. When it came to
walking, cooking, washing or softball she seemed to have inexhaustible energy. She was a source of freshness, health and
cleanliness to all around her. In the woods she would heat a
kettle of gruel over the open fire, and at our "home" she was
an untiring scrubber. One day she began to occupy herself, all
of a sudden, with the social question. This seemed to happen

under the influence of one of the leaders, but soon we noticed that she worked more and more in the slums, and after a few years she joined the Communist Party. I lost contact with her until one day when her name appeared in newspapers all over the world. Single-handed, she had liberated her husband, a young Communist worker, from a prison in Berlin. It was an incredible Wild West story; somehow she got into the Moabit jail and threatened an unarmed guard with an unloaded revolver. A successful hold-up carried out by a girl in a jail in the middle of Berlin! The police never found them, though much later I heard that during the Hitler era she was deported by some South American government back to Germany. According to another version, she was killed in Russia during a purge.

The second story is that of Friedel Fränkel. Friedel Fränkel was a short, broad-shouldered boy with ugly, coarse features, wiry hair, a low forehead and a long upper lip. He looked like a bull calf of the Aberdeen Angus breed. He looked bluish-black even when he had just shaved. He was an employee in one of the best Munich stores. Friedel showed very early contempt for all that was called Capitalism, which was quite a lot. The more he read Dostoievsky, Tolstoy and the writings of the early Halutzim (Zionist pioneers who established co-operatives; they were, incidentally, influenced by Tolstoy), the less he found their ideas compatible with his career. Curiously enough, and this is the reason why I write about him, his attitude towards Marxist socialism was just as bitter. It was mainly his study of the great Russians and his simple and peasant-like way of reasoning which brought him to that conclusion. He was stubborn. He wanted to have nothing to do with the socialists who, he thought, were intellectuals whose main function it was to chat in cafés and studios while the workers had to fight on the barricades. As to Dostoievsky, to him Western capitalism and Marxist socialism were practically the same thing and towards the socialists among us he was rather sarcastic. He was not intelligent, in fact he

was a little stupid, but he was original and followed a straight
line. There was no one else among us whose ideas were exactly
like his. With stubborn self-restriction he did what he thought
was right; he gave up his promising position in the store and
became an apprentice to a cobbler in a suburb. His relatives had
hoped for a rocket-like career, as a retail merchant-king; they
were bewildered and offended. The moment he made his first pair
of shoes all by himself, he sailed for Palestine, settled in a
village, and founded a family. His was the story of a successful
narodnik (as those Russian intellectuals who "took to the people"
used to be called). When he is an old man and succeeds in getting through all the political earthquakes while his colleagues in
the retail business are killed or dispersed over the globe, somebody ought to write his history. It could be done in the style of
Tolstoy's folk stories, under the title "The Cobbler from Munich."

Rudi Herz was a boy of the same generation. He was a child
of an environment which is unique and can never be quite described, the "better" Jewish middle-class. I believe his father
had to do with the textile industry. There has never been a
Sinclair Lewis to describe the peculiar void, the lack of purpose,
the absence of anything which would give roots or blossoms to
this environment—the colorless "goodness," the efficiency without inner goal, the peculiar anemia deprived of the red blood
of Jewish tradition, and transfused with the saline of a political
liberalism. Rudi Herz began—also, it seemed, suddenly—to delve
into Hebrew, Scripture and Talmud, and to associate himself with
an Orthodox community. His parents found him with *tephillin*
in the morning, wrapped in a prayer-shawl. He kept all ascetic
exercises, and very soon no longer partook of his parents' meals
and began to eat from his own plates. He changed from a business clerk into a strict ascetic who sat in the evenings stooped
over huge volumes of Talmud. This, however, was not enough.
He, like Friedel, found his occupation in discrepancy with what
he studied in his books. He quit the career which his parents had

chosen for him, and became a farmer. He was one of the first leaders of the farming schools for Misrahi, the Zionist movement of Orthodox Jews. He is now one of the leaders of the *misrahi chalutziuth,* those Orthodox Zionists whose central theme is a movement back to the land and to handicraft and life in co-operatives. Incidentally, he had a genuine inner relationship to art, particularly the Primitives and Renaissance painting. He always had reproductions of medieval altar pictures and of Giotto on his walls. All this belonged to him in a way I cannot define—a Jewish-Orthodox farmer with a Madonna of the early Rhenish School!

Three young people illustrate the doubts which were shaking the young generation, and the various roads which we took. They show the mood of bewilderment and restlessness which had seized a great part of Jewish youth ten years before the catastrophe. They are examples of brave ones who acted as they thought right. For the majority, to which I belonged, the Youth Movement was half play; we followed the line of least resistance. The leader who had converted Erna to Communism became a well-paid business executive in the United States. Today, when I think of the invisible Church, I see those three young people who, during the first grumblings of a cataclysm, followed their pure hearts and remained steadfast. I particularly see Rudi Herz with his ascetic features and his black skullcap, and behind him reproductions of Giotto and Michelangelo.

I was the only other one who had turned to religion. My experience was quite different from that of Rudi Herz, whose parents admired him for his conversion. I too began to live the life of an Orthodox Jew. I got up one hour before school time and, after having said the appropriate form of benediction, I wrapped myself in the prayer-shawl. Then, again with the prayers of benediction, I put on the *tephillin.* These are leather straps to which a capsule is attached. This capsule contains on a small parchment the famous Biblical passage: "Hear Israel the Lord thy God is one. Thou shalt love thy God with all thy heart, all thy soul and all thy power. . . ." It also says, "Take my words well to your heart . . . as a sign tie them to your hand and as a band between your eyes . . . write them onto your doorposts and onto your doors. . . ." Consequently pious Jews the world over, during Morning Prayer, tie these words written on parchment onto their left wrist close to where one feels the pulse; a second capsule is tied to the forehead; another capsule is permanently nailed to the door.

After the *tephillin* have been put on, the Morning Prayer begins with the words: "How beautiful are thy tents, O Jacob, and thy dwellings, O Israel. . . ." The Morning Prayer is a long and tedious affair to anyone who does not read Hebrew fluently. If one attempted to dwell on every word, it would take hours. Actually it has a harmonious liturgical structure, with the Psalms, the repetitive formulas (comparable to Litanies), the "Hear Israel" and the Eighteen Prayers. The latter are a liturgical text which is contained in each one of the three prayers of the day— the Morning Prayer, the Afternoon Prayer and the Evening Prayer. Pious Jews make these three devotions every day. They often do this with astounding rapidity, but not at all irreverently; they get into the spirit of the liturgy without having to dwell on the meaning of each word.

When I first came home on vacation, my parents and Grandfather exchanged glances of bewilderment. I used to get up long before breakfast and, in my room underneath the gable of the house, in solitude I began to put on the prayer-shawl and the *tephillin*. It takes a long time of repeated performances to tie the *tephillin* around one's left arm and one's forehead quickly, in routine fashion. Then the entire Morning Prayer faced me like a huge body of water. The trouble was that I could read Hebrew only with considerable effort:

As long as this soul is in me I thank you, Lord, my God and God
of my fathers. Master of all creatures, Lord of all souls. Blessed art
thou, O Lord, who returnest the souls to the dead. . . .

Thou who makest the blind see, who clothest the naked, who
freest the prisoners, who comfortest those who mourn, who hast
made the earth so that it renders all that is necessary to man and
also to myself. . . .

Lord of all the worlds, not on the grounds of any virtue of ours
but relying on thy infinite mercy. . . .

But we, thy people, the fellows of thy covenant, the children of
Abraham, to whom thou hast assured thy love on the mountain of
Moria, we, the descendants of Isaak, his only son who was offered
to thee on the altar, the community of Jacob, my firstborn son whom
thou, out of love, has named Israel and Yeshurun. . . .

Thus it went on, through many Psalms of David to the Hymn
of the Celestial Host, to "thy servants of many kinds" who

chosen in love, carry out the will of their creator, they open their
mouths in purity and holiness in order to sing hymns and praise the
holy name of God, blessed be He. They all take up the yoke of the
heavenly kingdom and sing with their creator the holy song of praise.
With a joyful mind, in pure tongues and in holy devotion they
humbly say: "Holy holy holy is the Lord Sabbaoth, all the earth is
full of his glory."

From this it went on to the "Hear Israel." By the time I had
finally reached the Eighteen Prayers the end was in sight. To
those of my friends who had grown up in the orthodox religion
all this was pleasant and they said everything by heart. I had
always that dragging sensation. In many places I did not understand the words, and towards the end I was glad to get through.
When I came downstairs, nobody was left at the breakfast table.

I kept strict dietary laws, as much as I could in a household
as impious as that of my parents. I kept even my own set of
china and cutlery, and soon I was surrounded by a cloud of
ascetic detachment like a yogi. At dinner after having eaten I
would remain at the table and, with a black skullcap, say the

long benediction which follows every main meal. They all tried
to get up before that, or to look away. They behaved very much
like a family of which one member has gone insane. Father tried
to see it all in a humorous light and teased me goodheartedly.
He addressed me as "Rabbi." Grandfather was annoyed, and
Mother was deeply distressed. When she first sent me to the
Kohen family, she had asked Frau Kohen not to influence
me in the direction of Jewish orthodoxy. Frau Kohen had
promised, but she could not prevent the atmosphere of orthodox
Jewry from reaching me. And now this! It was as if I had turned
on some dark machine of superstition upstairs in my room every
morning. That entire world of Spinoza, Goethe, Voltaire, Heine,
Uncle Julius, political liberalism, and the Age of Reason seemed
to be denied by an act of lunacy. For some obscure and repellent
reason I had turned my back on progress. I am sure Mother was
afraid I was going crazy.

A family council was called. Uncle Julius made a special trip
and the family delegated him to talk to me. He came into my
bedroom and told me that all this was perfectly idiotic and impossible. He told me about his trips around the world; there were
hundreds of millions of people who believed one thing with
absolute conviction, and hundreds of millions who believed another with the same degree of conviction. He told me particularly
about his experiences with Hindus and Mohammedans. The gist
of it was that religion was a purely relative cultural phenomenon.
Anyone who, as a Western educated person, found absolute
truth in one religion, must be either insane or imbecile.

I found his argument about the many religions very strong
and said that I did not know anything about Hindus, Buddhists
and Mohammedans but that we Jews had a special mission in
the world. He said: "That's what all the others say, too." The
thing that annoyed me was that he did not acknowledge me as
an even partner in the discussion, and kept insisting on his age
and his greater experience. I was fifteen, and he was forty-one,

and therefore he believed I had to listen to him without argument.

It seems extraordinary that, within the Young Jewish Movement, Rudi Herz and I were quite isolated. Those who had become Zionist spoke of the rejuvenation of Jewry, of the reestablishment of a Jewish homeland, of the soil of Palestine, and of the revival of the Hebrew language, as if it were something like the rebirth of Yugoslavia, or Ireland or Czechoslovakia. The specific element of the Jewish religious tradition was missing. Many were enthusiastic Socialists. The Bible, that is to say the Old Testament, came in only as cultural tapestry, very much as if a Scandinavian country were to revive a study of the Edda. Socialism, on the other hand, was embraced with religious fervor, and it represented for most a realm of justice and charity far transcending its actual political meaning.

Equally peculiar was the fact that we were all very much under the influence of Christian writers like Friedrich Wilhelm Foerster and the Russians. Friedrich Wilhelm Foerster is a German pedagogian, very close to the teaching of the Catholic Church. He was a radical Pacifist; so much so, that after the First World War he denounced to the Allied Commissions anything which in the remotest way resembled rearmament, either technically or ideologically. In his pedagogic writings he exhorted young people to a life of heroic virtue, a life of self-denial and sacrifice. On account of his radical pacifism he was extremely endangered by German rightist groups, and it may have been for the purpose of protecting him that the radical socialist Government of Bavaria made him Bavarian minister in Switzerland. Although he was not a Catholic he was in the habit of quoting such writers as Saint Catherine of Siena and Saint Teresa of Avila.

We were even more influenced by the religious writings of Tolstoy, his legends and his folk-stories, and by the great Christian figures of Dostoievsky—Prince Myshkin and Alyosha Karamasov. Friedrich Wilhelm Foerster's heroic asceticism, for exam-

ple in his *Guide for Youth,* exerted considerable influence on
many young members of the Misrahi, the Jewish Orthodox
Youth Movement.

As far as my stab at Orthodoxy was concerned, I very soon
yielded to the pressure brought upon me by my family. I have
a strong suspicion that I used it as an excuse to discontinue
Morning Prayer, Afternoon Prayer, Evening Prayer, and the
sacrifices involved in the dietary and the Sabbath laws. I had
an alibi: it created too much friction and unrest in the family.
My faith cannot have been as strong as that of Rudi Herz and
that of my Misrahi friends; or I would not have given way.
There were many conflicting influences, and I was ready for
compromise. After all, not even Friedel Fränkel understood why
religious forms and the liturgical life were necessary. Perhaps
even my Marxist friends were right; or Mother and Uncle Julius,
Voltaire, Heine, the *Berliner Tageblatt,* and Progress.

If I thought that Mother was more accessible to the national
ideas of the Jewish movement, divested from their religious
context, I was very much mistaken. I argued with her. I said
that it was very fine for Romain Rolland or Bernard Shaw to
condemn national or racial ideas but that the people in the street
and my classmates regarded us as an alien people. It was unrealistic to listen to a handful of European intellectuals, instead
of accepting the fact that we were not regarded as Germans in
Germany or Frenchmen in France. She would have to admit
that Einstein was also very learned, and he was a Zionist. Whenever he was asked for his nationality, he proudly stated he was
a Jew. She said she did not care how great a physicist Einstein
was; nationalist philosophy in any form, whether Jewish or
Japanese, was detestable to her.

I was torn by conflicting motives. On one hand I admired the
noble super-racial, truly European spirit of such people as Romain Rolland and Friedrich Wilhelm Foerster, which was shared
by my mother. On the other hand I thought it ignoble and

cowardly not to identify oneself openly and emphatically with a despised minority. There seemed to be nothing very noble about the fact that so many Jews had a blind spot for their Jewishness.

This was in the early Twenties, and in the Ukraine around that time occurred one of the worst pogroms of the pre-Hitlerian era. It was carried out during the course of the civil war in Russia, under General Petljura, one of the leaders of the White Army. Thousands of Jews were killed, among them old people, women and children. We, the members of the Jewish Youth Movement, canvassed the Jewish families in Munich in a campaign to raise money for the victims of the pogrom. In the light of what occurred to us later, I remember my experiences as a canvasser very well. The Ukraine must have seemed very far away; the horrible fate of the Jews struck quite a few of their brethren in Munich as something remote and foreign. Even those who gave me money reacted as if I were begging for victims of a mining accident in South America. German apartment doors have a small window just big enough to allow one eye to look through, and a safety chain. A single eye would gaze at me, and the door would open slightly with the safety chain on. I made my little speech about the Ukrainian pogroms. Quite often, I am embarrassed to say, the door closed again without the safety chain being taken off; one heard a shuffling of steps, and there was no further response. Little did we realize what was to happen ten years later.

5. Franz Burger

THOSE post-war years in Europe were times when the soil of history seemed to be plowed and receptive for any kind of grain. Germany was more than ever a world of contrasts and obscure tension. In the Ludwigstrasse in Munich one saw old generals martially decorated, like stuffed horses on wheels, while nearby in a Schwabing bookshop an etching was exhibited: the Crucified, nailed to the Cross by scoffing soldiers of the Reichswehr—"To the Memory of Karl Liebknecht." The teachers were already stuffing us with Nibelungengeist and political sauerkraut.

They all did it, except Franz Burger. He came from the Inn valley near Wasserburg, a region which had always received a stream of immigrants from the south, originally Romans, and much later artisans from Italy. He had been a Catholic to begin with, and I believe he had studied for the priesthood. When I knew him he was estranged from the Church but he was one of those creative, serene-tragic Mediterranean humanists who sow the seed of culture wherever Fate puts them.

He was our teacher in German and Latin. Under his guidance the *Annals* of Tacitus became documents of vital interest. Ovid and Virgil came alive. During the German lessons he read with us the poems of Rilke and Werfel. He even told us about Freud, Adler and Jung, as far as we eighteen-year-old boys were able to take it in. I remember Goethe's *Tasso* with which we did part-reading like actors on the stage, single poems by Goethe, André Gide's *Prodigal Son*, Horace, and especially Virgil.

One day, when he spoke during the history lesson of industrialization during the last century and of Karl Marx, an elderly pedagogic official appeared for inspection. Our teacher carried on quietly as if nobody were there for inspection. After that we were sure something was going to "happen," but nothing did. He was admired by everybody, including his enemies.

We knew that there was something sad and painful in his life. His wife was insane, and he kept her at home. Often I visited him at his home, especially later after I had left school, and I shall never forget that weird picture: Franz Burger, the humanist, in his library, a large room with huge bookshelves all around the walls, a room which exuded an atmosphere of spiritual shelter; and somewhere hidden in a room behind there was a pale, delicate Ophelia who appeared suddenly, when cne least expected it. The daughters, Marcella and Melitta, were beautiful, proud and downcast at the same time. Thus, the world of this man who was to make such a lasting impression on all our lives was a strange mixture of Goethean detachment and Dostoievskian demonism—a symbolic image of those post-war years in which we grew up.

During the last years of his life he was seized by some horrible disease, the nature of which was never quite known. He developed a severe spastic condition of his legs combined with cerebellar symptoms. He became very thin. His beautiful head became more transparent and ghost-like, and his deep-seated eyes shone like huge dark lakes. In the few years that were left to him he could neither stand nor walk. But he did not want to rest. His pupils fetched him, on their own accord, every morning in a wheel chair, and after school they took him home.

Thus it went on until his last few weeks. When I saw him then he was bedridden. It was spring, 1933. The Hitler Government consisted then of a coalition which was called conservative, and which impressed most people as an embarrassing episode. Burger gave me then, a week before his death, a peculiarly lucid forecast of all that actually came to happen.

When I think of Burger today a flood of seemingly disconnected impressions and sensations comes back to me. First there was the big handsome man with such a fascinating head that people in the Leopoldstrasse would turn round to look at him. Then there was the man fatally ill, lying on the pillows. On one side there was the German Gymnasium [high school] with its cloud of cultural mist and sweat; on the other was this man who came out of the cloud like a strange, mythical messenger. He instilled in us the religious sense of justice present in those socialists of the early industrial period—Marx, Engels, and

Lasalle; and he used to warn us not to mistake the philosophical materialism of the writer Karl Marx with the moral conduct of the person. "A man who lives in a London attic and saves money for a theater ticket is not a materialist in the sense in which the bourgeoisie uses this word." It is true that most people who understand the inherent evil of the philosophy of historical materialism have never experienced the transcendental dynamism which characterized all early socialists. It was Engels who once said that people think a materialist is a man to whom eating and drinking are the only important things in life.

Burger had one weakness: a secret love for Bismarck. He shared this paradox with many German liberals of his time. Perhaps it was due to the fact that Bismarck was the first man to oppose Kaiser Wilhelm the Second. Alas, those charming Bismarck lessons! Living today in a world of partisanship, forced on us by current events, it is perhaps difficult to imagine the logic immanent in that phase of humanism.

Once Burger asked me who my favorite poet was. I answered: "Liliencron." He was really disappointed, because Liliencron was a Prussian Junker who wrote "healthy" poetry, a sort of provincial Kipling, whose work was pervaded by the smell of horses and leather. Burger would so much have liked me to share his love for the *Duino Elegies* of Rilke, or for Franz Werfel. Like many adolescents, however, I was shy of everything that was twilight-like. If poetry had to be, then I preferred the horses and stables of Liliencron.

It was 1924, one year after the failure of Hitler's and Ludendorff's beer cellar *putsch*. Germany was already in the throes of an infectious disease to which it would finally succumb. Around this time Rilke's room in a boarding-house near our school was ransacked by the Bavarian police. He swore never to return to Germany and I believe he never wrote another German line until his death.

Just as the generals were displaying their medals, our classmates wore daggers, revolvers and arm-ribbons. It is incomprehensible to me that, in spite of their admiration for Burger and their scorn for the Nibelung professors, not one among them adopted Burger's social and cosmopolitan pathos. I gave such fellow-students Romain Rolland's *Jean Christophe* and Henri Barbusse to read; I spoke to them of Gandhi. However, Rolland and Gandhi were "aesthetes" who represented Judaism and weakness to them. Judaism and weakness were expressions of one single thing which they could not define. They appreciated Barbusse, but only as a naturalist painter of battles and of soldierly life. This made it possible to forgive him his social and political conclusions.

It often appears that everything revolutionary has somewhere at its roots an impulse of justice, no matter what degree of brutality it reaches in the end. To be sure there were perhaps a few fellows who were sincere in their protest against the Versailles "dictate of shame." Apart from those few, however, I saw examples of rebellion without aim, of a cynical liking for revolution, and a love of protest and force for their own sake.

Even today, when I think of those eighteen-year-olds, I have the feeling one has while facing a man with some uncanny mental disturbance. The writings of Nietzsche or Dostoievsky or Rauschning about the German "Protest for the sake of protest," and the "Revolution of nihilism" may seem like historical speculations. But I can say that I really saw it operating among the youngsters in Munich during the post-war years.

At that time, ten years before Hitler, there were social rules and regulations about the Jews similar to what one saw ten years later all over the country. Jewish children learned, as a matter of course, to take a position comparable to that of the Negro below the Mason-Dixon line. A friend told me that he and another boy, the only two Jews in the class, always stood apart during recess because nobody ever spoke to them. During a school trip to one of the lakes there were only two rowboats on hand; they had a boat to themselves.

It was not quite so bad in our school. It became still better when Franz Burger became our class professor. One day he asked me to give a lecture on the Jewish problem. He asked the leader of the Nazis to prepare himself for opening the discussion. This leader was a giant of a boy who made a cult out of "thunder of steel," "Front experience," and dying and yet there was something sultry and expansive about his emotional life; with all his war philosophy he would read poems about his mother with tears in his eyes, and faint during vaccination.

I was not looking forward to my speech. My adversary prepared himself with the usual "data" about the "Protocols of Zion" and such things. One could never know beforehand what "scientific material" he might bring up. It so happened, however, that the day chosen for our discussion was one of the high Jewish holidays. Burger refused to change the date and decided to give the lecture himself while the Jewish boys were absent. Thus, on the Jewish New Year in the autumn of 1924, while we were praying in the synagogue, our teacher made a brilliant speech in favor of us during our absence. From then on, our position among our classmates was even more improved.

In our class at that time there were four Jewish pupils. Three of these, including myself, were more or less Zionist and one belonged to the *Kameraden,* the German-Jewish group who devoted themselves to "German culture." It is interesting that the Nazis were friendlier to the three of us who were "consciously Jewish" than to the poor lad who gave his annual class lecture about some German war poet. They identified Zionism with racial segregation of the Jews, and they were right in doing so. Therefore, they thought they recognized in all this a part of their own national ideology and developed a benevolent attitude towards us.

6. *Mother*

I NEVER understood why Mother was never radical on any one of these issues. She was not outspoken enough for my taste, at any rate. All her sympathies were with the Independent Socialists and Pacifists. I remember the following example.

We all were deeply moved when the first premier of the new Bavarian Republic, Kurt Eisner, was assassinated by a Monarchist, Count Arco. Eisner, incidentally, was the one who had sent Professor Foerster as Bavarian Minister to Switzerland. He was one of those revolutionaries who are quite out of place in the game of practical politics: I always remember that he wrote an essay on the Ninth Symphony. He was one of those idealistic Marxists with a thin "materialistic" veneer that could be found all over Europe in the early post-war years. He was certainly an incongruous figure in a Bavaria which was rural and petit bourgeois with not much industrial proletariat. However, to Mother and me he was an embodiment of the ideas we stood for. One day, while on his way from his office to the Parliament buildings, he was ambushed by Count Arco and killed instantly. I learned of it accidentally, overhearing a conversation in a street car, and I reacted with the violence of youth in the face of injustice and brutality. I could not understand why the entire world did not feel and think like Liebknecht, Jaurès, Eisner, Barbusse, the radical socialists and the radical pacifists. I was stunned and bewildered to see violence destroying these people; it was like being overwhelmed by the mystery of iniquity. Is it perhaps this utter incomprehensibility which leads young people to accept the Marxian dialectics of history, because by this cold scientific system the disquieting mystery of Evil seems to be explained away? On hearing the news that day, I rushed to the place of assassination. There was a spot of fresh blood on the sidewalk and in front of it a poster: "Proletarians, take your hat off before the blood of Kurt Eisner!" Most people passed by. A few stopped and stood there sheepishly. No one took his hat off. Soon meetings were being held by students of the University of Munich demanding mitigation of the punishment of Count Arco. He was celebrated as a hero and as a liberator from tyranny. Mother felt that they should be as mild towards him as possible. This I simply could not understand; things had to be black or white.

Similarly, although she condemned Zionism on principle, she admired many of my Zionist friends. This, too, seemed illogical to me. There was Reha Freier, for instance. Reha (short for Rebekka) was, when I first knew her, quite young. She was married to a Rabbi. She was beautiful, of a simple Biblical beauty, someone right out of the Old Testament. She represented a type which occurs in every political or religious movement, the sort of person who causes others to despair. She seemed utterly disorganized and full of unbelievably impractical ideas. Although she was a mother of five I am not sure whether she could have fried an egg or made tea. If she did it she might have kept her hat on, even her overcoat—and it would most likely be a man's coat. She was an extraordinary linguist, and she was able to keep an audience spellbound. Her Hebrew was beautiful. When she had, in an emergency, to travel to some Balkan country, she was able to learn, on the train, enough of the language to make a speech. Since she thought and lived on a plane of practical impossibilities, she actually carried things out which no practical person could have achieved. She was the first one to have the idea (long before anyone knew what Nazis were) of getting Jewish children out of Europe and settling them on farms in Palestine. She had this idea before the great American Jewess Henrietta Szold conceived it, or at least quite independent of her. When there was a pogrom in a Rumanian town, it was not impossible for her to travel there and appear before the mayor, demanding that they organize a transport of Jewish children, a special train and everything. It was her strong point to appear before the most unlikely people, wide-eyed and with flowing robes, speaking not in terms of committee meetings and majority resolutions but in the language which King David used in his Psalms. With this embarrassingly naive and direct method she occasionally had stunning success. My mother was fascinated by this woman who presented in every respect the opposite of her own disciplined and spartan attitude.

As a young married woman Mother had suffered a bad attack of rheumatic fever. After Ludwig's birth she showed increasing signs of heart disease. Like so many fragile and sensitive people, she was intolerant towards anything that smacked of self-pity, and much of her ascetic philosophy seems to have been an attempt to overcome her tenderness. This, at any rate, is the way the psychologists would put it. As we see so often in people who have this streak, she drew no line between hypochondriasis and common medical prudence. Thus, when she was expecting Ludwig, she knew of her heart condition but made a point of disregarding it. I remember so well that even on the eve of his birth she worked in the store, lifting bales of cloth. During the early years of Ludwig's life she became short of breath but practiced numerous tricks to conceal it. She would go with us on hiking trips in the surrounding country, or to village church feasts, and would find some pretext to pause and catch her breath. These pauses increased in length. The women of the neighborhood told her to look after herself, but she laughed about it.

One evening in 1923 she asked me to play the piano to her while she rested in the adjoining bedroom. While I was playing, I suddenly heard a peculiar moaning sound from her direction. When Father and I got there she looked at us in a strange questioning way and muttered some incoherent syllables.

Her left side, arm and leg did not move. The doctor told us that it was a case of embolism. Her speech was restored within a few hours, but her left side remained paralyzed. Her left arm remained completely out of action, her left leg shuffled with the typical gait of the half-paralyzed.

The next two years entailed much agony. She laughed and cried more easily than before, and laughing or crying looked like a cramp of the face. She lost nearly all her hair. I had a suspicion that Father and Grandfather were embarrassed about her appearance, and that she felt it. Again she worked in the store. She even made business trips to visit wholesale firms in Munich. She refused to give in, and people had to pretend that there was nothing wrong with her. She had no illusions about the future. Father appeared irritated when she urged him to remarry in case anything should happen to her.

It was during these two years that she drew very close to me. Ludwig was only seven, and she was worried about what would become of him. It was probably then that I got my first glimpse into the meaning of anonymity and simplicity in the face of suffering. In January, 1925, just two months before my matriculation, she and Father visited me in Munich. I told her that the class, probably under the influence of Burger, had elected me to give the valedictory address at the final celebrations. However, I was in competition with another fellow, one of the "parallel class" (there were usually two or even three classes matriculating simultaneously in one school). In the event that I was the final choice, I had what I thought to be a very clever idea. I wanted to go up to the platform and speak to the teachers, parents and guests about the fact that we who matriculated were a chosen lot, chosen only by virtue of the economic or social strata into which we were born. Every pupil should know that, on the same day on which he was born, a boy was born in the slums. This boy might be in possession of the same mental and physical talents, but what would his life have been up to this moment? I intended to continue to describe not the course of our lives up to the solemn hour of matriculation, but that of one of those unknowns who grew up in our shadow. Finally, I would allude to the possible moral and political responsibilities arising from all this. I was very much impressed by this idea. It was quite unconventional, and I thought I was smart. When I considered all the stuffed-shirt professors and parents who would be in the audience, I was frightened by my boldness but the more I was frightened the more it appeared an unavoidable duty. I liked to see myself as a courageous rebel.

My parents were in Munich only for two days. As usual they wanted to go to plays and concerts. The first night we went to hear *Parsifal.* I still see my paralyzed mother there, looking and listening. In the Prinzregententheater the orchestra pit is invisible, especially designed by Wagner himself. On the stage there moved some high-bosomed women and obese men, enacting some sort of unreal slow-motion tragedy. From the bowels of the theater came the wailing sounds of a music whose humid sensuousness and subjectivism is intended to indicate "religion," or something which the artist believed to be religion. It was a strenuous and embarrassing experience. The only bright spot was the interval with sandwich rolls and beer. The next evening we went to see a comedy *The Dead Aunt,* an extremely hilarious play, which dealt with the reactions of people to the death of a relative. Mother identified herself with the dead aunt, and as the evening progressed she recuperated from *Parsifal.* Even on the platform, while saying good-bye, she remembered the dead aunt and began to laugh her distorted spastic laughter. Speaking of the dead aunt, she asked me not to stay one day after matriculation, and to hurry home as soon as I could. She thought my great speech was not so important.

On March tenth, on the last day of the matriculation exams, I received a telegram; Mother was seriously ill and I should come home immediately. I took the next train. Two stations before our home-town I discovered one of our neighbors in the same carriage. He came over to me with swaying gait and his breath smelled of beer. "My most cordial condolence," he said. This is the German stereotype formula of courtesy. It meant that Mother had died.

In small Jewish communities there exists no such person as a professional undertaker. Even liberal communities, which otherwise are lax in formal religious tradition, adhere to the old custom of the "Holy Brotherhood," that is a group of men and women who voluntarily attend to the dead. This is regarded as an important act of charity. In case of the death of a man there exists a group of men, in case of a woman there is a group of women. Their business is to wash and clothe the dead man and keep a nightwatch at his bed during the night he remains at home. In all religions, when it comes to matters of death, even the most liberal groups and individuals tend to retain traditional customs.

The Catholic cemetery was close to the center of the town. The Jews had a small plot of land which was situated on a hill, in the middle of fields, quite far from our town. Everything Jewish was a matter of curiosity and weird fascination to the non-Jewish people. Hence it often happened that boys would climb over the walls of the Jewish cemetery. In order to prevent this the top of the wall was spiked with glass fragments. There was neither chapel nor morgue, it was just a bare plot of land without buildings. The Catholic morgue had a little sideroom for the Jewish dead. As is well known, Jewish custom forbids anything decorative associated with funerals. The dead must be buried in unadorned boxes. Not even flowers are allowed. This serves to stress the fact that in death there is no class distinction, and symbolizes the equality of men before God. Thus, when I saw Mother, she was resting in some sort of unpainted oblong crate. I still see the bare sideroom with an unlit pipestove in the middle, the cement floor, the crate, Mother's face with the mouth a little open, the eyes closed, and yet not sleep-like, with an expression of remoteness, as if looking away from all of us. The funeral was a huge affair. It looked as if half the town had turned out. I do not know how much this was due to curiosity, and how much to the popularity of the dead person.

The cortege gathered near the precincts of the Catholic cemetery, then we walked behind a horse-drawn hearse for about two miles along the highway, then along a dirt road up to the hill. The entire Jewish cemetery seemed full of people; boys managed to cling to the wall, notwithstanding the glass fragments. Somewhere in the middle we were standing, a group of men with our hats on. Grandfather, as usual, was quite pedantic about the details of the ritual. He seemed to conduct everything. The Cantor made a speech which was obviously taken from some book of speeches, and had no personal relation whatsoever to the deceased. Father and I said the Kadish, "Glorified and sanctified be thy great name. . . ." Ludwig was only nine, he was not supposed to say anything. He just stood beside me with his hat on. Then we threw the first clumps into the pit. My grief at the time seems to have been surprisingly short. I had just finished high school, and I had to make a decision about the future. It was a time of transition and of many excitements. When a girl friend in Munich met me for the first time after my mother's death, she approached me with a deadly serious face and stretched her hand out. I had to stop and think for a moment to realize what it was about.

During the following year Grandfather, Father and Ludwig lived in that house like three sailors marooned on an island. When I was at home, it became even stranger. Since I was then nineteen and Ludwig only nine, there was the impression of four generations of men. It was a house of four males who appeared to walk around with an air of aimlessness. When I later read in the medical literature of the behavior of men in high altitudes, the "first stage" always reminded me somehow of us four in that house. In a sense, the atmosphere really had lost a certain amount of oxygen; all this in spite of the fact that we still had Therese, our faithful old maidservant, and Mother, after all, had been quite out of action the last year of her life.

Grandfather and Father seemed to watch one another more than usual. Father told me that he intended to remarry, mainly on account of Ludwig; Mother had asked him to do it. I even knew of some of the candidates. It seemed peculiar that Father discussed all this with me. The fact that his remarriage was something planned for the welfare of the entire house, appeared to make it a business item, something subject to hazards and accidents, and this again reflected on Mother. My parents' marriage had always been one of the fixed points of my childhood cosmos. Now, retroactively, it was made a product of chance.

Finally, after a little more than a year, my stepmother appeared on the scene. She was just about my mother's age. She was a roundish jovial person with a great treasure of affection. Grandfather erected a wall, but she pretended not to see it. I tried to address her as "Mama," which in our neighborhood was a rather formal and stiff way of talking to one's mother. She brought a second piano into the house (she was a piano-teacher), and very soon after her arrival we played the Bach D-minor Concerto and some duos. Whenever during the music anything went wrong, I got impatient and pounced on her; she laughed. But the "Mama" hurt her deeply, I soon found out. Ludwig never called her anything but "Mother," and he meant "Mother." It was quite wonderful to see him so quickly transformed. It was as if patience had returned to this house, patience and kindness and warmth. After a short time that cold element of the fortuitous and accidental disappeared. In fact, at times I had a vague feeling that Mother, our real mother, had been instrumental in sending "Mama" along. Soon I stopped calling her "Mama" and called her "Mother."

II

MEDICINE

7. Medicine

WHEN I look back today at my years as a student of medicine in Munich, Berlin and Frankfurt, I see that the true influence did not come from the curriculum of learning but from something outside. Karl Jaspers has pointed out that all academic learning presents one of three elements. First, the pure transmission of knowledge, of factual material. Secondly, the teaching of the Master. This means that the personality of the teacher is truly formative, much more so than a mere acquisition of facts would be. This element is still quite obvious in such subjects as painting and music and sculpture, but it used to be present everywhere. When a medieval student went all the way from Ireland to Paris to study with one of the theological doctors, it was not only because he was unable at that time to obtain it in a printed correspondence course. When Freud traveled to Charcot, he got more out of it than neurology. When Harvey Cushing went to study under Kocher, he experienced more than a course in surgery. There is something, even apart from technical tricks, which you cannot take down in notes. It is a formative principle which disappears with the death of the professor, though one can still discern it in a diluted form in those who belonged to his school. Thirdly, there is the Socratic method, a lively exchange between professor and students; the results obtained are the outcome of that method.

Medical science, at least the preclinical parts of it, could easily be handed out in an impersonal way. In fact, it is being handed out in such a fashion in many schools. However, Medicine is an art as much as a science. It is, apart from factual knowledge, based on attitudes, on intuition and on wisdom.

In spite of the false scientism which followed in the tracks of science the medical schools and the universities in general still had a strong humanist hangover, particularly on the European continent. Therefore it rarely happened that one student did all his studying at one school. There was the ancient tradition of migration. If Medicine were nothing but a compilation of factual material, it would not be necessary for the undergraduate to attend a different school ever so often. Moreover, there was no fixed curriculum. If you wanted to take Special Surgery before you had had General Pathology (although this is an extreme example, and you would be foolish to do so), you could do it. You could learn certain subjects at home from books, and during the time allotted for lectures in that subject you could have listened to lectures on the history of art, or on philosophy. There were hardly any written exams. Therefore it was much harder to "cram" for an exam according to some point system. It was up to the professor to see how much true understanding of the subject you had. Perhaps this was a remnant of an aristocratic way of teaching and learning—aristocratic not in a political, but in a humanist sense. The University was not yet a technical school but a *universitas*. All this had, of course, its discrepancies too; it made for snobbery, and for that false intellectual feudalism which became so sadly apparent when the Nazis were in power. Moreover, since there was no control on attendance you could go and drink beer instead of listening to a lecture. If your father had money, you regarded it as a matter of honor to live like this for a whole semester or two.

However, in addition to all the technical knowledge, the "extra" element of humanity and art made the medical schools lively and exciting, paradoxical and stimulating. In Frankfurt we had as a teacher in anatomy a Swiss with a long, flowing beard who in his free time wrote books on pacifism and on Gandhi. On the other hand, the famous professor who taught us this subject in Munich was particularly interested in anatomy for artists. He produced about two thousand lantern slides of nudes to teach us what he called living anatomy. His taste in art was somewhat strange and seemed to include everything academic and cheap. When he described the relief of the hand, he began to speak of "mothers' hands" and started crying. This happened about once a year. He would strain our imaginative power by assuming that the amphitheater was the womb, and that we were to "follow him on a walk around." Presently he conjured up some fairyland which would have been, in addition to its didactic significance, an ideal hunting-ground for Bachofen or for Freud. With all that, these experts in their fields transmitted, with a wealth of detailed morphology, a profound sense for *morphe* itself.

In Frankfurt our teacher in physiology was the celebrated neurophysiologist, Albrecht Bethe. On hot summer days he took the entire class to the swimming-pool, and in between swims he demonstrated muscle physiology in the living. There was always a certain amount of improvisation and freedom which elevated the matter of teaching into something creative.

Of all the basic sciences, the most exciting ones were those associated with biochemistry. I was extremely fortunate to receive my chemical grounding from Richard Willstätter, famed Nobel prize winner for his work on the green pigment of plants; my biochemical training from Embden, one of the pioneers in the chemistry of muscle contraction; and my pharmacology from Straub. All these men seemed to be in the possession of dazzling magic when it came to the matter of teaching. When I look back at every one of those lectures, I feel like some old opera addict when he ruminates over his evenings at the Metropolitan. For years I thought that my work would have to be in that particular line of science.

However, I received the strongest and most permanent impression of my undergraduate years through Volhard, the internist in Frankfurt. Volhard combined in an ideal form the three elements of academic teaching which I have mentioned. He had the personality of an exuberant and expansive artist of the Renaissance. He had originally intended to study for the Lutheran ministry, then for a naval career, and finally decided on medicine. He did everything in some strangely large and strong style. He was a perfect illustration for Thomas Mann's type of man in whom health is the force of creation. He had that same intensity of sensory perception, of smell and of touch which Thomas Mann ascribes to his earthbound creative geniuses. He raised a family of ten children (something so rare among the educated that he became famous for this alone), and seemed to be eternally fascinated by women. He tried to remember all the students personally, and those whom he favored he addressed by their first names and with the familiar "thou." He had preserved many of the artistic-intuitive and shrewdly computating methods of the great clinicians of the nineteenth century, and he claimed to be able to diagnose any, even the most complicated type of valvular lesion of the heart, without even touching the patient.

This was no idle boast. He trained us systematically to observe. He never gave any formal didactic lectures (you can learn all this from books) but confronted us with a patient at the beginning of the hour. It was amazing how much one could *see* without examining the patient or without knowing anything about the history. The entire diagnosis and the decisions as to therapy were evolved by some sort of parliamentary method. He planted his questions so shrewdly that in the end we actually thought that we had produced results. He would come in with an air of distress, as if he felt lost about some clinical problem and needed our help. To make it more attractive he used this method particularly whenever he had been called in to consult over the sickness of some "person of high standing" abroad. As a result, no student ever forgot any of his lectures.

Like all great personalities he seemed to be full of contradictions. He is known all over the world for his work on cardiorenal diseases. He wrote the largest monograph ever written on this subject, a truly Teutonic affair of two thousand printed pages. After he had written it all in longhand during his "free time," the publishers lost the manuscript and he had to write it over. He had a profound attachment to the basic sciences associated with clinical medicine, particularly to physiology. Once he made a speech in which he claimed that modern medicine has so wonderfully progressed that one could make diagnoses from laboratory reports, without ever seeing the patient. This from him who was a true artist when it came to clinical diagnosis! Those who did not know him, and deplored the mechanistic trend in modern medicine, were infuriated. He seemed to love everything that could be tabulated or presented in mathematical formulas. Yet he was the only German internist who gave ancient homoeopathic methods a try-out. Even then he was interested in that complex no-man's-land which is now called "psychosomatic medicine," and he wanted me to work in this field later in his hospital.

He was a good violinist, and on hot days he would sit with three of his sons, all in bathing trunks, and play string quartets in his garden. After having incurred his wrath over something or other, we placated him by playing chamber music in his house. He was a staunch conservative, and we used to hate what seemed a reactionary outlook. Yet when the Nazis were in power he was more decent in his attitude towards his Jewish co-workers than several of the professors who had previously excelled by their political liberalism. When censorship was tightest he sent me his portrait with a personal inscription to London—an unwarranted gesture. Needless to say, he was finally removed from office. After the war he was reinstated by the Allies.

When I think of such teachers as Volhard, I seem to know the answer to the problems of academic education. It is solved only by personality in the Goethean sense, by that element of soul added to the lifeless body of mechanical transmission.

After graduation I worked as an interne in Berlin in the neuro-logical department of the Moabit Hospital. Kurt Goldstein, the director of that department, is well known for his brilliant attempts to overcome an atomistic and mechanistic approach in the field of organic nervous diseases. In no medical subject did the mechanistic trend of the machine age have greater and more genuine triumphs than in neurology. If you wanted to think of the "human body as a machine," here you had your legitimate chance, with electro-potentials manifesting themselves in an intricate network of neurons which "fire," inhibit, and release one another. The diagnostic procedure is indeed the same as that by which a garage mechanic finds out where the motor is failing. The greatest achievements in modern neurology are based on a body of observations which underlie this ingenious concept.

However, Goldstein was one of the first to point out that the disturbances of cognitive and expressive functions which follow circumscribed injuries of the brain cannot be explained on this basis. He and the psychologist Gelb had followed single cases of brain-injured soldiers for years after the First World War. They tried to replace the mosaic-pattern of brain function by a different approach; that means that they looked at these disturbances in an entirely new way. The injured man was not a machine with one link broken in a certain place. There were basic modes in the functioning of the mind which were affected no matter what the anatomical localization of the injury might be. The whole thing was extremely involved, and since the atomistic theory of a neuron mosaic had proved so exceedingly useful regarding the "lower functions," such as locomotion and sensation, the main problem consisted in finding a new working concept. Consequently the chief of the department spent hours in discussing rather abstract problems while he was confronted with a patient.

The Moabit Hospital was one of the large municipal hospitals of Berlin, situated in the middle of one of the slum districts. It consisted of a main building with various additional ones, and numerous one-story huts. All this was sprawled over a huge terrain. At times it was quite comfortable to be able to go by ambulance to one of the more remote buildings. The interne quarters were located in the main building facing the street, just one story above the Admitting Office. It was the rule that the internes themselves had to carry out the routine examinations of urine and blood. Thus, every morning at ten o'clock after ward rounds, we appeared in the main laboratory, and under the supervision of an old laboratory technician we did the various routine procedures of boiling, precipitating, staining and microscopy. We envied the senior resident staff who were not obliged to do this. At meals there was a strict order according to which we were seated. At the head of the table there was one of those Chief Assistants who were not married and therefore "lived in." I beheld him only from afar. Then there followed a hierarchic scale, all the way down to us.

The sick people had their contacts in an order which was exactly reversed to this hierarchy. They had the nurses all the time, the Internes frequently, and the remaining staff less frequently—up to the Chief of Staff of a department who would exchange only an occasional word with any single patient. However, the Chief appeared god-like at the ward rounds, encircled by post-graduate workers many of whom had writing-pads on which they marked his sayings. Nearly everybody admired and envied the Chief, and aspired to be a Chief himself sometime. There were also some who just wanted to be ordinary general practitioners. They also took notes but only to learn how to do a good piece of work. In retrospect I realize that I must have regarded these people as "poor fish." To be a Professor was the thing that counted. Among the senior resident staff there were some who possessed a stunning quantity of knowledge about their specialty, book knowledge as well as personal experience. Yet, for some technical or personal reason, they had never attained an academic appointment. Some of them were in the odor of Superior Knowledge; they knew more than the famous Professors. Whatever may have prevented their academic advancement they failed to achieve the Title, nor did they care to go out into practice. They stayed on in the hospital, middle-aged gentlemen, always carrying with them a nearly imperceptible nimbus of resignation and ever so faint embitterment. We regarded them with a mixture of admiration and pity. To linger as a poor relative outside the gates during the Academic Banquet, this seemed to be the prototype of tragic failure, a living reproach against the injustice of society.

All this and our whole life were singularly dissociated from the life of the community around us. The Moabit Hospital was surrounded by endless rows of tenement houses, with overcrowded flats and small, cave-like stores. Wherever you looked there were endless flights of streets with that combination of old brick, advertising signpost, fire-escape and washing-line which, all over the world, is the face of the City of the Poor. There lived the people whose lives spilled over into the hospital. We received them when they were sick or injured or delirious or dying, or when they were bearing children.

When we were not on call we went paddling on the Wannsee, or dancing in one of the open-air restaurants in the fashionable parts of Berlin. When we were on call we invited girl friends, or had parties, at times in the room of one of the senior staff. We talked about science and politics. Experimental Medicine appeared to be only one aspect of Dialectic Materialism. When we did not talk about Science and Politics we discussed one another. This we did incessantly and with apparently infinite patience. Everybody analyzed everybody else. In the world of my childhood nobody had cared to discuss anybody else's motives. To be sure there had been such a thing as gossip, quite a lot of it; but this was quite different. We sat around, for hours and hours, and dissected with a seemingly detached scientific air one another's weaknesses, loves, hatreds, aspirations and despairs.

There is a lot of this going on today wherever young "intellectuals" meet. Present-day psychology with its particular idiom lends itself extraordinarily to this sport. In Burger's time I had shied away from all modern forms of psychological analysis. Now we all were inebriated by some miasma emanting from a mixture of Freud, the Russian novelists, Mann, Gide, Joyce and others. We were smart boys and girls. Although there remained nothing mysterious about any given individual, there was actually never an end to our talks. This is the most extraordinary feature about it. We talked until the small hours of the morning and began to talk again next evening. We talked and talked. Whenever we were on duty, and had no work in the wards, or no girl-friend engagements—we talked.

When I was a small boy and someone in our town stammered or had a peculiar twitch, I felt compassionate or, more often, secretly made fun of him. Now when someone stammered or had a twitch, we felt neither compassion nor mockery. We *knew why* he stammered or had a twitch. We had him all down. We took him apart, looked inside, and instantly knew what made him stammer. Then we left him there and took up the next. One case led to another, like eating peanuts.

At times, our discussions would be rudely interrupted by a rap at the door: "Doctor Stern, one apo!" *Apo* was one of the abbreviated catch-words which made up the intricate jargon of orderlies and internes. What the orderly wanted to indicate by "one apo" was that a sick man with apoplexy, brain stroke, had arrived by ambulance. With a sigh I would grab stethoscope, reflex hammer and flash-light, and descend to the ambulance. Inside the ambulance the air was sticky, with a mixture of the smell of leather, human sweat and gasoline. An old man was there, covered by a red woolen blanket and tied down with leather straps. When the beam of the flash-light touched his face he turned his head and moaned. I "went over him," as we called it, quickly and with a few movements, to test his reflexes and take his blood pressure. Then I would phone orders in advance to the ward, to have everything prepared. I drove on with the ambulance, fulfilled my duty, and went back to the interne quarters to go on talking.

When we spoke of our patients at all, it was in terms which must sound strange to an ordinary man: "There is a fellow Braun over in building E who has the most peculiar blood sugar curve." "How is Schmitthammer?" "His albumen-globulin ratio is going down all the time." Such answers were often determined by the sort of "research" an interne was doing. The life and death of the people in the slums around us was alien to us and reached us only in small fragments of abstraction. It was rather symbolic that the last thing we saw of a man were little glass slides with colored bits of tissue and a number (his post-mortem number) written on it.

Needless to say that there were some among us who did heroic work, particularly in situations of emergency. But this had nothing to do with the process of de-humanization and mechanization in the medical curriculum which has, if anything, advanced since those days.

The man who made the most lasting impression on me while I was working in Moabit was Ernst Haase, the chief assistant of the Neurological Department. His interest extended far beyond the technical aspect of medicine. Ernst Haase was a rather tall, gaunt, cadaverous man with dark eyes. He had his office right in the slums of Moabit, though he was a highly specialized neuro-psychiatrist. He was a man with a profound social consciousness and that peculiar air of sheer human kindness and wholesomeness which was so characteristic of many of these people. At the same time he possessed what one used to call, in cheap novels, "hypnotic" qualities. In fact he could have been a very fashionable ladies' psychiatrist if he had so desired. I have never seen anyone so much liked by the poor people. When the Nazi revolution came I was certain that he, a Jew with his social consciousness, would be one of the first to land in a concentration camp. When I met him and his family again much later in 1939 in London, I learned to my amazement that he had never been in hiding for a day, not even during the general round-up of Jews in that fateful autumn of 1938. He was never molested; God only knows what protected him.

Twice a week Haase ran a municipal clinic for drug addicts and alcoholics. There I worked as his assistant. The hours were from six to eight but frequently we worked until well after midnight. There I found myself in a strange and extraordinary world, entirely different from anything I have ever seen before. We saw a continuous stream of clients. There were mothers with children who had just left a home destroyed by an alcoholic. There were drunkards, morphine and cocaine addicts, the hopeless, the destitute, those who had cynically and rebelliously isolated themselves, bound to a life of increasing solitude and destruction, and those who had succumbed to the deficiency of a loveless world. This was a cross-section through the darkest layer of the city. It was that fringe of life where human existence is ultimately atomized and surrounds itself with a void, a space of negation. It would take a whole book to describe all this so that the reader would be able to re-experience it. In the middle of this Haase would sit, seemingly unperturbed. He combined the physician and the superb social worker in one person. Sometimes drunkards would suddenly appear on the scene with loaded revolvers. In this sort of situation Haase was at his best.

Haase, in spite of his excellent training, seemed to believe in the scientific aspect of Medicine only in a relative way. He was a keen diagnostician, but apparently he did not believe in the absolute separation of the doctor's profession from that of the social worker. Once he had diagnosed and localized a neurological lesion he wanted to know where the patient's children obtained their supper. At the conferences he looked unashamedly bored. There was a very large area of "research" which he almost seemed to despise. But in that endless stream of misery which flooded the Center for Alcoholics and Drug Addicts, he was like a rock of salvation. In every case, no matter whether it was that of a "better class" alcoholic who now slept under bridges, or an East Prussian village girl who had ended with prostitution and cocaine, he penetrated right into the core of the psychological and social situation. When it came to find the rational solution, he seemed to have unlimited resources of imagination and "know-how." He drew an appallingly small salary for all this but I often noticed, when he believed himself to be unobserved, that he slipped money into the hands of some alcoholic's wife.

I never quite recovered from these experiences. That means that I never recovered the undergraduate's boundless admiration for science and for the absolute sacredness of research. When I returned to Volhard, one year after, I was changed. The graphs, tables and formulas had lost their absolute value. I had discovered the other side of medical practice. Although I had more scientific training later, I never forgot those experiences in Moabit. They seemed to have put the abstract scientific aspect of Medicine into its proper place. It is just one side of a profound and complex development that with many of us science and art in Medicine are no longer integrated. As science in general, medical science has gained in extensiveness what it has lost in intensity. You can perceive the twilight of a humanist medicine if you listen to those conversations of internes about their patients. When "Smith" is described as "Bloodsugar 100.2,

NPN 73, BP 210 over 115 . . ." we get not just a practical ab-
breviation of the clinical chart, but something much more significant. Smith, the patient, has been conveniently reduced to a
formula.

If you had asked me during my student years what my philosophy was, I probably would have answered you without hesitation. I was convinced of the truth of dialectic materialism. I used
to belong to radical student groups, and we were all interested
in such things as collecting money for the famous British general
strike in 1926. There was nothing in the social or cultural sphere
which did not readily fall into the pattern of either Marx or
Freud. There was no disturbance that could not be diagnosed
that way. Theoretically, at least, it could all be remedied. I must
have had a blind spot for most of the deficiencies inherent in
these systems. With reference to the Marxist attitude toward
religion, however, I remember to have entertained certain doubts.
I wondered about that vast area of individual misfortune which
was not determined socially and economically, all that which
modern existentialists call the "marginal situations," injury, sickness, death. There seemed to be a gap somewhere, and there
were situations in which you were left in the lurch. I used to
bring this up from time to time in discussions, but it did not
worry me more than that; it was just a little blotch in the picture.

8. Kati Huber and Others

WHICH memories are important for this story; which ones
can I leave out? Let me put together, in any event, those images
which give an impression of happy and carefree years, a time in
which it appears in retrospect as if politics and the social ills of
our time, philosophy and religion were all remote forms of ab-

stractness. Life then was something like the blue lakes, the gay
meadows, the bright blue sky of Bavaria.

At the Café Gassner in Munich a number of us met regularly
at a certain table for lunch. There was Peter Kohnstamm, son
of the famous neuroanatomist and psychotherapist; Walter Seitz,
now Professor of Medicine in Munich; Hans Bethe, now Professor
of Mathematical Physics at Cornell University and world famous
for his theory of solar energy production (later he was chief
mathematical physicist at Los Alamos); Erich von Baeyer, cellist,
painter and medical student; a few others, and I. A lot of our
conversation, in those days, struck us as sparkling wit. I have a
dark suspicion that we thought of ourselves as geniuses, or at
least somehow set apart from the rest of the student body. It is
now consoling to think that in the case of Bethe this was true.

I remember Hans Bethe, Peter Kohnstamm, and myself going
on a Sunday trip to the Benedictine Monastery in Andechs for
the scenery and the beer, both of which were famous. It was a
bright June morning. In the train Bethe began to recite comic
poetry and then, by heart, the railway schedule of the Deutsche
Reichsbahn which to him was a meaningful symphony of figures.
Peter and I were preoccupied by the girls in the compartment.
Bethe said: "I wonder how one could come to a quick and abbreviated form of arithmetic with the duodecimal system of the
Assyrians and Babylonians." We arrived at Andechs, climbed
the hill of the Monastery, sat on the lawn under the old chestnut
trees and drank cool beer. The place was crowded with farmers,
men, women and children who, in their best Sunday clothes,
flocked towards the white church. There was also a stand in
the open air at which the faithful bought rosaries, candles, little
statues, and pencils with glass beads at one end which showed
a picture of Saint Benedict when one held them against the light.
By this time Bethe had worked out an arithmetic system by
which one can multiply and divide numbers in groups of sixes

and dozens as quickly as we commonly do it in groups of tens. He used a round beer-mat made of cardboard to write out the explanation. I felt hopelessly behind Peter's quick puns and repartee and Bethe's duodecimal arithmetic. On the way down we played a guessing game, and Bethe had to guess the word "anachronism."

Many memories of this period have to do with "house music." Chamber music, the music of small ensembles of string and wind instruments or of these instruments in association with piano, has been written by the great masters primarily to be played, rather than listened to. The fact that people listen to it is a complication which has to be reckoned with. In many corners of the world there still exists the tradition of chamber music which is several hundred years old. The initiates speak a common language, they recognize one another by certain mannerisms. After years of experience one can, from their physique and demeanor, distinguish cellists from violists, and oboists from string-players. Cellists always start right from the beginning in their shirt-sleeves, pianists take their coats off after having played a full piece in three movements. As experience grows one knows exactly where and when difficulties and mistakes come in. In a famous quartet by Mozart for piano and three string instruments I know exactly where the violist will come in, one bar too early; I sense it about ten bars beforehand and brace myself for it. I also know to which violist this will happen, and which will remain free from sin; it shows in their faces. A few years ago I said to Mr. Rudolf Serkin: "I want to ask you about a certain technical problem in Beethoven's trio Op. 97 . . ." Before I could name the difficulty, he interrupted and said: "That mordent in the first movement; you play it best as five equal notes."

We often took trips in collapsible boats on the Alpine rivers— the Isar, the Salzach and the Inn. We were usually mixed groups of boys and girls. Once on a canoe trip from Salzburg to Passau we spent the night in the sleepy town of Braunau. In Salzburg we visited the Mozart house, and I remember my feeling when I touched that famous little spinet, just to play a chord on it. When we arrived in Braunau in the evening there was a man with formidable whiskers near the landing-place who told us that we were in the birthplace of Adolf Hitler. This was, of course, years before the Nazi revolution.

The Brahms B-major trio, Beethoven's B-flat major trio ("the big one"), the two Mozart piano quartets, the two Schubert trios, the warm summer nights on the bank of the Isar, the lilac of the Englische Garten to be stolen towards the small hours of the morning—all this blends in memory into a poem of happiness. The stars seemed to stand still, and Brahms' syncopations and plant-like asymmetries said aloud what the ancient walnut trees outside the window were saying silently. I had been an anti-Brahmsian because of my adolescent devotion to Romain Rolland's *Jean Christophe* until the cellist of our chamber music ensemble, Erich von Baeyer, persuaded me to play Brahms.

Erich was heavy-set, of bear-like muscular build, with a thick thatch of smooth straw-like hair and enamel-blue eyes. His hands were characterized by baroque muscular bulges. Apart from his cello playing, he was an exceptionally gifted painter and an expert draftsman. When I met him for the first time, he made a rude remark about the shape of my ears and proceeded to draw me on a paper serviette. Usually he said very little and, apart from his good scholastic record as a medical student, there was no indication that he ever reflected. He once silently climbed a difficult rock in the Dolomites with pick-ax and rope, and then, dangling his partner over the abyss, finally said: "Now I have your life in my hands." This was considered a good-hearted joke, and it really was. His humor was that of a big dog.

Erich would perch his massive frame on a small chair, and

after having repaired a broken bow with the help of his teeth and a little carving-knife he would begin, sweating and gasping, to play the cello. Presently the chords and melodic sequences of Bach's solo suites would roll through the night. The landlady's room, furniture, knick-knacks and all, were transformed into a huge vibrating organ. In this music there was the sureness, power, lassitude and beauty of nature itself. If Erich had taken up the cello as his profession he would, I am certain, have ranked among the first. Even so he was better than many professionals. He did everything with the keen sensory organic receptivity of an artist; abstraction was alien to him, sometimes interesting and at other times repulsive. He was one of the first students who grasped intuitively the true nature of National Socialism. He did it with his eyes. He went to National Socialist meetings, and came back with a collection of drawings: drooping bellies, fish eyes, and thin-lipped faces.

We became friends from the moment of our first meeting. He reflected too little, I reflected too much; it was, actually, only through art that we understood one another. He was baffled by my conscious Jewishness and at times, I think, he felt it was something similar to what the Nazis had, only on a more intellectual plane. However, he sensed that there was some danger to the values of Europe. At that time there were gatherings of German and French pacifist students in the German-French border zone. Unfortunately these affairs were isolated gestures by comparatively small groups of high-minded people who tried to perpetuate the spirit of Briand and Stresemann. Erich went to these gatherings on his motorcycle, with cello, pencils and carving-knife. He was a favorable representative of German youth because the Gothic beauty emanating from that cello belied the ferociousness of his appearance. However, all he brought back with him were greetings of good-will and a caricature of André Gide.

This was rather characteristic of the numerous attempts to

save Europe which we witnessed around that time. The men of
Locarno, particularly Briand and Stresemann, were genuine in
their efforts to stem the tide of rising nationalist passion. There
were exchanges of lecturers and artists and elite groups of students between France and Germany. However, no matter
whether Thomas Mann lectured in Paris or Georges Duhamel
spoke in Berlin, or Erich played his cello in a Lorraine village—
the seed never sank into the ground. There was a peculiar esthetic
remoteness about all these attempts, they lacked resonance
among the masses of the people. Just as Cézanne and Matisse
were appreciated by a small number of intellectuals while the
people in general adorned the walls of their rooms with atrocities
from the department store, European consciousness had lost its
roots in the urban masses and had become something like an
esoteric luxury. In fact, it looks as if this remoteness of true art
and the disappearance of a true cosmopolitanism had a common
origin. There was that peculiar symptom of double vision, of
dual attitudes and ambivalence which is so characteristic of our
time. It is a commonplace to state that nationalism is incompatible with Christianity, and that there is nothing more appalling
than nationalist Christians. However, we usually overlook the
fact that an anti-Christian internationalist, such as Nietzsche, is
just as atrocious as a nationalist Christian. Only his atrocious-
ness is much more subtle and sophisticated, and it takes much
more to point out the incongruity and paradox of his position.
The great Christian mystic Dostoievsky who was at the same
time a vulgar pan-Slav politician, and the noble cosmopolitan
Nietzsche who at the same time "finished" Christianity in pam-
phlets which overflow with a unique form of tawdry arrogance,
were twin brothers of the nineteenth century.

Some of the leading artists and intellectuals of Germany and
France shared Nietzsche's duality. They rediscovered Europe
and hated petty nationalism, but their Europe lacked content,

it was a vague concept of some sort of esthetic harmony. How could this sort of thing ever have taken root in the people?

However, there was no plural consciousness, none of that complicated intellectual bookkeeping about Erich, who soon invited me to stay as a guest of his family in Heidelberg.

They were most extraordinary people in a most extraordinary setting. His father was a Professor at the University there, a well-known orthopedic surgeon. Among his ancestry there was the most varied collection of names one could find in encyclopedias and *Who's Who*. Their house was situated just above the river Neckar close to the Old Bridge. It was a rather old house, probably the most perfectly decorated private house I have ever seen. Its beauty was obviously due to a slow growth over generations. One of the celebrated ancestors had been Tischbein, the painter friend of Goethe. Furniture, paintings, sketches, musical instruments and books looked as though they were strewn about by a careless spirit, without obvious planning, without the air of the museum, yet perfectly harmonious. All this was the work of Frau Professor. There was a large glass veranda and a sloping garden behind the house. In this garden the students of the University put on open-air performances of Shakespeare.

I usually came for chamber music. If I were unfamiliar with a piece, I was given the score and put in a room on the top floor where there was an upright piano, out of hearing. After being given a certain amount of time to look at the score, I was allowed to come down to the music room. Erich used to have an excellent string ensemble. I remember particularly one violinist, the wild-looking wife of a Russian painter, whom he used to fetch on the spur of the moment from her husband's studio, transporting her back and forth on a motorcycle.

There seemed to be a gesture of careless improvisation about everything. There were always friends at dinner, or "aunts" who were not really aunts. It was impossible to know who really belonged to the family in the strictly biological sense, and it did not seem to make any difference. At times there was an impression of snobbery, for there seemed something planned in the way in which Thomas Mann or Adolf Busch "dropped in," but one was quickly reassured because everybody dropped in. A physics student from a village in Hessen appeared one morning at breakfast, and it turned out that he had spent the night in one of the small rooms on the top floor. I was astonished, but nobody seemed to give any thought to it; the Professor, who hardly ever spoke, asked him with a slight twinkle whether he was satisfied with the bed.

One day when our viola player was unable to play, Erich's youngest brother came from one of the upper floors to substitute. He handled the instrument rather adeptly but vanished after completing his task. When I inquired next day, I was told that he had gone skiing in the Alps. He was a handsome young chap, the child prodigy of the family. He was a nuclear physicist.

In contrast, the oldest brother was the picture of a German professor out of *Punch*—stiff brush hair, metal-rimmed glasses and all. He was a psychiatrist. It was a long time before I heard him say anything. I know that he was a follower of a German philosophy which had its roots in Kierkegaard's existentialism. He worked in a mental hospital and had Spartan habits. The apparent dissociation between the members of the family was remarkable. They all stressed this a little, it seemed to me, as if in willful parody.

One day I had to pass through a room in which a tall young girl was sitting. She was surrounded by big drawing-boards, raw leather, the implements of lettering, and leather tools. She was bent over a huge piece of parchment, doing some lettering in raised gold. I noticed that she was strikingly handsome. She was working without looking up, and in the corner of the room sat a man who silently watched her. Erich said: "This is my sister."

He looked at me and laughed as if he expected me to be bewildered. Later when I walked through the room and nobody
was there, I saw that it was beautiful work. The lettering was
of strong classical simplicity. The accuracy, the special setting,
the craftsmanship showed beauty and strength of creation.

Next morning I saw the girl again. She appeared while I was
playing the piano (I thought she had come through the wall),
and watched me. I introduced myself in a provincial manner.
Her name was Liselotte. To cope with the situation, I asked her
to play a duet with me. She said that she got clammy hands at
the thought of a duet and that she could not play, but she did
play. It was a short and simple piece, the second movement of
the fourth Brandenburg Concerto, in Reger's arrangement. When
she disappeared again, Erich came into the room and said: "I
presume you love my sister."

The Professor was a huge and hulking man, always slightly
stooped, with beetle brows which overshadowed his blue eyes
like awnings. He came out of his library for short meals and
watched his family silently as one looks at an aquarium. In order
to appear interested in orthopedic surgery, I once asked him
at lunch to explain Perthes' phenomenon of the hip-joint. (I had
read only the day before that such a name existed for some very
special symptom.) At first he did not answer, which made me
feel embarrassed and I looked down at my plate. Presently he
took a match box, three matches and a fork, and constructed
before my eyes a model of a pelvis with a diseased thigh-bone.
He made it move, first in one way, then in another, without
uttering a word. I guessed that the first movement was normal,
and the second one abnormal—Perthes' phenomenon.

After lunch he took me into his study and showed me a model
demonstrating the mechanics of joints. It was the puppet of a
Hitlerian storm-trooper who marched and gave the Fascist salute.
At that time storm-troopers were still funny. Later I observed

that the Professor sat for hours in his study in front of a desk without any book. All of a sudden he would pull out a carving-knife and a few wooden blocks and strings and make a little man. I was told that these little men were models which demonstrated an entirely new and ingenious theory of muscular mechanics. When he was invited to make an official speech at the International Orthopedic Congress he arrived with a large suitcase from which he pulled a number of wooden men, mammals and arthropoda. He made them stand, walk, bend and roll, and he made them do the most astounding things with any given joint.

There prevailed in those years in Heidelberg a rather highbrow attitude of esthetic aloofness. There was a conglomerate of philosophers, historians, and sociologists who seemed to regard the social disease of Europe as one would sit in front of an over-heated bowl of soup. Quite a few people of this intellectual *jeunesse dorée* came to Erich's house. They laughed about Hitler but they talked in a precious and ambiguous way about Hegel, and the "idea of the state." They made round mouths and drew their shoulders up when they spoke. The Professor, like all people of his type, was fascinated by the abstract which was strange to him; nevertheless he had a keen perception of smugness and insincerity. On such occasions he remained silent for some time without moving his huge frame, and it was not even certain whether he had heard anything. Then he would remark that, in his opinion, Germany as a political unit ought to be destroyed. After something like this he usually withdrew to his study.

The dissociation in the lives of the various members of the family seemed to be largely counteracted by the presence of Kati. Technically, Kati Huber was a domestic servant; in actuality, she provided something like a collective conscience for the family. Nobody appeared to know where anybody was at any given time, except Kati. She had the omniscience which hotel desk-porters pretend to have. She was able to tell you that Herr Professor was having a nap, Frau Professor was at the linen cupboards, Fräulein Lisi was doing bookbinding in Schlierbach, Herr Walter was visiting a hospital.

Kati Huber was a semi-illiterate peasant girl from a village near my home. She had come into the family more than thirty years before as the children's "nanny" and she had brought them all up with the same methods of care, reward and punishment which she knew from her own childhood. She had no idea what all these Professors and Doctors were up to, but that did not give her any feelings of inadequacy. Her religious upbringing gave her the conviction, never formulated, that everybody has his appropriate place in life. The so-called "inferiority complex" and true humility are two opposites. She treated fellow-domestics and visiting Nobel laureates to her crude little jokes with naive equality. Her warnings and criticisms were usually given in the form of proverbial "sayings"; many of these aphorisms contained dark and incomprehensible metaphors, and it was never certain how much of this was ancient folklore and how much freely improvised variations by Kati Huber. She lived a life of piety and went to Mass every morning at six o'clock. By the time I knew Kati her strength was already reduced, but she was still an important institution. She was respected and liked by the children, probably most by Liselotte. I felt that Liselotte's anti-intellectual rebellion was in some way intimately associated with her affection for Kati.

Liselotte had left school at the age of fifteen and secretly entered the services of a small bookbinder in the town. Her job was to open the shop in the morning, tidy it up, and to get beer for the master at lunchtime from the nearby inn. She kept this up for some time until her father discovered it, and sent her to a famous bookbinder's school in Weimar. There she was the only girl among craftsmen. Moreover, her colleagues came from craftsmen's families or from the working-class. They were mainly Communists. She learned to look at her own class from down below upward, but in a way different from that of Kati Huber. They became proud of her, and asked her to their meetings. She was taught to discuss the problem of social justice, to drink beer and to sing round-songs. While she learned the craft of bookbinding and lettering from the masters, she also pursued her one favorite study, that of Giotto, Cimabue and Fra Angelico. She went to Italy one spring to study all the paintings on the spot, and returned to Heidelberg and opened a studio for bookbinding and lettering.

One bright morning in 1932, a Whitsunday, Erich and I were sitting at the breakfast-table in the house in Heidelberg. He looked at the cloudless blue sky outside and said: "Let's go to Paris."

We packed a few things and mounted his motorcycle. The roads were white, dusty and hot. In two hours we were past the French border. When we stopped in a village for lunch, we found entire families of three generations in the restaurant sitting around big tables with white table-cloths. The children had starched white collars, neatly parted hair, long pressed pants, and looked like miniature grownups. Everybody had claret with his food.

A buxom woman, the innkeeper's wife, served us. She said in French: "There is not a single French boy of your age who would have a motorcycle like you. We French are economic and careful people. You Germans come over in the most flashy cars and motorcycles, and then you claim you cannot pay us any reparations." We laughed an embarrassed laughter.

At tea-time we arrived in Verdun. I had not put any hat on in the morning and had not felt the sun because of the air which kept whizzing past. Now I had a terrible headache and looked like a lobster; it was a minor case of sunstroke. Because of our

experience with the French innkeeper's wife, we tried to conceal
the fact that we were German. First we went into a teashop. Then
we bought a dictionary in order to find out the French word
for aspirin. The dictionary said *"aspirine, f."* However, in spite
of *aspirine,* I began to feel every small pebble on the highway.
In Meaux I let Erich continue alone and took the train. In the
evening we met again in Paris. We visited a Frenchman who
had at one time been Professor at the University of Heidelberg.
His wife was in the garden behind the house. She was tall and
beautiful, with an old wide-rimmed straw hat and a rather old-
fashioned costume. I still see her standing there, playing with
her children; there was something archaic and at the same time
foreboding about her appearance, as in certain paintings of
Picasso.

On our way home, after a few days' stay, we stopped in Fon-
tainebleau. We saw an old-fashioned hotel with a plaque outside
which said that Napoleon III had dined there. We entered and
found ourselves in a big dining-room in the style of the Second
Empire. There were many small tables most of which were
occupied by old ladies of a peculiar sort we had never encountered before. From their conversation with the waiters we
thought they spoke English. Their hair seemed blue, and many
of them were sitting alone, accompanied only by lap dogs. We
were thunderstruck to discover that the cheapest menu cost
what would correspond to eight dollars. I wanted to leave but
we decided to stay and eat only soup. The waiter told us that
one had to have the entire menu. After a while he beckoned us
to follow him, and took us past various *salles* into a small room
next to the kitchen. Here there were many men in dark blue
uniforms eating. The waiter explained that they were the chauffeurs of the people in the big dining-room in front, only here
the same menu cost two dollars. The chauffeurs welcomed us
with noisy cheer and explained to us that the people in the
dining-room were Americans. They took it for granted that we

were chauffeurs too and asked us whom we drove. I pointed at
my friend and said: "He drives me." This statement was greeted
with great applause, and we were offered wine. The chauffeurs
told us in rapid French a lot of things about the Americans. The
waitress came along and said to us: "I suppose that your masters
in the front room are going to pay for you."

That haphazard decision at the breakfast-table to go to Paris;
the goddess in the garden that evening; the beauty of the house
above the Neckar; the nuclear physicist and the Existentialist;
Liselotte with her bookbinders, Giotto and Fra Angelico; the
Shakespeare plays; the giant Professor with his ingenious toys;
Kati Huber—all this blends together for me now as the last eve-
ning-glow of Europe. One is almost inclined to think that this
could not have gone on; it was tinged with that trace of death
which is said to be immanent in beauty as long as we live on
this earth.

9. Medicine Again

FROM 1931 to 1932 I was Resident Physician in the Medical
University Clinic in Frankfurt under Professor Volhard. For
some reason, which even today I cannot understand, the professor had called me back from Berlin and I became Lecture
Assistant. This was a distinction among the Residents. It was
the duty of the lecture assistant to prepare the daily lecture in
Internal Medicine. He had to select the patients according to the
diseases which were to be discussed, or those patients who prevented a clinical symptomatology of striking didactic value. The
lecture assistant was placed like an acolyte next to the professor
in the center of the amphitheater, and he remained there during

the entire lecture. In many universities it was he who recited the patient's clinical history before the professor began to discuss it.

In Anglo-Saxon countries one distinguishes between clinical and didactic lectures—that is, between lectures in which patients are demonstrated and their histories discussed, and lectures in which, after the fashion of textbooks, clinical medicine is taught in an abstract form. This distinction does not exist in German-speaking countries. The two elements are combined. No clinical condition is ever discussed without being illustrated by the demonstration of a patient and a discussion of his history. Therefore the clinical teachers depended a great deal on the sort of illnesses of which cases were available on the wards. This increased the element of flexibility in the academic teaching of medicine, and made the schedule less rigorous.

Every morning at eight I appeared in the Chief's private office and presented a list of patients for teaching purposes. Strictly speaking, it was a list of illnesses. Like a chef who proposes the menu of the day, I would say: "We have today a mitral stenosis, a cirrhosis of the liver with ascites, a cancer of the colon, a chronic pericardial adhesion, and a spastic hemiplegia," and he would reply: "Always the same stuff. Can't you get something different once in a while, not ever?" At nine o'clock the lecture began. The history was read and then the bed was wheeled into the amphitheater.

Volhard had an unorthodox method of teaching, quite unique even compared with other German universities. Frequently the patient was brought in without any preliminary introduction. The professor raised his hand in an imploring manner, glanced all over the audience, and then looked long and pensively at the patient. Presently there was a hush over the big room, and one could have heard a pin drop. The only thing one heard was the patient's breath. This silence went on for several minutes which seemed like half an hour. The master looked as if he was oblivious to the world. Suddenly, as if collecting himself, he addressed the students who had been called down to the floor of the amphitheater: "What do you see?" This was the first sentence spoken and it presented the first words of an involved ritual. There was again silence because usually nobody answered right away. Until the very end of the procedure all technical helps such as X-rays, laboratory findings, charts were banned. We were supposed to be physicians, true physicians in a Hippocratic sense, devoid of all the props of modern technology, and the first act was the act of seeing.

Presently, a voice would rise from the middle of the amphitheater: "There is dyspnea. The respiration is thirty-five per minute." The professor remained pensive and immobile as if he had not heard. Someone else said: "Pallor around the area of the mouth," and again someone remarked: "Club-shaped fingers." Things became more involved when a student in the first row discussed the appearance of the veins of the neck. After the students had observed the most minute details, including the pulse of the carotid and the appearance of the nail-bed and duly described what they had seen, they were allowed to feel the radial pulse. After they had seen asymmetries in the expansion of the chest, they were permitted to feel the circumference of the ribs during the rhythmic movement of breathing. Usually students were allowed to touch only after everything that was to be seen had been seen. It was quite extraordinary to experience the varieties of tactile sensation. There was, quite aside from the world of sight, an entire world of touch which we had never perceived before. In feeling differences of radial pulse you could train yourself to feel dozens of different waves with their characteristic peaks, blunt and sharp, steep and slanting, and the corresponding valleys. There were so many ways in which the margin of the liver came up towards your palpating finger. There were extraordinary varieties of smell. There was not just pallor but there seemed to be hundreds of hues of yellow and of gray.

After looking for five minutes, and after sniffing, feeling, listening, the students began to compute the data. This was the great tradition of classical medicine of the nineteenth century, a sort of craftsmanship of the senses. Now the diagnostic picture began to arise. The signs became meaningful in their context and in association with what we had learned about, let us say, the physiology of circulation or the biochemistry of sugar metabolism. Only when the students, at the end of the parliamentary discussion, had come to a definite conclusion were they finally presented with X-rays, graphs and figures.

All this was conducted by the professor, and accompanied by the most extraordinary histrionics. Other German professors in clinical medicine, particularly those who had attained international fame, had in their teaching an impersonal, God-like manner, and conducted themselves with pompous solemnity. When a Geheimrat wanted to show lantern slides, he bellowed "Dark, please!" and you saw a visible trembling go through the row of assistants. These assistants were seated on a bench at the Geheimrat's right hand, in hierarchic order, from the associate professor down to the voluntary assistant physician. At the command "Dark, please" it was as if the Captain had shouted: "All hands on deck!" Everyone went into action, at the projector, at the window blinds, and so on. Then they all fell, in the manner of marionettes, back in their seats waiting to be re-mobilized at a word. This atmosphere prevailed in most German teaching centers.

With Volhard it was quite different. The to and fro of discursive teaching was accompanied by volleys of cajoling, sarcasm, flattery, ridicule and praise. At some stupid reply he would wince as if from physical pain. Yet he retained an amazing degree of natural authority. This was due to his overpowering physical presence and his amazing, universal knowledge of detail in

which he was always far ahead of the most widely read among
his co-workers.

Curiously enough the patients enjoyed these teaching sessions.
Perhaps they were welcome interruptions of the hospital routine.
At any rate, there is no doubt that Volhard succeeded. He instilled in us something which one might call clinical sense.
Furthermore, by his colorful and highly personal way of repre-
sentation, he fixed clinical pictures in our memory with extraordinary lucidity. Pneumonia, typhoid fever, various types of
cardiac lesions or of nephritis represented not just textbook
categories but acquired the vividness of drama. Pathology, "the
science of suffering," knows some mysterious and fascinating laws
of development, some sort of weird negative counterpart of the
laws which underlie growth and creation.

Every day at eleven o'clock there was the clinical conference.
The Chief and, all in all, perhaps thirty people were seated at
a long green table. The large number of clinical workers was due
to the fact that there were always quite a few voluntary assistants, foreign guest workers and visitors present. The professor officiated at the head of the table. Administrative, clinical
and scientific problems were discussed in an informal, random
manner. All cases of death had to be reported by the resident
physicians, and were discussed at length. "Literature" was dis-
tributed by the Chief. These were innumerable reprints of scientific papers which had to be reviewed at certain gatherings once
in a while in an evening at the professor's house.

I have already said that he loved the extreme. While he had
been professor in Halle and already world-famous he refused to
have an automobile and did all his consulting practice on a
bicycle. However, he insisted on being the only citizen of Halle
to ride his bicycle on the sidewalks. For this prerogative he
had to pay so many fines to the police that the money accumulated to a substantial sum. Finally, the Prussian police gave in,
and he remained the privileged bicyclist. When he came to

Frankfurt he obtained a Maybach, the German equivalent of a Rolls-Royce, with chauffeur and all. Transitions like this, from bicycle to Maybach, were quite characteristic, and in retropsect I must say that they symbolized the atmosphere in which we lived, while working under him, an atmosphere of the expansive and the contradictory.

There was a large amount of laboratory research going on. Volhard had conceived, rather early in the Twenties, the hypothesis that chronic high blood pressure could be caused by a substance which originated in damaged kidney tissue; that the high blood pressure, in turn, damaged the kidney more, thus establishing a vicious circle. This hypothesis was proved not in his clinic but, much later, by the ingenious work of Goldblatt. Nevertheless, the fact that the professor tried to prove a very definite though hypothetical point and that all his experimental co-workers were trying to ferret out a certain chemical principle gave the research department the intensive air of sleuths-and-hounds. At least this was the way he wanted to see it. I, too, by a peculiar combination of circumstances was given a bio-chemical problem for my Doctor's thesis. The specific problem itself, incidentally, was absurd and uninteresting but, even apart from this, I maintained by main interest in Neurology and Psychiatry. All the large medical university clinics had in those days a sub-department devoted to the neurological and psychiatric borderline problems of internal medicine. Usually one man was especially trained for this type of work.

In the Twenties there had begun the interest in what is now called psychosomatic medicine. The Heidelberg neurologist von Weizsäcker was one of the first to emphasize, in a grandly conceived and daring theory, that the dualism of "organic (i.e., anatomically visible) versus psychogenic" in medicine no longer holds, and that in all organic illnesses there are deeply hidden psychological mechanisms at work. When in the Twenties Thomas Mann's *The Magic Mountain* appeared, with its astounding insight into the mental roots of an illness as "anatomical" as pulmonary tuberculosis, there were many medical people who began to focus on this huge uncharted field. Even surgeons, usually the most mechanistic in the profession, congratulated the novelist on his work, and confessed that their outlook on illness had been changed. Of course, all this was strongly affected by psychoanalysis which had for quite some time begun to influence medicine as well as the arts.

Volhard wanted a trained neurologist on his staff but entertained at the same time some vague idea of what one now would call psychosomatic work within the Department of Internal Medicine. For these two things he had me singled out. He called psychoanalysis a *schweinerei* because of its preoccupation with sex, but he did not mean by this to imply a judgment of value. Thus, while he was distributing medical reprints for review and he came across, let us say, a psychoanalytic study on bed-wetting he would say: "Here comes something dirty—Stern, this is for you!"

The evenings would approach on which the papers had to be reviewed. This was done in the professor's residence, and was associated with beer, sausages and potato salad, and with a great amount of leg-pulling and general rambunctiousness. It went on like this interminably, from bone-marrow reactions caused by bacillus abortus to the influence of hypnosis on water-metabolism. The only one who could endure this fare without the slightest sign of fatigue and with what seemed to be mounting attention was the Old Man himself. He followed it all, criticized, dissected, conducted, argued and commandeered—a scientific Jupiter, with an air of omniscience. In spite of this, there was no hint of pompousness, and when we chaffed him, or pointed out some stupidity he had committed in the course of an argument, he roared with laughter until tears rolled down his cheeks. In the small hours of the morning he packed a large number of us into the Maybach, got hold of the chauffeur and took us to a hotel bar in Wiesbaden where he treated us to Rhine wine.

During this time I must have forgotten the social and human approach to medicine of which I had first become aware under Haase's guidance in Berlin. Volhard himself showed a fervent passion for knowledge combined with a cool detachment when it came to the social aspects of a case. It was the same sort of childlike pagan detachment, almost with a faint note of cruelty, of which Goethe and Leonardo were capable while looking at Nature. When looking at these people it seems as if the laws of truth and the laws of charity lived side by side in mutual independence.

Besides being the lecture assistant, which was certainly no full-time occupation, I worked in a cardiological ward and in the laboratory. The head nurse in the cardiological ward was a blonde middle-aged woman, an ardent Catholic from Westphalia. She devoted herself with extraordinary fervor to the welfare of each patient, and I remember that I had an awkward feeling in her presence. I know for certain that I felt her silent disapproval of our jovial "scientific" detachment. She was, although not really related, more or less like a member of the household of Professor Friedrich Dessauer, the famous leader of German Catholicism. There was another person, a senior physician, Doctor Hildebrand, incidentally also a Catholic, who showed a very human approach in his work in the ward. Although there was perhaps nothing heroic or extraordinary about all this, and it was less impressive than what I had experienced in the Center of Alcoholics in Moabit, yet it all is prominent in my memory because the general atmosphere, to which I myself contributed, was "scientific" in a "superior" manner.

Professor Dessauer was one of those incredible figures who arose in Germany during the sunset of German history, just before the present night fell. He was chairman of a "Department for Physics Applied to Medicine"; today we would call it a department of biophysics. In those days his establishment was unique in Germany, perhaps in the world. It occupied itself with all those aspects of research which lie on the borderline between physics and medicine. He had been one of the early pioneers in the field of X-rays and radium. However, he was one of those encyclopedic German types and could, without any difficulty, in fact with equal facility, have been chairman of a department of Physics or of Medical Therapeutics or of History or of Political Science or of Economics. He was a member of parliament in the Catholic Centrum and belonged to the parliamentary nucleus of that party. He was deeply religious, a mystic and ascetic. He was a thin and fragile man with a huge dome-like forehead. Like all the earliest pioneers in the field of very hard electromagnetic waves, he had acquired cancer of the exposed parts of the skin. Thus his hands and face were withered, and when one first saw his tremendously high wax-colored cranium, surrounded by a wreath of brown curls, the hollow face resembling that of a pale starved child, with deeply set intense eyes, and his thin, tapering, truly cadaverous hands, one had the experience of something almost purely cerebral with a trace of physical appendage. In contrast to this he had a strong, warm, mellow voice, and hearing him speak on ultraviolet rays or on Christian socialism, one could not get rid of the feeling of a friendly apparition.

He had a truly overwhelming power of oratory. While Volhard was at his best in a small circle of students whom he seemed to mold by sheer physical action, an artist and creative improviser, Dessauer made his greatest impression in formal lectures to a large audience in a big auditorium. Even people who had never been interested in physics or in political science or in history sat on the edges of their chairs and forgot to sneeze or cough. I shall never forget a lecture on cosmic rays. He had built some contraption in which gamma rays of cosmic origin could be registered by a Geiger counter. The click of the counter was amplified by a loudspeaker. I still see the eerie apparition (the "Professor" out of a story by E. T. A. Hoffmann) from whom emanated the oratorical flow of a scientific Bossuet. He interrupted his speech; the audience sat motionless in absolute silence; and every minute or so a click was heard over the loudspeaker, a friendly little tap from outer space.

This was less than one year before Hitler came into power. Professor Dessauer, one of the leaders of a democratic Catholicism, was then very much exposed, and his complete and utter fearlessness in all his public political appearances was in striking contrast to his physique. He was not only a profoundly religious Catholic but also, I believe, the descendant of a Jewish family which had been converted a few generations before. Any stormtrooper could have annihilated him with one hand and, later, they nearly did.

In spite of such vivid impressions in my immediate surroundings, I was not in the least influenced by them. On the contrary, I maintained what I now think was a very foolish and unrealistic philosophical attitude. I remember particularly a conversation with one of my friends who was engaged to the daughter of one of the refugee Menshevik Russian leaders. While I again held forth on the principles of dialectic materialism, he told me a few very concrete things which happened to his fiancée's family under the Bolsheviks. I shrugged my shoulders with a "That's too bad" attitude, and pointed out to him that there is "no surgical operation during which there must not flow a certain amount of blood." To think that I, who had never made the slightest material sacrifice for any one of my numerous convictions, said that. However, I was soon to get a first-hand experience of the inner dialectics of modern revolutions, at the receiving end.

In those days I was greatly disturbed by the lukewarm attitude of the leaders of liberal thought in Germany. Perhaps I felt that National Socialism could be counteracted by a radicalism of equal violence. While recovering from an attack of influenza early in 1932, I collected my wits and wrote a letter to Thomas

Mann. I remember its contents very well; I must have felt a great deal of disquietude at that time. I started out by praising his lucid rationalism. This was the more remarkable, I said, since he had apparently been sorely tempted by the magic of German romanticism and irrationalism (which was quite clear from the things he had written on Wagner). I indicated that he had succeeded in coming back to rationalism but not to the rationalism of the French thinkers of the eighteenth century. His rationalism was tried in the fire of German irrationalism of Wagner and Schopenhauer and purified in all those currents which had contributed to the rise of Nationalism. His was a return to rationalism on a higher level, a phenomenon which showed the spiral movement of history. In retrospect this part of my letter sounds to me like sophisticated apple-polishing, but I am sure it was meant sincerely at the moment. However, I then proceeded to take the famous man to task for his ambiguous attitude in all questions pertaining to the social revolution. I wanted him to commit himself. I pointed out that there was a parallel between the cultural skepticism of Freud and that of Karl Marx. Since Mann had recognized the great purgative element in the former, it would be only fair to recognize it also in the latter. I told him how distressed I (one of his admirers) was to see that in the *The Magic Mountain* he lumped Marxism together with Catholicism by presenting them in one and the same person, Naphta, an unsympathetic person at that. How could he! And he presented his own political philosophy in the pleasant, humane and humanistic person of Settembrini whose European liberal attitude was as far removed from Marxism as from Catholicism. This, I thought, was highly unfair to Marxism, and it was this sort of thinking which had contributed much to the misery in which Germany found herself at the moment.

It was not long before I received a lengthy reply. Although Mann wrote most of his letters in longhand, this one was typewritten; he explained this by saying that he was recovering from an attack of influenza and had dictated the letter. Since I have forgotten most of the contents of his letter, it is even more interesting to note what I remember. First, I remember that the famous man called my letter very intelligent, and he hoped he would meet me sometime personally. It is not difficult to see why this should have impressed me. Second, he remarked that people got erroneous ideas of his position on certain questions because he also changed his standpoint as time went on. He quoted, somewhat cryptically, Goethe who once said that "when people think I am still in Jena I am already in Erfurt." Third, he indicated, though I do not remember the context, that "the Catholic Brüning might still save Germany."

It was around this time that Professor Volhard decided finally that I should go away for post-graduate studies in Psychiatry and Neurology. Thus, in the summer of 1932 I went to Munich to work as a Rockefeller Fellow at the German Research Institute for Psychiatry.

10. *The Psychiatric Institute*

THE German Research Institute for Psychiatry was a tall building, modern after a fashion, situated in the outskirts of Munich. Its grounds adjoined those of a general hospital. Its wards were actually located within that hospital, and the building of the institute proper was entirely devoted to research. It was a so-called Kaiser Wilhelm Institute. The Kaiser Wilhelm Society was the largest German association for the support of research, comparable in many ways to the Rockefeller Foundation. It supported research in fields as far apart as plant physiology, eugenics, nuclear physics, and psychiatry. This particular institute was the first institute for psychiatric research, I believe, anywhere in the world. It had been founded by Kraepelin, the patriarch of classical descriptive or "school" psychiatry. Very early Kraepelin had conceived the idea of combining under one roof all those branches of science which he regarded as ancillary to psychiatry. Consequently the Deutsche Forschungsanstalt für Psychiatrie mirrored in its very organization the scientific approach of the turn of the century towards psychiatry. On the ground floor there were the offices of the clinical department and those of the department of genetics, the science of heredity. On the second floor there was a department of Serology and a department of Spirochete Research. The entire third floor was occupied by the department of Neuropathology, devoted to the microscopic study of the abnormal human brain. On the fourth floor there was a department of Biochemistry. There was something cosmopolitan about the place, interwoven with a quaint Teutonic element. The cosmopolitan atmosphere was due to the fact that the institute, particularly its neuropathological department, enjoyed an international reputation and attracted research fellows from many countries.. At one time we had guests from the United States, Canada, Brazil, Scotland, Poland, Czechoslovakia, Switzerland, Turkey, Estonia, Spain and Sweden. Although a part of the Kaiser Wilhelm Society, the institute had received its financial foundation from James Loeb, the American banker of German-Jewish extraction, and from the Rockefeller Foundation. In addition to this, the head of the department of biochemistry was an American scientist who conducted its proceedings by proxy, and appeared only on visits. All this gave to the place the air of an enclave of pure science, free of national and political boundaries. On the other hand, in marked contrast to it were certain German elements, particularly in the department of genetics and in the clinical department. Ever since the end of the last century, all those people who had been attracted to human genetics had some affinity, conscious or unconscious, with a biological, racist outlook on human affairs. Racism presupposes that a man's way of living is largely determined by some innate qualities which he receives from his ancestors; hence there exists in this world noble and mean persons, not by their free choice but on the basis of the chemical structure of their chromosomes. Marxism, on the other hand, postulates that a man's conduct is determined largely by the social and economic qualities of the environment into which he is born. In either case man's freedom is denied, in the first by some intrinsic principle, in the second by something outside ourselves. Consequently there were, even before Hitler, in the genetics department some scientists with a geneticist bias which had originated in the racist, anti-semitic literature of the Nineties, just as there had been in Russia, even before the Bolshevik revolution, geneticists with an environmental or Lamarckian bias. In either case the persons had not become racist or Marxist as a result of their scientific findings, but had gone in for human genetics because of a preconceived political idea.

The clinical professor was a thin short man with dark piercing eyes and a sharp profile which somehow conveyed the tension of a half-opened pocket knife about to snap. There was something Spartan-soldierly about him which covered a delicate sensitive core. He was known to have in his possession a collection of German romantic poetry in neat flexible Moroccan volumes. He belonged to the so-called phenomenological school of psychiatry which is derived from modern German philosophy. Its central idea had something to do with the question of how much one can understand a patient's actual, conscious mental symptoms by re-experiencing them, by putting oneself into the sick person's mind, so to speak. It emphasizes a sharp distinction between this method, and the method of interpretation of symptoms. Therefore, it set up a marked contrast to psychoanalysis. Although this school was theoretically interesting and more important than it would seem today, it remained completely sterile from the point of view of the treatment of patients.

The professor of genetics was a square heavy-set individual, with a chunky head, white brush cut and white goatee. He had done some interesting work way back in 1910 on the heredity of insanity. Ever since then he had apparently lived on his reputation. However, many years before anyone knew anything about Hitler he had begun to advocate the sterilization of the mentally afflicted. Curiously enough, this seemed originally not altogether incompatible with his Swiss Protestant background. It is quite possible that he had conceived it not only as scientific (which it was not) but also as humanitarian and philanthropic.

On the staff of the genetics department was Doctor Leo Mager. He was slim, blond and blue-eyed. We knew that he belonged to the Nazi Party and had a "low number," i.e., a party card number which indicated that he had been one of the early Nazis. It was rumored that in the event of Hitler's seizure of power he was slated for a very high position, probably Minister of Health of Bavaria. His blue eyes had a peculiar staring gaze, he walked with a stiff staccato gait, looked Nordic, and behaved in general like a ham actor impersonating a Nazi. He refused to sit at a table with me or any other Jewish doctor, and when I entered he left the room. He had, incidentally, developed a mysterious theory on the origin of certain diseases, and had been given a considerable research grant to prove it. He claimed that the distribution of these diseases was related to geological properties of the land. His research grant included large traveling expenses, and he drove all over Germany, sampled soil, and drew complicated maps in which he indicated graphically the incidence of sicknesses in the population, on one hand, and certain properties of the soil on the other. The relationship seemed to become more complex as his research progressed, the figures and maps were hard to understand, at least to me, and even to this day, whether his theory is valid or not, in my mind it remains associated with his theories on the influence of the Jews, or the Freemasons, or the Catholics on world history.

There was another man in the genetics department who fascinated me in the beginning, merely by his appearance. Doctor Schulz was short and round, with a huge pumpkin-like head, and enormous cheeks which were furrowed by parallel saber scars, tokens from his student years. He had jug-handle ears, and the way in which his jowls protruded in the direction of the shoulders gave the impression that he had no neck. I often watched him saunter through the corridors, with his feet turned outward in a Chaplinesque manner, and I used to watch the foreign doctors' reaction to this apparation, the caricature of German Academic Man. In the doctors' dining-room he always sat beside Doctor Mager, and therefore I began to associate the two in my mind. Doctor Schulz was quite aware of his appearance; he claimed that he owed his life to it. During the First World War, he told us, his company was smoked out from a dug-out by a group of French soldiers, and every German emerging from the entrance was bayoneted. However, when Schulz appeared, the French said: "Voilà, un cochon!" and let him live.

The chief of the department of research on spirochetes, Professor Brosam, was the example of a true specialist. Spirochetes are delicate silvery microorganisms of corkscrew shape, and one variety of them is the infectious agent of syphilis. It was said that the professor knew by heart five thousand references in the literature on spirochetes and from talks with him I am quite prepared to believe it. But he did not seem to think or talk about much else. His appearance was the opposite of the delicate structure to which he had devoted all his life and energy. He was huge, with a bald round head, a face that looked as if compressed by a blast, and an accidental vegetation of mustache. His limbs were enormous, and his long arms seemed to dangle uselessly when he was not making microscopic slides. He had huge animal colonies and spent night after night working in the animal house, infecting little beasts with syphilis; I never found out exactly for what purpose. He once had invented a stain for spirochetes in the brain which subsequently had become world-famous. As happens so often, his name became identified with the field in which he had gained his reputation, so that in the end the matter of creativeness became completely irrelevant. In his case there was something bizarre and uncanny about it.

On one occasion, one of our clinicians discovered a little ferret in his basement. Not knowing what to do with it he gave it as a present to Professor Brosam. This seemed reasonable enough because Brosam was the only one with large-scale facilities for animals. Half a year later Brosam read a paper at one of the medical meetings which began with the remarkable statement: "About six months ago one of my colleagues had the great kindness to hand me a ferret which he had found in the basement of his house. There I was, confronted with the problem of how to make the best and most extensive use of this animal. After deliberating for two days, the idea occurred to me that I could infect it with syphilis." It had taken him two days.

I had my own headquarters in the department which was devoted to the microscopic study of the sick human brain. This was the part of the institute in which I was supposed to begin my career. I was made assistant to the head of that department, Professor Spielmeyer, on the terms of the Rockefeller grant. Apart from having to do research on "Idiocy" and "Circulatory Disturbances," my main duty was to instruct the research fellows. There was a spacious bright laboratory with comfortable glass-topped working tables. There were a certain number of guest workers from various countries, and each was allotted a certain amount of space, a microscope and other facilities necessary for this kind of work. After an introductory period of training, I had, for a large part of the day, to wander from microscope to microscope in order to instruct the guests. Frequently there were not two from the same country.

Doctor Adam Opalski, now professor of neurology at the University of Warsaw, had his working place next to mine.

Opalski was a short, squat, muscular man, and most people might have spotted him as Slav but would have mistaken him for a cavalry officer. He made an extensive study of the abnormal anatomy of the ependyma (the inner lining of the brain), and for this purpose studied microscopic sections from two thousand cases. Except for certain areas of the cortex, i.e., the surface of the brain, which resemble one another too closely, Opalski was able to identify any area of the brain under the microscope. To him this was something like a sport, and at times he did it on the basis of bets. Soon he taught me to do the same; in fact, most of what I know about the normal microscopy of the brain I owe to him. Later, he and I staged competitions of this kind for the benefit of the guest workers. He would glance into the microscope, at a medium or high-power magnification, slap the bench, and say: "This is the small-celled part of the anterior nucleus of the thalamus" (a certain area in the interior of the brain). He was one of those people gifted with an almost mysterious sense of morphe, the structure of created things. His brother was professor of astronomy, also in Warsaw, and he himself was able to translate in his mind all these plain microscopic sections into three-dimensional concepts with a functional meaning.

The brain, like any other organ, consists of microscopically small particles, the cells. Unlike other organs, for example the liver, the appearance and function of these cells is not the same in any two different spots. There are about two billion nerve cells in the superficial layer of the brain alone. Each one of these cells looks approximately like an octopus. It has a body with a nucleus, and processes which resemble tentacles. Frequently one of these processes is much longer than the remaining ones. In this case, it is usual that the short tentacles conduct nerve impulses *towards* the cell body, and the long tentacle conducts them *away from* the cell body. In other words, each single cell can be compared to a sort of telephone center. The short processes receive incoming calls, the long process sends a call along to another cell.

If a person does something simple, for example, if he moves his little finger, a large set of these cells in the brain is required. If one tried to describe the wire connections which correspond to such a thought and its transmission to the muscles of the hand, one would have to write an entire book. Such a motor impulse going out from the brain *towards* the muscles of one's little finger is continuously accompanied by reports from these muscles coming into the brain. This means that, while the little finger is moving, reports are being received by the brain about the position of the finger joints, the tension of the muscles, and so on, at any given moment of the action. In fact, the brain cells are able to send proper orders out into the executive organs (in this case the muscles of the little finger) only if they receive continuous incoming calls about how the orders are being carried out. From this little example alone it can be seen that the wiring must be of infinite and wondrous complexity. In fact, even people who have never worked in this field will readily understand why so many research workers in the medical sciences throw themselves into their work with a selfless fervor which resembles religious devotion. In the department of neuropathology there were not only psychiatric and neurological guest workers but also pathologists, that is, people who devote their work to the study of morbid anatomy. The normal and abnormal anatomy of the brain is so complicated, and particularly the methods of investigation are so involved that most anatomists refrain from dealing with it to any extent unless they have been trained specially for this task.

When I walked from one microscope to another, I traversed immeasurable distances as far as the people with whom I had to deal were concerned. There was, for example, a Japanese animal pathologist from Mukden who studied a peculiar form of brain disease occurring in silver foxes. I shall have to talk more

about him later. Next to the Japanese was a Nazi psychiatrist
from Northern Germany. Once a week we assembled with the
clinicians in an amphitheater, microscopic slides were projected
onto a screen, and I had to discuss them.

The chief of our department, Professor Spielmeyer, and the
chief of the serological department, Professor Plaut, formed the
counter-balance to all the Teutonic elements. Both were scientists in the better sense of the word, open and cosmopolitan.
This had not always been so, at least not in Spielmeyer's case.
Shortly after the First World War he had made a remark in the
foreword to a textbook which had been generally interpreted as
bitterly nationalist. But since then he had broadened more and
more so that he actually arrived at detesting any form of narrow
provincialism. Professor Spielmeyer, a tall, lean man with fair
hair and blue eyes, came originally from Northern Germany.
Plaut was from an old Southern German Jewish family. It was
Plaut who had been closest to the great Kraepelin and had accompanied the latter on a famous world tour which led them to visit
almost all psychiatric centers, including lunatic asylums on tropical islands. Spielmeyer had been on lecture tours in North and
South America. It was due to all this that Spielmeyer and Plaut,
the two friends, had succeeded in creating that undefinable
atmosphere which goes with the catholicity of science.

One of the Rockefeller fellows in the biochemical department
was Lydia Pasternak, daughter of the Russian impressionist
painter, who had been one of the intimate friends of Tolstoy.
He was the first to illustrate *War and Peace* and *Resurrection,* in
close collaboration with Tolstoy himself. The walls of the doctors'
dining-room were decorated with several lithographs by Leonid
Pasternak, signed by the painter himself. One of these lithographs was Tolstoy's portrait.

It must be obvious that the doctors' dining-room was an unusual place. When I come to think of it, it seems quite remark-

able now that nobody ever talked shop. But I learned the most
varied things there. Doctor Essen-Möller, an unbelievably tall
and bald-headed Swedish clinician and geneticist, now professor
of psychiatry in Lund, introduced me to the after-dinner sport of
lifting a raw egg up from the floor with the aid of a dessert spoon.
He and Lydia Pasternak, neither of whom spoke German as their
mother tongue, composed ingenious poems in the style of Christian Morgenstern, a profound German mystic, who has written
poetry of a bizarre childlike humor, somewhat like Lewis Carroll.
Some of the clinicians used to sit over their coffee in what, to me
now, seem like endless huddles about Kierkegaard and existentialism. I can still see American doctors from the Mid-West, a
doctor from Brussels, and a Chinese psychiatrist from Peking
sitting in on this with an expression of open curiosity, but I
found out that in spite of the heavy Teutonic terminology they
actually understood what it was all about.

The most extraordinary phenomenon (I had occasion to recall
it later in all its details) was a couple of Nazi doctors from the
Rhineland who held forth on the so-called "Theory of Permanent
Revolution" of Trotsky. This theory was familiar to me from the
"political" activities of my student-days but that it should be expounded by these people was something entirely new and quite
astonishing. After listening to their discussions a few times I
said: "Gentlemen, I understand that you draw a good deal of
your theory on political strategy from Trotsky. Does it not strike
you as extraordinary that you—Nazis—quote Trotsky, a Bolshevik and a Jew, as if he were your evangelist?" They turned to
one another, laughed, and looked at me as one would look at a
political yokel (which I was). That their reply should have been
such a revelation indicates our political naiveness at the time.
To begin with, they belonged to a then quite powerful wing in
the Nazi party, which was in favor of an alliance of Communist
Russia and Nazi Germany against what they called Western
Capitalism. They claimed that very few of the Nazi leaders were

really anti-semitic, and that anti-semitism was quite consciously used merely as a political tool to obtain the support of the petite bourgeoisie. It was quite possible, they said, that Hitler took his anti-semitism seriously but most Nazi leaders were not even interested in the Jewish question and employed it only in the way indicated. As to Bolshevism, it was the same. The anti-Bolshevist campaign was initiated only in order to obtain support from big industry, particularly in France and England. From this they proceeded to develop their own dialectics, which were, in an eerie and weird fashion, similar to, and yet slightly different from, those of Marxism.

I cannot quite understand today why this overwhelmed me. I had already dimly perceived a change in the image of Communism. It was as if the original passion for justice, that religious sense of identification with the poor which had been so apparent in figures such as Henri Barbusse and Vera Figner, had given way to something new and altogether opposite. Another generation seemed to have arisen, scientifically-trained engineers of destruction. The means had become the end. Ernst Haase had already told me, from his experience of close contact with Russians, that a new social machine was no longer related to the thirst for justice which had, at least in part, underlain the social revolution. We did have a vague idea of things which, a few years later, first came into the open in André Gide's book *Retour de l' U.S.S.R.* But only here, in the doctors' dining-room, and in conversation with Nazis, did all this crystallize into a simple insight. It was extraordinary to listen to these cold, thoughtful lectures. All that remained was the most cynical Machiavellism; when one was not listening very carefully, one was never quite sure whether they were talking Nazism or Bolshevism, and in the end it did not matter much. This experience was startling and has remained with me until today. I was not at all surprised at the Non-Aggression Pact in 1939, and I was extremely sur-

prised when the German-Russian war was interpreted in the
American press in 1941 as an ideological war.

It also seems in retrospect so obvious that a cold intellectual
approach to matters which are actually of the spirit is one of the
deadly sins of our time. There we were sitting, talking away, on
Kierkegaard, on Existentialism, on Dialectic Materialism, but
without the moral decisiveness, the *raison du cœur* which all
these questions demand. Most of us lived the same life, a life of
libertinism and *laissez-faire,* and therefore any subject on which
we touched in our intellectual pursuits became equivocal, amorphous and meaningless. One can see precisely the same thing
now among many intellectuals in North America. Many of the
people in that dining-room were later forced by fate to make a
moral decision, to live a heroic life and (in some cases) to die
a heroic death. But it took much time and agony.

Not at all sophisticated or Machiavellian was the Communism
of Herr Eisinger. Eisinger was the chauffeur of the institute. He
had a tower skull (an abnormality not infrequent among the
Alpine races) which gave him, falsely, a feeble-minded appearance. His task was to drive the chiefs in a limousine, and to run
errands between the institute and various hospitals and firms of
supply. He growled like a bear whenever he was given an order.
He was quite open with me, and whenever we drove into town
together he was more talkative than usual. Eisinger gave me a
clear and precise forecast of the political future of Europe. While
we were transporting jars with brains through the magnificent
Arch of Victory and Leopoldstrasse towards the Institute he explained to me that it was a good thing that England and France
rearmed. If they did not, and Hitler came to power, there would
be war. He spoke a broad Bavarian idiom. He told me that quite
a few of the professors at the Institute were *rindvieher* (cattle)
and implored me not to believe them. He also told me that he
and the Herr Cooperator (assistant parish priest) of Sendling
were on the Nazi blacklist. It seemed that the S.A. District

Leader of Sendling, a Munich suburb, had informed Eisinger
that he and the assistant parish priest would be shot on the first
day of the seizure of power.

11. *Herr Eisinger*

I MUST have done something to my back at the time, I have forgotten what. At any rate I was lying on my stomach with a
couple of electrodes for diathermy over my back when another
patient in the physiotherapy department of the Schwabinger
Krankenhaus said: "Hitler has become Reichschancellor." This
seemed to be a statement of utmost importance, and my first reaction was to get up from the table, go home and pack, or at
least do something about it. But since nobody in the room seemed
to get as excited about the news as he should have, I remained
quiet.

I had a feeling of tingling warmth in my lumbar area, and I
pretended to go on dozing. The physiotherapist, an old man
with a round peasant face, made a few dark hints to me. At first
I did not understand, but during subsequent diathermy treat-
ments he indicated that the Bavarian youth in the Alps were
prepared and ready to get going. They were secretly organized
and armed to defend Bavaria, and put "our king" back on his
throne. They just waited for their password to be given and
Hitler did not stand a chance. The more often he spoke about
it, the more detailed did his account become; and gradually I
also began to see the boys with rakish green hats adorned with
woodcock feathers secretly gathering near the mountain lakes by
moonlight. Incidentally, he did have something there. In March,
1933, it was a question of a few hours and the Crown Prince
Rupprecht would have been proclaimed king by a *coup d'état*.

Bavaria would have become a Catholic monarchy separated from a Hitlerian Reich. However, all monarchists seem to be as thoughtful, slow and methodical as my friend in the physiotherapy department, their techniques are not as up-to-date as those of their adversaries, and the final outcome is well known.

Gradually, the Institute began to show changes. At the first scientific meeting Brosam gave a lecture. The topic was syphilis, and the professor said it was historically certain from the Old Testament that Moses simply killed off all patients with venereal diseases. A more humanitarian attitude towards the sick came with the ascent of the Aryan peoples. At the mention of Moses everybody glanced furtively at Professor Plaut whose appearance, incidentally, was in no way suggestive of prophetic Israel. It so happened that Brosam had always been a personal adversary of Plaut. One might have expected the transition to be more subtle, but it was not.

It seems that the professor of genetics had, for a long time, drafted a legislation for the sterilization of the unfit. This was, as I said, quite independent of party politics. In fact, similar legislations had been drafted in other non-Fascist countries. However, in 1933, Professor Rüdin, probably to his own surprise, saw himself suddenly dragged out of scientific semi-obscurity into the limelight of the German opera. Presently he was made Reichsführer of all German psychiatrists, and he saw the sterilization law passed in its most radical form. I still feel that he was acting in good faith, at least at that time, and he did what almost any other professor would have done if his life's idea, no matter how bizarre, were suddenly carried out by a government, no matter how constituted. All schizophrenic, manic-depressive, feeble-minded patients, and I believe almost all psychiatric patients had to be sterilized by surgical operation.

Because of the extermination plants, the concentration camps and the killing of the mentally afflicted during the war, this earliest of the Nazi atrocities has received much too little attention in history books. Every case with a psychiatric diagnosis had to be reported to the authorities, under threat of heavy penalties, very much as in other countries in the case of certain contagious diseases. Sterilization Courts were set up, with a hierarchic structure of higher and higher courts, up to a Supreme Sterilization Court. There was an incredible amount of red tape involved in all this. The important thing to realize is that, more than any other Nazi undertaking, it had the semblance of scientific objectivity, and here for once the "Aryan" and the "non-Aryan" were treated with complete impartiality. The premise, namely, that all these illnesses were determined by an inherent factor, was utterly false. But granted that the premise was true it could be mathematically computed by what time the German people would be free of mental illness. I mention all this because there are many people in the Western countries in favor of sterilization, even if not to this extent, and particularly because this gave me the first inkling of a society managed on so-called scientific principles.

There were some extreme instances. I remember the case of a housemaid, a devoutly Catholic spinster in her early forties who had broken down with a severe attack of melancholia. She was immediately slated for sterilization. A gynecologist, Doctor Albrecht, objected to the operation. He reasoned that the combination "melancholy, devoutly Catholic spinster of over forty" abolished all chances of offspring anyway, and that, on the other hand, such an operation, because of its profound meaning to the patient, would considerably diminish all possibilities of recovery. The case passed various levels in the pyramid of Sterilization Courts, but in the end she was sterilized. There were often heart-rending scenes on the part of patients and their relatives.

We are appalled at the wholesale killing of the mentally-afflicted in Nazi countries, at the experiments carried out in mental hospitals, but it happened not infrequently to me later, in a different cultural environment, that I heard similar desires expressed by people who believed whole-heartedly in Democracy and even fought for it. In mental hospitals you pass rows and rows, hundreds and hundreds of chronically demented men and women, drooling, staring into empty space, crouched motionless or rocking incessantly. In many cases their condition goes on for decades before they die a spontaneous death. Suddenly someone next to you is heard muttering out of the corner of his mouth: "At times I often ask myself, why don't we really let them die a peaceful death, at least the hopeless ones, would it not be so much more humane?" It really does not make much difference whether the thought is spoken out loud by someone else, or passes as a faint shadow in the depths of one's own heart, or appears as a fact reported from a faraway country. From a strictly pragmatic point of view, lacking a metaphysical concept of Man, there is no reason at all against such a step. We, in a non-dictatorial environment, are clinging to many patterns because of a Christian heritage, of which we are no longer conscious and not because we actually believe in the Christian doctrine of vicarious suffering, or the Hindu teaching of karma, or simply in man's immortal soul. In fact, most of us do not believe in any of these things. Thus, we cling with one hand to modern pragmatism, and with the other to the Hebrew-Christian philosophy. But the gap is widening all the time, and there will be a moment when one hand will have to let go.

Death, the Greek philosophers used to say, is the origin of philosophy. They should have added Insanity. And the chronically insane and the idiots, challenge our morality and gauge the inner dynamic tension of Christianity. There was a famous Lutheran pastor, Bodelschwingh, who built up a huge colony of feeble-minded, idiots and epileptics in Bethel in Western Germany. During the war, when the Nazis carried out the slaughter of all mental patients, Pastor Bodelschwingh insisted that he would be killed together with his inmates. It was only on the basis of his international fame that the politicians let him get away with it, and let him and the inmates of his colony live. This was a kind of last-ditch stand of Christianity.

The clinical director began to show statistics (I still see him write figures on the blackboard in a quiet and systematic way) which proved that since the introduction of Labor Camps, the number of psychoneurotic individuals encountered in the hospitals had considerably diminished. It was meant to indicate that the new era had brought a boom as far as the mental welfare of the population was concerned. Here, too, the State had sanctioned something which presents, poorly expressed, a widespread popular idea, namely, that milder psychiatric cases should be brought to their knees by a more disciplinarian attitude. It was quite extraordinary to watch this thin, sensitive man become enthusiastic (so at least it seemed) about his figures which symbolized the triumph of a soldierly Spartan life over the intricacies and agonies of the human soul. It occurred to me that he must be weak.

Incidentally, speaking of the clinical conferences, I am reminded of one amazing scene. A man was brought in who had been picked up as a psychiatric case in one of the medical wards. He had been admitted there on account of a stomach ailment. A psychiatric consultant had been called in for the following reason. There had been, as it is often seen in public medical wards, a rather close contact between the patients. Our man had used this contact to spread his ideas, those of a conscientious objector. He had "preached" (so the clinical report said) to his fellow patients, and to the nurses and internes he appeared to be a crank. The assistant read this history and presently the patient was brought into the conference room. He was a rather tall, thin, soft-spoken man with a sallow complexion. The fact that he was in his pajamas, dressing-gown and slippers, and we were all dressed, some of us in white doctors' coats, seemed somehow to put him at a disadvantage during the ensuing conversation. However, he did not seem to think in these terms. On the contrary, he was most affable and pleasant. As usual he gave his history very much as it had been reported. He told of the First World War and of his experiences in the trenches. There, in combat, he had suddenly come to the insight that killing people meant killing people, regardless of the circumstances, and that it was against the law of the Gospel. He said that he had resolved right there and then to tell everybody about this, his belief, and that since returning from the front he had attempted to devote his life to prayer and good works. He felt it was his moral duty to spread this idea. It was only natural, he said, that we as psychiatrists would look at all this from a different point of view. He understood that most of us were bound to think that he was crazy. He would never hold it against us, regardless as to what conclusions we came about his case, and what practical steps we might take. While the professor "explored" him, he maintained this most natural friendliness. After he had left the room, the professor summed the case up and came to the diagnosis of schizophrenia. I was startled. This meant not only insanity, but it implied, automatically, sterilization. There was never any discussion. During the entire scene I had a most painful sensation of familiarity, some sort of *déjà vu*. I could not remember, for the life of me, where I had seen this before. At this moment something strange happened. I was walking back from the hospital wing to the institute in the company of Doctor Bruno Schulz, the man with pumpkin head and the saber scars. It was dark, a dismal oppressive winter evening, and nobody spoke. All of a sudden I remembered. There is in Tolstoy's drama, "The Living Corpse," a scene in which the hero, a religious conscientious objector, is being examined by a panel of psychiatrists and declared insane. That very moment Schulz turned to me and broke the silence:

"Do you know what this reminded me of? Tolstoy's 'The Living Corpse.' There you'll find a completely analogous scene."

During the subsequent conversation, I got my first glimpse of one of the noblest and most beautiful souls I have ever encountered. Schulz came originally from Braunschweig. His background was Northern German. He had been the German beer-drinking and saber-fighting student. It seems, however, that the front experiences during the First World War had a shaking impact on him, perhaps not exactly in the same manner as in our poor patient, but somewhat similarly. Like many people of a Northern German Protestant background, he had been decisively influenced by the Russian religious thinkers. As far as I know he was not religious in any formal sense, but he simply lived a life of charity. It emanated from him. There are several Jewish physicians on this continent who owe their lives to him. The word "underground" activities had not yet been coined in those days, but this is what Schulz was engaged in all the time. His appearance was Germanic in a ludicrous manner. No German professional man has ever appeared in a political cartoon looking as bizarre as Bruno looked in reality He was generally considered a funny man. He had his hats specially made for him in Braunschweig and, like Mark Twain, he did all his writing in bed. Like many geneticists he was a good mathematician and he entertained something like a mystic relationship to numbers. He believed firmly in the theory of serial clustering of chance occurrences, a statistical theory which comes close to a science of superstition. He carried on a scientific correspondence with the famous statistical mathematician Weinberg, who has contributed much to the mathematical theory of genetics. This correspondence was written entirely on postcards. As some people play chess by mail, Schulz and Weinberg exchanged series of postcards which were covered with formulas on some technical aspect of the theory of probability. Looking at his superficial appearance one could see that nature had equipped Schulz with the most perfect smokescreen for almost any sort of secret activity. Later, he often discussed with me the possibility of emigrating. But his appearance and his lack of gift for languages must have inhibited him. Looking back, it was better that he stayed. Not only do I know of many Jews whom he helped, he also applied a brake to the psychiatric Reichsführer. Moreover, he often had to examine patients clinically for the question of sterilization, and he committed extraordinary distortions to save them from the knife. I know now that he had numerous close escapes but he was the psychiatric Reichsführer's assistant and, more than that, he had a unique camouflage.

It was in connection with Doctor Schulz that it first dawned on me that the Great Dividing Line in Europe, in fact in the entire world, is not the line between Right and Left. All of us who grew up in the intellectual atmosphere of the Twenties were sincerely convinced that people who were politically to the left of the middle acted under a moral incentive. Indeed, as I have said, in most radicals there had been during the early post-war period, underneath it all, a love of justice and a compassion for the multitude. Conversely, it was held that people were conservative out of material motives for conservation, no matter how much some of them were able to deceive themselves. In this respect the Nazi years taught us a lesson. It happened not infrequently that you met a friend whom you had known for years as a "staunch liberal," and he turned out to be eagerly ready for any compromise to save his skin. On the other hand, we saw people whom we had disdained as "reactionaries" go to concentration camps and to the gallows. In the beginning it seemed confusing. But gradually the issue became clearer, and it was obvious that the only thing that counts in this world is the strength of moral convictions.

How dangerous and misleading it is to think in purely political categories! Political terms achieve the same power which certain words hold in the archaic-magic world of the primitive. There are some people who use the word democratic for a society which upholds the moral traditions of Europe; other people speak of democratic but mean technocratic. To them a society

which is stripped of all transcendental values is truly democratic
and the traditions of a Christian society are out-dated and "reactionary." It is interesting that I do not know to this day about
Schulz' political convictions. He might have been a social demo-
crat ("left wing liberal"!) or a German-Nationalist ("reactionary"!)

Doctor Leo Mager also turned out to be a surprise, although
this came about in a different way. Doctor Mager belonged to a
small group of Nazis who really believed not only in "National"
but also in "Socialist," although the latter in an obscure petit
bourgeois meaning. This group felt itself betrayed from the beginning. At any rate, it was strange to observe that very soon
after the seizure of power, just when his great chance would
have come, Mager returned his party membership card. First
openly and later secretly, he worked very much like Schulz
against the new masters. He often berated me because "Jewish
World Power" (this concept was still a remnant from his Nazi
days) did not act more vigorously against Germany. Jewish
World Power and I were shamefully embarrassed. In his case I
also know that he helped numerous people under most dangerous circumstances. During one of the purges in the course of the
war he escaped to Switzerland.

At the very beginning of the Nazi era there was still an element
of cops-and-robbers about it all. On the very day after Hitler's
seizure of power, on the first of February, 1933, Herr Eisinger
went to see the S.A. leader of Sendling. He kept his fist in his
right coat pocket in an ominous manner and said: "You threatened to kill the Herr Curate of Sendling and me on the first day
of the new regime. Here I am, kill me." According to Herr
Eisinger's version, the leader receded a step and merely said:
"You know I didn't mean it." As Herr Eisinger repeated the
story a few times, the leader's reaction became more panicky:

"He grew as pale as a sheet, walked slowly back toward the
wall, never taking his eyes off my pocket, and he said, 'You know

perfectly well, mein lieber Herr Eisinger, that I never meant that seriously.' "

Right after that ominous first of April, 1933, the day of the anti-Jewish boycott, all my Jewish friends, all those who had graduated with me, in fact all Jewish professional people "except for world war veterans" lost their jobs. The clause ". . . except for world war veterans" was intended to give the impression of a just and humane decision, and one could see that this was the psychological effect it had on our professors, technicians, dish-washers, janitors and charwomen, all except for Herr Eisinger and a few other people. A few months later the Jewish veterans lost their jobs too, but without anyone ever hearing about it. It was right at the beginning, in April, that Professor Spielmeyer called me into his office and said:

"Don't think of leaving. I want you to stay on. After all, you are paid by the Rockefeller Foundation, and if they dare to touch you, I'll see to it that no more American money will come into this place, and believe me, they know that very well."

This gave me the feeling of becoming a hostage, a pawn for bargaining, and I did not like it. Moreover, the fact that all my Jewish friends lost their jobs one by one gave me a feeling of isolation. I was not elated at all; on the contrary, I felt like be-ing left behind in the enemy camp. I told Spielmeyer so but he gave me an involved theory the gist of which was that "this Gov-ernment could not possibly last more than a year." He had in-teresting details to tell about Downing Street and the Polish Government and the Quai d'Orsay and Economics, but even then I had a faint but accurate premonition. History has its own immanent apocalyptic laws of progress, laws which seem to be surprisingly independent from what we read in the daily news-papers. I was then dimly aware of something of that sort, al-though I might not have been able to express it in so many words. However, I resolved to stay on for the time being, and I began to look around abroad.

The Forschungsanstalt was a funny place. Except for the Reichsführer for Psychiatry and Sterilization, the professor for spirochete research and a few of the clinicians, one could just as well have been working in Geneva or in some small University in New England. The fact that the Reichsführer was surrounded by Schulz and Mager and Spielmeyer and Herr Eisinger seemed to neutralize him.

Herr Eisinger's exploits seem in retrospect extremely bold, and it is hard to understand how he got away with them. It was already required by law that during any public speech of Hitler the loudspeakers in all institutions and factories had to be turned on, even during working hours, for the employees to listen. Herr Eisinger accompanied every speech with a running comment for the benefit of the listeners, the janitor, the glass-washers and the charwomen. I can still hear him interpolating unequivocal remarks such as "'stretching his hand out to France for lasting friendship,' *heilige Maria, Mutter Gottes*, listen to *der Depp der damische* [that crazy fool], nobody believes him."

12. *Home*

Most people think that the anti-semitism which we encountered under Hitler, is the same anti-semitism as one encounters anywhere else—in drawing-room conversations, in universities, in clubs, in railway compartments and in church groups, in the unwritten laws pertaining to the allotment and hierarchy of jobs—only exaggerated to an utmost degree of injustice and cruelty. This is a serious error. Quantum physics teaches us that energy, in its transformations, does not increase in a continuum but by "jumps." There is something similar about Evil.

In Bavaria, during the Wittelsbach monarchy, there had been

a little of what we later called the "good old pre-war anti-semitism." Jews labored under handicaps similar to those under which numerous racial and religious minorities labor in other parts of the world. They were barred from certain public offices, if not constitutionally, at least by an unwritten law. There was the element of the "Christ-killer" and all that in some of the children. But as a whole most of the Catholic people (and they constituted the majority) shared the views of Herr Josef Filser quoted in the first chapter. The old king liked the venerable chief Rabbi of Munich, Doctor Werner, who was not infrequently seen at court. Herr Fränkel, an extremely Orthodox Jew from one of the oldest Munich families, was made Royal Councillor for Transport and Trade. Catholic children earned a little pocket money by switching the electric light on and off on Friday nights in the households of Orthodox Jews. The Regensburg cookbook in which pious Frau Maria Schandry included numerous recipes for Lent and Christmas, also gave with complete impartiality, and not without fondness, the recipes for certain bakeries and dishes which the "Israelites" consume on Friday night and on Passover.

All this had changed after the First World War. With a wave of chauvinism a new brand of anti-semitism appeared which I mentioned in connection with my school days. The Jewish Youth Movements and the Zionism of the young people were a reaction to this. During this time my parents received a large amount of literature, mainly periodicals, which seemed to emphasize that German Jews were Germans. The Jewish Community in our town resolved to build a synagogue, a real building, something like a Protestant church, which was to replace the old embarrassing prayer-hall inside the brewery. There was at least one community meeting every year concerned with the plan of that synagogue. It struck me that those who were interested in the building, including Grandfather, did not seem to care for it so much from a religious point of view (one could serve God equally well in the old prayer-hall) as from a desire for something like collective prestige. There would be a solemn opening, the mayor of the town, the official representatives of other religious congregations and the representatives of various *vereine* would appear; there would be a brass band; there would be speeches; and there would be, last but not least, a detachment of Jewish war veterans. (This last point seemed to have an importance which was quite disproportionate. The question of how many people have fought in a war, and how many have been killed, seems to be one of the most important in the social struggle of minorities. When, before the Second World War, a British submarine remained submerged and its entire crew was lost, I read in one of the Catholic London papers a statement as to how many of the sailors on board were Catholics. This may have arisen out of the same sentiment; at any rate I do not understand why anyone would care for such statistics.)

The building of that synagogue never came about. But at those community meetings Grandfather and Herr Kommerzienrat Gross used to speak of the plans of the new synagogue with eagerness which had nothing to do with the Zeal of Thy House. It rather implied that it was about time to display something; what exactly, nobody knew. This was precisely what we in the youth movement meant when we spoke of "spineless, undignified, cringing assimilation." In the face of increasing anti-semitism the older generation seemed to repeat anxiously and with increased frequency: "But look, we are exactly like you," while we said: "Yes, we are different from you, we are Jews, and if you want to know, we are proud of it!"

Now things in our little town were different. When I left Munich and the Institute to visit my home-town for the first time, during the Nazi era, Father received me at the railway station. It was evening. The station platform was dimly lit. There was the usual cluster of people behind the ticket barrier, and looking from the car window, I spotted Father among them. He was slightly stooped, his hands in his greatcoat pockets, and he peered searchingly towards the train. I had seen him like this hundreds of times before. Yet, without any physical detachment, he was detached from the crowd. Or did I perceive something which was not there? There was his sudden smile of recognition. After I had passed the barrier and he embraced me we seemed to be, by this simple gesture, more isolated from the people around us.

Herr Weigl, the bicycle dealer, said: "Guten Abend, Herr Stern," perhaps louder and more forcefully than had been the custom. Presently I smelled again the old familiar smell of the railway station, a stale smell of soot, human beings, sandwich parcels, glue, paper and apples. Father said: "Nun, wie geht's? Tell me something!" There had been times, in my teens, when I might perhaps have said to myself: "Why does he not, once in a while, use a new phrase, just one new one?" This time I felt like moving up more closely to him while we crossed the hall and walked towards the town. The people around us, Herr Weigl's loud greeting, and the smell of the station conveyed a new strangeness. Father said: "He is decent," referring to Herr Weigl, and I felt incredibly embarrassed.

On the Bahnhofsplatz was an enormous sign in enamel: "In this town Jews are undesired." I had known of the existence of these signs in all German towns, on all places in front of railway stations; but the moment I saw it I realized that, somewhere deep down, I had entertained a dim, ill-defined belief, bizarre and illogical, that our town might be an exception. We passed the lumber yards which adjoined the Station Avenue. In the shadow, just outside the pale of the big arc lamps, one could see the quadrangular piles of wood. Their silhouettes looked like rows of fortresses. This is what they had been to us when we were children, little forts in which we hid for hours, waiting for the enemy gang which was camped in other lumber fortresses up on the height of the Taubenberg. We went along the main street, the Ludwigstrasse, past the huge elaborate monastery of the Redemptorist Fathers. (When I was small Mother used to tell me that it had cost a million marks to build it.)

In the light of a street lamp, Judge Deigendesch passed us and took his hat off. Father took his hat off, perhaps a trifle more eagerly than usual, and bowed, perhaps just a little more deeply than usual, or did it only appear to me like this? "He is also decent—one of the decent ones," Father remarked, and I felt again the same embarrassment. As we neared the railway bridge there was a streamer across the street: "The Jews are our misfortune." I tapped the wide stone railing over which I used to run barefoot as a boy, the glistening steel lines deep below. One had to do this with one's eyes fixed on the sidewalk of the bridge, and the purpose had invariably been to achieve a mild and agreeable throbbing of fear. This evening it was too dark for the rails down below to be seen but I looked at the signal lamps getting lost in the distance, and they seemed to be at one with some world through which Father and I had never walked before.

We passed a few more people, some of whom said, "Guten Abend, Herr Stern," and the ceremonial repeated itself. We passed all the familiar places. There was a bierkeller with a bowling alley. There we used to sit on summer evenings at tables with our sandwiches, drinking beer and eating big white radishes. On a square not far from it was a big showcase, brightly lit, and above it a sign: "The Jews are our misfortune." I knew those showcases. They displayed a weekly paper which was entirely devoted to enlightening the population on the Jewish question. There were detailed stories of, let us say, a Jewish lawyer of Magdeburg who assaulted his non-Jewish secretary; or an Orthodox congregation who kept German girls in the cellar of their synagogue for the purpose of commercial prostitution; statistics of the part played by the Jews in the Russian revolution and in the organization of "Wall Street." Of course, Father and I did not stop to read it. Perhaps in passing it we walked just a little more quickly. We knew the kind of information which was displayed. We glanced furtively out of the corner of our eyes and remarked simultaneously that nobody was standing there reading it at the moment. "I never see anyone stopping there," Father said.

We passed another square, in the middle of which was a fountain with a bronze gilded Saint Sebastian, tied to a bronze gilded column and pierced by bronze gilded arrows. At this square Herr Steiniger, one of the competitors of our firm, had his store. "You would be surprised—he is not decent at all, he does not greet any more." Presently we passed Frey's, another competitor's textile store. "He still greets, good sort."

When we finally arrived at home Mother was standing in the corridor behind the store, at the landing of the stairs. She had her kitchen apron on, which meant that she had prepared something special for me, otherwise she would have left that to Therese.

"Where did you stay so long?" she asked.

"We've made something special for you," Therese said, emerging from the kitchen.

"Pot roast and maccaroni," Mother added quickly.

The table was set with shining linen. Ludwig was sitting in the living-room reading a book by B. Traven.

"Well, well, at last," Father said after we had entered the dining-room, and he gave me a hug and a kiss as if I had returned after ten years in Central Africa.

"Wow, sauerbraten and maccaroni," Ludwig remarked.

"That's for you," Therese beamed.

Those were the rituals of homecoming, unvaried and precious since I had first gone into the Big City Far Away as a boy of ten, to return only on vacations. During the supper Father said that one of the apprentices in the store had joined the Stormtroopers, that Herr Ruhland had assaulted Herr Neuberger and the police had looked the other way, that Herr Gruber would not work for us any more, and that the butcher Vogl was decent.

"In the street they greet you as before"—meaning the Vogl family. It was obvious that the mankind which surrounded Father was simply divided into two breeds, those who "greeted" and those who had stopped greeting.

Doctor Marlinger was decent, Doctor Lagally did not greet any more, one Gebhardt family was friendly, the others had stopped greeting. The parish priest who had never "greeted" before began to "greet" now ostentatiously. "Awfully decent of him, that's something you've got to admit." Father, ever since I remembered him, seemed to be vaguely conscious of his naiveness; he tried to defy us and at the same time looked for approval. The human cosmos of the small town had become to him a dualist system, made up of those who kept on exchanging ordinary courtesies with him, and those who had stopped doing so. This was more involved than it sounds. "Herr Drexel stopped right on the Market Place to talk to me the other day, so, incidentally, did Doctor Marlinger." This was one step more advanced than "greeting."

"Listen to what *he* did," Mother said, referring to Father. "The Storm-troopers went around to every Jewish store and put the official labels to the show windows: 'Do not buy from the Jew!' He just went out in open daylight, in front of all the people and tore those labels off. The only Jew in town to do such a thing. They could have hanged you for that, and nobody could have done anything about it!"

"Ah, nonsense, hanging! Do you know"—he turned to me—"who the chairman and the vice-chairman of the party are?" He named two young men, both of whom happened to be sons of unmarried women from the lower class. "Take *that* as food for thought," he said.

I did not know what he wanted me to think but it occurred to me that illegitimate children in small towns are exposed to extreme and bizarre forms of humiliation, and that here the Revolution was displayed with simple crudity, with its raw flesh so-to-speak. It seemed all too primitive for History, the faraway Goddess.

"Think of those two chaps sitting up there in an office, in upholstered easy chairs, and with secretaries," he said.

Before we all retired Ludwig went downstairs into a niche near the cellar door and pulled a switch. Mother explained that he had installed a gadget by which he could interrupt the current of the doorbell during the night. There were people in the neighborhood who stuck matches or putty into the bell button at any hour in the morning between one and seven, and we were no longer in any position to ask for the protection of the police.

I lay awake for some time listening to the sound of the running water in Saint Florian's fountain. I had a sense of foreboding. The feeling I had that night seems now much more natural and less strange than it actually was, because of the many things that came about since then. In reality, nothing very much had happened at that time. That there were some people in town who stopped to say hello; that there was a showcase with pornographic leaflets, or that there were some big posters on display; that there were hooligans ringing doorbells—all this was of the order of nuisance and bother, with just a touch of the vulgar and unsavory. It seems trivial in the light of intervening memories. Yet that night—I cannot explain why—I suddenly sensed that all this would end only with our complete and utter destruction.

I looked through the window. Nothing could be seen. It was the same sleeply quaint little town, under a night sky. And yet it was as if we were huddling on the barque of our childhood, and around us there was an evil force which seemed to be in tune with infinity.

13. Exit Leo Nikolaievitch

THE FEW Nazi guest workers in the Institute behaved as if they found themselves in enemy territory. Even those who did talk Nazism, somehow seemed to fail to fit into a recognized pattern. I remember a biochemist, a blond and somewhat anemic youth with an open candid look, who at the dinner table expounded to me the neo-pagan Germanic Religion.

"I used to be terribly anti-semitic, you know, until I came to study the writings of Doctor Hauer. Then I found out that what we hate in the Jews is not the Jews. It is Christ and the Christian religion. This religion is something so utterly alien to the very spirit of the European peoples that they revolt with their entire being against it. But although they feel a revulsion they are not aware of its true origin. Hence that irrational hatred of the Jews, because people vaguely feel that it is actually a Jewish way of feeling, thinking, acting, a Jewish norm of living that has been stuffed down their throat for the past two thousand years. Once you have found out that it is actually Christianity which is the painful foreign body in our flesh, something curious happens, you stop hating the Jews. You regard them with the same kind of sympathy or antipathy as you might regard any other foreign nation."

I asked him in what way the Christian, or rather Hebrew-Christian, way of thinking was so alien and indigestible for the Northern European nations. He replied that the moral teaching of the Bible imbued the people with a disastrous sense of anxiety and guilt. "The New Testament claims to have done away with fear, but it builds up a sense of fear even more dramatically than the Old Testament. It's only a continuation of the same thing."

He claimed that the Indo-Germanic peoples had a much higher idea of the ultimate destiny of man. You had only to read the description which Tacitus gives of the German people of the pre-Christian era to realize that. "There has been one revolt against the shackles of an alien thought—that was Luther. But with Luther it was still unconscious—Luther did not realize himself that what he was actually fighting was not Rome; it was an element that had arisen long before the Catholic Church and far away from Rome, some kind of desert mentality which was grafted upon the mind of the Aryan peoples and had thwarted and dwarfed it. Thus Luther made the mistake of reviving instead of abolishing that spirit, although the unconscious root of the Lutheran rebellion lay actually in the depth of the Aryan mind." Hitler was even worse, he said, for Hitler deflected the anti-Christian forces into vulgar Jew-baiting, and by doing so removed, perhaps forever, the chance of the revival of a truly Indo-Germanic spirit in Europe.

I asked him, since he had such an Aryan chip on his shoulder against the Ten Commandments, how he would prevent children from lying and stealing and murdering. He told me something, which I have forgotten, about the Indo-Germanic mentality, and that he would certainly do anything to prevent his children from getting acquainted with a desert deity who appears under thunder and smoke on a mountain. The reader must realize that this was a clean-looking, sympathetic young man, and no Nazi ogre. On the contrary, he was the sort of young idealist who might easily have landed in an actively anti-Nazi camp, and perished there. I have lost track of him, in fact I have forgotten his name. The point is that he expressed something, under the quaint make-up of a Teutonic *weltanschauung*, which, under varying disguises, many people say today in many places of the world. Moreover, he expressed quite clearly what I believe now to be the true background of the entire Nazi revolution.

Gradually the Psychiatric Institute became suspect. Professor Spielmeyer, scientist of world renown, descendant of a Northern German family of pastors, struck up a peculiar kind of alliance with Herr Eisinger, the chauffeur. Leo Mager saw to it that not a single portrait of The Leader was hung up in any one of the offices, although this was now the rule in all public institutions. One never heard "Heil Hitler." Doctor Margarete Bülow, the chairman of the doctors' dining-room committee intended, at all costs, to maintain the dining-room as a clean, aseptic enclave. There had existed for a long time, slowly and gradually accumulated by the doctors' efforts, a record collection. This collection was unique of its kind at that time and in that sort of dining-room; it contained everything from Bach partitas to Brahms concertos. Doctor Adele Juda began to act as if that collection had assumed an extraordinary importance and meaning.

From the windows, just beyond the trees of the Englische Garten, we could see the factory chimneys of the Maffei Works and the Bayrische Motoren Works smoking again, day and night; far away in the fields, in the direction of Schleissheim, one could perceive an even rhythmic crawling movement, tanks, armored vehicles and mounted guns. The charwomen, glass-washers and animal keepers stopped working, and watched intently. It was as if a supernatural power communicated with their little lives and showed in their faces. There were wonderment, tension without aim, and paralyzed fascination. Gradually more and more began to say "yes" to all this, as if their "yes" were outside the laws which underlay logical assent.

Herr Eisinger could still be seen talking to small groups of two or three, but he stopped his running comments on radio speeches. His face, with tower skull, Hitler mustache and all, showed faint traces of pessimism. "They are all *rindvieher*," he told me but it appeared to come out of the mouth of a sad clown. The janitor began to say "Heil Hitler," an outward sign showing that Herr Eisinger's authority was broken.

It was around that time that the Nazis began a campaign against vivisection and cruelty to animals. The air of make-believe, of a diabolical yes-and-no, of whirling and whizzing ambiguities, was increasing, and soon the stokers, professors and storekeepers were surrounded by an optical wall which separated them from reality. Herr Eisinger began to collect material to report Brosam to the authorities for "cruelty to animals."

One day Professor Spielmeyer, Herr Eisinger and I were riding in the car which belonged to the Institute. I had balancing on my knees a jar with a human brain floating in formalin. Eisinger spoke to us as to two intimate friends. "Listen to what happened to me the other day. I had lent my camera to a friend who wanted to take a picture of his kids. Know what happened? Without ever telling me about it he had a secret Communist printing set-up in his basement." He did not give Doctor Spielmeyer or me any time to think about this last statement, and continued quickly. "The police came on a *razzia*, arrested him and his associates, and took all his implements away, including my camera which I had lent him in good faith." There was again an increase in tempo. "Hoppla, I said to myself, Eisinger, you won't let these fellows get away with it. You know what I did? I went straight into the Polizeipraesidium in the Ettstrasse, and did I tell those fellows off! To take away the camera of an innocent working-class man . . ." Here he paused. "Only because I am good-hearted enough to lend it to a fellow who makes me believe he wants to take pictures of his family. No, sir. You know what they did? They apologized! 'Herr Eisinger, it was an oversight; you understand the circumstances.' I got my camera back."

Herr Eisinger's stories no longer sounded funny. Although their veracity was undoubted, the world of cops-and-robbers no longer existed. It was a kind of pretense. There was something similar about the dining-room. The egg-from-the-floor act still evoked laughter. Lydia Pasternak and I became increasingly popular, because we were Jews. We became sensitive to our rôle as mascots. Keeping us preciously no longer prevented that enclave from being dissolved. One could still sit at night and listen to the partitas. But all that which went on within a circumference of a hundred feet seemed to pervert even Music herself.

The führer for psychiatry and sterilization felt endangered and compromised by the reputation of the place as a "hornets' nest of reaction." Around this time the murder of Dollfuss occurred. Numerous Nazi doctors fled Austria and sought refuge in Germany. All the psychiatrists among them were allocated to the Institute, and a new era began. The spell of the dining-room was finally broken. Forceful young men appeared, dark and brooding, and handsome in a sensuous fashion. One of them remained after dinner, sitting at the piano, playing free improvisations which sounded ominously like *Das Rheingold*. Soon there were two camps, the Nazis (whom the staff members called "Austrians") and the old guard. Doctor Margarete Bülow appeared sad. The cell had succumbed to osmotic pressure. After-dinner conversations were suddenly broken off when someone opened the door. We began to talk shop, on cerebral changes in epilepsy, and on the chemical structure of cerebrosides.

One day one of the "Austrians" took all the Pasternak pictures off the wall, and replaced them with one photograph, The Leader's portrait. Doctor Margarete Bülow ran to Doctor Schulz. They drafted a note of formal protest, not because The Leader's portrait was hung up (that was too dangerous a thing to do and would have meant the concentration camp) but because changes had been made in the dining-room without consulting with the fräulein chairman. But the deed was done and Tolstoy lay, face down, on a laboratory bench. A secret meeting was

called, and Doctor Schulz read us the drafted protest. Everybody present wanted to sign. It was strange to see how these
people who apparently had suppressed a sense of shame over
their enforced passivity got incensed, and suddenly risked their
jobs and their future over an issue which lacked all practical
significance. "Lydia and you must not sign on any account,"
Schultz said to me, "because you are considered biased, and
moreover you would certainly be arrested and put into a concentration camp if your names were found here." There was a
long and proud list of signatures which, for obvious reasons, I
shall never forget. From a practical point of view it was foolhardy and senseless; all that came of it was that the Gestapo
received a little dossier for future reference. There was a general
exodus from the doctors' dining-room. Everyone, except for the
"Austrians," ate in a nearby restaurant. Then the führer for
psychiatry and sterilization made a move; he apologized on his
part for the incorrect demeanor of the "Austrians." Several
people, including Doctors Schulz and Mager, never entered the
dining-room again. The little incident was heavily laden with
symbolic significance. Exit Leo Nikolaievitch. Enter Adolf. A new
era had begun in all our lives, not only in my life as a Jew, but
in the lives of Doctor Spielmeyer, and the janitor and Herr
Eisinger, the people around us, and the nations of the earth.

III

THROUGH THE INTERIOR

14. *An Unusual Barter*

THE Psychiatric Institute gave us the best that classical psychiatry could offer. In these institutions of research, the sting was taken out of all this, the animal was tamed. In the department of genetics, in thousands of files, stored on shelves, in cupboards and in crates was the disease of generations. It could be reduced to mathematical formulas, to graphs of predictability, and it seemed to lose all the passion and the fortuitous chance of suffering which had been experienced in each single "case." In the Department of Clinical Research we observed human experience and behavior. We created precious categories. In the Department of Neuropathology there were hundreds of museum jars with brains, and thousands of microscopic sections, in colorful stains, mounted on glass. Most of us got out of this some sense of assurance and power. Sickness, insanity, begetting and dying—all seemed to be objectivated and made to conform with the cleanliness and brightness of our laboratories.

During all this time one of the great mass psychoses of history was taking its course, right in front of our windows, and the destructive force erupting from the depth of life was something to which our very frame of reference was not applicable. In spite of the fact that I enjoyed my work I was, nevertheless, aware of the void. In order to know Man I had to study myself.

It was around this time that I was introduced to one of

our foremost analytical therapists. Doctor Rudolf Laudenheimer was like some sort of anticosmos as compared with the Psychiatric Institute. He had originally come from the school of classical psychiatry, like all therapists of the analytical school at that time. As a young man he had been lecturer in the department of psychiatry in Leipzig, under Flechsig, a famed brain anatomist. He had been working in areas in which Internal Medicine, Human Physiology and Psychiatry overlapped. However, at the dawn of the century he broke with traditional psychiatry of the academic school. He had, since his student days, been associated with a group of writers and poets who later rose to fame. He had been in contact with Freud at an early stage, later with Jung. At any rate, in the middle of a promising academic career he broke off in a way which was baffling to those who knew him. He and his wife took a loan and rented a small farmhouse. For some time they had to live there with one patient. This, their historical first case, was a rapidly deteriorating General Paretic—a man afflicted with a syphilitic disease of the brain which at that time was still incurable. Frau Laudenheimer described vividly how they lived with their patient in the semi-wilderness, how they bathed him, fed him, cleansed him and how they waited through his endless attacks of restlessness and yelling.

Soon after the paretic, a few more patients had arrived, this time persons who were in need of psychological therapy. After a few years a small sanatorium was begun, and after a few more years more buildings had to be added until the enterprise had grown into one of the best known private sanatoriums in Germany. Ten years before I first met him, the Doctor had retired, at the height of his fame, into private practice in Munich.

Frau Laudenheimer had been a girl from the East Prussian countryside; she must have been strikingly beautiful in her young days, and even now one could see her beauty under the mask of age. The apartment was furnished with very good taste. There were warmth and nobility of style.

Doctor Laudenheimer looked like a Jewish nobleman. His silvery hair and beard, and his penetrating, melancholy eyes, made many people who first met him think of Freud. His wife was tall and strong, there was something fierce in her beauty, and her gray mop of hair seemed to radiate like a forbidding crown whenever she let her temper go. He was rather reticent when not in intimate company, she spoke incessantly as if she wanted to crowd out silence. This somehow appeared to be associated with the fact that she had no children. There is a peculiar tragedy about childlessness, a dim, just faintly perceptible form of sadness which is never quite expressed. Such people, deprived of a certain form of creativeness, seem to be, in another way, more in harmony with the sadness of creation.

In the evening Frau Laudenheimer told Sanatorium stories. She paced up and down the floor and spoke in the words and with the gestures of a famous Prussian General, whose wife had just been admitted in a state of depression during pregnancy. Or she was transformed into an obsessive-compulsive novelist who is helped by the nurses to unpack his suitcase. Or she propped herself up in front of the grand piano and began to sing Brahms, as a celebrated singer would when, as a patient, she was about to entertain fellow patients. Her eyes, her heaving breast and her wild hair looked more and more Wagnerian as she struggled along with Brahms. Her voice was cracked and tinny but she pronounced each syllable formidably as one used to in the theatrical classes of the nineties. This Great Sanatorium, a strange combination of opera, Wild West drama, and Magic Mountain, was an inexhaustible source of entertainment. It was something utterly different from what her husband had actually been doing all these years, different from the agony of each single patient. However, she knew that perfectly well. Whenever her eyes began to gleam threateningly and it looked as if she had

identified herself perfectly with her rôle, she suddenly began
to laugh, shook her gray hair and the spook vanished completely.
The Doctor looked at all this silently and with good-humored
tolerance. There was no maliciousness in it, nor any of the resentment of past glory. Here in Munich, the house was still a
center for artists, musicians, writers, scientists, and the practice
was still flourishing.

Laudenheimer's main interest, outside Medicine, had been the
History of Art; so much so that even during the middle years
of his life he had still been toying with the idea of changing his
occupation altogether. It was fascinating to observe how he
spoke, in connection with what seemed to be "specific psychiatric
problems," of Goethe or Manzoni, of James Joyce or Chinese Art.
I realized for the first time something of which I had perhaps
been conscious dimly and in a shadowy form; that the "problem
of human behavior" cannot be tackled in the artificial isolation
of laboratory and clinic, or by all those scientific methods which
reduce the infinity of life to sterile quantification. This was not
a matter of sour grapes with him, because he had earned his
original fame with strictly scientific investigation. Nor was it
anything like sophistication; he had the humility of all genuine
people. It was rather a natural transcendence; he had his roots
in the soil of the nineteenth century but he spread his branches
towards something which seemed to be beyond the twentieth.
He rejected almost instinctively all determinism, whether of
Freudian or Marxian or any other coloring. I remember him
saying: "If I did not believe in the Freedom of the Will, I'd
give up being a physician." Although he was a Jew by heritage,
he had been brought up as a Christian since childhood: he, too,
had that elevated Protestant humanism which I have seen in
others of his generation, enlivened and warmed, as it were, by a
Jewish sensitiveness. Although his clinical approach had been
molded decisively by Freud, he belonged to the circle around
C. G. Jung. However, like all humanists, he was pluralistic

almost by nature, and he made one forget everything about
"isms." Just as Haase and the experiences in the Moabit slums
had sown the ferment of social consciousness into my medicine,
he added the ferment of what I would now call a personalist
attitude.

There prevailed at that time among the young Germans a
peculiar brand of irrationalism. This was a reaction against a
rationalist pragmatism which had been handed down to them.
Bios, Life, was extolled as something that had a primacy over
logos, the Spirit. Even those who were avowedly anti-Nazi used
to sit over their after-dinner coffee in the Psychiatric Institute
and talk about D. H. Lawrence and Ludwig Klages, the German
philosopher of the *bios.*

I think that with D. H. Lawrence it had been a vigorous rebellion against an emasculated bourgeoisie, rather similar to that
of Nietzsche. With Klages it had become a form of shadiness,
one of those specifically Teutonic forms of the European illness.
Thomas Mann was one of the first to recognize the danger in all
this (perhaps after having first discovered it inside himself) and
he spent half his life combating it. For many people there
seemed to be a dark fascination in this magic brew. Something
similar could be seen in some of the followers of Jung. It was a
strange form of mysticism, a mysticism which opposed itself to
Reason.

Although Laudenheimer belonged to the circle around Jung,
he escaped this danger, perhaps because of his profound affinity
to the classical, perhaps because of his strong though ill-defined
Christian belief, perhaps because of his Jewishness. It seems almost as if a Jew cannot be an irrationalist; Bergson's apparent
irrationalism was actually the deep personal struggle of a man
of the nineteenth century for the Metaphysical, and found its
solution in Christianity.

During one of my first conversations with Laudenheimer, he
said to me: "When you go home today, bring a copy book and

begin to collect all your dreams." This advice was given with the
air of a routine procedure, as a dentist tells his patient to buy
poultices and apply them three times daily. When I returned,
he said: "Lie down on the couch over there, relax and close your
eyes." He made a further proposal: "As a form of payment, I ask
you to play Beethoven sonatas to me four times a week."

During the subsequent two and a half years I spent a considerable time lying on that couch, relaxed and with my eyes
closed. There were not enough Beethoven sonatas I was able to
reproduce half adequately. A good deal of Mozart had to be
added, and Schubert. I think he loved Schubert more than anything else, and since Schubert sonatas are very beautiful and
very long, and since one of them does for a whole evening, and
can often be repeated, I was delighted. He said: "I am like old
King Saul. I don't want your money, I want music."

Thus started the strange procedure of an analysis, on the basis
of an unusual barter. A good analyst is everything—father, re-
cording machine, Mephistopheles, Virgil and Beatrice, all in one.
I was slowly and painfully taken through quagmires and seraphic
regions. Among the numerous things which changed in my life
during this time was an extraordinary fact: when I first lay down
on the couch I was a convinced dialectic materialist; when I
arose from the couch for the last time I was absolutely convinced of the primacy of the Spirit.

15. Bones to Philosophy

THE National Socialist Revolution had, not only materially, a
devastating impact upon German and European Jewry. It acted
like earthquake and flood because the masses of Jews were, in
spite of years of gathering clouds, psychologically and ideolog-

ically utterly unprepared. Most people think of us as cunning, foxy, with a great amount of practical foresight. The years after 1933 proved us to be as sentimental in our attachments, as emotional and stupid in our practical decisions, as much given to wishful thinking and self-deception as any other people.

It was a great paradox that one of the vilest and most cruel racial persecutions in history hit a people which was amazingly well integrated into the cultural life of its "host." For the German Jews, as is well known, were the most assimilated and most deeply rooted Jews in Europe, perhaps with the exception of the Italian ones. This natural fact was unfortunately used by certain political groups. When Eastern Jewry had to migrate due to the horrible pogroms of fifty years ago, certain groups of German Jews locked their doors to them. No wonder that this caused much bitterness and misunderstanding on the part of the Russian and Polish Jews; they came to look upon the assimilation and cultural deep-rootedness of the German Jew as some sort of treacherous camouflage which it certainly was not. Out of their bitter experience, prejudice and resentment were carried over to a second generation and to this continent; even those of us who never dreamed of any discrimination among ethnic groups have come up against this sort of thing. A few Eastern Jews felt something like the glee of just retribution when the German persecutions started; it never occurred to them that the forest fire would spread to Eastern Europe. In the end all were united in an apocalyptic flame, in a terrible communion of death.

In the beginning, however, one could still discern groups and different psychological reactions. The large number of middle-class families, most of whom owned retail stores, began to sit back, listen to the Swiss and Austrian radio and to every little scrap of story or anecdote that resembled a small-scale Nazi defeat. Much calculation was going on, on the basis of some form of classical out-of-date economy, as to how long "they" could carry on. Since the new government did not have "solid business foundations" it was believed to be doomed to bankruptcy in the good time-honored style of the bourgeois world. Most of those who deceived themselves in this way had in the end to emigrate without any material goods whatsoever; they were swallowed up in such centers as Shanghai. The more fortunate ones were able to reach the big cities of North or South America, or go to Palestine. Others, particularly those who had no relatives, or childless couples who did not have anyone to break the path for them, underwent the fate of concentration camps, sealed cattle-wagons and extermination plants.

A large number of the young people belonging to these families became Zionists. The Zionist Youth Movement for the first time in Germany was no longer led by a somewhat isolated, detached group with a *weltanschauung;* all of a sudden it became a powerful means of solving an urgent practical problem. They established a well-organized *hach-sharah,* training camps for farming and craftsmanship, so that youths would not arrive in Palestine altogether unprepared and again be swallowed up by some city civilization such as is represented by Tel Aviv.

Skilled academic workers, physicians, scientists and artists found employment abroad. They seemed to be least affected by the deluge. Of all the Jews they seemed to have experienced ideologically and materially the least impact. There was no sign of reorientation. They seemed to think, feel and work very much in the same way in hospitals, institutes and factories as they had been wont. However, there was a current of restlessness and a shift of values underneath the surface. Although they were taken in by countries in which freedom had persisted, the more sensitive among them retained a profound feeling of uprootedness and insecurity just as one has the sensation of rocking and vibration after a stormy sea voyage. They felt that the peculiar nineteenth-century brand of liberalism and unrestricted individualism which was characteristic of the social strata to which they belonged was a hollow structure. On the other hand, they recognized the immorality behind that new irrationalism of Klages and Spengler. Most of them had no roots whatsoever in Jewry. Its positive values, its great traditions, its spirit were entirely unknown to these people. A senseless and cruel stigma was all that Jewry had become to them.

There was a particularly small group of those who had identified themselves so much with German culture, not only the Germany of Goethe but the Germany of Bismarck, that their forcible exclusion struck them as an explosion strikes a child. They groped blindly around in some sort of no-man's-land. Among these were the first cases of suicide of which we heard.

Socialists emigrated to the Western countries and resumed their activities; but most of those whom I happened to know did it in a rather abstract, literary sort of way. It seems almost that in order to be creative and useful in the labor movement one has to grow up in the country in which one works. Although the problems and worries of the working-class seem the most uniform and international phenomenon in today's world, in order to help effectively New York garment-workers, or Yorkshire miners, or Norwegian lumberjacks, you have to have been among them almost from childhood.

In all this uproar, bewilderment and confusion, the most realistic and positive way seemed to be that of the Zionist Youth. These people felt that they were born into a new life. The German turmoil was an almost welcome pretext for them to shed the clothes of Western Jewish bourgeoisie, the position of economic intermediators which it held in a capitalistic world, its pale abstract existence in the foam of a drying-out current of civilization. Maybe they had got too big a dose of Teutonic pessimism with reference to Western civilization in general, and this played an unconscious part in it. That does not matter now. It is amazing with what eagerness all these children of a long purely commercial and intellectual tradition took to manual work on the soil and in workshops. Ludwig played a leading part in this movement. I believe he got his first stimulus from me. For his plans were not laid yet, the Nazi Revolution coincided with his matriculation from high school and it just needed the hint of a suggestion to make him choose his life work; it was profoundly different from anything he would have done if life had gone on in a conservative undisturbed way.

This was a healthy, optimistic and wholesome crowd of youngsters; they were, with the exception of certain purely religious groups, the only happy and well-adjusted people I encountered at that time in Germany. They all seemed happier than they would have been if, under normal circumstances, they had taken the unavoidable career of traveling salesmen or of textile merchants. Some of them seemed, with cynical humor, to regard the advent of Hitlerism as a boon. Incidentally, the training farms were favored or at least not molested by the Nazis during the first five years, as was everything which in any way contributed to the emigration of the Jews. It sounds paradoxical, but it is true that this group of young Jews was the only group with a genuine, wholesome enthusiasm at that time in Germany, at least among the people I saw. Among the Nazis there was too much compulsion, over-organization, and among those who were eagerly "in it" there seemed to be that faintly perceptible but constant sultry background of psychosexual maladjustment which has been described by many observers.

By a most extraordinary coincidence, I was the only Jewish physician of my age in a non-Jewish institution in all Germany who was not affected by the "Aryan" laws. This was due to the fact that at the time of the Big Change I was holding a position under the Rockefeller Foundation. Thus I stayed, but since I could not change my profession I took part in the activities of the Zionist groups. We arranged courses on history, on Hebrew culture, or anything we were able to do with the children.

Nevertheless, even then, as it had been the case ten years

before, pure Zionism with the somewhat noncommittal appendix of "Jewish culture" left me dissatisfied and with the definite sense of a void. Don't mistake me. I am, of course, not speaking of the practical achievements at the time. I know that my brother and all my friends have done more for suffering and endangered people than I shall ever be able to do in all my life, and that was all that mattered then. There was Reha Freier, of whom I have spoken before. I want to mention her particularly because it was she who founded the German Youth Alijah; nobody thinks of her today, and all the credit and fame for getting European Jewish children into Palestine goes to others. How shall I ever be able to do what these people have done?

No, it is not that. It is not the question of the immediate practical necessities. Perhaps even then I felt at the bottom of my heart that a mere withdrawal into a national culture was not a solution for the Jews, and what we needed in the end was a universal solution, a solution which was equally applicable and equally binding on those poor devils around us who persecuted us. Moreover, there was the question of the Jews themselves, that big majority for which there would never be any space in Palestine. What about them? Should they be cast off as the injured parts of the bodies of certain animals are cast off? To bridge this gap in Zionist ideology Ahad-ha-Am had put forward his idea of Cultural Zionism. Palestine was to be a cultural center for those who were unable to live there. The Jews in the diaspora should receive their creative impulse from Jerusalem. However, was this not a religious concept under disguise, and if not, was the concept of cultural communication rather shallow and abstract? Whatever my actual reasoning process may have been at the time I saw once more that a national solution of the Jewish problem was no solution at all if it was not at the same time a religious one. Here was the perfectly unique case of a people which was unable to solve its difficulties (what a euphemism!) in a purely "realistic" way.

Something essential was missing. The fate of the Jews was inextricably interlaced with the fate, in history, of their God. This much I knew.

Thus I went back to the Orthodox Synagogue. I argued that if anyone was in the possession of the crystal of truth, no matter how deeply buried in accidental superstructures, it must be these people who had been huddling around something for several thousand years and through all weathers. I was distrustful of Jewish Liberalism and the so-called reformed Synagogue because of all the possible distortion and dilutions of the Word which must have occurred during an assimilation of Jewry to a benign, somewhat colorless and noncommittal Deism of our Western society.

There had been similar tendencies before and my case was by no means unique. I have spoken of Rudi Herz who ten years before had abandoned the liberalism of our general environment and been converted to the strict Orthodox position. The most famous case was that of Franz Rosenzweig, a highly spiritual personality who had adopted Orthodox Jewry as a young man. He exerted considerable influence on German Jews towards Orthodoxy. His most famous work is a peculiar word-for-word translation (with many extraordinary neologisms!) of the Old Testament which he edited in collaboration with Martin Buber. There is also Ernst Simon, who, I believe, has worked a good deal towards reconciliation with the Arabs in Palestine on a religious basis.

Then I was not at all concerned with these examples, in fact, I believe I knew little about them. Since I had left the Synagogue ten years before I had gone through a philosophical Odyssey but not, as it seems now, with the burning urgency which characterizes the seeking of truth. After having been caught, like almost everybody else, by the magic fascination of Schopenhauer's world, I had abandoned myself to Kant's triumphant rationalism and afterwards to Hegel's dialectic and its particular offspring, the dialectic materialism of Karl Marx. There had not been any "problem" for some time.

Perhaps we should not deny the merits of Hegelian dialectics if we remain aware of the fact that they are limited and that they will yield correct results if applied within limits—to the surface layer, so to speak. They work very well with the partial aspects of a given problem, aspects which are artifically isolated. But they never work with the whole of a phenomenon. Under no circumstances can we ever "explain" such a phenomenon as the fate of the European Jews during these last twelve years on the basis of economics, or social psychology, or psychoanalysis or any other science.

It is either meaningless, or, if it has any meaning at all, this must be of a transcendental nature. This was then and still is my firm conviction. It would be easy to prove that once you have experienced this truth everything else follows logically. We shall see what I mean by "everything else."

Here I should like to remark parenthetically that the great fault of our time is not so much woolly thinking in itself but that artificial isolation of partial aspects of wholes, when truth can be attained only by contemplating a whole. This is where at a later stage present-day philosophy helped me a good deal, particularly what little smattering I had of modern German phenomenology and of Whitehead.

16. *Milk to Faith*

IN THE Orthodox Synagogue I was received by my old friends as if I had never been away. It seemed strange, and it was at the same time consoling to me, that all through those ten years these men had been going on praying their regular three times a day and "learning" in their free time. I do not deny that the emotional frills of religion, the icing on the cake, were quite important. To re-experience the atmosphere, to hear the familiar tunes, to relive again the rhythm of the week and of the year, to be again imbedded in the stream of the liturgy gave me a feeling of security and shelter in those days.

On Sabbath afternoons there was a study course of the Prophets conducted by a young man of my age. We took the original text in Hebrew and accompanied it by the traditional exegetic literature such as Rashi and certain texts of the Midrash, Besides this we also studied some medieval Spanish-Jewish mystical literature, eschatological writings of tremendous grandeur and beauty. This, however, was more in the way of recreation besides the "work." Those were wonderful days. I lapped it up, to use an idiomatic expression. I was like a man who has been living for a long time on canned food who suddenly gets home-made bread and vegetables freshly picked in the garden. If there was, in the midst of this mad and tumbling world, Life and Truth—this was it. I knew that with all the fibers of my heart.

Incidentally, most of my friends of the *halutziuth,* including my brother, had a strongly anti-Orthodox bias, and most of them saw no necessity at all for religious tradition in any form. Their prejudice was associated with the fact that most Orthodox rabbis held rather conservative and reactionary views with regard to all Jewish questions. The attitude of these boys towards the religious tradition can be best illustrated by a little conversation which my brother had with a stupid overseer of a synagogue. (I happened to overhear this dialogue.) The man asked my brother whether he was fasting (it was Tisha b'Av, the day of the destruction of the Second Temple). My brother replied that he was not.

The man said: "And these are the people who want to build up Palestine!"

"Palestine won't be built up by fasting," replied my brother.

This was the general attitude. Quite a few of those who had been studying in Yeshivoth stayed, by way of demonstration, at home on the Day of Atonement and took their meals.

Professor Büchler, the head of the Jewish college in London, told me in this connection that he once acted as guide to a group of parsons of various Christian denominations through the co-operatives (*kvutzoth*) in Palestine. After having been through a few of these, the ministers of religion asked him: "But tell us, Dr. Büchler, where are the houses of prayer?" And he had to admit that there were not any. "Jews in the Holy Land—and without synagogues!" They just couldn't understand it.

Those boys and girls who in their lives showed extraordinary examples of self-sacrifice and of a profound sense of justice and charity did not realize that they themselves were actually living on the immense treasure of Orthodoxy. The attempts, in the Western world, to live on pure Ethics deprived of all form are barely a hundred years old. They have not yet been tried in the fire of time. This much we can say: Orthodox Jewry has preserved Judaism unadulterated in its purest and richest form over thousands of years. Pure Ethics is an artifact isolated by a purely rationalist, "modern" process from the huge organism of tradition. Even if we do not see anything wrong with this fact in itself we must admit that, historically speaking, the burden of proof lies with those who are the enemies of Orthodoxy.

To go back to the study group. I have said that the drama in history which I have witnessed myself, the fate of European Jewry, was either meaningless, or else its meaning was transcendental. There is no other alternative. Now if you believe in the existence of God the first possibility is excluded, and that agony of horror which we have witnessed in our time must have a meaning which transcends all materialist dialectics. Since I believed in the existence of God, the answer was obvious.

From this the next steps in my development followed quite

clearly. If all that was going on around us had any hidden meaning, where was I to look for it? If I had not been studying the Prophets at that time, I would still be looking around in helpless confusion. There were men of the remote past, separated from us by two and a half millenniums, who spoke of the drama of history in dark and at the same time colorful, in meek and at the same time overpowering words. These words had withstood the test of corroding time, and they were obviously spoken to you and me. The element of grandeur and power was the only thing I found which matched the grandeur and power of the catastrophe going on around me and, what is more, it was obviously meant to match it. Anyone who has lived through those years when man's face was distorted either in senseless hatred or in a cry of agony can make a simple test. First read a clever and scholarly article on "The Jewish Question," and then read any chapter of Isaiah or Amos, and you will know what I am talking about.

It was around that time that I became convinced of the absolute truth of Revelation, and this conviction too has remained unshakable. Some people among those who read these lines will be disappointed. Because, although I said that I am deeply convinced of the transcendental meaning which is immanent in the historical fate of Jewry, I did not know that meaning. I believe I am closer to it than I was at that time.

I must admit that in the beginning I, like many of us, had a somewhat childlike and simple idea about it. I thought that these catastrophes in Jewish history happen as a punishment, and that the terrible persecution had befallen us because most of us had forgotten that we were Jews and had abandoned the ways of God laid down in the law. This is a rather simplified and anthropomorphic version of the prophetic concept of history. Its absurdity becomes obvious when you consider events in the light of individual cases. My own grandmother, Mother's mother, who lived an exceptionally saintly life, died at the age of eighty-six in a concentration camp. What was she "punished" for? No, if the suffering of our people had a meaning transcending common historical and social concepts, it could not be expressed in that simple formula.

Simultaneously with my conviction of the absolute divinity of prophetic Revelation, I became convinced of the profound significance and central position of the Messianic idea in Jewry. I began to believe in the truth of a personal Messiah as I am convinced of the reality of the paper on which this is being written. In the light of what I have said on Revelation this statement sounds rather superfluous. And yet, it is not quite so. For, in many phases and currents of post-Christian Judaism, the Messianic idea has curiously lost its central position. It has moved over to the periphery and has become pale and ill-defined.

With regard to the Messiah, various views are held by faithful Jews. The most widely held view is associated with the glowing picture of the Messianic Age which is given by the Prophets, a picture of peace and complete fulfillment. "Without the Messiah, no Peace on Earth" means to them at the same time "Without Peace on Earth, no Messiah." The Messiah is signified here, in this world, by the lion lying with the lamb.

Characteristic of the Jewish attitude is the remark which a friend of mine, a Yeshivah student, made to me in Munich during the Abyssinian war: "They say that their Messiah has come nineteen hundred years ago, and just now they are slaughtering one another with the most advanced and cruel weapons."

Very characteristic also is the Hassidic story related by Martin Buber. A Rabbi who happened to be in Jerusalem heard the great trumpets blow, and there was a rumor that the Messiah had come. The Rabbi opened the window, looked around and said only: "I see no change."

I held the same opinion quite firmly. In an ill-defined and yet quite certain way that mysterious meaning of our collective suffering and the Messianic idea were closely connected with one another. I remember that when I was in London the Rabbis used to preach that the Jews were persecuted as the bearers of the Messianic idea, and they left it at that.

17. Frau Flamm and the Yamagiwas

IN SPEAKING of the Forschungsanstalt, I have not spoken of friends who came into my life at that time, and who were to play a very decisive rôle. They were Frau Flamm and the Yamagiwas. The latter were a Japanese couple, a doctor and his wife. He was a veterinary pathologist, head of an Institute for Animal Pathology at Mukden, and the son of the world-famous pathologist Yamagiwa, the discoverer of experimental tar cancer. His wife helped him here and there with odd things in the laboratory. Since one of my regular duties was the instruction of our guest workers in neuropathology and neuroanatomy, I came in close contact with this remarkable couple. I soon noticed that they were regarded with feelings varying from distrust to hatred by all the other Japanese. This, I found out, was due to the fact that they were ardent Christian converts and pacifists. The other Japanese were more or less fanatical Nationalists. Mrs. Yamagiwa must have struck them as a particularly distasteful specimen because her father had been a well-known artillery general in the Russo-Japanese war. One of the other Japanese fellows, an ultra-Nationalist, had found a simple explanation for it. He took me aside and told me quite confidentially that in Japan a woman like Mrs. Yamagiwa would generally be regarded as hysterical. She was, he said, utterly un-Japanese, to a degree which to us must be quite inconceivable. It sounded familiar to me; this Japanese was an ideal object for Nazi propaganda. Once when I told him that I was going to visit my grandmother, who was then still free, he asked me whether she was living in Palestine. At first I did not understand. Then it occurred to me that propaganda had succeeded in making these people see in us Jews some sort of second-generation Germans.

To the Yamagiwas I was from the beginning a definite object of curiosity, and it did not take me long to find out why. Except for a pastry cook in Mukden, I was the first Jew they had ever met. They had heard a good deal about it in their Lutheran Bible class in Tokyo. Whenever Saburo Yamagiwa and I were not entirely occupied by neurotropic virus diseases in animals he cornered me about the Jews. I must admit that during those years neuropathology was not always in the center of our interest; we were much too much distracted by all the strange things going on around us. Thus, Yamagiwa succeeded in persuading me to get a Hebrew edition of the Old Testament into the lab and to translate to him straight from the Hebrew whatever little I knew. Thus whenever we were tired of the cyto-architecture of the human midbrain we put in ten minutes of discussion on Isaiah. Strange happenings in a research laboratory, but then I must say everything was in a stage of mild derangement in those days.

Frau Bertha Flamm was one of our technical assistants. For a long time I knew her only for her extraordinary technical skill in making silver impregnations of nerve cells or microphotographs. She occupied, on account of her talents, a special laboratory of her own and we rarely saw her. When we met her at all she was rather silent and seemed inaudible in her movements. She was quite natural, without any aloofness or pose, in spite of her obvious detachment. In fact there was an air of goodness and warmth about her, and although she was isolated and remote she seemed to be the confidante of all the lab girls. She had, for instance, tea by herself in her room but you could usually see one of the girls keeping her company and whispering something to her. She was the type of Alyosha Karamasov, the person who does not belong to the gang, and yet is liked by every single one for his own special reason; that was exactly her position. Here, too, I soon found out that it was not all neuropathology.

Associated with her remoteness there was some strange fascination. Everybody knew a little bit about her, and when you pieced the bits together you had at least the outline of a picture. She was thirty-six, and had a daughter of eighteen. She herself had been a moderately well-known actress as a young girl. She lived apart from her husband in one of the poor districts of the town, in an apartment of one of the dense and narrow dwellings that huddled around old St. Peter's. This was in the center of the old city of Munich. As if to make it a bit more romantic, there lived with her an eighty-year-old washerwoman, Frau Weiss, who, it was said, had adopted her when she was a little child. Frau Flamm went to early morning Mass every day on her way to work, and in the evenings she did household work for mother and daughter. She was extremely meticulous and patiently pedantic in her histological and photographic work, and usually worked overtime. Curiously none of the other lab girls regarded this as unfair competition because nobody ever doubted her motives. She lived a life of heroism in small things. Maybe stories of heroic goodness without glamor tend to sound sentimental and tawdry, and that is why people don't like to read stories about saints.

There are several reasons why I speak of Frau Flamm and the Yamagiwas in one breath. First of all they were both primarily interested in religion, and their tender hearts soon met in a profound friendship. Secondly, Frau Flamm, too, seemed to regard my scanty and recently acquired knowledge of the Old Testament as a source of information vital and burning. Thirdly, all three of them were quite naturally, without the glimmer of a doubt, convinced of something which it had taken me a long and involved struggle to see—the hidden significance of the Jewish tragedy which we were experiencing. They did not seem

to know exactly what it meant, but that it reached in its significance beyond the natural plane was obvious to them. I thought
I had made a startling discovery but they knew it all the time;
it appeared to be linked with something they had learned at
school.

I was glad that they did not try to convert me. And yet, it
seems now that there was something in the situation which prepared a profound evolution in the depth of my soul. For a long
time there was nothing extraordinary in it. Here we were sitting,
a Protestant couple, a Catholic and a Jew, and whenever we were
not looking at microscopic slides or discussing world politics,
we talked about religion. These people were an island because
they had preserved human decency. This in itself was a consolation. And yet, in my state of spiritual restlessness, the situation contained at the same time an obscure challenge for me.
Here were people of the Japanese and the German race who
thought the same thoughts as I, and felt the same feelings as I—
entirely different from the pagans around us but also different
from those of my Jewish brethren who were agnostic or irre-
ligious. Here I was, in the midst of an ocean of treachery, vile-
ness, cunning and cruelty, separated by two thousand miles from
the Land of Canaan, and by two thousand years from the Second
Temple—and found people of strange nations who had the words
of David and Isaiah engraved in their hearts. This was a miracle.
I felt it to my innermost depth but I refused, somehow, to admit
it in its fullness and in all its implications.

Two things happened during that time which proved to be
very important. One was a chance remark made by the young
man who conducted our Sabbath afternoon Bible class. I think
it was at the time when we discussed those particularly "Messianic" chapters of Isaiah. He said: "You know, occasionally,
when you contemplate these two thousand years of Galuth [dis-
persion] without even any remote hope of return, you are almost
inclined to wonder whether Jesus was not the Messiah after all."

For "Jesus" he used a dark word which orthodox Jews occasionally use, perhaps out of some superstition. Of course, he discarded the thought, it actually had occurred to him as something silly but, as it happens with chance remarks, it stuck with me. My immediate reaction, perhaps already on the basis of my experiences, was: "How do you know he wasn't?"

One evening in December, 1933, I was walking through the streets of Munich, my heart full of the disquietude which accompanies spiritual journeys, and even more by the disquietude caused by the mounting persecution, when my eyes fell on a leaflet pinned on the notice board of a church. It announced Advent sermons to be preached by the Cardinal on "Jewry and Christianity." It had never been my habit to look at notice boards of churches; in fact, it was the first time in my life I looked at one. Since I had just been pondering that very moment about the question of "Jewry and Christianity," I first had the feeling you have when you are deceived by what psychologists call an affective illusion. However, I believed what I saw, and the following Sunday evening my brother and I went to St. Michael's Hofkirche. There was an enormous crowd of people. We were pushed and carried to some place not far from the pulpit. I believe that most people came because they gathered from the title of the sermon that something was going on against the Nazis. This was a rare occasion, probably the first one of its kind.

At that time the Nazis had not only started their onslaught against the Catholic Church and the confessional Protestants, but they had also made big strides in integrating Christian tradition into their system. This was not easy. The Old Testament had to be discarded as alien to the Nordic spirit, and Christ declared an Aryan and anti-semitic, in order to be acceptable to good society. It is difficult now to believe the extent to which these currents had penetrated into the minds of the intelligentsia and the middle-class city dwellers.

Cardinal Faulhaber's sermon was actually very simple and unsophisticated. All he did was to clarify the birth certificate of Jesus of Nazareth who was a Jew in the flesh, and to reassert the oneness, the complete organic unity of the God of the Church and the God of the Patriarchs and Kings of Israel. He made only a few brief hints as to the preservation of the Jews after the Resurrection. He referred to Saint Paul's ideas on the subject as revealed in those famous chapters of the *Epistle to the Romans*. He also quoted some other Cardinal (I believe it was Manning) who, while preaching to Jews in a synagogue, said: "Gentlemen, where would we be without you?"

The sermon came as if it had been specially timed and written for my personal consumption. It had a profound, irrevocable influence on me. I remember well that, with the few meager hints he gave of the Paulinian idea with regard to post-Christian Judaism, he opened up an entirely new vista. I felt like a child who had known its own house from inside and from the garden, and who is now, for the first time, shown it from far away as part of the landscape.

Every Jewish child is taught that his religion is the mother religion of all monotheist religions, and that this mother has given birth to two daughters—Christianity and Islam. The mother is older, and usually wiser and more venerable than the daughter, and it is somehow or other implied that the Christian sect is Judaism in a modified and somewhat diluted form. Here, in the church and during the sermon, in the midst of this extraordinary setting of Munich in 1933, I suddenly realized for the first time in my life that things were not as static as all that. Did not the Prophets imply that through the Messiah the Word was to be carried to the "farthest islands"?

There was no use denying that this had happened. Contemplate for a moment the fact that there had once been a tiny people at the periphery of the Roman Empire, submerged within an ocean of a thousand creeds, which jealously guarded the

precious treasure of Revelation within the walls of its City—and
here I was standing two millenniums later and listening to those
who did not belong to Israel in the flesh but defended the God
of Abraham, Isaac and Jacob, of Moses, Isaiah and Job as if
their own lives were at stake.

My first claim, my proud assertion, all that which had been
an anchor in the storm of persecution, namely that the election
was "ours"—seemed suddenly to be taken away from me. I must
admit that I was caught up in a great inner turmoil and confusion.
My first reaction, during my conversations with the Yamagiwas
and Frau Flamm, had been pride. This pride was not very well
defined but it was approximately the idea: "What would you
be without us?" Most Jews conscious of their Jewry have this
vague sentiment at one time or another—the pride of the first-
born, the pride at the discovery that Christianity has emerged
from Jewry, as if we allowed them generously, so to speak, to
live on our heritage. All this is felt in a vague and ill-defined way.

Now I was shaken out of my inner sureness by the following
fundamental and indisputable facts. Firstly, there were two
parties who unanimously and in perfect agreement maintained
the racial wall around the God of Sinai—these were the Nazis
and the Jews. Let there be no mistake. Jewish religion up to
this day is based on the axiom that Revelation is a national
affair and that the Messiah to the Nations has not been here
yet. Do not be misled by the fact that Jews in their personal
ethics are anything but exclusive and racist. Do not be misled by certain noble Talmudic principles such as "The just
of all nations have a share in the world to come." This latter
idea has no bearing on the question discussed here; it deals
with what to Jewish antiquity was the "invisible church." Do
not be misled by fine cosmopolitan sentiments and actions of
reformed Judaism which are often prompted by noble hearts
but at the same time by much vague thinking and by a lukewarm dilution of the most profound and world-shaking elements

of the Judaic treasure. No, there is no getting away from it. Revelation was still contained within the precious vessel of the Nation; I only had to look at our liturgy to see that this was so. Jewish religion was racial exclusiveness. Mind you, it was racial exclusiveness in its noblest, most elevated form—in its metaphysical form, so to speak. It was a racism exactly opposed to that of the Nazis, but it was racism just the same. It was racism with the highest, divine justification—as long as its one basic premise was correct, namely that the Anointed One was still to be expected.

Secondly, Jesus had come not as the "founder of Christianity," of the "daughter religion"—no, he had come first and foremost to us Jews with the claim of being the Messiah, the Son of the living God. The question then whether he was what he claimed to be had still to be answered with a clear Yes or No.

Thus I found myself suddenly in what seemed to be very dangerous waters. Having grown up in a materialist world, having worked for years in scientific laboratories, a type of work in which an agnostic and materialist position was more or less implied, I had proudly re-stated, at least before myself, the absolute reality of the things of the spirit. The bold and defiant cry of the seventeenth-century mathematician, Pascal, that God is "not the God of Philosophers but the God of Abraham, Isaak and Jacob" had become my own.

And now, not long after the beginning of my journey, I was facing the eternal question: "And who do you say that I am?" What was even worse was the vague feeling in the back of my mind that this question had to be answered fully, and without any possibility of evasion or compromise. There is a common German proverb, "Whoever says A must also say B." I had said A, and all of a sudden there seemed to be a B to it, and I had the dim notion that I might have to say it.

Actually the B was very remote just then—much more so than

would perhaps appear from the way this story is related here. In fact, the more I felt irked and later haunted by question B the more I seemed to cling to the stark overwhelming reality, to the call of the Jewish communion which had become the tragic communion of Fate. I intensified my study of Hebrew as far as I could besides the work at the laboratory. I took part more frequently in study courses and in the services at the synagogue. My intention to go to Palestine became more serious. I wanted to do something constructive in spite of the fact that, contrary to my brother's case, an occupational re-orientation was out of the question.

During that time I was frequently in the house of one of the leaders of the orthodox congregation in Munich, Eugen Fränkel. He was a true example of Jewish piety, and his house breathed the very spirit of Jewish tradition. This man was overwhelmed not only by the sorrow of the persecution but by the personal sorrow of chronic suffering (there was a young daughter bedridden for years with some hopeless progressive disease). But he had the translucent spirituality which I have often witnessed in the Orthodox and which seems to be so utterly unknown to most people who discuss the "Jewish problem." In his demeanor, in his actions, thoughts and feelings, he seemed to personify the spirit of the Torah. God dominated and permeated his entire life, from the Washing of the Hands to the stirrings in the innermost depth of his heart. His daughter's agony was double agony to him, yet I have never seen Job's "The Lord has given, the Lord has taken" *lived* as much as in his life. It was his natural gesture, so to speak, and not a strenuously acquired and debatable philosophy. There is an ancient Midrashic tradition that the author of the Book of Job was none other than Moses himself. This legend has always had a deep and touching significance to me. Does it not mean that the writer of the Law which seems to imply that suffering is nothing but wrath and just punishment knew all the time that suffering has also an altogether different aspect?

I had at one time looked after the daughter while she was in the hospital. Thus I was invited to spend the Friday evenings in Dr. Fränkel's house, and this I did almost regularly. I also saw the daughter quite frequently on Saturday afternoons. The Friday evening ceremonies, the round-songs after the table prayer, particularly the Psalms, and Dr. Fränkel's informal chats on a few lines of medieval exegetic literature—all this provided part of my background at that time. I am still convinced that this is the only form of Jewish life worthy the name. Dr. Fränkel had a son who was a well-known biologist, a "pure" Zionist without much religious allegiance. I was unable to understand his position, and particularly why he had doubted what seemed and still seems to me today the very nucleus of the Jewish life. Incidentally, the father had originally maintained the strictly orthodox view with regard to Zionism. Basically the orthodox had been anti-Zionist, because it was generally held that the Jews should not return to Zion unless the Messiah had come to lead them there. Later, however, a compromise was found. Settlement in Palestine and the cultural re-orientation connected with it was no longer regarded as incompatible with orthodoxy. Those orthodox who held this view were called Misrahi. I remember that it had been quite an event when old Fränkel was converted to Misrahism by his children. This had happened many years before the time of this story. In the winter of 1935 Dr. Fränkel proposed my name as that of a possible leader of the Young Misrahi group. At that time, however, I had experienced a little the sensation of Dr. Jekyll and Mr. Hyde. However, I regarded it as a hopeless undertaking to acquaint Dr. Fränkel with the ideas that went through my head. He was so deeply rooted in tradition that he would not have understood me, and I would only have hurt him. I am sure he would have been disturbed and bewildered if he had known about my

evenings at Frau Flamm's house. Perhaps he might even have
doubted my honesty, although he was too charitable to do this.

Frau Flamm lived in that section of the town in which the
poor and faithful had been living for centuries. I believe that
there is something similar in all big Catholic cities in the world.
In countries like Bavaria the basic layer in the structure of the
Church besides the farmers are the little tradesmen and their
families, the cooks, washerwomen and maids. There may be much
smallness, rigidity and resistance to progress but, at the same
time, there is perhaps the greatest treasure of anonymous sanctity.
These people always seem to be concentrated in certain areas
where the apartments are narrow, dark and overcrowded. There
is always enough of mustiness and the smell of poverty in the
air to make everything appear just pleasantly unhygienic. [A
self-confident man from Hammersmith once said to me: "They
say that Roman Catholic countries are dirty."]

In one of those houses, on the third floor, in a dark and some-
what hidden flat lived Frau Weiss, the old washerwoman, and
Frau Flamm with her daughter, Ruth-Maria. In Frau Flamm's
room we had many evening sessions. It so happened that when
I got to know her she was studying Soloviev. Among German
Catholics during that time there was a strong interest in the
Eastern Church and a trend towards union. I remember that the
only decoration in Frau Flamm's room besides a reproduction of
El Greco's Madonna was a portrait of Dostoievsky. I do not
know exactly what I learned then about Soloviev. The only
book I remember I borrowed from her was his famous essay on
Plato.

During those evenings with Frau Flamm and her daughter,
or with the Flamms and the Yamagiwas, there was a harmony of
spirit which equaled that of the Friday evenings with the
Fränkels. There was no doubt, it was the same atmosphere of
peace and understanding. You will say, "Well, that sort of thing

is always present whenever you meet decent people—no matter of what philosophy or religion." No, that was not it, there was something else. It was really the spirit of Judaism I rediscovered in this strange setting, enriched by remote peoples, and cleansed of its purely ethnic elements.

It was not quite the situation of Dr. Jekyll and Mr. Hyde. In fact, I remember very well that Frau Flamm and the Yamagiwas loved and understood the world of Dr. Fränkel, and encouraged me in my endeavors to embrace Orthodoxy. What a strange phenomenon! Yet Dr. Fränkel would not have been able to understand their world. Thus, I made another important discovery. Christianity confirmed and believed everything which Jewry believed but added one fundamental assertion which Jewry rejected. Heresies are based on denials. In this sense Christianity was no heresy from Judaism; it rejected nothing essential but made a new positive claim.

It was about that time that I went to see Martin Buber about my increasing spiritual difficulties. I told him that I had been studying the Epistles of Saint John, and that I found there the spirit of Judaism expressed with such purity and in such overwhelming intensity that I could not understand why we did not accept the New Testament. I reminded him that he himself had once called Christianity the "first Hassidic movement" among the Jews. To this he replied that it was true that the Epistles of Saint John were Judaism at its highest, and that he could well understand my enthusiasm. "However," he said, "if you want to accept Christ and the New Testament, the maxims of the Epistles are not enough. You must also believe in the Virgin Birth and in the Resurrection of Christ from the dead." These things are hard to believe, he said. He began to talk of the giving of the law on Mount Sinai, and whether God really pronounced the ten commandments Himself in His own voice. He wanted to indicate that this, too, was hard to believe. He became quite pensive and said something to the effect that we do not know how to take this description of the miracle of Sinai, and whether the people actually *heard* God. "Perhaps there was only one word said." To me it did not make any difference with regard to the nature of the miracle whether one word or a thousand words were said. Buber's answer disturbed me greatly. I realized that my newly acquired interest in the New Testament which had developed into a profound attachment was actually a rather emotional and romantic sentiment. Buber had put it very clearly. In questions like these, vagueness and compromise were excluded. To me as to every Jew the very concept of the divinity of Christ was something utterly alien and incomprehensible. It was incompatible with the spirit of the Old Testament, and a blasphemy. "Nobody sees God and lives." ". . . Because that thou, being a man, makest thyself God."

In retrospect it is interesting that I could not at all understand why the Voice of Sinai as a true physical phenomenon, something which was actually heard, presented a problem to Buber. He was much more logical than I. Because if that Voice was possible, then the Incarnation was possible too; both phenomena were on the same level. His doubt, on the other hand, had something to do with a general paling and lack of fresh immediate concreteness in matters of faith which is so characteristic of modern non-orthodox Western Jewry. This is due to the assimilation of Jewry, on a cultural plane, as the carriers of agnostic humanism. It seemed to me that Buber, whose original merit had been to open up the treasures of Hassidic piety for the western world, had become a victim of the same process. He was not aware of this. I remember that once, during a conference, he told us: "Several of the young Jews in the Youth Movement came to me and said: 'When we take up a prayer-book we have difficulty in saying *ata* [thou]. It is impossible for us to address God directly just like that!'" If I understood his subsequent remarks correctly, he meant to say that this was a wonderful sign of religious awakening, the experience of immense distance and awe. In reality, however, Jews who find difficulty in addressing their Father in Heaven directly in the second person singular present a very sad picture indeed.

I must state here in anticipation it took me very long, nearly ten years, to accept the divinity of Christ. The more I came to believe in Him as a Messiah the more He remained at the same time the historical person, the prophet who exceeded and fulfilled all prophecy. One calls this sort of thing Arianism. Had He not Himself warned us: "Call me not Master . . ."? For a long time I believed that old Tolstoy was right; he wanted to strip the Gospel of the supernatural altogether. I agreed with him that the Church which upheld and defended this supernatural element of the Gospel misused this very element in order to keep the poor ignorant, dependent and oppressed; those sects, however, which preserved nothing but the ethical nucleus of Scripture seemed to stand for true charity and justice.

I suppose everybody who comes to accept Christ reaches this goal in his own particular way. It looks as if this uniqueness were associated with the ultimate secret of the personality. Somewhere in the back of my mind I knew all the time that there was something wrong with Tolstoy's position, and that is why I was not satisfied with it. If the divinity of Christ was an error or a lie, certain formative forces which radiated from this very idea and fertilized the depth of the soul were impossible to explain. In a certain inverted and paradoxical sense Tolstoy was right. For without the divinity of the Messiah the simple piety and heroic sanctity of some of our peasant maids were somehow unthinkable, but so were Chartres and Grünewald, and Bach and Mozart.

This experience of the "historical argument" was very intense and, it seemed, quite personal. I discovered much later that Pascal wanted to make it the foundation stone of a great and lofty form of Christian apologetics. It is obvious from the *Pensées* that he intended to build on this indisputable fact the scientific evidence of Christianity. One of my great teachers in Medicine used to say that in order to be a scientist you have to have only one talent—to be astonished at the proper time. The scientist Pascal was astonished at an obvious and simple fact. Just as the Prophets had predicted it, the fruit of Israel had burst at a definite historical moment, the seeds had been flung to the far corners of the earth and had brought forth plants a thousandfold. It seems that Pascal planned a gigantic apologetic work because he, a mathematician and physicist of the Cartesian epoch, was aware of the dangers of modern positivism. He may, in nights of mystic fever, have sensed the wave which was to flood and drown the Western world.

However, we do not know. History is acted in Time, its very matter is Time, and being tinged with Time it is tinged with not-being, with Death. With this our present-day existential philosophers are only varying what Plato and Saint Paul have expressed before. They have rediscovered it under the fear and dread which pervade modern man. If history's very essence were time it would be a formless and structureless matter unrolling itself like permanent finality, a horrible antagonist of eternity. Indeed materialist dialectics, if it were brought to its logical conclusion, would come precisely to this image of history. The only phenomenon which invades history with an element of timelessness is Prophecy. The prophetic view elevates history and enlightens it with Eternity. Eastern Christian thinkers, with their Platonic tradition, such as Soloviev and Berdyaev saw this very clearly. The great Eastern religions leave history aside as a chaotic structure. Only in Judaeo-Christianity do Time and Eternity meet in History.

This is the miracle which overwhelmed Pascal in the seventeenth century. Perhaps with him it was only a "thought." However, for men living in times of seemingly chaotic transition it is an immediate experience, something affecting them in their very being. We have an extraordinary example of this in Saint

Augustine. He was shaken by the transcendental forces immanent in history. When one reads certain parts of the *Civitas Dei* one almost feels as if this had been the very nucleus of his conversion.

However, at the time which I am discussing here I knew nothing about either Pascal or Saint Augustine, at least nothing about the way in which the "historical argument" or the immediate experience of history had overwhelmed them. I emerged from the Synagogue, from our study course on the Prophets, and I met non-Jews who thought my thoughts and felt my feelings, who seemed to glow under the radiation of *shehinah*, the very seat of the Word. Somewhere deep down I felt that all of us Jews who reacted to nationalism around us with national vigor were closer to the Nazis than these people who believed in the God of Abraham, Isaak and Jacob.

There was no getting away from it. If this German woman and that Japanese couple were right, then I was wrong. For if the Messiah had come nineteen hundred years ago then Revelation was no longer enclosed in the precious vessel of the *am ha' amim*, the people of peoples. Then the true bond between the four of us was beyond the blood of the nation; it must have been provided by Him.

If they were wrong, then the Nazis were right. If they had falsely accepted the word of some obscure Jewish preacher of nineteen hundred years ago as the word of God then they were, as many of our Nazis believed, the victims of some monstrous fraud.

Here you have a neat problem. Just try and let one of our scientists, our historians, sociologists, solve it. It is one of those formidable "either-or" problems of Kierkegaard, one of those stinging questions which go on paining you in the depth of your existence until you have given a clear answer.

There were times when I doubted my sanity. Everywhere around me I saw people who were wiser and better than I, and who did not see what seemed to me the essential alternative. Here I was, one of my people in the middle of the most dreadful persecution we had ever suffered and, like a faint shadow, the possibility arose of leaving this community of destiny. This seemed madness. It seemed madness the more since it was my natural urge to stay with those with whom I was born to suffer. Was the swastika not a modification of the Crucifix under whose sign we had been tortured before? This is what it seemed to be if one took history on the natural plane. Perhaps all this was a "build-up," carefully framed by my subconscious to camouflage an escape from Jewry.

I was easily able to dismiss this thought because I saw that during persecution it was only the "race" that counted. Christian Jews did not fare better than their brethren. On the contrary, they often fared worse because socially and politically they frequently belonged nowhere.

Modern man can no longer take spiritual realities at their face value. His is the tragedy of Hamlet. He does not only experience; he reflects. And once he tries on himself all those up-to-date tricks of psychological investigation, he is lost. He lacks naiveness and is distrustful towards himself; soon he sees himself hopelessly entangled in an inextricable network of purely psychological references. Then comes the great turnabout; the only thing which is real, ultimate Reality, appears as something relative, as a pure mirror-phenomenon; and the network of references appears as something very real. At that moment the great negation is completed. This is one of the spiritual pitfalls of our time. I suppose each cultural epoch has its own specific form of negation, and the process I have just described is rather specific for us who are alive right now.

18. Anguish of Regeneration

No MATTER in what dangerous straits my people were I knew that, as far as ultimate truth was concerned, I could not make *ressentiment* the basis of my future life. I know that many of my Jewish fellowmen make this mistake. They say: "I am not a Jew in a religious sense but we have been despised and persecuted so much that a decent man could not possibly . . ." This is what Nietzsche called *ressentiment.* It is one of Nietzsche's indisputable merits to have shown the uncreative and destructive qualities of *ressentiment* in history. Mind you, this motive is very understandable and may be justified under certain circumstances but it contains a nucleus of pure negation.

Intermingled with *ressentiment* there is a good deal of pride, not only of wounded pride but of pride pure and simple, of a feeling of national superiority. I do not say it is present with those people whom I have just quoted but I know it was very much so with me.

The great German Lutheran writer, Ricarda Huch, once remarked that for the Jews to become converted to Christ means an extraordinary sacrifice. Not only, says she, must the individual die with Him in order to live; it is the whole people that must die with Him. By some mysterious twist of fate the Jews are the only people which cannot remain a people and be Christian at the same time. Christ extolled a double sacrifice from His people; not only the individual Adam has to die to be dissolved in Him—the group too has to be dissolved.

This is one of the most profound remarks ever made on the so-called Jewish problem. It touches the very center of it. The Jewish contemporaries of Christ who rejected Him knew that by accepting Him they would sacrifice the nation. The one and only condition under which they would have accepted Him, He had to refuse. He could not be their "national leader," and this in spite of the imminent danger from outside. This was a super-human demand. It seems a natural right of every nation to defend itself in times of danger. In the case of the Jews the word of the "seed that falleth into the ground . . ." referred not only to the individual but to the group.

The Jews maintained the idea of racial integrity at a time when it had lost its transcendental meaning; for "all was fulfilled" in Christ. If death, as Berdyaev expresses it, "gives meaning to life," here the ultimate death of a nation will give meaning to its life. But before that happens our people is condemned to live on as some sort of a ghost representing the idea of racism. It seems that in modern times the fate of the Jews becomes more and more intimately associated with the fate of the racist idea. Only when the problem of the un-Christian national segregation is solved, will the "Jewish problem" be solved too.

It is interesting to see how Christians (I do not mean non-Jews but those who profess to believe in Christ and follow His gospel) react when facing the Jewish problem. It is those who are still tortured by nationalism who are anti-semitic. This is what psychologists call projection. They hate their own demon in something they see outside themselves. Read carefully Dostoievsky's anti-semitic pamphlet. There is, page after page, a tone of irrationality and of passion which cannot be explained on the basis of the subject he is dealing with; that is his attitude towards Jewish nationalism. Like all great hatred, this is self-hatred. All the motives he projects into the Jews are, deep down, his own. Just replace the word "Judaism" by "Panslavism," and you know what I mean. Dostoievsky was one of the deepest Christian thinkers of the nineteenth century but there was one way in which he succumbed, like so many other men of that

century, to *chthonic* or "earthly" forces—in nationalism. That
was his impurity. That is where his own world is incompatible
with that of Alyosha and of Myshkin. And what does he do?
He bursts forth in an epileptoid fury against Jewish nationalism.

This touches closely upon the secret of why Jewish shortcomings, Jewish vices, Jewish impurities are hated more than those
of other people. Because the physical existence of the Jewish
people is, from the point of view of the metaphysics of history,
an incongruity. The Jews are here, they are living, whereas the
ultimate meaning of their existence as a people is that it should
transcend itself. This is perhaps the reason why not infrequently
Jews who approach Christ struggle more against His final embrace than anyone else. In all those Jews whom I saw approaching the Church and remaining with one foot on the threshold
there is, besides a thousand natural obstacles, besides the fear
of cowardly betrayal, besides the anxiety of isolation, something
else; there is a seemingly invincible horror, something which
reaches deep down beneath the social and biological strata of
the personality, something that seems to arrest the pulse and
make the blood curdle in the veins, there is a cosmic fear, a
panic of death and dissolution. It is as if the agony of a people
were compressed into the space of an individual existence, as
if the agony of all peoples were contained in the night of
Gethsemani. This is where being and becoming reach those
timeless spheres which are contained in History.

According to the biogenetic law of Haeckel, the embryo's development is a condensed and rapid version of the development
of the species. In a similar manner every Jew who is conscious of
his Judaism and is converted to Christ goes, in his lifetime,
through the spiritual destiny of his race. Hence this particular
intensity and agony of development, hence this profound anxiety
which is nothing but primeval fear of death and of birth. I
think it is ultimately on the basis of this fear that we can explain
some of the paradoxical attitudes, the writhing movements

which we witness in people like Franz Werfel. Read this passage written not long before his death: ". . . [the] Jew who goes to the baptismal font deserts Christ Himself, since he arbitrarily interrupts his historical suffering—the penance for rejecting the Messiah—and in hasty manner not foreseen in the drama of salvation, steps to the side of the Redeemer, where he probably does not at all belong, according to the Redeemer's holy will; at any rate, *not yet*, and not here and now." This is what the panic of total eradication will do to our thoughts. We all go through these and similar mental contortions before we have torn up all our earthly roots and let ourselves fall into space and into the great embrace.

If I speak of the ultimate significance of the dissolution of the Jews, I mean it in the Paulinian sense. I do not speak of "assimilation as the only rational solution" of the Jewish problem. This idea is a typical product of nineteenth-century liberalism. It is the very counterfeit of the conversion of Israel. A religious Jew who chose to be burned at the stake by the Inquisitor rather than let himself be baptized is obviously closer to God than a modern Jew who is baptized to solve the problem of anti-semitism for his children.

Jacques Maritain once said that the Nazis adopted certain elements of the Old Testament and applied them in distorted form (racism) and the Communists did the same with certain elements of the New Testament (the brotherhood of men). In the light of this thought, it is interesting to see how these two movements approached the Jewish problem. The Nazis, in denying the historical significance of the coming of Christ, tried to re-establish a pre-Christian status, and produced a diabolical caricature of the segregation of the people of Israel. The Bolshevists, during of political pantomime of a Messianic fulfillment, attempted some peculiar state of assimilation of the Jews. At least originally (things have developed differently during the Stalinist period) the Bolshevists gave our poor Christians of the West a lesson in racial tolerance, not only of the Jews but of all minorities. However, this solution presupposes a purely naturalist concept of Man. It is logical only if we believe in nothing but the materialist dialectics of history, it is one of the practical shortcuts so characteristic of modern materialism and nominalism. It may have, like communism in general, begun in individual impulses of a longing for justice but it ends up in that form of equality which is a feature of machinery, of a world of machinery in which human life loses its creative significance.

Thus, the orthodox Jew who rejects Christ vigorously is much closer to the Christian than enlightened intellectuals who keep the "sayings" of the "great social reformer" Jesus on their bookshelves next to anthologies of Confucius. Because, by their vigorous denial, the Orthodox constantly re-state the potentiality of a true Messiah and of His divinity. Whereas the others, no matter how good their intentions may be, rob the God of History and the God of the thornbush of His devouring fire. If one believes in a concept of history which is not materialist, then one must admit that the dynamics of spiritual development is constantly fed and upheld by the dialectic antithesis which exists between Synagogue and Church. Forces of evil have separated the two. How much would be won, even today, if Christians could have a glimpse of orthodox piety. That monstrous phenomenon, religious anti-semitism, could never appear again. If a Hassidic mystic and a follower of Saint John of the Cross could know one another, not separated by a barbed wire of social and political prejudice but in a spirit of charity, they would be amazed how akin they are in their striving. However, for some strange reason that does not seem to be possible. Nevertheless, it is, as we have said, just that dialectic tension which is of creative significance. This is, undoubtedly, one of the meanings implied in Chapter IX of the *Epistle to the Romans*.

It was a perturbing experience for me, just when I had rediscovered Judaism, just when I had become immensely proud of my spiritual heritage in the middle of the most plebeian stupidity, just when I had found something absolutely certain while others around me were choking in the fear created by a world of shifting uncertainties, to see that I might have to abandon what I had found. Today I know that there was actually nothing I had to give up. On a spiritual plane Christianity is Jewry. It is Jewry led to its fulfillment. There is no essential truth of the Old Testament which the Christian denies.

At that time I was, like most of us, so enmeshed in social and political concepts that I did not see this simple fact, and I did not want to see it. I had an almost triumphant feeling about the stupidity of our persecutors. Since the word "Christian" today is synonymous with "non-Jew," I made great use of the confused issue and said, like many of my fellowmen: "See . . . the Christians . . . how they behave?" As to those poor real Christians around us such as Frau Flamm, the Yamagiwas, our good and noble Dr. Schulz—it was just too bad for them. Whenever Frau Flamm spoke to me of Christianity, I felt as if I had to look through the window, like the Rabbi in the Hassidic story, saying: "I can see no change." As violently as I had been hit by the experience of what I called the "historical argument," I seized upon the historical counter-argument. Perhaps the Messiah had been realized in that small group of people around me, but what about mankind in general? Where was the lamb feeding with the lion? I had only to look through the window to see every bestiality, every horror, every stupidity ever committed by Babylonians and Egyptians. The peoples were still the *goyim*.

It was only gradually, in the course of years, that I began to realize that Freedom of the Will, the greatest gift bestowed on man by God, was not abolished by the appearance of the Messiah. If that central historical event nineteen hundred years ago had changed the fundamental ontological structure of man, then there could never have been any idea of man, nothing—as I would put it today—corresponding to the second person of the hypostatic union. If Christ by his very appearance had created a complete social change on earth then the Messianic idea would be a *contradictio in adjecto.* [Incidentally, the post-Christian development of the Messianic idea among Jews is by no means uniform. I believe that there is, for instance, an interesting Midrashic tradition of the Messiah sitting unknown to everybody at the Gate of the City and dressing his wounds.] To transform the world mechanically by an extraneous event would distort the *te' munah,* the *image* which man represents. Therefore those of us are utterly wrong who, like the Hassidic Rabbi, look through the window and say: "With towns and villages of innocent people bombed, with millions of innocents thrown into machines of annihilation, it simply cannot be that there was a Messiah here on earth."

The more I became convinced of this, the more I felt that reasserting the Jewish position meant agreeing with the Nazis against the Christians. My remote feeling of triumph was nothing but a dangerous form of pride. I believe that the position of post-Christian Jewry is somewhat the same as that of the Prophet Jonah. After his message is delivered to the *goyim* he remains outside the walls, grudging with God. To be a Prophet and in his function of a Prophet not to be associated with the idea of the nation is so horrible that he would rather drown than fulfill his mission. It is the enemies of his people whose conversion is at stake, and to sacrifice his national pride for the conversion of others is more than his human nature can take. There seems to be profound symbolic significance in the fact that the Book of Jonah is the reading on the afternoon of the Day of Atonement.

I saw then that the fate of my people was intimately associated with the fate of Christ in the world, that there were people around me who held in their hearts the God of Israel, although they were not Jews; and in the intensity and profundity of their lives I saw the Messianic prophecy of Isaiah fulfilled. This was the beginning of a new outlook on life. Something old had burst, though I did not want this fact to be true. Something new had sprung up. I did not know where I was being led. But I felt that insight meant obligation. I knew that there would come a time when I would have to make the big jump into the unknown.

Under the indescribable dread of persecution, I began to see the meaning of the mystery of Israel. However, no matter how intense this experience was, it only initiated a change in my life. Christ is not only the Messiah to Israel. If He means anything then His meaning transcends all national destiny, it would affect you as a person even if you were alone on this planet. Experience may stir you up in your depths and make you receptive. But if you were left like this you would be nothing but a hollow recipient. Marx said about Hegelian dialectics something to the effect that philosophers have thus far interpreted the world but it is for us to change it. In the same manner we can say that after having interpreted our destiny we have to change ourselves.

At the end of January, 1934, just two months after the Cardinal's sermon, I was seized by a severe influenza. When I tried to get up I could not. My limbs felt like lead, and I was unable to walk for a distance of fifty yards. The doctors told me that the hilum of my lungs showed a peculiar knotty swelling and that my sedimentation rate was way up, one hundred and thirty. The fever, they said, was negligible. I was told to take it easy, and I remained in my room in an attic in Schwabing. I felt so sick that I was unable to move. After three weeks I went to the Students' Health Service. They fluoroscoped me and told me that I had to go immediately to a students' tuberculosis sanatorium in Agra, Switzerland. When I got there I found out that the place was, although in Switzerland, a German Nazi enclave. Back I went to Munich.

I presented myself to Professor Lydtin, a well-known chest specialist. He said: "My dear boy, what you have got is miliary tuberculosis." I had learned that miliary tuberculosis is one of the few hundred per cent fatal illnesses. He looked at me and quickly added: "Don't be afraid. If this had been able to kill you, you would already be dead." Then he gave me a long lecture about extremely rare types of miliary dissemination over the lungs in which there was some peculiar allergic tissue reaction which enabled the body to vanquish the illness. "Of this form only two dozen have been described in the medical literature— and to think that you are one of them." He took me in front of the X-ray showbox, and there, radiating in a milky light, was the picture. A huge hilum-like cumulus cloud, and all over the lungs as far as you could see, snowflakes. "Now I understand why you feel so rotten, the worst feeling you must have had was before the tissue reaction appeared." I did not believe any of the things he told me except "miliary tuberculosis" and I was certain that it would kill me. Even if it would not kill me—a German Jew, in the academic profession in 1934, afflicted with illness—I found myself suddenly at the margin of existence. It was a death sentence with a peculiar type of execution. I looked back at my life and found it singularly meaningless. I looked ahead and was seized with fear.

They sent me to a private sanatorium in the Black Forest. For months I lay in bed and saw nobody except the nurses and doctors. Then I lay outside on the gallery for several hours, twice a day. I spent about ten months on my back, thinking all the time. On the mattress to my right was a young man of a Prussian noble family. He was a philosophy student, and had studied under Heidegger. His entire life history, since childhood, had been interspersed with episodes of tuberculosis. He was very stoic about it. He belonged to the Confessional (anti-Nazi) Protestant Church and was a good Christian.

On my left was a sociology Professor from Louvain. He was one of those Catholics who sympathized with the Nazi movement, out of a romantic idea about the Holy Roman Empire or something like that. I pointed out to him how incompatible his position was with Christianity and told him about the struggle of the Catholics in Munich. He became quite attached to me and his attitude seemed to change entirely. However, a few years ago I heard that he was a collaborator with the Nazis in Belgium during the war, and was condemned to death after the liberation of Belgium.

Von Lössl, the young Prussian, always had a volume of Aristotle in the Greek original with him. I used to read the Old Testament in Hebrew with the aid of a Hebrew dictionary. We exchanged bits of Bible and Aristotle. Von Lössl gave me lectures on "being," of which I understood nothing. He tried to be more explicit by using the Greek terms from the original. With this method I understood even less. He told me that he intended to study Saint Thomas under Gilson or Maritain in Paris. Nevertheless, when Lemans, the Belgian, was not present he told me that the Jesuits had secret trap-doors in the Vatican into which they lured their adversaries; underneath the trap-doors were cellars full of skeletons.

In July, 1934, the snowstorm picture of my lungs had become denser, and the Doctor stopped showing me my X-rays. However, in September they began to clear up. By that time I had had much opportunity to think and to study something about *being* in spite of the fact that Lössl's Aristotle was somewhat obscure. At the end of 1934 my lungs were clear and I was able to return to Munich, even though it was winter.

19. The Wrong Schmid

FOR MANY years life moves forward as something fortuitous and inconclusive. It is as if destiny had withdrawn itself into a far corner. Then there come months when everything seems to be tinged with the infinite. Lives are extricated from the haphazard stream and symbolize what is beyond the accidental. Thus it was in Munich, as it had been in Heidelberg and in Paris. There was a peculiar, almost painful, intensification, as if everybody had been forced to present all that was in him, in a condensed meaningful way, before we were finally called by destiny.

I had come to Munich with several introductions. There was a circle of musicians, with which Frau Masser made me acquainted. Herr Masser was a banker, attached to the Dresdner Bank. When the Dresdner Bank dismissed all its Jews, including those in prominent positions, Herr Masser came home with the news that he was pensioned. He thought that this was fair, and that business people had a better chance than those of us who were in the professions. This pension was some hint of Justice, a remnant of fairness. It saved the music-room with the Bechstein grand piano, an island of beauty and friendship to be preserved until the flood would have subsided. There was one child, a boy of eight who could not go to school any more because he was Jewish. What should become of him?

Shortly after the news of the pension arrived we had some chamber music in the large music-room. Late in the evening Frau Masser played one of the Bach solo suites for violin. Her sad eyes, her handsome face, the Bach with its virile romanesque beauty, all this seemed to leave the Dresdner Bank and the pension behind. It was as if she owned a magic carpet by which she could save her little boy instantly, on the spot. But, beyond, Herr Masser knew, there were the strange cities of Australia in which a man of fifty-three would be ground into the milling stream. "Out there" it looked like certain perdition. There was no doubt. Herr Masser was enough of an economist to know that the Nazis could not last long. He showed it to me in figures. The debts of Germany were appallingly high, even without full-fledged re-armament. Frau Masser said that she would rather take her fiddle, and no money at all, and go to Australia. Incidentally, it was often the women who sensed the greatness of the impending catastrophe and who wanted to take chances.

The Massers acted as if their disagreement were accidental. Herr Masser did not like Bach. He said it was dry stuff, and he whistled Offenbach operettas to tease his wife. As a matter of revenge, on Herr Masser's birthday, she sneaked up to the bedroom door while he was still asleep and began to play a Bach solo suite. On our music evenings Herr Masser got the stands ready, unpacked the instruments and saw to it that the musicians were well regaled. He was proud of his wife, and said that he would be content to be an usher and live on his pension. There was a strange game of mutual half-humorous, half-tragic deceit going on. Thus, the pension developed into something unlimited by human whim, like Time itself. Wolfgang, the little boy, stayed at home; the Massers kept on waiting and making music.

In our ensemble was an excellent viola player, an elderly high school teacher, short, with a round protruding stomach. He came from one of the oldest Munich families of generations of schoolteachers. He appeared silently, took his appointed place, played beautifully, said little, wrapped his viola in a silk scarf, packed it in the case and vanished silently. His name was Käsbohrer. Like every true musician he was strict and forbidding when it came to exactitude of performance. In the middle of a passage he sighed or threw a hand up like a disgruntled stationmaster (this precisely was his appearance). Presently he pulled an old reading-score out of the pocket of his luster jacket and pointed at a combination of legato bows and staccato dots. Either it was because he was the only non-Jew and therefore accentuated the element of isolation, or because we were too sophisticated and nervous by comparison, or because he was so silent and matter-of-fact; there was something unreal about Käsbohrer. He took his place in our midst like a ghost. After a few weeks,

however, I found out. Someone told me that Käsbohrer was a
staunch Catholic. When the Nazi persecution of the Jews began he made a vow to make music from then on only with
Jews. This was his form of protest.

Frau Masser said to me: "You must meet Julia Menz and Willi
Schmid." Julia Menz, the famed harpsichordist, and Willi
Schmid, music historian and critic, were both Bach experts.
Julia Menz gave concerts abroad and when Frau Masser spoke
of Julia flying from India to Java, I realized that Julia was Frau
Masser's other self, her ego by desire. In this way Frau Masser
must have been flying in her dreams, from India to Java, from
Australia to New Zealand. There was still some world in which
Bach's sequences sounded as if in a pure atmosphere, far away
from Hitler and the Dresdner Bank and pensions. Frau Masser
and Herr Käsbohrer kept insisting that I must meet Willi Schmid
and Julia Menz. They meant to arrange for it at the next possible occasion. I never met either of them.

In the case of Willi Schmid the reason was quite extraordinary. On June 30, 1934, during the famous purge, he was taken
away from his house and shot. No reasons were given. On the
same day it was discovered that he had been the victim of a
mistake. The SS guards, in their great zeal, had mixed up two
people of the same name. A storm-trooper by the name of Willi
Schmid, apparently one of the traitors of the party, had been on
the black-list. The mistake was barely discovered when it was
corrected. The true Willi Schmid was also shot the same day.
In those days for every person who perished and for every person who was saved there seemed to be an element of the seemingly fortuitous, that puzzling element of chance, of hit and
miss. There is no reason why I should not have been killed in
a gas-chamber and the Massers should not be alive in Canada.
But Willi Schmid's case, the story of the two names, seemed so
blatant that it kept haunting me for years.

Perhaps it was the bizarreness of his story, perhaps it was the obvious symbolism implied in his common name; at any rate, whatever it may have been, I began to feel about Willi Schmid precisely as the Friar in Thornton Wilder's *The Bridge of San Luis Rey* felt about the victims of the collapsed bridge. I began to become interested in any data about his life which might give a possible meaning to such a murderous coincidence. A few years later Willi Schmid's friends published a collection of his essays, letters and poems, and a biographical obituary by Father Peter Doerfler, Bavarian priest and writer. This book was published in 1937 in Germany; it contains little that would compromise Schmid politically—anything of that sort would, of course, have prevented its publication. Yet there were a few sentences which could be interpreted in such a compromising way. On the other hand there were remarks which can, if one tries, be read as if Schmid belonged to those intellectuals who strained themselves to find a bridge toward Nazism. In other words Schmid was perhaps an example of those "non-political" Germans who represented a puzzling and disquieting phenomenon in a world in which political and moral issues are too closely intertwined for the comfort of one's immortal soul.

The story of his childhood sounded rather like the romantic biography of a Southern German poet and musician. His spiritual food was Goethe, Stifter, Moericke and Latin and Greek poetry. There were people who later remembered him as a schoolboy sitting in a Munich streetcar with a volume of Virgil or Catullus. It was the custom that the boy who led his class should give a speech at the commencement exercises. He was chosen to do this but, instead, performed a cello sonata by Richard Strauss.

He began his university years by studying philosophy and romantic philology at Munich, later the history of art in Rome. When the First World War broke out, he enlisted as a volunteer. The war left him stranded, like so many others, barely alive. Typhoid fever in Serbia, an abdominal gunshot wound at the battle of the Somme; both left him an invalid for years to come.

During those years he studied pedagogy, art history and music, and in 1923 received his doctorate with a thesis on Don Bosco.

In 1924 he first began to edit old choral works and Mozart's church music in Pustet's *Musica Sacra*. At the same time he found employment as music critic on one of the Munich papers. During the following ten years he was most productive, unearthing ancient pre-Bachian music. His journeys of research took him to Berlin, Prague, Paris, Milan, Turin. He made some most delightful discoveries. Even the month preceding his death yielded valuable findings in monasteries at Ravenna, Cividale and Padua. However, deciphering those scores alone did not satisfy him. He studied the old instruments, especially ancient types of viola, like the viola da gamba, and soon he was able to perform the music. This he did together with other violists and with Julia Menz. Moreover, it was he who supported and stimulated Wolfgang Graeser during the reconstruction of the *Art of the Fugue,* Bach's gigantic musical testament which, up to that time, had consisted of seemingly unconnected fragments like a rubble of stones that has to be rebuilt into a celestial temple.

When I tried to look at him against the background of the weird, ghost-like chiaroscuro, Munich, 1934, there was one thing that struck me very forcibly and at once—that was the curious mixture of a somewhat simple patriotism with the "European" attitude. This seemed to be inherent in him, not acquired on some intellectual detour. This peculiar brand of *Europäertum* was quite characteristic of Bavaria. It was still manifest in peasants and the "simple folk," even in this century. No doubt it was a residuum of medieval cosmopolitanism. While the intellectuals of Europe were gradually getting rid of nationalism, the peasants of Southern Catholic Germany had not yet accepted it. With them there was a feeling of friendship for, or at least never any really hostile feeling toward, Latin peoples. This Latin and European affinity was, as everyone knows, the main

reason why Bavaria originally did not display any enthusiasm
for Bismarck's imperialism.

While reading little essays of Schmid's on Paris, Verona or
Gmund, on Casals, Picasso or Slevogt, I had a familiar sensation
which I could not identify at first. Ah, there it was—the same feeling one has when reading Mozart's letters from Paris, Rome, Dres-
den or Prague, or the diary of some medieval traveling craftsman.
It is a European cosmopolitanism which has its roots in the soil
of cultural tradition and is not acquired by philosophical speculation. Schmid said in one of his most beautiful essays ("The
Catholic Element in Mozart") that Mozart's music is *naturaliter
christiana;* just as one could say about people like Schmid, that
they are Weltbürger by nature, sometimes in spite of narrow
provincialism. As far as he was concerned, it was some sort of
Latin patriotism which was obviously irrational, certainly not
political, on the contrary, something of an "erotic" nature (in
the sense that he himself occasionally used this word). Let us
quote from an essay called "Parisian Impressions":

The general picture of the streets, the way the girls walk, the
students argue with one another, the workmen have their meals, all
this is somehow pervaded by a Latin atmosphere. I am resting in
the shade of the plane-trees near the Quai on the Island of St. Louis
and I am watching the fishermen. Their stoic calm is the same as in
the days of Bouvard and Pecuchet, the same as depicted by Daumier
who lived in that pretty little ancient house next to Baudelaire. Once
more you hurry to see your Watteaus in the Louvre; once more you
experience that feeling of happiness when facing the early Greek
relief which a benevolent philologist has christened *l'exaltation de
la fleur.* Strolling across the Place des Vosges you pass that grandiose
Victor Hugo—Parisians celebrating enthusiastically the *centenaire du
romantisme* do not distinguish very much between him and the really
great Delacroix. Again you buy the same fresh wholesome fruit from
the ladies of the Halles. Everything is as it used to be. You are again
surprised and amused by the church of Sacré Cœur; its architecture
is like majestically blaring brass music. However, while I gaze from
the Eiffel Tower over Paris in the mild, veiling light of the setting

sun I am reconciled with everything. I am greeting Les Invalides, the Seine and Notre Dame. There it is, Paris has caught me again.

There was nothing very original about all this and I had read similar things in other essays on Paris. And yet when one held these lines against the background of a certain petit bourgeois Upper Bavarian element in the book, they began to glow in an enchanting light. From there I penetrated a little further. The most remarkable feature of this man was something else—the perfectly homogeneous synthesis of artistic and spiritual or, better, of musical and religious values.

The word "synthesis" is not quite correct, for it implies that these elements once existed separately. In his case one could not conceive of them separately; this was a definite impression which the essays, in themselves not very significant, conveyed. Music was religion, allegiance to something; and religion, on the other hand was deeply interwoven with its modes of artistic expression. "*Musica sacra* penetrated and tempered *musica vulgaris*, the firstborn, with its creative breath," Schmid said. This profound organic relation was apparent everywhere, in his essays on Mozart and Bach as well as in that article on Paris. There he finished up in his own home, as it were, with the Benedictines of Solesmes and with the Gregorian chant, after having dealt with interesting technical details on Landowska and Casals, and on Cortot's interpretation of Couperin and Debussy.

I had the feeling of approaching more closely the tragic secret; the symbolic paradox of such a life and such a death. Nietzsche, not the neurotic of the "blond beast" and the "Antichrist," but the other Nietzsche, the prophetic historian, often proclaimed this as the specifically German tragedy, namely that political power and spiritual greatness exclude one another entirely. The Germany of Bismarck and that of Bach cannot live side by side; while one is in bloom the other must needs perish.

On a bright June morning in 1934 the storm-troopers entered

the house of a man with the common name of Willi Schmid.
Did he protest? Did he swear to his innocence? This I do not
know. He was taken into a police yard, put against the wall
and shot. Immediately it was seen that there had been a mistake.
A mistake? It did not matter whether there was really a mistake,
or a "mistake" faked by a personal adversary. The latter possibility is excluded, according to people who knew the situation.
It did not seem to me an accident at all, it was not "one" Willi
Schmid who fell a victim. It almost appeared to me as if his
common and typical German name, marking him for his fate,
was no mere coincidence. No, he and his name symbolized that
German element which was murdered "by mistake" in that most
senseless of all revolutions.

After Nietzsche had become mentally deranged, there was
found among his possessions a peculiar document—a warrant to
arrest and shoot Bismarck. Bismarck was to Nietzsche the expression of a Germany he hated deeply, the Germany of military
might. This silly, grotesque little incident sounds like the reversal
of the tragedy of Willi Schmid. Here a personal individual event
and the super-personal, symbolic destiny are but one. Here
Thornton Wilder's Dominican would not find it difficult to decide
between chance in its cold mathematical aspect and fate in its
high significance.

They found among the numerous little notes and excerpts on
Schmid's desk, a quotation from the letters of Saint Bernard to
Pope Eugene the Third. *"Ordinatissimum est minus interdum
ordinate fieri aliquid"*—"It is quite regular that sometimes something irregular should happen." This idea appeared quite frequently in Schmid's writings, the apparent irregularity of things
which are regular in a higher sense, the perfection of things
which are imperfect on a natural plane. For example, he says
about Mozart: "The fact that the Requiem remained unfinished
appears to have a mysterious significance, as it has in the case
of unfinished Gothic cathedrals, of Bach's *Art of the Fugue,* and of

Saint Thomas's *Summa*." What a strange way of writing a motto about one's own life.

I came to believe that he was able to live through those last hours of cruel darkness with some inner light. In a beautiful essay on a Bavarian Franciscan, Sister Maria Fidelis, he had spoken several times of the vicarious suffering of unknown individuals. Curiously enough, he touched on this idea in connection with the history of post-war Germany:

> Christ's sacrifice is of infinite value and lacks nothing. We, however, are often not worthy to partake of it. We can become worthy of it through our suffering and through the suffering of others. Oh, highest mystery. . . . Her life of sacrifice coincides with the storm which shook our country during the post-war years. We who hear about God's mysterious work in her soul feel as if we had been aided by a stream coming from this well.

After all, no one ever will know the secret of his last hours but again it seemed as if I could now apply the last sentences of that essay on Sister Maria Fidelis to the writer himself:

> Such a hint . . . is not meant for the curious. Their desire to be thrilled by the miraculous is not fulfilled in this case. However, some others will be humbled by the ever-new miracle of Christ's working. They will be humble and grateful that our country was considered worthy of something sacred at a time when Antichrist seems to rule the world.

20. *Jonah*

Early in 1935 Professor Spielmeyer died. This happened only two months after my final return from the sanatorium. Then I knew that it was very dangerous to wait longer, and I looked for a position outside Germany. From the time before I left Munich for London, there was one scene which, for obvious reasons, has left an indelible trace on my memory.

It was in the assembly house of the Jewish Congregation of Munich. We were all gathered in the bare, office-like conference hall. There were representatives of all Jewish youth groups, and a few rugged individualists who were not affiliated with any particular group. Martin Buber had come to give us a brief course of instruction. The whole affair was planned to last twenty-four hours, and was intended as a model course. A new type of collective study of Scripture was to be demonstrated, and Buber had chosen the Book of Jonah as his subject.

Martin Buber, a man of middle height with a wavy black Assyrian beard and a big mane of hair, was seated at a desk surrounded by eager boys and girls. They were grouped like a parliament, although this had obviously not been intended. At Buber's right were the *werkleute*. This was a group of young German Jews who more than anyone else followed Buber's ideas, although one could not say that Buber had any real system which one could have followed. These *werkleute* were recruited from the liberal, "enlightened" Jewish middle class. They corresponded to an original group, the *kameraden*, which had undoubtedly been the most "German" one within the entire Jewish Youth Movement. Most of them were children of those well-to-do businessmen who used to wear silk hats when they visited the reformed synagogues once or twice a year, on the holiest of holidays.

Only a few years had passed since the *kameraden* had been sitting around campfires and reciting Goethe, Rilke or some obscure poet from the Northern German heath. During recent times, however, these young people tried to go back again to the source of Jewry, which the reformed synagogues could not give them. The world of traditional Orthodoxy was closed to them, strange and perhaps even repulsive. It is Martin Buber's indisputable merit to have offered a drink of the purest wine

from the vineyard to those who had grown up in the world of
Goethe and Rilke and who would never have found their way
through the brushwood of Orthodox formalism. Although Buber
had never intended to found a school, the *werkleute*, by accident, so to speak, had become his enthusiastic disciples. It is
said that they built up fine co-operative farms in Palestine.

In that part of the hall which was facing the desk there were
groups of *habonim*, formed out of the fusion of two groups, one
of which had always been Zionist, and the other neutral but
with Zionist sympathies. I had years ago belonged to one of these
two groups. Now the *habonim* seemed to be interested in ex-
tricating as many young Jews as possible not only from Germany
but also from the unhealthy atmosphere of commerce, intel-
lectualism and assimilation. They had several camps in the
country in which, during that phase by agreement with the
Nazis, young Jews were still prepared for emigration. These
people from the Jewish urban milieu were taught to till the soil,
to make clothes and shoes and to live in the *kvutzoth*, the co-
operative settlements of Palestine. Ludwig, then one of the
leaders of the *habonim*, happened to be somewhere in Northern Germany at the time. The *habonim* assumed a rather noncommittal position in Buber's course. These people, who had
mostly grown up in a German cultural atmosphere, had an intensive program of Hebrew studies; nevertheless they were little
interested in religious problems. Co-operative socialism, agri-
culture, and the Hebrew language were all that mattered, and
this complexity of interests was loosely linked with some vague
ideas on Hebrew tradition and culture. The majority of them
were anti-orthodox.

Left of Buber were the *misrahi* and other Orthodox. There
were some who looked pale and lean, with dark glowing eyes,
bloodshot from waking, praying and studying. I knew them very
well because I belonged to their synagogue, and took part in
one of their study groups. They seemed to live in a world of

their own. They wore black skullcaps and they hardly mixed with the others. During recess or in the evening they suddenly got up and, without the least embarrassment, said the Eighteen Prayers as if nobody else were around. To anyone who listened it sounded like a mechanical repetition of formulas, and this impression of ceremonial rigidity was emphasized by stereotyped movements, the bowing at certain words, the three paces back and forward at the beginning of the prayers. It was not quite clear why these people had come at all. Most of them seemed to know more about the etymology and the exegesis of the text than Buber himself. In spite of this, for some reason they rarely took part in the discussion.

Once only, towards the end, was there a quarrel. Even today the point under discussion seems important. For those who do not remember the Book of Jonah sufficiently, I should like to review it briefly: Jonah receives a special order from God to admonish the Gentile inhabitants of Nineveh who had succumbed to a life of sin. He wants, however, to evade his duty, and he flees (hence the adventure with the whale). But circumstances force him to land in Nineveh. There at last he carries out his divine mission: he predicts with prophetic certainty that Nineveh will perish within forty days. The Ninevites believe him, are converted, and change their mode of life for the better. Therefore God does not carry out the plan which Jonah had prophesied —He preserves Nineveh and its people. Jonah is extremely disappointed that his prophecy is not fulfilled. He settles outside the city and sulks about God and men, especially God.

The traditional interpretation of the Book of Jonah is as follows: Jonah, the only one among the Prophets who had to preach exclusively to Gentiles, was a proud Jew. To preach the word of the Lord to the enemies of the Jews, the inhabitants of Nineveh, hurt his feelings of national dignity. Therefore, he attempted to get out of his mission altogether, and later when the people of Nineveh were converted and saved, he stayed grudgingly and in isolation outside the walls of the city. This interpretation of the Book of Jonah has a meaning which I have already indicated.

Martin Buber, however, gave an entirely different interpretation: Jonah had received the order to predict the destruction of Nineveh. As a prophet, however, he knew beforehand that there would not be any destruction. In the eyes of the people of Nineveh he would appear as an impostor, because what he predicted with certainty would not occur. This was the reason why he tried first to dodge the issue altogether, and later, after he had played the rôle forced upon him, withdrew with a grudge.

All this was perhaps Buber's personal exegesis. At any rate, the way he proposed it sounded very modern and psychological. Now to an Orthodox Jew traditional exegesis is as ancient and as binding as Scripture itself. Therefore the *misrahi* presently began to open fire and a heated discussion developed in which the *habonim* and *werkleute* joined, although they knew nothing about it and did not care very much. The Orthodox insisted as if their life were at stake. I recall vividly how clusters of fanatically debating people remained after the *misrahi* and other Orthodox had already said their *maariv* (evening prayer).

The scene was outside time. Here were young Jews in the middle of Germany, an island engulfed by contempt, hostility and danger. If some SS leader had been in the mood for it, all of those who were there could have disappeared forever in a concentration camp, the same night. Nobody seemed to give it any thought. At that moment the only important thing was the significance of the written word.

How could I forget those two days? We hardly stopped to eat; everyone had the feeling of the keenest intensity and concentration. Everyone knew that "in the coming year" he would be "in Jerusalem" or in some strange land. Some, I fear, were deported to concentration camps and killed.

For me it was the last time that I was in close contact with the world from which I came.

"*Should I ever forget thee, Jerusalem. . . .*" Oh, how I should like to be able to see them all once more, my friends of those days, and tell them the story of a journey which seems to have taken me infinitely far away from them, but in reality has led me right into their midst.

IV

ENGLAND

21. *London*

WHEN I arrived at the pier in Harwich I had to queue with a large number of people who were scrutinized by an immigration official. When my turn came, the man asked me whether I was looking for work in England. I had been briefed and said: "No, I am going to stay for a two weeks' vacation with friends." He asked me to show a letter of invitation. I had been briefed for this too. Triumphantly I reached into my pocket. But, alas, I could not find the letter. Feverishly I reached into all my pockets. The crowd behind me became impatient. The immigration official finally decided to take the rest of the people while I looked for my letter. When all the people had boarded the train, he took me once more. "Don't you have any letter at all? Some letter, at least, to show who you are." I felt reassured and pulled a letter out. It was from Frau Spielmeyer and was addressed to a Neurology Professor in London. "The bearer of this letter was the last assistant and favorite pupil of my late husband. He is looking for a research job in England. . . ." The interpreter read this letter to the immigration official. The official shook his head, and said: "I am sorry, but you go back to Germany. . . ." The train had been waiting for me, and now the engine whistled. The interpreter looked intently at my hat, took the immigration man aside and whispered. Then they both looked at my hat. Finally the immigration man said: "All right, go."

✦

Now I was one of the Refugees. First we settled imperceptibly, like dust, in the huge cities of the Western world. Then there were corners in which the dust tended to collect, and in which it was easily seen. There were streets full of us: Greencroft Gardens, London, N.W.; Washington Heights, New York City. Many, however, settled like dispersed particles in Paddington, Ealing, or Hendon. Each one of us carried an invisible wall of strangeness around him because those summer evenings of our childhood in Königstein or in Starnberg were incommunicable.

There were times when you had to approach your neighbor. On a Sunday morning you needed small change in order to get the slot machine of your gas-heater going. The neighbor handed you the coins politely and to him you, in your dressing-gown with a towel around your shoulder, were the German-Jewish Refugee next door, part of that penetrating anonymity of the city, like the fog.

Parents arrived, and grandparents. Old men, patriarchs in their stores in Reutlingen or Chemnitz, or in their offices in Magdeburg or Ulm, whose lives had been part of the seasons and of the fragrance of Suabia or Saxony, turned into strange boarders and roomers. Their happiness was the joy of escape, something that evaporated unnoticeably and was absorbed by the city. They fell into the arms of Generosity but Generosity was no mother. It was a nurse with the odor of antisepsis.

All, even the oldest among us, learned the language. However, the city gave us only the hand-me-down, the second-rate words, instruments of practicality as useful and comfortable for the life of strangers as the underground, the bus, the park and the public bath. The infinite in language is something quite beyond public convenience. In our new land it had ripened underneath the gables in the Cotswolds, over brooks and heaths of Northern England, and over the wharfs of London for an eternity before we presented our passports at Harwich.

There was a new form of happiness and strength to be able to "get along" so soon in stores, on busses, in the laboratory, with patients. We used, with great dexterity and cunning, inexhaustible variations of nouns, adjectives, verbs, sentences, while all the time Language gazed upon us remotely. Our native language had become that of the Enemy. It was somehow associated with that thing behind us, that monstrous Anti-Mother, that dark and demoniac crater from which we had come. Hence, most of us tried frantically to hide everything that could ever remind us of it, even the

> *"Füllest wieder Busch und Tal*
> *Still mit Nebelglanz"*

which expressed the irretrievable melody.

When I arrived in London I obtained a research scholarship from the Medical Research Council at the most famous neurological center in the English-speaking world. A Jewish family which had founded that particular research scholarship had made a provision that a German-Jewish refugee was to have it. "Queen Square" was as much of a microcosmos of Britain as the Psychiatric Institute in Munich had been one of Germany. The consulting and teaching physicians exuded the atmosphere of Harley Street and of that mixture of sobriety, pragmatism, dryness and brilliant lucidity which is so characteristic of Anglo-Saxon science. There is no medium in which Neurology can thrive better, and therefore it was not surprising to see that the "Queen Square" people had brought that branch of medicine to its perfection, and maintained it on that level. The Homburg hat, the pin-striped trousers, the tightly rolled umbrella, and that doctor's leather case seemed to go well with a neat, intricate network of neurons which ran smoothly or fused and stalled somewhere outside the world of human suffering and passion.

In the bowels of the hospital were the ancient laboratories. The neuropathological laboratory was a huge room, the height of a church, with an entire wall consisting of an enormous window. The room resembled one of those old-fashioned woodcuts of laboratories one might see in an 1890 edition of the *London Illustrated News*. But even inside the building, one worked in the London air of mist and fog; our boxes for microscopic slides were always covered with a velvety layer of soot.

The technical staff seemed to mirror humorously the world of the "big shots," at least as I beheld them. There was the histological chief technician, a little man by the name of Anderson who had originally been a Yorkshire miner. He carried on his small body the head of a professor, different only by that imponderable something which attempts to devaluate, by some trace, the features of all intelligent people who are born in poverty. He had been working in the mines since the age of nine, and his fingers showed the characteristic "beatings." During the First World War the Dean of the Medical School and Chief Pathologist had discovered him in a base hospital, and since then Anderson's genius had been devoted to that delicate craft of microscopic staining. He had invented new staining methods, and had even published a successful small manual on the subject. Anderson worked at the head bench, and talked, sang and whistled incessantly.

Besides that England of recumbent reticence which is always represented in Continental magazines by a long-legged man with a shag pipe, there is an equally characteristic England which is unbelievably garrulous. The chief pathologist and his chief assistant were representatives of these two Englands.

The laboratory was a place in which philosophies clashed. I was bewildered to see that Anderson, with all his past and present, was a Conservative with just the trace of an inkling of Fascist sympathies. One of the lab boys belonged to the left-wing labor group, one boy was a staunch Catholic, the biochemist was a devout Baptist with the characteristic liberal tradition of English non-Conformism. The young research workers were physicians who came from Scotland, Ireland, Australia, the United States and Canada. While everybody was busily impregnating nerve cells with metal compounds or azo dyes, gently bathing microscopic sections in small glass vessels or titrating or centrifuging, there was a continuous repartee in what seemed to me many tongues. Incomprehensible remarks whirred past my head, released short salvoes of laughter or intricate chains of argument. At times the lab boys seemed to become exceedingly hot-headed. Conservatism appeared shamefully stripped of its glory by Socialism and Liberalism. Or the Catholic Church was squeezed mercilessly within a forceps of Nationalism and Marxism. Tempers flared and periods of silence followed. It only needed an interruption like the familiar call, "Tea is ready," and everybody sat down with an air of perfect amicability as football players do during half-time.

The relationship between the various levels of professional hierarchy was characteristically different from anything I had ever seen on the Continent. Between chiefs, assistants, technicians and charwomen there were walls which it took me a long time to notice. Yet the doors of the Dean's office were always open, towards the laboratory and towards the corridor. When the technician needed slides from that office he walked straight in, did not stop whistling, and the Chief did not lift his head from the microscope.

When I made my first appearance, there was no secretary to announce me. I had to place my hat—an impossible Continental affair with an umbrella-like brim—right on top of a celloidin microtome. I did not even find the time to take my greatcoat off; it was a huge gray Munich greatcoat, resembling an igloo. Everybody went on working, carefully giving the appearance that my presence was unnoticed. Yet I am certain to this day that my hat and greatcoat, and the fact that I attempted frantically to remain on the Chief's left side while walking, brought me the scholarship. Oddity was highly appreciated.

This, incidentally, I found confirmed throughout England. For instance, later when a lab boy had to be hired and there were many applicants, one pale dysplastic chap with a red frozen nose and bluish amphiboid extremities—one of those boys from London slums whose very appearance seems to call for more food and sunlight—got the job. His name was Bradshaw, and he had come by bicycle all the way from Clapham Junction to apply. The Chief christened him "foetus," not at all maliciously; it came as close to the true features as any designation could. Thus, Bradshaw was more or less permanently added to the collection. It was not so much the case of average people having the fun of selecting cranks; everybody, in order to be somebody, had to be a bit of a crank. This complicated system may well be the salvation of England within the type of world civilization which is about to develop.

All of us, even research workers with international reputation, had to do our own manual work, the cutting and imbedding of tissues, the handling of the ovens and microtomes, and the staining. Anderson, like many people from the north of England, had once sung in choirs and was expert on Handel oratorios. Thus, in order to enliven the tedious and monotonous work at the laboratory benches, when we were not engaged in arguments, we sang. Anderson conducted, and it happened not infrequently that a prominent neurologist from abroad who was being taken around in the hospital, found the entire laboratory, doctors and technicians, singing the "Hallelujah" chorus from *The Messiah*, while shaking tiny pieces of tissue suspended in various metallic solutions.

22. *Primrose Hill*

I DID not attempt to regard myself as one of them. The Jewish tragedy in Germany had made me conscious of false façades, and I sometimes saw camouflage even where there was none. Of course, there was the elderly German-Jewish refugee who spoke only English, even within his family, and wore plus fours and played golf. I did not want to be "one of them"; I had seen to what this led. However, Bradshaw and I were both accepted for the very reason that we were "different." Something else kept all us refugees psychologically corralled: our fearful gaze into the crater in which the others were still struggling. While to those around us Hitler was one other incident of European barbarism, an abstract political phenomenon, we knew that individual lives were gradually being extinguished. It was not the "Fascist problem," or the "Czech question," or "Chamberlain's moral victory" or "Chamberlain's moral abasement." These were abstractions, easy to cope with. But there was the hemiplegic old man in Eisenach from whom they took his housekeeper. There were my grandmother, uncle and aunt who were not allowed to leave the house before dusk, the same people with whom I had gone on gay hiking trips in the blue mountains of the Rhön. Letters increased which, under disguising words, showed that laughter and smiles had altogether disappeared, that Herr and Frau Masser were sitting with their eight-year-old boy in their attic, silent, wondering what I might be able to do. It was as if vises were closing imperceptibly around a hundred thousand necks. This kept us apart because it could not, in its concreteness, be re-experienced by "others."

Frau Masser's letter was written with the despair of the death-sentence. But letters have to be dealt with by committees. I am only Number 73 in the queue, it says so on my little card. The lady behind the desk tells me that I have to fill Form D but that I have to come again and queue in front of Room 6 where I shall get Forms A and B. If Frau Masser's wealthy uncle can bring proof within the next three days that he can guarantee her support in case of accident or illness, we might push her case through within the next three months. No, an uncle in the United States is of no use because his guarantee is of no avail to the British Home Office. In that case I have to fill Form C. The room where I obtain Form C is closed now but I can get there next Monday. Meanwhile the vise has closed by one thousandth of an inch. Where will it be when I return after three months?

Frau Masser has beautiful features and can play the Bach violin solo suites better than anyone I have ever heard. But this means nothing to the lady behind the desk and I do not blame her. The lady is kind, and it is only out of kindness that she sits there. She has dealt with the seventy-two people before me similarly, and there is nothing else she can do. In the files in front of her is compressed a multitude of lives full of love, pain, and happiness. Perhaps there are other Frau Massers who play Bach solo suites and have little boys, God only knows. But Form C must first be signed by that uncle and confirmed by the Home Office. The Home Office is overburdened with cases like this.

I am doing "research." I am interested in tumors of the thalamus, an area in the center of the brain. I am also interested in the Red Nucleus in Man. The Red Nucleus is a peculiar motor area in the human brain. Many people have wondered about its function and have made experimental studies on rabbits. However, the human Red Nucleus differs from that of lower forms, even from those of anthropoid apes. Perhaps its morphological change comes about parallel with the development of upright gait. I imbed brains in celloidin. It takes four weeks before I can make microscopic slices and stain them. Anderson and Doctor Cumings, who watch me sitting at the microtome, are obviously wondering about me. They know that my brother and my parents were left behind.

I go back to Room 6 at the Committee, with Form C filled out and signed. Meantime an entirely new regulation has come out. The Home Office has waived Form C altogether. Could we not try to get the Masser family into Australia?

If only I could get Frau Masser over here by magic into that large house near Hampstead Heath in which the people have so many rooms that are not being used. They could sit around the fireplace in the evening and listen to her playing the Bach solo suite or, if they do not like that, to Mendelssohn's violin concerto. They would listen to the beautiful music and watch her beautiful head. They would say, "We are glad to have this woman here, we are going to put her and her husband and her son up in that top-floor room. There is no difficulty for her, with her music, to find a way in the world."

Frau Masser remained unknown to those people. Meanwhile her letters became more imploring and more frequent. Perhaps it was really a question of Form C, the British Home Office, the Australian High Commissioner, the wealthy uncle's affidavit. Perhaps it was something else that kept her and her family back. After all, a great many people had found their way to Great Britain, more than to any other country in proportion to the population figures. But Herr and Frau Masser perished.

My little address-book had the names of all those whom I knew to have emigrated to London before me. One of the names was Liselotte's, who had left her bookbinder shop in Heidelberg. At the time when I came to London she was working as a bookbinder at the Warburg Institute.

I met her at the Cumberland Hotel for lunch. She looked me over, my umbrella-like hat and the igloo greatcoat, and asked me whether I was here on a special mission; in that case my disguise was very poor. I told her that nobody ever looked at me in the street. She said that in England nobody looks at conspicuous people in the streets; it was not done. She said that what had happened to Hitler regarding the Jews had happened to her with Germans; it was a horrible thing to say, but she could smell Germans. I said that I doubted that she could smell anything German in me because I was no German—I was a Jew.

I said that we were a segregated people, segregated by a mysterious fate, and that we ought to practice severe dietetic and other religious laws to keep a fence around us. This segregation had something to do with our mysterious *raison d'être*, and that a Jew must first go through persecution to be able to grasp this. I told her about the work my brother was doing with Jewish youth in Germany. She said that this was all wonderful, she had hardly ever met any Jews who were conscious of their Jewry. Most of the Jews whom she used to know, for instance among the university professors, tried to disguise their Judaism and be something they were not. At this I lowered my voice, glanced around the tables to see whether anyone was listening to us, and said that I wondered if Lewis' in Oxford Street was a Jewish store, because I had intended, from the time of my emigration, to buy only in Jewish stores. At this remark she became silent again and looked me over.

After a pause she said: "I don't know what's wrong with you boys who come out. You are all carrying something around you. I call it the cloud. There is a cloud around you. I had it too; only with me it was of a different sort. But we all leave that place over there with the cloud around us. It takes some time to get rid of it."

In order to reassure her I told her something else which was more comprehensible. I said that I seemed to be in a panicky fear of succeeding in the new country, or at least my wishes were two-pronged. It was the hesitancy of being born into a new world, the fear of birth. In the beginning I had discovered to my

dismay that with the wish of obtaining a job, I secretly harbored
the wish not to get it. There used to be a famous Munich come-
dian, Karl Valentin, a gawky and cadaverous man, who had
identified himself with an imbecile petit bourgeois to an extent
which was uncanny. He used to play the scene of a man in front
of a dentist's office, hesitating to push the bell and saying: "If I
knew for certain that he was not at home, I would ring." This is
often our attitude when we are confronted with new steps in life.
However, once emigrated, you had to ring the bell; there was no
going home.

With the mention of Karl Valentin a lost world was conjured
up; the world of the small people and their real life, the beer
halls, the market-women around St. Peter's, the infinitely funny
and likeable Bavaria which we had known when we were children. For a moment there was a rift in the cloud. We struck up
loud, thoroughly Continental laughter, and tears rolled down our
cheeks. Liselotte told me that in England one did not slap one's
knee, at least not in hotel dining-rooms.

She was living in a rooming-house adjoining Primrose Hill.
This is one of the places at which many planes of London seem
to intersect. One walks up there through Camden town, an area
in which working-class people live in narrow gray streets with
small shops. The grayness was disquieted and pitifully enlivened
by huge colorful walls of Oxo, Guiness, and Bovril, and by the
glistening canyon of the London, Midland and Scottish Railway.
You also can walk up to Primrose Hill from St. John's Wood, or
through Regent's Park, straight from the fashionable homes in
the neighborhood of Baker Street. All that is so close seems
worlds apart, but once one is up there, one is on a hill overlooking London, and the distance produces the peaceful illusion of
equality. Her room overlooked the trees on the hill.

She told me how she had come to emigrate. One morning her
father received a letter from the university authorities that he
was dismissed. They had discovered several Jews among his an-

cestors, so that he was exactly half-Jewish, all told. "According to this," she said, "I was only twenty-five per cent non-Aryan, you know." However, even her father with his Mosaic ancestors could have stayed, had it not been for his political convictions. So they used the Aryan legislation as a pretext to give him the sack. Liselotte herself received a letter from the Reich Commissar of Arts that she was permitted to continue her work. The house in Heidelberg was abandoned, terraces, garden, Neckar, Shakespeare plays and all. The Professor was betrayed and vanquished by the little wooden model of a stormtrooper which he had carved during those silent afternoons. He moved to an industrial city in the Rhineland and started a private practice. Spitefully he opened with it a little workshop in which he made braces and flatfoot supports with his own hands. Contrary to what the Reich Commissar for Art must have assumed, Liselotte did not make much of her seventy-five per cent. She left Germany.

In London she lived first as a guest of a leading British surgeon in Harley Street. There were seven domestic servants and in the morning, on waking up, she got her tea and *The Times*. There was dinner every night in evening dress. After three weeks, she moved out and took a small room near the Thames. There were days when she had no money left for the next meal. During the first two years, she had eighteen different jobs. She acted as a tourist guide for Germans (she showed me a linen cuff which said "Fremdenführer"). The pay was small and she had to live mainly on tips. The Germans all wanted to see historical spots, which she provided freely. At a certain place on the Isle of Wight, she never forgot to say that here a meeting between Napoleon and Lord Nelson had taken place.

At one time she posed for an advertisement of stockings, and after that she took part in an advertising film for the Savoy Hotel, "A Day at the Savoy." A stranger named Harkness and she had to play a couple living at the hotel, from breakfast to retiring. Harkness in his dressing-gown poured coffee and passed her toast with eggs and bacon, all in a room at the Savoy. After they had had breakfast the scene had to be shot again, and then they went off horseback riding in Hyde Park. After she had taught German at a girl's school, she found the position of bookbinder at the Warburg Institute.

We went to the house on Primrose Hill and I looked around the room. There was a beautifully lettered quotation from the German Romantic philosopher Schleiermacher, something about God in Nature. Hanging on the wall was a quaint Würzburg wine bottle and, on the same nail, a large rosary ("a farewell gift from Kati Huber," she told me). There were many hand-bound books, the collected works of Tolstoy, several volumes of Sigrid Undset, Goethe, Nietzsche, E. T. A. Hoffmann, Jean Paul, and a volume of essays by Bergson, beautifully bound. She showed me some of her lettering. She came from a German school of lettering which descended directly from Johnston, the man who had been the master of Eric Gill. She herself had never met Eric Gill.

I looked at the books and said: "Listen to me, I am serious. Don't think that this is going to be The Cloud or that I am crazy. . . ." And I began to tell her about my experiences with the Catholics in Munich and about the Yamagiwas; that I had discovered a new Judaism, and that it was Christianity; that I was in a great dilemma because here were my people and here was Jesus, the Christ who had come to us as well as to those who wanted to exterminate us. I had come to believe with Saint Paul that the true Jews of today were those Gentiles, like Frau Flamm and Doctor Yamagiwa, who followed Christ.

After I had finished she said: "Never mind, it *is* The Cloud and you *are* crazy. . . . Why are you not happy about your beautiful Hebrew tradition?" She said that she had never had any religious belief in a formal sense. However, in her darkest hours in London she had taken to reading the Psalms again and the Book of Job and they were a profound consolation. Compared with the power and grandeur of the Old Testament, the Gospel

was just sugary lemonade and the Saint Paul a traveling sales-
man.

All this sounded like a famous passage from Nietzsche. I found
out later that she had never read it. As a matter of fact,
Nietzsche had only expressed what a large number of Germans
with Christian background felt. This was probably a revolt
against the sweetened, unheroic, sofa-cushion variety of Christianity cultivated by the middle classes of the nineteenth century.

"Look here, you don't understand what I mean," said I, and I
started all over again. I said that her distinction between Judaism and Christianity was only a matter of public school terminology; that Christianity itself *was* Hebrew tradition, even Martin
Buber said so. That once you have understood the Messianic
spirit of Isaiah, there was an organic transition, a transition of
growth right into the Gospel.

But she remained adamant. She added that Luther was the
worst of all of them. "If I ever were a professing Christian, I
would be a Catholic." I answered that the Lutheran revolution,
if not Luther the man, was understandable when one considered
the externalized form of Christianity of his day. She would not
hear of it. Perhaps she was trying to appear clever.

There was something strange about all this. I, a Jew who had
discovered the Gospel, attempted to persuade a "Gentile" who
had discovered the Old Testament. The situation showed clearly
that thinking and talking meant little if unaccompanied by acting and living. Whatever our views may be, we had come
from roots far apart; she from an over-sophisticated academic
tradition, I from the merchant's house in the small town; she
from a liberal Lutheran, I from an "enlightened" Jewish background. We both had been instilled with Goethean humanism
but our revolts against the bourgeois tradition had taken entirely
different routes. We both had known the life of "freedom," the
perfect libertinism of European youth of the twenties, and the
hangover of nothingness and spiritual despair. No matter what

our views were, her indomitable courage and her straightness of
action expressed reality much more clearly than all my talk.

We were both equally endowed with a sense of style. It should
not be surprising that we first resolved to get married during a
moonlit night in the churchyard in St. John's Wood. However,
the so-called Nuremberg laws made our marriage dangerous for
our relatives at home. We had to think very seriously of reprisals.
This, on the other hand, made it more adventurous, and belonged
somehow with the Full Moon and Churchyard.

I went to the town hall on Haverstock Hill. There were several
floors with dismal corridors. On one door was written: "Deaths."
The next one said "Marriages." At the desk I found a man of
drooping appearance, with steel-rimmed glasses. I addressed him
by stating that I was of German nationality and one hundred
per cent non-Aryan, my future wife was twenty-five per cent
non-Aryan on account of the fact that her father had two non-
Aryan grandparents. Therefore our marriage, on the basis of the
Nuremberg Laws, was criminal and punishable by at least twenty-five years of prison for the less-Aryan partner, that is to say
myself. "Now I happen to know," I said, "that there exists a mutual agreement between Great Britain and Germany on marriage
laws. That is to say a marriage which is illegal in one of the two
countries is automatically illegal in the other."

The drooping man who had listened without interrupting said
politely: "Would you mind repeating all this?" After I had explained in more detail, particularly about the percentages, he
said: "My dear man, Great Britain is legally bound to such an
agreement only as long as both countries' marriage customs are
within the reasonable boundaries of morals. Sit down, young
man. Let us suppose for a moment that Germany had introduced
polygamy or a law according to which widows have to be
burned. . . ." In the end he advised me, for the sake of our relatives in Germany, to keep our marriage secret and to live under
separate addresses.

Once, when we walked down Oppidans Road, we saw a rotund pink-cheeked lady of about sixty standing in front of a house whose fence was newly painted in sky blue. "Here comes Destiny," said Liselotte. "Ask her whether you can have a room." The lady's name was Mrs. Silk. She said that she did let rooms, but only to special friends. However, after a little while she told me that there was one room free which I could have.

23. On Hope

THE NEW COUNTRY began gradually to engulf us. Everyone knows the atmosphere of the happy, wholesome family in Charles Dickens' novels, that family in which the young lad finds a haven of refuge after having been subjected to the cruelty of stepmothers, spinsters, headmasters and schoolmates. Precisely such a family were the Silks. Mrs. Silk had looked me over the same way as the Dean of the Medical School had done before. Then she had added us to her collection.

Oh, those bucolic breakfasts on Oppidans Road. Those merry nights with the logs singing in the fireplace, and Mr. Walters, a ginger-haired, long-legged young man, explaining everything about Chamberlain and Halifax. Evelyn Cooke, in between the incoming and outgoing boat (he was a ship's doctor), studied the Choral Preludes and the *Well-tempered Clavichord*, the latter with vocal accompaniment. Claude Silk, one of the sons, had been a medical missionary overseas. There he had lost his wife, who caught pneumonia while nursing a native. He returned with five children, and with five hundred dollars in his pocket. There seemed to be numerous other ladies and gentlemen, all with equally fascinating life histories. I never knew how many belonged to the family. Everybody seemed to be related to everybody, if not by blood, then at least by Mrs. Silk's maternal bonds.

She had that untiring, relaxed, effortless industriousness which appears to give the guest a moral right to sit longer than necessary at the breakfast table in order to thrash out some important point on the toasting of bread, the curing of bacon, and (alas) Chamberlain and Halifax. Her maternal rotundness protected us from demonic forces; even passionate and obscure quarrels among the boarders and the family seemed to lose their sting. That family was ill-defined in its frontiers; somehow we belonged to it and played our part.

Claude was a towering man with circular outlines, a huge peasant head, and big brown eyes. He wore a cassock with a leather belt and crossed himself when saying grace. He did not take any permanent job after coming back from overseas but deputized for other Anglican clergymen.

It was never quite clear how many of the people paid for their board; economics was subordinate to something else in the order of things. The crucifix was hanging there, the fireplace was burning, the framed cross-stitch patterns said something about Jesus and love and Jane Silk, 1883, as if all this were destined to be used by anyone who happened by. There was the spirit of ancient Catholicity, draped in a few pieces of national costume. I never knew what value that costume had in the eyes of those who wore it. When I spoke once to Claude about Roman Catholics he said: "Many of us admire them, some of us envy them."

However, the intrinsic suffering and passion of Europe were alien and remote. The sultriness and the neurosis and the animalism which contributed so much to the German revolution—all that could just as well have been part of Gehenna, for no inkling of it penetrated Mrs. Silk's house. I was obviously the victim of something which was not cricket; that was that. When Chamberlain saw Hitler, Mrs. Silk was satisfied. It was the decent thing to try anything to preserve peace.

Thus, in spite of Claude and Evelyn, and John, and good old

Mother Silk, and the biochemist and Anderson and Bradshaw and the Committee, we felt that between us and Germany had arisen a huge smooth wall of rock. When we listened carefully we could still hear those trapped ones inside—grandmothers, uncles, aunts, Herr and Frau Masser with their boy. We heard faint knocking here and some scratching there. There was nothing to be done. "Dear Sir, re: Mr. Ludwig Masser, File No. 723921 RS, In reply to your personal inquiry at the Committee on Feb. 19th, we advise you that the Cuban Government admits families with a temporary permit under the following conditions only. . . ."

The complexity and abstractness of human life in our time seemed to strangle the hearts of men. Mixed with the feeling of freedom and hospitality was the shuddering exposure to fear. This is the way a person must feel who, having escaped a shipwreck, spends the night alone in a lifeboat. What has become of those behind? Is this the same cold night through which all other ships are sailing while the passengers are snugly tucked into their beds? No wonder that, with all the warmth of Charity, we saw with heightened intensity the large City ground into a molecular mass of loneliness. All that I had once seen in Moabit, those lives spent by the poor in thousands of equal rooms, that infinite cacophony of voices, the posters for beer and those for life insurance, the implements without creation, the rapidity of communication without communion, all this blended into a piercing noise of negation.

It was in this mood that I came in contact with Saint Thomas for the first time. I read a book, *On Hope,* written by a German Catholic layman, Joseph Pieper. In this book the author expounded the teaching of the Angelic Doctor on the virtue of Hope. Until that time, Hope had been to me, as it is to most people, something purely natural and an everyday emotion. I remembered that in my childhood I used to see cheap symbolic oleographs representing Faith, Hope and Charity, and I used to

wonder how Hope got into it. Hope seemed to be related to
wish rather than virtue.

The book started off with the Christian concept of the *status
viatoris*, Man in the state of a wayfarer. The opposite of the *via-
tor* is the *comprehensor*. Man who has comprehended, who is in
possession of the beatific vision, is no longer "on the way." As
long as he is alive, however, he is in the state of a traveler.
Human existence contains an element of "not yet," and this element has a dual significance; on one hand the absence of completion, and on the other hand a direction towards completion.
This absence of completion contains a negation; it puts Man continuously into the dangerous proximity of nothingness. The dark
abyss of freedom is the freedom to choose negation.

Willful choice of negation is possible. Since Man, says Saint
Thomas, is a creature endowed with Reason, no natural means
can prevent him from sinning, "because he originates from nothingness, and therefore he has the power to turn towards nothingness." Only when the *status viatoris* is abolished and the *status
comprehensoris* is entered, is Man united with the Absolute Being
and the freedom to choose nothingness is "tied." From this dynamic polarity between the *status viatoris* and the *status comprehensoris,* from this "direction towards" completion which is implied in the *status viatoris,* Saint Thomas, or rather Herr Pieper
expounding Saint Thomas, evolved the theology of Hope.

To me it opened up, through a little gap, a gaze into a lofty
Christian anthropology. The three streams of Hope, Faith and
Charity were shown in their true perspective, not from below but
from above. They assumed their full, wide, all-embracing significance which transcended whatever they "meant" emotionally
on a natural plane. The dark antipodes of Hope were Despair
and Presumption. Both destroyed the *status viatoris,* the "not yet"
of human existence. Despair transformed it into naught, and
Presumption faked comprehension. In both instances, the stream

of becoming was arrested and transformed into petrifaction and death.

Hope as well as Despair, transcended their natural meaning and became infinitely deepened in Christ, the true image of Man. "Since our Redeemer," says Saint Thomas, "has created and perfected Faith, it was of equal salvation to us that He introduced us into Hope. This He did by teaching us prayer by which our Hope is directed towards God." Despair chooses Nothingness, Hope pierces Nothingness. "Even if He should kill me, I put my hope in Him," says Job. Since Hope has been heightened by the act of redemption, the potentiality of despair has been immensely deepened, too. If you want true Existential Philosophy, in the deepest sense of the word, there is Existential Philosophy for you.

These few sentences perhaps do not explain the shaking influence this book had on me at the time. Pieper not only supplemented Saint Thomas with the quotations from the early Fathers of the Church but with many references to modern philosophy, particularly that of the Existentialists. This resulted in an anatomy of despair and anxiety which surpassed anything I had come across in natural psychology. It was just as if a mathematician had tentatively introduced a factor, and saw that the formulas "worked." At times in Euclidian Geometry one makes a trial start with an arbitrary assumption, and comes to evidence. This was about the way I felt.

Someone once remarked that you should try experimentally to live for one day as if the Gospel were true, even if you do not believe it. In the same way I invite you to think of the nature of Man as if Christ had been God-Man and died for your and my salvation. The whole of anthropology as conceived by philosophers and psychologists is at once deepened in a very peculiar way. It is as if a great, but albeit two-dimensional, picture received a third dimension and came to life. If, as Auden once remarked, it is the function of the poet to introduce order into chaos, then God is our poet.

I used to sit on a bench on Primrose Hill and look over all the City of London. If it were true, I used to think, that God had become man, and that His life and death had a personal meaning to every single person among all those millions of existences spent in the stench of slums, in a horizonless world, in the suffocating anguish of enmities, sickness and dying—if that were true, it would be something tremendously worth living for. To think that Someone knocked at all those millions of dark doors, beckoning and promising to each in an altogether unique way. Christ challenged not only the apparent chaos of history but the meaninglessness of personal existence.

In the autumn of 1938 a Jewish boy shot a German Embassy official in Paris. This was followed by the first nationwide round-up of the Jews in Germany. For several days the newspaper vendors kept shouting something about murder. This time, I knew it was the real thing. Reha Freier arrived, I do not know how, and we sat waiting and talking, like the relatives of miners who are trapped in the pit. All she knew was that my brother had been arrested while coming to the rescue of a children's camp. He was taken to Buchenwald concentration camp.

We ran around in the streets, we sat in a little Lyons' tea shop, in the musty offices of the Jewish Agency, then inside some railway station, we went to the Committee, and to another Committee, again to the Agency. There was nothing practical we could do. Reha said the persecuted were stronger than the persecutors. They seemed to be full of triumphant joy, she said, and I should not worry. While they were being loaded into wagons, they sang the Psalms in ancient Hebrew melodies. As long as I was sitting with Reha Freier in those smoke-filled rooms, in front of teacups and cigarette butts, although we could do nothing, I had at least the feeling of being in contact with my brother because she was the last one to have seen him in freedom.

One evening, I began to talk to her about Christ, about the significance of His life and death, about Christians, about the

Yamagiwas and Frau Flamm, and about the Cardinal's sermon
and Saint Paul. At this time I was already so certain that I must
have sounded very convincing.

Like all of us, she had what you might call a cold admiration
for the human person of Jesus.

"I do admit," she said, "that there is some strange mystery by
which His suffering and death have drawn millions of people to
Him for two thousand years."

I had kept all my thoughts back for a long time. Then it poured
out of me under much pressure. The darkness, bewilderment and
discord of the Christian epoch in Jewish history dissolved the
moment you saw that one thing. The Christians who hit Jews
were hitting Christ their brother. The Jews who rejected Christ
rejected their own God, their own supernatural essence. As long
as Christ crawled like a wounded man in the no-man's-land between those two fronts, no political measures would ever solve
the "Jewish problem."

Reha became pensive and said: "All this sounds as if it must
become very important to us Jews sometime."

She, a Zionist, a rather emotional Zionist at that, who spoke the
beautiful Hebrew of Isaiah and of the Psalms, said that she could
not believe in any Jewish concept of God as propounded in Scripture, and that Buddha and Confucius were just as much or as
little relevant. Later in the evening she said: "It would all come
so natural to us Jews, wouldn't it? There is something about that
story of Mary the Virgin Mother as if it were especially written
for us, and I could just see how we all would go for it."

In those days I went for the first time to a Catholic Church to
pray, to the church of the Dominican Fathers in Hampstead near
to our house. I went there every morning before work. I prayed
at the altar on the right side. I had no idea what it was about,
but somehow I believed in the power of prayer. I do not remember how I had come to believe in it but the efficacy of prayer had
become something quite unshakeable to me. There was a peculiar

intensity about it, because there was no immediate practical help which I could give to my father and my brother.

24. New Year, 1939

AFTER six weeks the first news trickled through: Ludwig was free again. Curiously he was one of the first seven people to be released. The Nazi authorities had asked for a panel of Jews who would be most important for a practical organization of a mass emigration of their people from Germany. Ludwig held a key position in the Zionist movement and in the organization of *hahsharah*, the type of farming settlement in which Jewish children were trained for Palestine. Therefore his person must have been important for the Nazis' aim, to get as many Jews as possible out of Germany in the shortest possible time. This was the reason for his liberation from the concentration camp among the first seven people out of the several hundred thousand who had been arrested in those autumn days.

After his release, it took quite some time before I could get direct news from him. His letters were short and cryptic but one thing was quite clear—he did not want to leave. With his twenty-three years, he was one of the few "senior" ones left with that multitude of Jewish children who waited to be admitted to Palestine. His presence was needed, and he had apparently the feeling of the captain on a sinking ship. I pleaded with him, I called him names, I implored him to think of his parents' peace of mind. Finally, towards the end of 1938 I had word that he was coming to London, albeit only on a visit.

My wife, our oldest boy, then a baby, and I were in Cambridge for a few days after Christmas. I had word that Ludwig

was expected in London on New Year's Eve, so I left my wife
and the child in Cambridge and hurried back to our flat.

It was the night of New Year's Eve and I was alone in the
flat, when the bell rang and Ludwig came in. He looked thinner
than ever. We embraced one another without a word. He grinned
and kept his hat on. He sat down and said: "Play me some Schubert." While I played Schubert, he went into the kitchen and got
a large box of cornflakes. He ate the entire content of the box
and said: "Play me some *Well-tempered Clavichord*."

While I played, he got another box of cornflakes and ate them
too. During the whole time we hardly spoke a word and he insisted on keeping his hat on. Finally he took it off. It was like a
ceremony of unveiling. He was proud, and at the same time somewhat embarrassed, that his head had been shaved.

It was a strange way in which we greeted the year 1939
in that little flat on Oppidans Road. I still see him sitting there
with his hollow cheeks and his shaved head, listening to Bach's
preludes and fugues. After he was through with all our cornflakes, we sat and talked until dawn. From what he told me and
what I heard later from others, I was able to piece his story together.

He happened to be in Berlin in the headquarters of the Zionist
Youth Movement. Berlin was one of the few cities in which there
was still a possibility of hiding oneself, probably only because it
was so large. Ludwig had just decided to do that when a telegram arrived from some children's camp near Kassel indicating
that the children there were in trouble. Though realizing the
futility of it, he took the train. When he arrived late at night the
Stormtroopers were already waiting for him at the station. The
night before the S.A. had "stormed" the camp and beaten the
children up. Ludwig and all the youngsters above a certain age
were taken to Buchenwald.

Although the Nazis made even atrocities a streamlined, organized job, this time there was bitter chaos. The camp was in a

horrible state because within two days thousands of Jews had
been brought in from all over Central Germany. For several days
they had no food at all. Many had already spent several days
and nights standing up inside municipal halls, gymnasiums, fire-
stations or warehouses in their towns and communities, before
they had been transported to the camp.

In the camp there was *"Appell"* twice a day. This meant that
people had to stand for several hours lined up in their yard.
The old ones collapsed and were kicked to stand up again,
or were carried away. After several days there were two meals
consisting of potato soup and black stale bread. On account
of the completely unsanitary conditions there was soon an epi-
demic of diarrhea. Ludwig wanted to spare me most of the
details, but this one he told me. There was only one latrine
which consisted of one huge cesspool; spanning this was one
solid beam to sit on. The guards laughed at people thronging
this place. Many of the old ones were too weak to keep their
balance and fell down into the cesspool.

Everybody entering had his head shaved. There were a great
number of upper respiratory infections leading to pneumonia,
particularly in the aged. People were soon discouraged and
demoralized. Ludwig saw this and organized among his own
group little get-togethers with lectures on subjects of Jewish
history and a course in Hebrew. There was such a general confusion and disorder that the guards did not notice such group
formations or did not mind them. (Almost ten years later I
experienced a most extraordinary coincidence. In an American
psychological publication, *Journal for Social and Abnormal
Psychology,* I came across an article written by a German-
Jewish professor, dealing with observations on mass psychology
of internes of concentration camps. The author himself had spent
those days in Buchenwald. He spoke of the general demoraliza-
tion and claimed that there was one group of young Jews who
were a notable exception. This was a Zionist group who, under

a leader, got together and formed something like a study circle. The point was that in situations of such extreme stress only those remain upright who have a goal strong enough to maintain their moral tension. In the description I recognized my brother.)

Ludwig told me that hunger bothered him more than anything else. As he grew weaker he developed delirious fantasies which had to do with cornflakes. There was a young Rabbi from Munich whom we thought funny because of the manner in which he used to give talks at ladies' tea parties about Jewish Ethics and such things. Ludwig used to imitate him, and succeeded in looking like him when he said: "Oh." This Rabbi was the one who shared his bread ration with Ludwig in the camp.

Uncle Julius was also taken to Buchenwald. The masses of people were so enormous that he heard of Ludwig's presence only when the loudspeaker gave the names of the first ones to be released. Ludwig got out just before his sickness became serious. He arrived one morning in Berlin, his head clean-shaven and without a hat. He had a little money in his pocket, and he told me that he was in a tortured state of indecision as to what he should first buy, a hat or cornflakes. He finally decided on cornflakes and walked home on foot because he was not allowed on streetcars.

In 1939 we finally succeeded in getting my parents out of Germany. Uncle Felix, far away in Chicago, had been able, with affidavits, money, and guarantees of one sort or another, to help us cut through the barbed wire. Later, I found out that he did similar things not only for his brother but for numerous people, among them people of whose existence he had never heard.

Our parents arrived one evening in May. Father looked tired and harassed but he was happy about the plane trip from Frankfurt to London which had been of utmost importance. Father and Mother topped off their last days in the old home by what they thought were luxuries. They had to spend all their money inside Germany, and they arrived with ten marks in their pockets.

Now they were sitting at the table in our small flat on Oppidans Road, their bags in the middle of the room. They kept reiterating, almost rhythmically, like panting animals, how lucky they were. Their new freedom was tainted with melancholy, but they talked well into the night. They told us about the goods they still had been able to buy and take with them—the silver, a few pieces of furniture, and particularly the linen. Father told me that he had learned English, and began to recite the story of a Herr Schmitt who visited Kew Gardens, and the conversation which Herr Schmitt had with Mister Brown, an Englishman who grew flowers.

Mother gave us all the details of what happened in those autumn days of 1938. A stormtrooper came and dragged Father into the middle of the street. He collected the children from the neighborhood, arranged them in a circle around Father, and said: "Now you all say with me in chorus—You dirty Jewish swine! One, two, three, you dirty Jewish swine." Most of the children failed to respond. All the Jewish men from our town were taken to Dachau, except Father, who was put into the town prison. We never found out why. Mother and the other women were put under house-arrest. Finally, after a week or so, they were freed again.

Three days after our parents' arrival, we learned that all their linen, the precious dowry of more than fifty years, and everything they had bought so lavishly in order to spend their last German money, was stolen in transit somewhere between Germany and England. Mother cried. Now, she said, they were stripped.

V

AMERICA

25. Mount Royal

At the beginning of 1939 I casually remarked to a Canadian neurophysiologist who was leaving for home: "If you ever should find a job for me in Canada, just send me a post-card." It was one of those things one does not really mean. Exactly three weeks later, however, a post-card arrived: "I have found your job."

Once in 1935 I had had the opportunity of obtaining a research scholarship at the brain research institute in Madrid, and a peculiar combination of circumstances resulted in my not accepting it, and obtaining a similar job in London. Half a year later the Spanish Civil War broke out. I have often asked myself what my future would have been had I accepted the first appointment. Shortly after I arrived in London, I got an offer to teach neuropathology at the Peiping Medical Union in China. We were very enthusiastic about going there, but when I learned that I could not have easily resumed my activities in London at an uncertain later date, the appointment in Peiping fell through. A few months later the Sino-Japanese war started. When I told Doctor Cumings that I was going to Canada, he said that this meant certain war. There is a beautiful story by James Thurber of a man who is fond of relating the most Providential hairbreadth escapes; in the end he is killed by a rock falling on him with astonishing accuracy under the most accidental circumstances.

My wife, our oldest boy (then one year old) and I arrived in Montreal on June 24, 1939. It was a Saturday afternoon. When the boat landed, all the bells of Montreal rang. We were told that this was the day of Saint Jean Baptiste, the patron of French Canada. In the streets we saw groups of marching men in very colorful uniforms, with music bands, who looked as if they were advertising department stores.

The manager of the Queen's Hotel was a jovial man with a cutaway. He spoke to us like a father, and as if he had expected our arrival personally for weeks beforehand. My wife was thrilled and asked: "How does he know?" I answered distrustfully, like someone who had made a serious study of life on the North American continent: "He doesn't. They learn this sort of thing in special courses." A room was reserved for us on the eighth floor. From there we looked over an endless forest of roofs, signboards and fire-escapes, with a thin rim of bluish haze which, we found out, was a faint indication of the St. Lawrence valley. The heat and moisture were such as we had never experienced before. It was as if the ceiling were closing imperceptibly down towards the floor, with us in between. The air in front of the window vibrated.

In the evening the telephone rang. It was a lady associated in some way with McGill University who had received one of the numerous letters of introduction sent ahead of us by an English neuropathologist. The lady called for us by car, showed us the campus, and took us to the top of the mountain. When we returned late in the evening, the telephone rang again.

"This is Mrs. Langdon speaking." She, too, had received one of those letters. "It must be ghastly in a hotel room, with a baby, on a day like this. Listen, my husband and I are leaving Montreal for a few days. Why don't you stay at our place? We are going to leave the key to the house under the doormat.

There is food in the Frigidaire." My wife told her that she was taking a great risk, since she had never seen us. Mrs. Langdon said she was prepared to risk it. The lady who had shown us around, took us to the Langdons' on the following day. For a few days we found ourselves the inhabitants of a beautiful house. There were wood-carvings on the walls, and pewter and silver in glass cupboards, old French-Canadian and English handicraft. Everything was laid out with taste. There was a cool lawn around the house. There was a hand-carved wooden crucifix, and in the bedroom we discovered an old yellowish photograph of a nun. There was a sentimental lure and temptation in all this; it was as if a corner of our childhood had extended that far. Such was our welcome on the New Continent.

I had obtained a working position at a mental hospital on the outskirts of the city. We took our apartment close to the hospital in an outlying suburban district. We got acquainted with a sector of life on the North American continent which is of greatest importance, and which will probably be of even greater importance in the future. This is the life of those people who are above the working-class, even above the white-collar proletariat in the European sense, and yet no longer bourgeois in the nineteenth-century sense.

Years ago we had acquired the Continental attitude of superiority towards all things American. At school some of our teachers made the cheap and arrogant distinction between "culture" and "civilization" which, I believe, goes back to H. S. Chamberlain, the son-in-law of Wagner. At that time we believed that America was Babbitt, Jazz and Hollywood. The first Americans and Canadians we met were the research fellows at the Psychiatric Institute in Munich, who had turned out to be people very sensitive to things of the intellect, and without our morbid tenseness. They were intelligent, open-minded, and lacked our heavy solemnity. Many of them had a surprising degree of natural charity and sense of community. Our inborn sense of the esthetic was alien to them, but they seemed to envy us for it with a humility which made us feel embarrassed.

Here, however, it was different. We found ourselves in a monotonous infinity of houses, ugliness insistent and threatening by the very fact of its seemingly limitless multiplication. The houses were jerry-built, rows after rows, creeping along like fungi mass-cultured by wealthy people who lived in cool stone buildings, far away from us. The houses were filled with settees; moonlit lake scenes with moose; mahogany radios; Jesus the Good Shepherd, souvenir de la Gaspésie; polished bedroom sets and so on. With insignificant variations the same uniformity prevailed on all sides. Thoughts were channeled into all this by radio and newspapers, as if an ocean were artificially aërated. It was as though the mystery of human existence itself were replaced by a Prefabricated Life.

In the middle of this, my wife settled with the determination of a brave soldier. We were poorer than those around us. We had to rely on my small salary, and almost half of it had to be sent to my parents in England. Before I was naturalized I could not think of being permitted to do some practice besides my other work. We had gone into debt to bring our old furniture with us. My wife built a small sheltered island out of our chests of drawers, the cupboard, the hope chest—most of it eighteenth-century handicraft from Franconia. All this, together with her works of lettering and binding, now seemed to have the function of watchful icons.

In spite of the fact that now we no longer wanted to be different, in spite of the fact that we made numerous friends, we felt segregated. Montreal shows, in a coarsened and seemingly static form, all the imprints and traces of the quarrels of the European family of peoples. At home in high school we used to have "living pictures," scenes in which an action was shown arrested at a certain point, in a motionless pantomime. When you look down from the top of Mount Royal, you can almost

directly perceive currents of European history of the last few
centuries in a petrified form. There are French who seem to
perpetuate the France of the time of Pascal, Monsieur Arnauld
and the Port-Royal, a France which had dodged the impact of
the Revolution. Here until a short time ago, political liberalism
and the Catholic tradition were mutually exclusive. As in other
Catholic countries, there is much voluntarily accepted poverty.
In the province there is the genuine rural culture, with the
family farm as a center. The clergy is suspicious of industrialism
and of the city, and one has a feeling that most of the Frenchmen
who live in the city rely on the soundness and indestructibility
of the village. Calvinist prosperity, at one with the rest of the
British Commonwealth, seems to look down upon all this with
amused self-assurance. This, in turn, spurs the French into national resentment of an incredible tenacity. To many of them
the Church itself becomes a vehicle of national exclusiveness,
obviously the opposite of what she actually is meant to be. In
between this are the Jews and the Irish, both of whom seem still
to bear the resentment produced by the suffering in their European home countries. Thus, the city is parcellated, and everywhere there are frontiers of distrust.

We did not have any feeling of "belonging." We felt like rabbits who turn up accidentally in the middle of a fox-hunt. Even
the Jews who were most charitable to us did not seem to grasp
the true significance of what was going on in Europe. Most of
them had the naive and understandable idea that if one only
was able to beat Hitler "and his gang" everything was solved.
The more sophisticated believed in a solution offered by dialec-
tical materialism. Some Catholic people let us feel anti-semitism
for the first time since leaving Germany. In Germany we had
been subject to the cruel precision of a huge anonymous machine; here for the first time we experienced anti-semitism from
person to person. At the beginning of the Hitler revolution I
remember having overheard a Jew in a railway compartment

remarking to another Jew: "You are lucky, living in a Catholic area!" But here the spirit of the Catholicity we knew in Europe seemed lost; it was as if these ethnic groups had brought along with them all their ancient animosities. There was no need to introduce any up-to-date form of racism, with all the ideologies of the twentieth century. It was all there in the form of preciously retained resentments of bygone times.

To the onlooker it appeared that the Church itself was incorporated into this maze of social and political petrifactions. Was it really true that we, Jews, Catholics and Protestants, had been huddling around our common God, in the darkness of persecution? The evenings at Frau Flamm's, the Cardinal's sermon, the brave Käsbohrer, Bruno Schulz and the "Living Corps," the old cook in Munich who informed me naively that "Our Lord Himself was a Jew"; all this seemed centuries ago. Gradually but surely it paled and faded away. I became almost convinced that I had been the victim of a wishful illusion. There was no drama of Golgotha. There was no cornerstone. Christianity was a haphazard temporal form of herding, there were tea socials, "charity drives," and the very Gospel itself had become part and instrument of political exigencies.

That Christ whom we had beheld! Had He detached Himself from all this, was He mercilessly removed from this place by the distance of time and space? Or was this His objectivation, an amorphous trace left behind by cosmic explosion? Those among us who, as Communists, had lived a life of sacrifice and danger out of "compassion with the multitude"—were they not infinitely closer to Him? Those who were among the rocks of Northern Palestine, renouncing the material benefits of the world of our childhood—were they not infinitely closer to Him?

During this time I got an occasional letter from Ludwig in which he described the life of his community. They were living in a poor co-operative without private property. In spite of the hardness provided every day by Nature, in spite of the threat

of Rommel's army, cowering just across the Egyptian border—
no, perhaps because of all this, there was a tone of joy and happiness in all his letters. They had removed another thirty acres
of rock; they had made an artificial fishpond in which they bred
European fresh-water fish; they had built a new community
house; he had introduced a choir and a small orchestra into the
school of which he was in charge. Compared with their way
of life our existence seemed to be the continuation of a lie which
we had wanted to flee. Their life seemed to be something real.
There is a round song, in Hebrew, of the psalm:

Behold how good and how pleasant it is for brethren to dwell together in unity;
Like the precious ointment on the head, that ran down upon the
beard of Aaron.
Which ran down to the skirt of his garment, as the dew of Hermon.
For there the Lord hath commanded blessing, and life for ever-
more.

"Brethren to dwell together in unity . . ." There it was again,
the lure of belonging. Providence had made me a Jew. There I
belonged with the fibers of my heart. There was the sheltering
warmth of blood. There, perhaps, was my task. How had I ever
come to doubt it?

And yet, far away at the back and just dimly perceived, was
another loyalty. Those Christians in Munich who had suffered
for us and with us during the night of annihilation, with whom
I had for the first time seen a super-national Israel—they seemed
to beckon me not to betray them. In that experience lay an obligation. I knew that there were ministers and priests in concentration camps. I knew that, with all the knavish brutality, there
were anonymous precious deeds of sacrifice in the name of
Jesus of Nazareth, the Anointed One in Israel, deeds of sacrifice
made by those who did not belong to us in the flesh.

There was no doubt about the natural place of my loyalty
and love during this most terrible moment in the history of the

Jews. I knew where I belonged by nature and by inclination. Here, in the New World, not broken by the apocalypse, everyone was still falling into his appointed place, within a frame of purely social and political categories. In fact nothing but that frame was visible. And yet, long ago, in those dark and dreadful days, for one moment the curtain of history had been torn open and we had seen the bleeding flesh of Christ.

For quite some time I thought that it was possible to remain a Jew and yet guard the secret of Jesus. I know that there are many who remain in this peculiar state. There are some very outstanding examples—Henri Bergson, Franz Werfel, Sholem Asch. It was impossible that, at this moment when our people was undergoing its agony, even Christ Himself would demand of one of us to become a deserter. Most of those Jews who remain with one foot at the threshold of the Church feel that, in such a moment of history, even Jesus would not have left the Jewish community of suffering. Yet there was something not quite clear in this thought. Because, during the Nazi persecution, for the first time in Jewish history since Christ, the Jews were not persecuted on account of their religion but only on account of their race. In fact, in Germany I had seen that Jewish Christians were frequently worse off than we who were also Jewish by religion. They were rejected by the "Christians" as Jews, and by the Jews as renegades. They shared the fate of Christ, of whom Pascal says that He is equally undesired by pagans and by Jews. Thus baptism as an escape from the fate of Jewry existed no longer. In this respect Hitler had, unwittingly, helped to clarify a spiritual issue.

During that time I spent many evenings in conversation with one of the Nuns of the Sacred Heart. I told her frankly that when I studied the New Testament, or Saint Thomas and Saint Augustine, or Pascal's *Pensées,* or Newman's writings, I saw a world which was entirely acceptable to me and to many Jews. Not only was it acceptable, but it represented in a pure light something which I perceived as our true home. However, this world, and the world of Christianity as it presented itself actually in front of our eyes, socially and politically objectivated, were two altogether different worlds. I did not even see any bridge. As long as this incongruity existed, it seemed almost to be the mysterious task of the Jews to keep out. I was approaching the paradox of which I spoke once before, the paradox of which, I believe, Werfel has been a victim.

At one time, I said, I had sworn that if I escaped from Germany I would do everything for the rest of my life to help the Jews. Now I had maneuvered myself into a corner of spiritual intricacies and paradoxes which appeared hopelessly insoluble. Moreover, I said, even if I embraced Christianity formally, there was still my wife and there were my children. To force my wife into anything which was alien to her would be atrocious. She was living a Christian life as it was, without ever calling it that.

The nun said that "helping the Jews" was not a problem to be solved on a purely natural plane. It would be very limited to think that I could help the Jews only by working on the land in Palestine, or by being a public promoter of racial justice, or by becoming a great Zionist leader. If I had really grasped the world of Saint Thomas and Saint Augustine, of Newman and of Pascal, I would have to admit one thing: that the pains and the blackout I was experiencing right now might be enough to "help the Jews," and might be infinitely more than what I could be doing in the practical order of things. If I did not understand this, I should leave Saint Thomas and Saint Augustine and Newman and Pascal alone.

The Catholic Church is a church of the multitude. Consequently the outsider, approaching her, faces a thick layer of mediocrity. We have associations of thought built chiefly on magazine articles, radio items and newspaper headlines. Whoever has experienced supernatural charity during the persecution on the Continent may stumble across a bigoted or anti-semitic priest—and with one such experience the vision of the Church seems forever gone. In Mozart's *The Magic Flute* the two people who are to be initiated in the Temple of Love and Wisdom are first repelled by rough guards; then they have to cross lakes of water and fire; and only after all this are they able to see the interior.

Thus, it took us some time before we saw the immense hidden treasure of anonymous sanctity in the Church; the spiritual power that flows to and from thousands of unknown souls every day. The stream of sacrifices made, for supernatural motives, by a multitude of working-class people, by religious in their communities, by priests and lay-people alike. In one superficial respect there is again a strange resemblance between the Jewish people and the Church: the misdeeds of one member are more broadcast than the sancity of a hundred others.

Gradually, we got to know many young priests with a profound and ardent social consciousness, with a sense of self-abnegation which I had seen before in some of the early social revolutionaries.

26. *Catechumen*

VICTORIN VOYER was the first French-Canadian whom I got to know more intimately. He was a post-graduate student who interned under me in a course of Psychiatry. For a long while we used to talk nothing but psychiatry. He accompanied me on ward rounds, and all I noticed for some time was his eagerness to learn, and our conversations remained confined to mere technicalities. However, he impressed me by his character; there was something wholesome, clean and straight about him. One day, after a ward visit to hundreds of chronic patients, he sud-

denly began to remark on the mystery of suffering. We climbed
up on a high window-sill and crouched there, overlooking seemingly endless rows of beds. He sounded emotional, over-enthu-
siastic with the mere process of ideation (as one is at the age
of twenty-six) and a little sentimental. However, he did say a
few things which made me become attentive. I told him what
I thought about this question, and he told me more about himself. He was obviously acquainted with contemporary Thomist
philosophy and with the personalist movement, and when he
discovered that we both shared the same interests he became
so enthusiastic that he nearly fell off the window-sill.

During subsequent talks he told me about his childhood in a
family of ten children on a Quebec farm; about their life of hard
work and poverty; how his people got him through the University.
His entire philosophy stemmed from that true simplicity of life.
He gave me the story of his parents. It seemed like an endless
story of small and bitter every-day sacrifices, willingly accepted,
and strangely enough there was an atmosphere of hilarity and
cheerfulness in all this. Worries either get you down or give you
buoyancy. This was an immediate extension of the world of Frau
Flamm and the old washerwoman, of the Kohen family—in
short, of all those families in which I had seen religion form the
organic basis of life.

All this determined his outlook to an astonishing degree. No
matter what we discussed, whether labor or the Jews, nationalism
or the war, there was the same warm spirit of charity and justice
which enabled him to penetrate to the core of the question without any intellectual stunts. He explained to me, without condon-
ing it, the social, economic and psychological background of
French-Canadian chauvinism. He himself was anything but a
Romantic or a Reactionary. Very quickly our friendship became
solid. I, the German Jew who had been reared in a country
thousands of miles away, who had participated in the mental
Odyssey of the years after the first war, and he, the boy from the

French-Canadian village; we spoke the same language, we
thought the same thoughts, and there obviously was something
powerful enough to overcome all these forces of social, political
and biological molding.

This experience was repeated, perhaps even more forcefully,
when my wife and I made the acquaintance of two people who
had a decisive influence on our further development, Jacques
Maritain and Dorothy Day.

There again, looking at the surface of things, you could not
think of two people more different. It seems, at first sight, that in
order to understand Maritain fully you have to understand
Europe, the Paris of the Schoolmen, and the Paris of Picasso, the
haute bourgeoisie of the Republic and the Revolutionary intelligentsia from the East, the world of Virgil and the world of Jean
Cocteau—in short the thousand ambiguities which seemed to
characterize the human intellect in our century. And there is
Dorothy Day, with her background of the non-conformist middle-
class family of the American mid-west. Nothing could be more
apart. Even in their conclusions there two people seem to be
equally at variance. Yet it is not at all difficult to see why their
influence on our lives should have been identical, so much so
that when I think of them today I have the feeling of a unity of
currents.

For a long time I had wanted to meet Maritain. In England
I used to plan long letters to him which I never actually wrote.
I thought that if there was one man in the Church who would
have an answer to many of my questions, he was the man. Nobody in the Church seemed to have had a more profound understanding of the Jewish problem. He seemed, from his own experience, to understand the hundred twists of our intellect which
were produced by our heritage of Marxism, Scientism, Freudism.
In London I used to think that, if this man has come through
the maze of all those experiences to accept Saint Thomas, there
must be something to Saint Thomas. It was that certain feeling

of assurance you have if you know that "somebody has been there before."

I was introduced to Maritain by chance. One day I mentioned casually to Mrs. Langdon, the lady who had given us our first refuge, that I was interested in the Catholic Church and in Thomism, and that I had been deeply influenced by Jacques Maritain. She told me that Maritain happened to be in America at the moment, and that he was going to be in Montreal in a week; she could see to it that I was introduced to him. One can imagine my feelings.

A week later I had to appear, at ten o'clock in the morning, in the house of a well-known French-Canadian family, to meet the famous man. Their home was furnished in the style of wealthy houses of the *fin du siècle:* there were huge rooms with recesses hung with heavy velvet draperies, richly framed oil paintings, alabaster sculptures. I was sitting in one of those grottos when a velvet curtain parted and Maritain came in, accompanied by the lady of the house who introduced us and left us alone. Since there were no doors, only draperies, I was childishly afraid that someone might be hearing what we said, although there was nothing secretive about it. I moved closely up to him and spoke in a low voice. It is peculiar that I do not remember our conversation with much detail.

Briefly I told him my story and he seemed to be deeply interested from the beginning. We spoke of reformed and orthodox Judaism, of Hassidism, of Dostoievsky's "Great Inquisitor" and the problem of iniquity in the visible Church. I told him about my spiritual experiences in London, and that I often believed that my conversion was nothing but a mirage produced by an unconscious desire to escape the destiny of a Jew. He implored me not to allow the precious fruit of my spiritual experiences to be corroded by psychological self-analysis, to believe in the genuineness of these insights which occur on a plane quite apart from that of primitive motivations. He spoke of the bleeding

wounds on the visible body of the Church; of the divinity of
Christ as a stumbling block for the Jews. He spoke in a peculiarly
sketchy way, in hints rather than statements. Yet there was an
impression of substance and clarity about everything he said.
He held his hands compact and made movements with his
fingers as if he were kneading material into thoughts. His head
was attentively bent, his eyes had a remote gaze; although it
was warm in the room he wore loosely around his shoulders a
muffler which had no function as a piece of clothing.

Since I spoke almost in a whisper he had moved up closely
and spoke also in a whisper. He asked me the most personal
questions about my spiritual life but there was not for a moment
the feeling of obtrusiveness or indiscretion. I had from the first
moment the deep impression of a strange and pleasant form of
personal directness which was the result of a great charity and
humility. As we sat in the somber salon in the midst of velvet
draperies and whispered about the *shehinah* and the divinity of
Christ, I became aware of the uniqueness of the situation. We
were stripped of accidentals of national and social origin, and
circumstance found strange neighbors huddling. In moments of
great intensity historical time ceases. I could just as well have
been inside the catacombs, a helpless catechumen whispering
to an apostle.

27. *Father Couturier*

Among all of us who were not allowed to participate in the
war, and had to watch it from a safe corner, there arose a peculiar feeling composed of suspense and guilt. It was *our* war
that was being fought. People who had grown up in the streets
around us in a suburban part of Montreal were being seared to

death by flames in mid-air and swallowed by tropical seas. They died for something which seemed only remotely associated with their lives in suburban homes, the assembly line of present-day existence. It was as if their deaths had already touched our hearts some years before, during the early agony of Europe and during those past days in Southern Germany. And we remained alive. To think that a man who lived on the floor above the drugstore at the corner of Wellington Street and Third Avenue was killed by a flame-thrower for something which seemed immediately related not to his own life but to that of Grandmother, Herr and Frau Masser, and Doctor Schulz.

Uncle Julius, the linguist and world-traveler, the international businessman, was now a worker in a valve factory in Stamford, Connecticut. He refused to make use of any of his business connections. He did hard manual labor for the first time in his life, and lived on the basis of an hourly wage, as his own factory-workers in Germany had done. I wrote to him and asked him why he did not, like other people, try to make a success in business; it would be so easy for him. He answered in a charming letter in which he described his daily life as a factory-worker, overalls, lunchbox and all. The letter was interspersed with quotations from Goethe, Schiller and Nietzsche. But he avoided my question. Uncle Felix wrote: "He reminds me of one of those penitent figures one finds in Russian stories."

I met a psychiatrist from California whom I had known in the Psychiatric Institute in Munich. "The first thing we ought to do after the war is over is to give people a rational outlook on life. The truth is that science is still being suppressed. People everywhere in the world are laboring under a sense of irrational fear and guilt. Unless we remove all the out-dated morality and religion of centuries, there will not be any peace on earth." This sounded familiar but I could not place it right away. "We gave the boys in the Navy personality tests, and I tell you that in my opinion over ninety per cent suffer from a guilt complex which

is produced by our cultural religious pattern." I told him that
the present world war was senseless unless seen in the light of
the passion of Christ. He had encountered me only during my
work on brain pathology, and looked at me with astonishment.
"If you really have come to believe stuff like that, you must be
schizophrenic." What he meant was that my ideas were crazy.
They were apparently also dangerous to the form of post-war
"cultural pattern" which he envisaged.

In the meantime, I went back to the nun at the Sacred Heart,
and she encouraged me to go on praying. One evening I began
again, after an interval of several years, to talk to my wife about
my religious search. Again she said, as she had said years ago
in London: "If I were a Christian at all, I'd be a Catholic."

"Look here," I said, "stop talking nonsense. If you want to be
a Catholic it is not enough to have a sentimental attachment to
Kati Huber, or to look at medieval paintings. I told you before
that this means believing in the divinity of Christ, and in the
Church."

I quoted previous conversations which she had long forgotten
because at the time they had meant much less to her than to me.
Once in the country, in Gloucestershire, she had said that Jesus
had been such a perfect and ideal person that a legend had
grown around him after his death, and people gradually came
to regard him as a God. "I wish you would stop quoting me, I
never remember from one day to the other what I say," she
answered.

"All right," I said, "there is a Dominican priest here from
France, Father Couturier, a priest-artist, and a friend of Matisse
and Picasso. If you really are interested, I'll arrange for you to
see him."

I had met Father Couturier through an introduction by Mr.
Maritain. It was quite true that Couturier was an artist and a
friend of Matisse and Picasso, but I was using this as a bait.

"How I hate to see people about something I know nothing about," she said. "But it sounds fascinating."

The following Saturday afternoon we had an appointment in the Dominican Monastery in Notre Dame de Grace. I left my wife with Father Couturier in a parlor. The parlor was glass-encased and looked like an oversized telephone booth. I could see the two through the pane. The priest was in a white gown. He was very tall and thin, with a small head, sunken cheeks and large, very lively gray-blue eyes. His short-cropped hair was gray. He had large expressive hands which he kept moving slowly, or hid in his large white sleeves. I could not hear what the two people were saying. He was leaning back with an amused and ironical air and she looked like an attentive schoolgirl, sitting straight at the edge of the chair. It so happened that I had a ski-suit and ski-boots on, and my steps were noisy on the stone-covered floor. I paced up and down, stopped to look at a map of the Archdiocese of Montreal, and at some rules and regulations printed in French. Then I went for a walk. When I returned, my wife emerged from the glass booth.

She looked excited and her face was slightly blushed. After we had said good-bye to Father Couturier, we walked a little in silence. I was very curious about her first reaction, but I did not want to ask. After a while she said: "I think I'd like to become a Catholic." That moment I had a very peculiar feeling which is hard to describe; I can come closest to it by saying, idiomatically, that I felt as if God had called my bluff.

How inadequately all this is told! Experiences which appear "emotional" and arbitrary are actually surface eruptions of developments which have been going on for a lifetime in the depth of a personality. It would be impossible to tell my wife's story. It is difficult to trace the sequence of one's own experiences. There is always a remainder one should leave untold. This is even truer when it comes to the lives of others, particularly those closest to us. But I have never seen anyone seized in the roots of his existence, as I saw it in my wife in those days. "Tell me," she asked me, "what did we talk and think about all the time before?" She pointed at the Gospel. "To think that this was the only thing that mattered, and I never realized it." On Whit Sunday, 1941, she and our two older children were received into the Church by Father Couturier.

Even then I doubted my moral right to leave the Jewish community by a visible sign. The issues of supernatural and natural charity, of natural and supernatural justice, of loyalty and of treason seemed so hopelessly entangled that I continued in a state of bewildered search.

28. *Jerusalem in Every Man*

WHEN we met Dorothy Day for the first time I had the same experience as with Jacques Maritain. We found everything again that had ever inspired us at any time of our lives. It was all there —the spirit of piety and peace I had encountered in orthodox Jewish families; Franz Burger's great heart and humanist generosity; the rebellious fervor of justice of some of the early revolutionaries; the sense of community, simplicity and self-abnegation of the Zionist Halutziuth; the sense of the beautiful which had enlivened those faraway days in Heidelberg and Munich; the lucid clarity, logic and common-sense which I had admired in my greatest academic teachers. Nothing was missing.

Something was added to all this, however, something of infinite importance. The limitations produced by the ethnic, social and temporal were removed, and there was something that transcended it all, something unifying which did away with immediate finality and promised further growth. Christianity never demands of you to deny anything positive you have ever loved. You find all of it again in Christ, but you find more. He does not want you to be nostalgic for the past, because the past is in Him. He asks you not to look back at the burning city lest you will turn into a pillar of salt. The Europe of our youth seemed centuries removed. Yet it was here, stripped of all that was arbitrary. What made it possible that this woman from the midwest and the boy from the Quebec farm, the philosophy professor from Paris and we ourselves, my wife and I, spoke the same language, and seemed to share the mysteries of our past, the suffering, the thousand eradications of a thousand bygone days, if it was not the One who united us with one simple gesture?

With Dorothy Day we had at once the feeling that we had always known her. If I could have, by some magic trick, taken her into my brother's *kvutzah* in Palestine, she would have understood right away (more deeply than in the common sense of the word) what they were doing. If I could have taken her into Haase's consulting-rooms in the slums of Moabit; if I could have taken her into Burger's classroom; or among the radical students in Frankfurt; or into the orthodox synagogue in Munich; or among the highbrows of Heidelberg, she would have *known* all this. But in addition she had something which they did not know; it was something like an other-worldly principle of purification and synthesis.

For those who do not know, I must explain that Miss Day is a onetime Communist. She is now the leader of the Catholic Worker movement. Among those in the present-day Church who have a vivid social consciousness, one can discern two different trends. There is one large group of people who feel that industrialization and Western urbanization in themselves are neither good nor bad, and that it is a duty of Christians to penetrate the city and the factory with the salt of the gospel. They are careful not to discard the impulse of justice immanent in Marxism and the Labor Movement. They feel that even our present-day technocracy can still be spiritualized. It took us some time to discover this sort of Catholic underground, a powerful movement among young people who are idealistic and ready for sacrifice.

On the other hand, there are those who feel that technocracy and industrialism have reached a stage at which they can no longer be reconciled with Christian principles. These are people who reject industrialization as such and attempt to by-pass it. The representatives of this group are the English Dominican Fathers, Eric Gill, Dorothy Day, the women of the Grail Movement, and Catherine de Hueck. They feel that the de-humanizing forces immanent in a technocratic society are too strong to be overcome in any way but by de-centralization or by the principle of voluntary poverty.

This perhaps sounds romantic and impractical. However, from knowing it, I should say that in a possible future society of pure pragmatism, both these approaches will be of equal importance. I have never tried to solve this problem. One cannot solve it by thinking. However, even if Dorothy Day and her followers were wrong in every single point, her merit will always remain the fact that she has transferred that peculiar immediate social consciousness of the early Communists right into the center of the Church, that is to say she has made innumerable Christians deeply aware of the social injustice right in our midst, Christians with the highest aim who otherwise would never have been aware of the urgency of the social question.

It is amazing to see how many young lay-people, priests and nuns, today have a spirit of identification with the underdog which is so familiar to me from intellectuals of bourgeois origin who, in the early twenties, gave away all their possessions and joined the Communist Movement. Many of those early Communists were Christian in their intentions, and would have done the same thing if, by some historical twist, the Marxist doctrine had not been associated with the elements of atheism and class-warfare. In fact, as various people have pointed out, the great socialist movements of the nineteenth century can be traced back to the Hebraeo-Christian tradition, but once this first impulse was spent, socialism merged into a de-humanizing managerial movement of which we may be entering only the first stage.

Now we see an amazing number of young Catholics who are taking up the social movement just at the stage where it was contaminated with nineteenth-century materialism, and they are baptizing it. One comes across these people in the most unlikely places. It is simply amazing to see in how many of them one can trace the influence of Dorothy Day or the European Dominican Fathers, even if the actual techniques vary as widely as the techniques employed by Mr. Nehru and Mr. Gandhi. Many profoundly religious people live an individualistic sort of Christian life, the life of "Christ and I closed up inside a bottle." They achieve a high degree of spirituality but the notion that the Negro problem, or the clearing of slums, or the problem of strikes in the coal-mining area has anything to do with religion, is quite alien to them. In the Middle Ages the visible Church was woven into the pattern of a society of castes. Consequently the great geniuses of Christian thought did not stress the problem of social justice in a way so that it can be transferred immediately to our time.

When the Reformation and the French Revolution overthrew that hierarchical society of castes, they identified the Church with that type of society and believed it not to be viable in any other social structure. It was just because the visible Church had been woven into that pattern that the principle of the brotherhood of man was taken up by the revolutionaries; it diffused, by a process of osmosis, from the Church into thousands of secular currents. This is the reason why the sense of social or racial justice is so natural to the convert who approaches the Church from outside, and he is bewildered to see that these ideas take such time and effort to become rooted in the consciousness of Catholic people. *His* great difficulty lies at the opposite pole. He cannot think of God in other but social terms, he cannot conceive of a Charity altogether detached from the social implications, a Charity which would still have to be lived if he were the only human being in the entire universe, if he were completely alone with God.

Now, however, we are at a turning-point of history. Things look as if the immanent moral *élan* of the great revolution had petered out, and that we shall have a scientific social apparatus in which the triad of Faith, Hope and Charity will be entirely replaced by a triad of Research, Insurance and Management. Whether the apparatus will be a Russian or American model does not concern us in this connection. It is no coincidence that precisely at this moment the Church reclaims all that has diffused into those secular currents; that she is re-assimilating the social elements of the gospel which had been disguised for instance in Marxism; that hundreds of young priests adopt the social teaching of the Church and become "radicals"; that the two poles of the gospel, the mystery of the personality and the mystery of the multitude, just begin to fuse again in the consciousness of the people.

Mr. Arnold Lunn once said that Protestant and Catholic piety approach the social problem in entirely different ways. The Protestant fights against unjust institutions—for example, slavery. The Catholic does not fight against the institution but identifies himself with the victim of injustice and lives with him, as Saint Peter Claver lived with Negro slaves. This statement is correct only as a historical observation, pertaining to a definite period. Right now we are witnessing a reintegration of those two currents in the Catholic Church.

The function of Jacques Maritain, Dorothy Day and others, has been to help in reclaiming land of Christianity flooded and carried away by secularism, drawing on the great principles in the social Encyclicals, and making many Catholics aware of crucial social issues. With us, however, their function was exactly the opposite. We had to be familiarized with other aspects of Christianity, those aspects which are alien to the outsider who brings natural social consciousness as his dowry into the Church.

I have said that in entering the Church one does not have to give up any single positive value one has ever believed in. You think of yourself as a traitor to your past. You think you have to leave Goethe behind, or Tolstoy, or Gandhi, or Judaism, or whatnot. But there is nothing which is good in all these things which you do not find again in the Church. Now it is ordered and synthetized. It is molten in Christ. Moreover, you do not have to accept anything which is repulsive to you in the Church, on a political or social plane. Nobody wants you to accept a totalitarian politician, or a priest who is obsessed by racial prejudice. All you have to accept is Christ and His Sacraments.

29. *The Print of the Nails*

I SURMISED from Dorothy Day, when I first met her, that she, too, must have had the "traitor complex" for a long time. However, from her and from other Catholics, lay-people, priests and nuns alike, I learned one thing: that you cannot come to grips with Christ as long as you think only in terms of social or political or ethnic references. You have to confront Him alone, divested of all this. Nor can you "figure it all out" intellectually. That comes afterwards. Faith, Hope and Charity are *acts*. They are by no means *non*-intellectual but they are much more than intellectual. They are not *non*-emotional but they are more than emotional. There is a German word, *durchleiden,* for which there is no good English translation. It means to experience and get to know something by suffering. To "suffer a thing through" with your entire being, rather than to "figure it out." This precisely is the lesson we received from people as highly advanced and widely different in their origin and in their avenues of approach as Jacques Maritain and Dorothy Day.

There comes then a moment when the question is no longer: "How can you enter the Church if you see how many of its members misuse it as a cloak for social injustice?" but rather, "How can you, if you have social consciousness and see the dynamite of social evolution stored in the Church, *not* enter it?"

The question is no longer: "How can you with your scientific training accept the doctrine of the Church?" The question is rather: "How can you who see how science is being used to construct a world which is no longer Christocentric, if you are deeply aware of the urgency to reintegrate the wealth produced by modern science into a Christocentric cosmology—how can you *not* become a Christian?"

There comes then a moment when the question is no longer: "How can you with your Jewish consciousness leave the Jewish community at the time of its most terrible persecution, and join a community in which there are many enemies of the Jewish people?" This question is, of all three questions, the most plausible one to ask. For this reason alone we may suspect that it contains a greater pitfall than the two others. To the outsider, on the plane of a low natural order, the Church itself is just another hostile camp. Indeed to some of its members it is an Irish institution (in the United States), a French institution (in Canada), and so forth. In the true mystical body there is no trace of an ethnic structure. However, my Jewish friends do not perceive that. Can you blame them? Their next-door Irish neighbors, or the priest around the corner, may be extreme nationalists. Now many of my friends have developed a Jewish national pride, since the time of the Nazi persecution. However, this is precisely the point at which the demands of Christ set it.

Rilke once wrote, around the year 1920, a remark which can be summarized as follows: "Supposing the Versailles Treaty were really an act of injustice against the German people, then we have two ways open. We can develop a spirit of more ardent nationalism and of revenge. Or we can do the opposite, we can discard all arms, even those of defense, abolish all remnants of an army, and try systematically to build up a pacifist state in the middle of Europe, a state that teaches a lesson in pacifism, no matter what the political constellations around us in the future may be. In the first case, Germany will most certainly be overtaken by a terrible fate. In the second case, she will experience a true re-birth."

To the Jew who lives in the post-gas chamber period of history, the alternative presents itself in a similar way. The Jew who has perceived Christ in the Church enters it not *in spite of* the fact that many of its members harbor an ignorant and prejudiced hatred against his people, but *because of* this fact. Here for the first time he is facing the demand of the Gospel in its terrible actuality.

In the late autumn of 1943, I went to see Father Ethelbert, an old Franciscan monk in Montreal, to ask him to receive me into the Catholic Church. I had spoken to Father Ethelbert on previous occasions. In fact I had had many talks with priests and nuns before, even in Munich and in London. People who roam around in the precincts of the Church for a long time become like bachelors who often get close to marrying but somehow do not find the turn. Tolstoy, speaking of bachelors, once said they become like beggars, meaning that they are like poor men who sit at the roadside while the stream of life passes by. I must have appeared like such a beggar to Father Ethelbert. At least I felt that I bewildered him. He understood many of my difficulties but much of it, many of the inner contortions of a European and a Jew and an intellectual, was alien to him. He reduced much of it to those simple principles of which he and I were both certain.

Father Ethelbert was a man of great simplicity. He, too, looked at me with that peculiar inward gaze I had seen so often in people who seem to look at something which is projected onto their retina from behind the eyes. He would say: "Look here, my good fellow . . ." then proceed to ask me a question and, without waiting for my answer, answer it himself. Then he would add, reassuringly: "That's right!" as if to confirm my reply, which I actually had not given. Perhaps he felt that my answers might be unnecessarily labored and complicated. It was a good thing for my vanity that he did not even seem to regard me as a rare specimen. He said that for instruction he would have to send me to Miss Sharp, a lady who lived at the Grey Nuns' convent. "Miss Sharp instructs our converts," he said. "She has a tremendous experience."

Miss Sharp was a blind and very old lady. She was a convert herself. "Now let's see . . ." said Miss Sharp, with that cheerfulness which dentists so often exhibit when they are laying their instruments out. She showed an utter disregard for the fact that I had acquainted myself with many of the intricacies of theology. I scarcely needed to mention to her that I firmly believed in the existence of God, when she set out to prove that existence to me. Her enthusiasm seemed to increase as she drove her points home. I do not think that it was so much the fact that her system was not adaptable to individual cases; I rather assume that the good Father had warned her of me as a dangerous freelancer. And this was a good thing.

One morning in December I said to Victorin Voyer, while we were in the ward: "Would you like to be my Godfather?" He jumped down from our usual window seat, slapped my back, pumped my arm, his jaw dropped and he began to burst forth with something which sounded like crying, laughing and talking all at once. The patients glanced at us in alarm.

There was a strange combination of Godfathers. My second Godfather was an old schoolmate of mine. I had met him in Munich only during our religious instructions which we received from the same teacher. He had been converted in Italy where he and his family had escaped from Hitler. I met him again, after twenty years, in Montreal and we discovered a strange parallel of destinies. Thus my spiritual protectors were a man from the French-Canadian village and a Jew from Munich. My wife and these two men accompanied me when I was received into the Church by Father Ethelbert on the Vigil of Saint Thomas the Apostle, December 21, 1943. It was only after my first Holy Communion, the next morning, that I looked at the missal to read the gospel of the day. It was the story of the man who insisted on seeing and touching the wounds of Christ so that he could believe in His divinity:

Now Thomas, one of the twelve who is called Didymus, was not with them when Jesus came. The other disciples therefore said to him: We have seen the Lord. But he said to them: Except I shall see in His hands the print of the nails, and put my finger into the place of the nails, and put my hand into His side, I will not believe. And after eight days, again, His disciples were within, and Thomas with them. Jesus cometh, the door being shut, and stood in the midst and said: Peace be to you. Then he saith to Thomas: Put in thy finger thither, and see my hands, and bring hither thy hand, and put it into my side; and be not faithless but believing. Thomas answered and saith to Him: My Lord and my God. Jesus saith to him: Because thou hast seen me, thou hast believed: Blessed are they that have not seen, and have believed.

VI

LETTER TO MY BROTHER

Someone remarked that Shestov was a Jew. "Hardly," said Leo Nikolaievitch, with doubt in his voice, "no, he is not like a Jew. Name me one single unbelieving Jew. There is none, not one."

Maxim Gorki, Reminiscenses of Tolstoy.

Some things lose their fragrance when exposed to the air; and some thoughts, when translated into language, are thereby robbed of their deep heavenly meaning.

Saint Thérèse of Lisieux, Story of a Soul.

30. Letter to My Brother

YOU SUSPECTED for years that I would end up as a Christian. When you finally heard of the accomplished fact you showed neither astonishment nor disapproval. Nevertheless, you told me in your letters on several occasions that you would like to know what I really think and believe. I am going to try to tell you. Do not expect from me a systematic exposition of Christian doctrine. This has been done much better than I could ever attempt. It is expressed in the clearest and simplest form in the Creed, and there is nothing I could add to it. Instead I am going to give you a few thoughts in a personal and (you will be disappointed) unscientific way. After all, you know most of the preceding story anyway. It was written not only to explain how I became a Christian but equally to help Christians understand their brothers, the Jews.

In writing to you, I am not trying to argue you into anything. As Newman has said, nobody has ever been converted by an argument. Even if I attempted to do so I should have to know exactly where you stand, and I don't. I think that you believe in some form of Fabian Socialism. I could give you a list of names such as Sidney and Beatrice Webb, and a few others, and ask you to tick off the ones whose names correspond to your philosophy. It really does not matter. The thing that strikes me much more is the fact that you live in a community close to the soil; you own no private property; in the first years of your settlement (I do not know about now) you went through great hardships. I remember your writing to me some years ago from a holiday trip. You told me that you were sitting on the slope of Mount Carmel, and you were very proud to use a fountain-pen which your community granted to you in your capacity as a schoolteacher.

You, with your intelligence and your many other personal gifts, could have been very "successful" in the West. But you live a life of voluntary poverty, whether you call it that or not. Unlike you, I own a car and life insurance. Our life is probably much more comfortable than yours. It is the life of an average family in a North American city. You see the paradox. You live, apparently on the basis of an a-religious philosophy, a life which corresponds to what my religion teaches me. I, on the other hand, live in a setting which makes life in accordance with the precepts of Judaeo-Christian morality a questionable and problematic task.

This is one of the strange contradictions of our time. Even if I attempted to convince you, this paradox alone would seem to weaken my argument and strengthen it at the same time. It would weaken it: the fact that the majority of Christians did not behave in a Christian way has always weakened the Christian argument. But it would also strengthen it. Because, if I took the time, I am certain I could prove to you that, no matter what philosophy you talk, historically the impulse of your action is, in the end, derived from Holy Scripture. You may believe in some form of Western rationalism (shall I tick off the name of Bertrand Russell?), but you are living on an income derived from the immense treasure of the Jewish-Christian heritage. The fact remains that you live in a co-operative community not far from Lake Genezareth, and when you talk you do so in the language of Isaiah. I talk Isaiah, but in the language of Bertrand Russell, a language that did not exist in Isaiah's time, and in a place four thousand miles away from Lake Genezareth.

You and I are so much alike in our way of acting and thinking that people used to remark on it. Therefore, there ought to be a way of communicating. It is so long since we have met that it is very hard to know what questions you might ask me if we were sitting in the same room. Some time ago I sent you a reprint of an essay on a religious topic, and you told me that you liked it. You detached yourself from your own opinions and granted me my premises. This gives me hope that I may be able to make myself understood.

Inner Resistances

The inner resistances you might have are manifold. There is, of course, the point I mentioned above, the outward manifestation of Christianity in many of the people who profess it. I have no real answer for that one. I hide myself in shame. However, do not forget a lesson which we know so well from the history of Judaism, that is the fact that Evil has more publicity than Good.

Moreover, if you did believe in Revelation you would see that this belongs to the very essence of the spiritual dialectics of history; namely that the nucleus of Revelation in its purity is immediately surrounded by objective evil. We have only to study the Old Testament, particularly the Prophets, to see that. On the other hand, all those elements which appear good in the anti-Christian revolutions are derived and borrowed from Christianity. This could be the subject of a historical thesis.

Other resistances are of a more subtle psychological nature. When you hear words like "Fall," "Original Sin" and "Holy Ghost," thousands of childhood thoughts and sentiments and the very smell of Sunday-school come up. These words all belong in the category of the stork and the sort of thing you used to believe in before you were smart. "Original Sin and Science—what utter nonsense," you are inclined to say. It seems so much more clever to use terms such as Ether, Planck's Constant, or the Theory of Surplus Value.

Let me dwell on this for a moment. A good deal of the resistance of enlightened and modern people against theology is not at all directed against the teachings presented by that discipline. If the same ideas were presented in a more abstract terminology, nobody would see much discrepancy with Reason. Some of my agnostic friends are great students and admirers of Aristotle and Plato. Now the idea of Original Sin was anticipated by Aristotle, perhaps even more explicitly by his teacher Plato, and ideas strangely similar have been introduced by many non-Christian thinkers up to the present time. But those thinkers use abstract and involved terms. They spare you that smell of Sunday-school; they do not repel you. Philosophers and mathematicians feel at ease only in the abstract. It is only the poet who calls a spade a spade. We who are still hypnotized by the mathematical sciences revolt at an idea, even a possible truth, if it is presented in poetic form. (I am using the word poetic here in its larger, ancient meaning.)

Freud, a genius who has presented some of the most profound observations on the psychological nature of Man in what you might call mythological form, was curiously sensitive to this. In one of his anti-religious writings he discusses the triad of Science, Art and Religion. He remarks that, while Science represents truth, Art compared with Religion is "harmless" because it does not pretend to be anything but a figment. This statement is erroneous but it brings us close to the concept of Truth. Some of the news which you read in this morning's paper is true in the sense of ephemeral verifiable facts. Now what about Shakespeare's dramas, Tolstoy's novels, Michelangelo's paintings and Haydn's quartets? They are immortal precisely because they express eternal truths about Man and the World, truths much more profound than any item in the newspaper.

This does not mean that I think that Original Sin and the Holy Ghost belong to the realm of art. William Blake once said that Christ and His Apostles were artists. Actually they were neither artists nor scientists but something different. What Blake, an Englishman of the early industrialist period, meant to imply was that we cannot confine the concept of truth to the scientific order.

Therefore, I ask you to forget for the time being your Sunday-school complex. The terms used in Hegelian dialectics and those presently used by mathematical physicists only sound smarter than theological terms. That in itself does not mean that they come closer to the true nature of things.

Professor Heidegger and Babette Klebl

Before I go on expounding my belief to you I should like to interpolate a kind of historical note which may seem to be out of place and which anticipates some things I am going to say later. I do not know whether you remember Babette Klebl, the maid in the household of Herr and Frau Hirsch in Munich. She came from Neumarkt in the Oberpfalz, and her sister was a waitress in the Lowenbräu. Babette was a daily communicant. In fact, at times Frau Hirsch disapproved of her going to Mass at five every morning because she was afraid that the lack of sleep interfered with her efficiency and made her cranky. I remember that Babette's life was one of hard work and of what appeared to be incessant prayer. She had her shortcomings; at times she actually was cranky. Moreover, it did not take much to make her infuriated, but she always regretted it soon, and I must say that the most impressive note about her, apart from her piety, was her humor. Babette worked in the kitchen and lived in a small room decorated with cheap holy pictures. In times of stress, of sickness and of death in the Hirsch family, Babette suddenly seemed to be the solid center of the household. When Otto Hirsch, a noble and promising boy, died at the age of sixteen, the only person in the house who seemed to have a profound inner relation to Death was Babette. I rediscovered Babette's portrait later in Franz Werfel's novel *Embezzled Heaven*. Even the young man's death and the maid's attitude are described there. This seemed a strange coincidence until I discovered that there were many people who recognized their own Babettes in that story. Babette must be legion. The Kaspar Russes and the housemaids have played an important rôle in the history of conversions.

In my wife's case the situation was quite similar. Kati Huber, born in Hundsacker near Straubing in Lower Bavaria, exuded the odor of hard work, the righteousness of the Psalms and the peace of the Gospel. She too was a daily communicant. She lived this life apparently untouched by the vicissitudes of a sophisticated and overcomplex family. You would be quite wrong in thinking that this is sentimental glorification. Obviously the Babettes and Katis have their own shortcomings and their secret passions. But their approach towards life transcends ours. While we were engaged in a continuous flight from ultimate reality (our intellect lent itself so well for this purpose), there existed among us all the time people who lived unknown lives of humility and charity. And, believe me, they did it with mystical fervor.

I remember how I used to be somehow aware of Babette's superiority and maturity. One afternoon, while she was cleaning the table, I said to her: "Don't tell anybody but actually I too believe that Jesus Christ died for us on the cross." I cannot quite understand why I said this. I was in my teens then, and perhaps I wanted to let her feel that I knew what went on inside her. My remark caught her off guard. She blushed, and her goiter shook a little—a sign that she was moved.

Every one of us who has escaped the European catastrophe knows that those obscure lives were of great significance for us. A great number of intellectuals, Liberal, Catholic, Socialist and Fascist, betrayed us. Everything seemed so complex; there were so many questions of political expediency that the cleverest Professors were hopelessly entangled in an infinite labyrinth of dialectics. Some tried to build bridges of Fascism as others tried to build bridges toward Stalinism. I remember some of my Jewish friends who were enraged about cruelties committed in Fascist countries but felt indifferent about the same cruelties committed in Russia. The opposite was true of many Catholics. As the international scene shifted so did allegiances and loyalties. It was as if the devil had led us to one of those distorted mirrors one finds in amusement parks; only that there was nothing amusing about it.

The Kaspar Russes and the Babette Klebls did not become confused. As bats find their way in the dark by the reflection of supra-sonic waves which they radiate, these people sent out into a dark universe a continuous radiation of prayer and sacrifice, and from somewhere out there returned a continuous echo. Thus, they remained oriented. And in this way they were able to reduce the most bewildering situation to a simple formula. Their world was mapped out by the Gospel.

When the Hitler era broke loose, all things seemed to assume a nightmarish quality which is impossible to describe to anyone who has never lived under a totalitarian regime. Then it was interesting to watch the way in which the intellectuals tried to understand the situation. Our sociologists began to talk about the in-group and the out-group. The Marxist dialecticians became entangled in an acrobatic apparatus which just did not seem to fit. Professor Heidegger, that same Professor who had given beautiful seminars on Saint Augustine, tried to find his place in a Nazi world by elaborating some very involved ideas on Hegel and Existentialism. Not so Babette Klebl. She said: "What do they want to do against the Jews? It will end badly with these fellows because our Lord Himself was a Jew." This statement was simple and intelligent. Berdyaev and Maritain did not actually say more. Only they said it in a more diversified and interesting manner. Babette had a metaphysical concept of history.

Nothing has convinced me more of the divinity of the Church than this organic continuity between the Klebls on one hand and the Berdyaevs and Maritains on the other; that, without the Church, the Klebls would not be ennobled and wise creatures they are; that Intellect, without humility, is the most destructive force in the world.

The Betrayal

There is nothing original in what I have just been saying. When you read Tolstoy carefully, particularly his autobiographical notes, there is no doubt whatsoever that his greatest source of inspiration was the life of simple piety among the peasants and nursemaids of his childhood. The old Tolstoy who advocated an abstract Christian morality, deprived of all sacramental channels, refuted his own argument. For such a bone-dry ethical system would never have remained vital among the people from whom he drew his inspiration.

Goethe, that belated straggler of the Renaissance and perhaps its greatest son, worked his whole life writing a tragedy which has, when you come to think of it, a most extraordinary plot. It is the story of a man with an insatiable hunger for intellectual satisfaction and prestige, a man whose personality contains a self-perpetuating machine of expansion which can be stopped by nothing short of physical death. In the course of his career he cheats a simple pious young girl. But in the end he is saved by the contrition and prayer of that girl. This plot contains, if you allow me to use a big word, the immanent drama of the West since the Renaissance. At least we hope it does.

To make my point clearer, I should like to come back to the story by Franz Werfel. It does not belong to the same category as Goethe's story, but it may illustrate better what I want to say. The heroine of that novel is, as you know, a maidservant. She has a nephew for whom she saves every penny to enable him to

study for the priesthood. She apparently succeeds. He writes to
her every so often from the seminary and later from the various
parishes in which he works. One day she wants to visit him but
does not find him at the given address. After a long involved
search she finds him in a suburb of Prague as a photographer,
living a rather shady existence. He has never been a priest. Now
during this scene the nephew makes his standpoint very clear
and he is, for the first time, sincere. He says that he was unable
to go through with the priesthood, it went against all reason, it
seemed such an outrageous lie—the entire world of the Gospel
and the Sacraments. Nobody with a modern scientific mind could
possibly swallow this stuff.

That scene has highly symbolic qualities. The repulsive
nephew represents, you might say, Hitler and Stalin. He presents, in a certain sense, also you and myself. We too have cheated
the maid. The point is that the ever-increasing rift between intellect and faith does not occur as a pure accident, outside the
moral order. The intellectuals have learned to say No so elab-
orately and in so many different ways that they can no longer say
Yes.

Form a Sentence with "How Can You . . ."

Today I share Babette's faith. I presume it would be very difficult to reach her degree of perfection, or the degree of perfection of any one of those souls through whom I have come in contact with the spirit of Christ. But the very fact that I am able to
share her faith is something which I regard as a great gift. In
spite of the preceding chapters I cannot quite explain how it
ever happened.

Now perhaps you will say: "How can you . . ." I do not know
whether you personally would say this but many people do. They
say: "How can you, as an educated person . . ." or "How can you,
as a man with scientific training . . ." or "How can you, with

knowledge of psychoanalysis . . ." There seems to be a great
number of How Can You questions. In all sincerity I do not even
understand why these questions are asked. This too I have in
common with Babette. But there is a point in which she has an
advantage over me; she is never asked, and therefore does not
have to answer.

Let us first take the one on psychoanalysis. Several things may
be meant by that question. What is most frequently implied is the
idea that psychoanalysis has been able to reduce all matters of
faith, in fact all transcendental matters, to natural motives. For
example, one can take the life history of Saint Augustine, analyze
it according to Freudian principles, and demonstrate the unconscious motives of his conversion. Then you have "explained"
how he found Christ and the Church. (I believe that someone
has actually done this.) But one can also take Nietzsche's life
history, subject it to the same analysis, and demonstrate how he
came to hate Christianity. I would not be a bit surprised if the
basic psychological mechanisms were the same in the two cases.
They frequently are. I could give you a very simple psycho-
analytical commentary on the story which I have told in this
book. If you are able to explain with the same method why one
man becomes a Christian and the other one becomes an anti-
Christian, there are only two possibilities. Either the psychological method is not valid to decide whether Christianity is true
or not, or there are no truths which transcend the material plane
of man's existence.

Looking at the history of the human spirit at long range, it is
a tremendous thing that psychoanalysis has rediscovered the
primary position of love in Man's world. This discovery was made
from a materialist platform, as it were. What else could we expect from a genius who is a child of the nineteenth century?
Lop a few of the accidental ornaments off and you have a
psychology which reaffirms and enriches the Christian idea of
Man. Psychoanalysis gives us an embryology of love. Chris-

tianity could make use of this very thing. Psychoanalysis shows us that the infant is more of a passive recipient of love than an active lover, and that it cannot bear hostility. As we become more mature, we are more able to love actively and we learn to be able to be rejected. Christianity teaches us that the climax of human perfection is to love infinitely to be able to be hated infinitely. This degree of human maturity has been reached perhaps only once in history, in the person of Jesus Christ. Psychoanalysis teaches us that *Amor* can be transformed into *Caritas*. So does Christianity. Later generations will see that in the rediscovery of the crude archaic traces of "love" in Man's physical nature, there occurs a decisive turning-away from that Manichaeism of which Western Man has been so dangerously ill. Moreover, psychoanalysis with its detailed care for the history of each individual and its emphasis on psychic injuries, reaffirms, more than any other discipline in psychiatry or psychology, the dignity of the human person. This is, in the end, one of the reasons why psychoanalysis has been rejected by Communists and Nazis alike. Freud's atheistic philosophy is a tragic historical accident, but it *is* an accident. His philosophical statements are amateurish and contradictory, and they can easily be separated from his psychology without doing harm to the latter. If you invert his materialist position you obtain an image of the psychological nature of man which is complementary to theology. However, the fact remains that psychoanalysis, like all great discoveries of the human intellect, can be used to make ammunition for nihilists or to provide balm for the wounds of mankind.

The question about science is even harder to understand. I have never experienced any conflict of that sort. Some time ago I read in a German history of philosophy that Pascal's early death was caused by the inner tortures he endured resulting from the conflict between Science and Religion. It is quite possible that Pascal suffered inner conflicts but there is no indication that

this was one of them. I presume that de Broglie is a Christian
and that Planck was a Christian. Pascal and Newton were Christians. It is possible that they were Christians *besides* being Scientists or *on account of* being Scientists, but why should they have
been Christians *in spite of* being Scientists?

God

On the contrary, I should think that an atheistic Scientist would
labor under conflicts. I was never interested in the usual
proofs of the existence of God. This is the one point in which I
approach Babette Klebl's simplicity rather closely. I often wonder how much good those proofs do, just as I wonder how much
a man can become convinced by an argument that goes on in a
class on art-appreciation. If I had to give a class on God-apprecia-
tion I should start off by talking about Science. People like
Science perhaps because of the apparent principle of certainty.
But I have often noticed that people love and admire the world
of Science because of something which is beyond the material.
An American psychiatrist remarked some time ago that at every
moment of our existence there are going on in one single nerve
cell processes of such infinite complexity that an assembly of all
the Nobel prize winners in Chemistry could not imitate them.
That remark was made in a connection entirely different from
what we are discussing here. I do not even know what the
speaker believes. But what he said is enough for Babette and me.
We need no further evidence. Of course you must realize that one
single brain cell is nothing. You have no idea what is necessary,
in the way of chemical interaction, to enable you to think "There
is no God." Those thirteen hundred grams of colloidal matter
inside your skull represent a flawlessly integrated universe. Complexity in itself might not impress you. A chaos can also be complex. But a meaningful harmonious complexity, that is another
matter. Some time ago a French biophysicist, in a popular book,

calculated the time necessary for one protein molecule to occur as a chance combination of atoms (that is to say, by a process comparable to throwing dice) and he found that the theoretically assumed age of the earth would not be enough. Not your brain, just one molecule of protein. I do not know whether his argument is correct, but Babette and I are satisfied that the universe is no meaningless chance occurrence. To me the very fact that you read what I am writing here and understand it (never mind whether you agree with me or not) is proof of a First Cause. It is the proof that you who read it have been created by a Spirit. *Cogito ergo est:* I think, therefore He is.

There can be no incongruity between Science and Religion, at least not in the sense of belief in a First Cause, a Creator. As far as that first step is concerned, Newton and Pascal not only cannot have labored under any painful conflicts, but on the contrary—whatever great discoveries they made in the Natural Sciences must have confirmed the first basis of their belief. Their belief, in turn, helped them to integrate their discoveries. Those discoveries would have remained amorphous chunks if the scientists had not in the back of their minds continuously carried the idea of a meaningful Universe. No fragments of a jigsaw puzzle mean anything unless you are convinced that they are part of a whole which will finally turn out to be a picture. Every good scientist has a cosmology. He may be dimly aware of it and carry it with him as an ill-defined shadowy image, or it may be elaborate like that of the great Christian thinkers of the Middle Ages, or that of the evolutionists of the nineteenth century. It has in fact been shown that the evolutionist view of natural history, as well as the Marxist view of human history, are distorted derivatives of ancient religious concepts of the history of Universe and Man, and can even be traced back to them. There is no scientist who does not try to fit his findings, which are by their very nature fragmentary, into the jigsaw puzzle of some universal idea. For this reason I think that a perfectly atheistic scientist (if there is such a thing) would have to labor under serious inner conflicts. Reason must be perfected by faith.

Christ

Of course, most of those people who believe that Pascal-the-mathematical-physicist and Pascal-the-theologian kept a double ledger would still admit a First Cause. They have nothing against a God who represents a Euclidian entity. What they consider as incompatible with reason is the God of the devouring thornbush, the God who admonished and threatened a little desert tribe and finally sent His only Son as a Savior into the world.

Every human being experiences in his life a tragic dichotomy, a painful dualism. I believe that all children are somehow aware of it. When we behold the harmony of the heavens, when we see a landscape in sunset, when we hear a Mozart symphony, we experience something like perfection. We should like to eternalize the instant and address it with Faust: "Stay on, thou art so fair." And then we experience ugliness and decay, sickness and death, hatred and murder. That medium of absolute perfection seems to contain an element which makes for continuous deterioration. The Church has the only answer to this terrible paradox. It says that those moments of beauty and perfection *are* potential eternity. However, this perfection has been corrupted in time by an act of choice which was made possible by the creation of Freedom.

I pointed out to you that your own brain is a cosmic galaxy of electronic orbits, something which ought to fill you with wonderment and awe. But your thoughts are variable. You might plan a garden, or you might think of killing your friend in order to marry his wife. With this we introduce a possibility which is not implicitly contained in an infinitely complex and perfectly harmonious machine. That is the idea of Freedom. The same

Creator who made such a thinking-machine possible added Freedom.

Since there is a divine Creator and Spirit it would be extraordinary to assume that He led an existence completely independent from, and outside, the world He has made. It stands to reason that He could reveal Himself in History. Thus we find in History a strange exchange, a tug-of-war, a highly dramatic struggle between God and a small people which lived in an area that marked the crossroads of ancient cultures. Very early there was an inkling, and the indications became increasingly clearer as time went on, that this small people underwent all those earthly and spiritual meanderings not just for its own sake but to bring forth Someone whose life would be of infinite significance for everybody in the whole world.

If you were a believing Jew you would have no objections so far, because up to this point the Jewish and Christian teachings coincide. However, from now on you would raise objections and they would be twofold. You might say: "Are we living in a Messianic age? If so, count me out!" This is what I used to say for a long time. The story I have cited of the Rabbi who looks through the window at the announcement of the Messiah, and says, "I see no change," is the entire spiritual history of the Jews in the past two thousand years. It is that sense of disgust and impatience which marks all the early Jewish social revolutionaries who were sensitive to the lack of justice and charity in contemporary society. Today I disagree with that Rabbi but I have a deep sympathy for him and for the early social revolutionaries. Theirs is a holy discontent. In fact, I think that this discontent is one of the metaphysical forces of history. When Jews use as an argument against the Church the story of the Inquisition they do not quote it only because they got hurt in the process. There is again, deeply hidden, that disquieting sense of the paradox. Thus, their Messianic skepticism and their very existence are a continuous reproach and sting in the flesh of the Christians. When Saint Paul

says that "blindness in part has happened in Israel until the fullness of the Gentiles should come in," he is not only prophesying
but he is exhorting the Gentiles. Fullness is not just something
numerical, it has also a qualitative meaning. Unless the Gentiles
come in in fullness, they cannot expect the Jews to see.

I do not agree with the Rabbi's remark. The prophecies have
been fulfilled. The Christ has been on earth in the historical person of Jesus of Nazareth. However, with His appearance as such,
society cannot be suddenly transfigured. That would presuppose
a peculiarly mechanistic view of history. If the appearance of
the Messiah just by its very happening converted the world into
a world of peace and love, as the throwing of a switch lights a
room, Freedom, which more than anything else made Man God-
like, would be denied. We would be like those puppet figures in
the ballet who dance automatically to the beat of the music and
become lifeless the moment the music stops. The entire drama of
Jewish history up to the appearance of such a Messiah (even if
it happened only twenty thousand years from now) would be entirely meaningless. In fact, the only Christ who is compatible
with a Judaic concept of history is the Christ who lived and was
crucified, the incarnate God who was haunted and tracked down
between party politicians and Roman imperialists, and igno-
miniously executed. His Peace and His Justice did not mechanically transfigure the world independent of our will, but it did
transfigure the secret depths of single souls. When Christ speaks
of the effect of His first coming, He chooses metaphors such as
"the leaven" or "the seed"; in other words He speaks of changes
which are slow or hidden or scattered. This does not mean that
we should not think of society and of politics in Christian terms,
it means only that everyone has first to seek the kingdom of God
(which is not of this world) and all those things will be added
unto us.

The Church then offers a definite concept of the nature of
Man and of the nature of history. It claims that the potential

Goodness, Truth and Beauty of this world were spoiled by the free act of Man, and that from then it was as if things contained something like a self-propagating element of negation, of nothingness. This can be best explained by an analogy which we find in the physical nature of the Universe. If you remember your physics you will remember that the second thermodynamic law modifies in a certain sense the law of the conservation of energy. It states that, although all energy is conserved, there is a higher probability of energy being converted into temperature than into any other form. This means that an increasing amount of energy will irreversibly remain temperature and that finally the cosmos as we know it is bound to die a "heat death." The tendency of energy to be converted into heat with a certain degree of irreversibility is called entropy.

In the world as we know it there exists, according to the Christian concept, something like a law of entropy. There is a negative process which we conceive as Evil, Sickness, Decay and Death which seems to have an intrinsic power over Beauty, Goodness, Truth, all those elements which imbue us with a sense of Eternity. The only means of reversing this process of "entropy" was the Incarnation. A second Eve appeared, the Blessed Virgin was immaculately conceived. Everyone was given a second chance. And God was incarnate. By His life and suffering and death, human history was inoculated with a new ferment, the only ferment which is capable of undoing that ever-expansive process towards nothingness.

If you were a believing Jew, you would have another objection. You would say that it is pagan to have any image of God whether in a human or in any other form. God did warn us frequently in the Old Testament not to make a graven image. But He did so precisely because He had already made an image of Himself, namely in Man.

People who do not believe in Revelation are irked by the idea of a God as represented in the Bible. They say that He is anthro-

pomorphic. They want a philosophical God, if any. However, the
specifically Jewish idea is not so much that God is anthropomorphic but that Man is theomorphic. There is an ancient discussion
of the *Rabbonim,* I believe it is Talmudic, in which the question
is under consideration: "Ma K'lal hatorah?" ("What is the fundamental principle of the law?") One Rabbi says: "Love thy neighbor as thyself," but another one counters: "There is a more fundamental one—He created Man in His image." This means that
Man in the original idea of creation is God-like. If that is true
there must be in God something to which the idea of Man is
analogous. The Christian idea is a little more specific, and calls
the something in God of which Man is, in a mysterious fashion,
an image, the Second Person of the Holy Trinity. But she is only
a little more specific about it than the Jews. Just meditate for a
moment on that rabbinic discussion, and you come quite logically
to that explicitly Christian notion of God. The idea of the Incarnation is nothing alien grafted upon the tree of Jewish tradition.
The Jewish spirit is profoundly incarnational. In fact, that holy
discontent which would like to see the whole of society transfigured, is psychologically part of that trend.

Four Possibilities

I have in my life experienced the most incomprehensible abyss
of Evil, and of suffering, as far as it affected those closest to me.
One of the sisters of our mother, her husband and their little son,
and Grandmother lived together in an apartment in an industrial
town in Western Germany. You remember Aunt Clara and Uncle
Max and little Richard very well. We were often guests in their
house and I used to go on hiking trips in the Thuringian mountains with them in the summer. They were simple, God-fearing
people and they led good lives. Uncle Max was an ironmonger.
He used to play the clown for us boys. On Friday night he
used to bless bread and wine, and on Saturday he used to

take us to the Synagogue. Their lives were good in the sense in which many people's lives are, and they might have died the death of most good middle-class people. Death looks so uniform to us onlookers although it may well be the most individual experience of each single person. At any rate, after a certain number of Friday nights, of hiking trips and of card games they might have died. Their friends would have felt sorry and there would have been obituary notices in the paper. They seemed to have been destined to live the lives and die the deaths of millions of those who now live around me. Of our grandmother, mother's mother, I have similar memories, though in certain ways more peculiar. She knew in her own way the quiet humility of sacrifice. I do not want to go into her life any further than is necessary to make her character understandable for those who did not know her.

One morning, late in 1940, they were all awakened at five, and told to be ready at five-thirty with as much as they could carry in their hands. They were packed into an overcrowded train and transported to the south of France into a concentration camp. While they were kept there their relatives in the United States tried to get them released. I wish I could write a separate book to describe their agony of fear, hope, physical hardships, desolation and inner darkness when, with the German occupation of Southern France in 1942, all hope was gone. Grandmother died in that camp. I still have some of her letters in which she tried to make us feel better. Aunt Clara and Uncle Max and Richard were deported East. People were thrown into those trains like potato bags, squeezing one another without adequate space to sit or lie down. They were given no food or water, and they had to evacuate as they were. Many of them did not arrive alive. But those who lived saw scenes of which we could not dream in our worst nightmares. Babies were killed by being smashed against trees in front of their mothers. Finally the people were shaven, stripped naked and killed.

I knew them. They were just as good as you and I, and in some respects they were better than many of us. Now here is something that might strike you as strange. The more I meditate on them, on those nightmarish last years, months and hours of their lives, the more I come to believe in Jesus Christ, the Son of the living God.

Let me make this clearer. Confronted with this horrifying picture of innocent suffering there remain only a few ways in which I can react. One is despair, moral nihilism and suicide. In fact, some of us who remained alive went this way. It does not take much to feel compassion for these suicides. For if the lives of those innocent victims ended with their death, I must deny God. If there were a God who allows this sort of thing, I should feel like Ivan Karamazov; I would not want to have anything to do with him. If my relatives who were tortured to death were annihilated at the moment of dying, if there is no meaning in their existence transcending the lives of their bodies then, obviously, God is worse than Moloch or Baal—or, much more simply expressed, there is no God.

There is a second possibility. I might have reacted, as I originally did, with an increased Jewish national fervor. Many Jews have done so and this reaction is even more understandable. I am not speaking of the settlement of the Jews in Israel, which was practically important, and may later from the viewpoint of the metaphysics of history, be very meaningful. I am talking only of inner data, of a nationalist ideology and of nationalist sentiments. I might feel quite gleeful at the suffering of the German people during the war. To some of them things happened which were similar to those which happened to the Jews before. For example, trainloads of thousands of Sudeten Germans were shipped from Czechoslovakia to Berlin. When the trains arrived it is said that only a minority of the passengers were still alive. One remembers how Nazified many Sudeten Germans had been in their attitude, and I must confess that there have been times in my

life when I would have said: "Serves them right. Now they are
getting a dose of their own medicine." I might not have put it so
crudely, but that is what I would have felt. I might have said that
the only way to get out of our misery was to become a powerful
nation ourselves, no longer to be always at the receiving-end and
to dish it out if necessary. Now it is obviously no solution to the
problem if, instead of my innocent grandmother, the innocent
grandmother of a Sudeten German is thrown into a train. But
apart from this, I have indicated in several other places in this
book that the meaning of Christ for the Jews, from the point of
view of the philosophy of history, is precisely the fact that for us
(and eventually for all peoples) there is no such thing as a
national solution. Jewish-orthodox critics of the Gospel, no matter how objective and benevolent, never cease to discuss the
famous quotation: "It is said unto you—love your neighbor *and
hate your enemy!*" They point out that there is not a single passage in the Old Testament in which Man is commanded to hate
his enemy. On the contrary there are several passages in which
charity towards one's personal enemy is indicated. The Jewish
scholars say that since all the other quotations from the Old
Testament are correct and this one sounds like pure invention,
it must have been interpolated at a later date. However, the
meaning is clear if we consider the significance of "neighbor" as
one belonging to the same people and "enemy" as a national foe.
Because, though the Old Testament nowhere exhorts us to hate
a personal enemy—when it comes to Moabites and Assyrians it
is full of the spirit of "let them have it back, and plenty." We who
have been, in a certain sense, the inventors of nationalist ideology
(at a stage of our history when it was functional and spiritually
justified) are asked to be the first ones to give it up. There have
been individual Jews who, out of a spirit of charity, advocated
and gave material help to the German people after the fall of
Hitler. These persons have anticipated a profound metaphysical
truth. If the Jews at the time of Christ, in view of the Roman oc-

cupation, had refused the "national solution" as He Himself did, they would have died as a nation but they would have died in Christ! They might have gone out into the world preaching the Gospel, or they might have lived a life of non-violence toward the Roman conqueror. In either case they would have lost their life as a nation in order to gain it. They would have transcended their racial destiny, and it is difficult to think what tremendous historical impulse would have come from a nation thus transfigured. Once when I was still in the throes of restlessness, before I entered the Church, I had a long conversation with a very learned, profoundly religious French-Canadian priest. This man shared the nationalist fervor which one finds among so many groups of racial minority anywhere in the world. In spite of his spirituality he was not free from that resentment which always seems to diminish the stature of a man. In the course of our conversation I pointed out to him how deep the traces of persecution and of anti-semitism are in every one of us, and that I could not believe that Christ would demand of me to join the ranks of those who, on the natural plane, are our persecutors. Everything in me, I said, revolted against the idea. He looked long and pensively at me, and finally he said: "Yes, if following Christ would require me to become British, I must say this would be a terrible demand." This sounds comical, and can be understood only on the basis of long-standing historical grudges, of subtle currents of hostility, irritation and spite, as they occur between racial groups. He continued to be silent for a while after his remark and I knew that he understood. Actually he brought forth no argument against mine. But curiously enough this little fragment of our conversation had a profound influence on my conversion. At that moment I knew in the depth of my being that we have to partake of the flesh and blood of Christ regardless of whether with persecutors or with friends. This and nothing else is the true and lasting remedy for hatred. It is a hard fact, but it is one of the many hard facts for which Jesus of Nazareth had to die on the cross.

I might have tried a third possibility. There were many years in my life when I would have looked through the eyes of dialectic materialism on the disaster which has overwhelmed us. I would have regarded this philosophy as the only true remedy. Now it has frequently been pointed out that there are actually two Karl Marxes. One of them was full of truly religious fury. He hurled curses at the capitalists of the nineteenth century and he uncovered the lack of justice and charity inherent in an industrialist civilization—very much in the manner of an Old Testament Prophet. His attempt to interpret history was in its motives much more spiritual than he realized. I suppose that an attempt to interpret history with the methods he used is better than no attempt at interpreting history at all. Many of the early Communists were followers of this Karl Marx, and their materialism was only a historical costume, the dress of the nineteenth century. Some of the Communists who were persecuted by the Czarist secret police are spiritually related to those Christians who today are persecuted by the Stalinist secret police. However, there is another Karl Marx, the streamlined Hegelian absolutist, the strategist of class-warfare. Unfortunately this is the Karl Marx who has been successful. And he has led to a world of horror equaled only by that other Hegelian grandchild, National Socialism. Yes, I remember very well when I used to talk of matters concerning human relationship and the future happiness of society in terms of production-level, the synthesis-coming-after-the-antithesis-to-capitalism, and lots of abstract things like that.

There is a fourth solution. This is a rationalist pragmatism which is becoming more and more prevalent in the Western countries. It is, you might say, a non-Marxist or "cold" form of materialism, a baby which seems to bear all the signs of a powerful future and of a good life-expectation. There was a short period in my life in which I would have adhered to this form of pragmatism. I might have said approximately as follows: "If we want to see in the future that no more innocent grandmothers, parents and children are tortured to death, there is only one way. Let us investigate objectively the roots of racial and of class hatred, with all the tools of present-day science, with methods of economic investigation, of sociology, of behaviorism, of psycho-analysis, in short with all the branches of science which occupy themselves with things human. Let us be as scientific and system-atic in the establishment of interhuman relationships as we have been in technology. Let us have some sort of international board of social psychologists to study and to control the relationships of groups of people. In order to be able to do this successfully we may find that we have to abolish metaphysical concepts of human existence because it is possible that those are the con-cepts contributing to tension. If we find this necessary let us be courageous and do it, let us sterilize the air and remove all germs of faith so that we may live more rationally and more peacefully in an aseptic scientific atmosphere. Human affairs have long enough been governed by Belief, let them be governed by Science and Usefulness. In the world of matter the road away from belief to science has led to the greatest technological prog-ress in history; why should we not make the same step in the world of human society? Once we freed ourselves from an an-cient cosmology the way was clear which led to Television and the Airplane. If we only freed ourselves from equally ancient concepts of the nature of Man we shall have a world in which human affairs, for the first time in history, will be governed by reason. In order to find out why man tortures man, and in order to avoid it once and for all, let us consult those who are objective about it—psychologists and social scientists." Thus I might have spoken for a short period in my life. In fact, if the signs of the times do not deceive us there is a great chance that, once Marx-ism is finished, we are in for a global experiment of this kind. To my mind there is only one form of society which is worse than the Marxist or the Fascist one—that is, precisely such a "scientific" society. Compared with it Germany and Russia would look like children's playgrounds. Man's life on this earth would come about as close to the idea of hell as anything on this earth may. Needless to say that there is nothing wrong with Economics or Political Science or Psychoanalysis or Social Science or any other similar subject. The great Russian thinkers of the nineteenth century, who were so distrustful of and hostile towards Science, mixed Science (which is precious) up with Scientism (which is destructive). It is this scientism as a norm of human life, without God as the center, which leads to a form of nihilism unequaled in history. Saint Augustine, himself an expert at decaying civilizations, once drew our attention to the meaning of the word "nothing" in Our Lord's terrible sentence: "Without me you can do nothing." This word is to be taken quite literally. Christ does not say: "Without me you cannot do very much," or "Without me you can do only a certain amount," or "Without me you can do only little." He says: "Without me you can do *nothing*." A Christless world, scientific or not, leads to utter negation, to nothingness. Germany and Russia have given pretty good examples of this. However, there are indications that secularism and pragmatism, which have by comparison led a rather amateurish existence outside Russia, may be shaped into some scientific-technocratic norm for human beings. This, not material destruction, would mean the end of Mankind.

The Solution

Thus we see four possible answers to the riddle of the abysmal suffering, which we have witnessed in our time. Not one of these answers is adequate. Each one of them misses the point. Despair is no solution; even if we wished to despair we cannot because we believe. Resentment is no solution; our dead ones themselves seem to warn us against such a spirit and it would so easily lead us to commit the same cruelties on others which were committed on us. Statism is no solution. Scientism is no solution.

There is only one way: Jesus Christ. If we are concerned with
the suffering of those innocent ones, we have first to look at Him.
If we are concerned with the Evil which has brought it about,
we have first to look at ourselves. Everything else is deception.
If I want to renew the world I have to begin right in the depth of
my own soul. This is the only true and permanent revolution
which I am able to achieve. Class warfare leads to another set
of oppressors and oppressed; national revenge leads to another
set of persecutors and persecuted; and the Board of Social Scientists for the Prevention of Intergroup Hostilities is the most dangerous mirage of them all because it makes us believe even more
that the decisive battle is fought far away from us, outside ourselves; it turns Good and Evil into two pale abstracts; it seeks to
de-humanize the issue.

There is something extraordinary in the suffering of Christ. It
seems to include all human suffering, and yet it can be "completed" by the suffering of individual persons.

It includes all human suffering. In the famous opening passage
of *Anna Karenina* we are told that "all happy families resemble
one another, but every unhappy family is unhappy in its own individual way." The same could be said about single persons. No
matter to what degree suffering individuals may resemble one
another, there always remains, somewhere in the depth, a nucleus
which is unique. In our work as physicians we listen to people's
life histories every day. And although psychological science gives
us insight into the intrinsic mechanisms of each one of these, although we are able to analyze, disentangle, classify, and name
the things which hurt people, there remains in each case a secret
element which cannot be reproduced nor re-experienced. It belongs entirely to that one soul. You would think that three
mothers each of whom has lost an only child represented three
stories of the same kind. They do only up to a certain point.
When that certain point comes we encounter a strange uniqueness. It is the same with dozens of people innocently executed,

or millions of Jews murdered, or so many people in forced labor camps, or so many millions with anxiety neuroses, and so on. I am not only talking about the subjective quality of experience which makes each individual a universe, I am speaking about something which, by its very nature, resists comparison. Suffering cannot be quantified.

There is only One Who unites all these secrets in His suffering, and that is Jesus Christ. The more you dwell on it, the more it becomes clear that in His agony He anticipated the hidden agonies of innumerable individuals. For centuries the Church has meditated on the Five Sorrowful Mysteries of the Rosary or on the Fourteen Stations of the Cross. And the more people did so, the more the Agony of Our Lord became revealed. It has innumerable facets. It anticipates, it contains your and my life in a singular way. Newman once expressed this idea of the Church in an unforgettable sermon on the Night of Gethsemani in which he unrolled before our eyes with poetic genius the universality and infinite multiplicity of the suffering of Our Lord. In our medical work we get to know this in its countless human mirrors. Everyone is familiar with that stage when the patient reaches something which is incommunicable, something which in this form does not seem to occur in anyone else's life. With this one aspect of his life he seems to be alone. But he is not.

We have all experienced scenes which seem to be fixed in our memory because of their stark terror. I remember how one night, eighteen years ago, as an interne, I had to inform a woman that her boy, an only child, had bled to death from a post-operative hemorrhage. It is an awful thing to say but in a hospital there is something "routine" about such an incident. Yet somehow, the scene in all its details is unforgettable, perhaps because of its simplicity; how the woman looked at the body of the boy for a while, and how she said to her husband: "This is our child." One of my relatives told me a story from Dachau. An old Jew who was rather sick used to walk around supported by his two

sons. One day he collapsed and was soon dead. A stormtrooper
kicked the body aside with his boot and said in front of the dead
man's sons: "One Jew less—all the better."

In our work as physicians we see people with beads of the
sweat of death on their foreheads; we see married couples in the
struggle of mysterious enmities; we see drunkards threaten their
children, and children in a despair of hatred against their parents. One of the first things we learn at Medical School about
our own attitude is not to get emotional or sentimental about it;
not to be too involved with our feelings. This is good advice.
In fact, those physicians and nurses who are matter-of-fact are
much more efficient and helpful than the ones who have their
feelings involved all the time.

And yet, we must realize that it is Christ Himself who is
present in all this suffering. It is He and His mother who were
there, that night in the children's ward. It was He Whose body
was kicked aside: "One Jew less—all the better." It was He who,
with our father, was mocked by the stormtrooper. It is He who
is present in the agony of millions of deaths and secret humiliation. This is neither sentiment nor melodrama—it is just a basic
fact. I am almost tempted to use the word "scientific" in this
connection, because it has nothing to do with emotions. It is an
axiom. Our Lord Himself indicated it, and the Church has upheld
it throughout the centuries. It is with this axiom in mind that
Pascal said that Jesus is still suffering on the cross.

And, I said, if we are concerned with Evil we have first to
look at ourselves. The Gospel teaches me that if I am concerned
with making the world a less cruel place to live in I do not need
that Board of Social Scientists. There is inside myself Evil to
work on, enough to last me a lifetime. Dostoievsky's Father
Sossima implores his monks that everyone should regard himself sincerely as worse than the one with whom he is dealing.
There is not only a Communion of Saints but also a Communion
of Sinners. Many present-day Christian thinkers have attacked

modern psychology, especially psychoanalysis, because those
who practice it frequently happen to profess an anti-Christian
philosophy. These critics forget that psychoanalysis has reaffirmed
that which the Church has taught all the time; namely, that
potentially there is inside every man a den of murderers and
thieves. Why these potentialities become manifest in your neighbor and remain latent in you, this is not for you to judge. The
veil which separates the potential evil in you from the manifest
evil of the man about whom you are going to read in tomorrow's
headlines is thinner and more mysterious than you think—this is
the catharsis which emanates from the great Russian writers of
the nineteenth century and from psychoanalysis, this is the true
purification of which modern man is so desperately in need.
But it is only an elaboration of an old truth. Every act contains
an element of timelessness, and every evil act contains an element by which I am endangered. For centuries every Catholic
child, man and woman has prayed: "I have crucified my loving
Savior Jesus Christ."

Now you will say: "First you discuss four possible solutions
and you reject them. We must not despair. We must not get
even. It is no good rebuilding society in any scientific way,
Marxist or otherwise. And yet, supposing it is true that all innocent suffering is the suffering of Christ, supposing that everyone
participates in the Evil to which the world is succumbing—what
of it? Instead of a realistic plan you discuss a couple of lyricisms."

What you are tempted here to call lyricisms, the truths of the
Gospel, are actually appallingly concrete. Consider for a moment
all the theories regarding man to which we used to adhere.
Society should be changed, world governments should be set
up, people should be re-educated but we ourselves are actually
not committed, or at least not necessarily so. It can all be done
by others, by political actions, by committees, by bodies outside
my individual life. When you come right down to it all this does
not hurt us much, it can, if need be, go on outside the immediate

orbit of our existence. If by lyricism you mean something pale
and abstract, something that does not touch you really, this is
lyricism.

But the Gospel demands our immediate action right now at
this moment, and in the place in which we find ourselves. It
says that our own soul, with the help of Grace, contains enough
potential energy to change the world.

The Church

My dear fellow, I keep on referring to History and to Science
and to Literature and whatnot. I do this because I want to remain,
as much as possible, on a ground which you and I have in common. But I can refer to those things only as analogies and ap-
proximations. Divine Revelation and Faith are categories quite
different from purely intellectual arguments. These categories
are alien to you. Therefore, no matter what I say, this letter will
leave a void between you and me. There is always something
halfway about it, and we get stuck in those analogies.

The Incarnation was not only an event acted out in historical
time. It left its indelible mark on the world. It was perpetuated
in the life of men. I believe Bergson once said towards the end of
his life that everything good that happened in the world since
Christ has happened through Him. The Incarnation was perpetuated in a very specific way in the Holy Sacraments, particularly in the sacrament of the Holy Eucharist, in the Communion of Saints and in the visible physical unity of the Church.
There are many saintly Christians in the world today who do
not believe that faith in Christ necessitates faith in those other
things. They believe that matter has been transformed once, as
it were, at the actual time when God took human flesh, and that
the subject was exhausted at that single historical event. That
disbelief in the sacramental life of the Church has two roots.
It is firstly based on an ancient and profound disrespect for

Matter, and secondly on the development of what the philosophers call Positivism which arose with modern science. It is possible that both these roots are two expressions of the same thing, and I believe that this disbelief corresponds only to an historical phase.

Non-Catholics think that revealed religion in general, and Catholic dogma in particular, are something which you get rammed down your throat. Again I am going to choose an analogy which does not quite explain what I mean. Let us suppose you said that a student of Music gets Harmony and Counterpoint rammed down his throat. You can try to compose without studying the laws which Bach and Mozart have expounded, just as you can believe in "some kind of higher being and the golden rule and all that stuff" without bothering about the statements made by Saint Augustine or Saint Thomas. There are people who have a wonderful natural musicality, and when they improvise music you find that, at their best, they rediscover spontaneously the theory of Harmony and of Counterpoint. However, you can always demonstrate that they would have done even better if they had studied those subjects. There are other people who know the entire theory of Harmony and of Counterpoint, but their own productions remain sterile. However, everybody, the most romantic composer and the most modern composer, keeps referring to Bach. It could not be otherwise. You can take a simple Euclidian axiom and develop all mathematics out of it. You can take a basic musical law and develop the *Art of the Fugue* out of it. Similarly you can take a phrase such as "God is Love" and develop Theology out of it. But you do not need to do it as a free-lancer; others have been there before. It has already been done by great mathematicians, by great musicians and by the Saints. Yet if the Church sees to it that Babette, in the way in which she lives her faith, is aided by the insights gained by Teresa of Avila, you feel a dark suspicion of some weird play for power. Non-Catholic Christians too live, to an extent of which they are usually not aware, on the wealth not only of the Gospel but also of the Doctors of the Church. The only really impoverished ones are our skeptic Western intellectuals. They refuse to practice the gift of Faith which would enable them to crown and perfect Reason. With Faith gone they are in the same position as that shipwrecked man stranded on an island with crates full of canned food but with no can-opener. He starved to death with all the cans in front of him. Likewise, the majority of our contemporaries are in possession of the heritage of Christianity and of all the immense treasures of Western spirituality—but they are unable to tap them.

In London I listened to non-Catholic preachers of various denominations. I was struck by several things. I never heard them say anything positive which was not compatible with Catholic doctrine. Every one of them, in his greatest fervor, seemed to emphasize and develop some special idea which I had also found inside the Catholic Church. The only points in which they were non-Catholic were points of denial. What originally had been impulses toward freedom seemed to have led to extraordinary subjectivism.

Although Catholic orthodoxy is the only form of Christianity acceptable to me, I do not like to talk about these things from the point of view of Catholic apologetics. During the persecution of Christianity we all experienced wonderful examples of heroism among Protestants and Catholics alike. I have myself experienced supernatural charity among non-Catholics. Moreover, our experiences have shown that the anti-Christian forces in history are so vehemently directed against anything which confirms and confesses Christ. At this moment a lot would be gained if people returned to Christianity, or in fact if they at least returned to the ethics of the Old Testament.

The Church is immutable in her teaching. There is only one supernatural truth, as there is only one scientific truth. What in the mastering of matter constitutes the law of Progress, in things of the spirit is the law of Preservation. I remember when I showed you the Papal Encyclical about the Nazis. You were quite impressed, and you said: "This sounds as if it had been written in the first century." That's just the point.

The Church mirrors the facets of History. The Gospel is always the same. But the life of the Gospel in the turmoil of the fourth century is seen in Saint Augustine. The life of the Gospel at the height of the Middle Ages (some people would say the early dawn of the Renaissance) is perceived in Saint Thomas. In the nineteenth century, the century in which the human mind began to rule systematically the material forces of the universe, the Church began to extol the Little Way, the mystic life in hidden "little people." This is the only logical answer to the threat of a coming managerial age. Christ always has the appropriate answer, and He gives it in His saints. I have mentioned how great intuitive geniuses, such as Goethe and Tolstoy, perceived the mystic significance of the "little people." The Church, quite independently, has emphasized that same point. But in doing so she only re-emphasized one aspect of her eternal doctrine. Every century the Church takes a red pencil and underlines certain words of the Gospel, words which happen to fit the occasion. "Many thoughts," says Father Sossima, "seem to lead us into a state of doubt. Particularly when we see the sins of men we ask ourselves: 'Shall we tackle all this by force or by humble charity?' Always decide in favor of humble charity. Once you have decided in favor of it you will conquer the whole world. Humble charity is a terrible force; it is the greatest force in the world; there is nothing like it . . ." Concerning the small inconspicuous acts of love he says: "Everything is like an ocean, everything is movement, and all things are actually in contact with one another. At one end of the world you cause a little motion, and from the other end of the world it re-echoes." This was written by a Russian of the nineteenth century, almost at the same time when Saint Thérèse of Lisieux lived that obscure life which represents the lesson for our present age. By that is not meant our practical philanthropy, the do-goodism of everyday life, which is important too but is only a beginner's exercise. The true thing is an intense, all-out transformation of our lives in the life and passion of Christ.

You remember that I remarked that I had a feeling of allegiance to the simple pious folk in Munich, and that this feeling of loyalty prevailed over my Jewish loyalty. I could not have gone back and said to them: "Look here, all this stuff about Jesus is nonsense. There is such a thing as Revelation but it is strictly a tribal affair. Forget about the Messiah . . ." And, as you remember, I felt I would side with our pagan torturers in speaking like this. But there was still something else to it. I knew that these people lived, or attempted to live, a life of heightened mystic intensity, the only life which offers salvation to man.

I shall never forget the morning of my first Holy Communion. Outwardly it was like any other morning in December. When I entered the church, the church of the Franciscan Fathers in Montreal, it was still dark outside. Inside there was that crowd of people you find in any Catholic Church in a downtown district of any large city. There were men and women from the small rooming-houses near the railway tracks, and from the areas around the shopping center. There were what seemed to be employees from a nearby hospital. Some of these were going to Mass after a night's work. Our lives—that of my wife, of my friends Albert and Victorin—had converged, and had converged with those unknown ones around us. And it was as if others were there: my parents, and Kaspar Russ, and the Kohen family, the Jews from the Canal Synagogue, and Jacques Maritain and Dorothy Day, and the pious old maids of our childhood homes. And there was no doubt about it—towards Him we had been running, or from Him we had been running away, but all the time He had been in the center of things.

Index